So Many

CHRISTINE WEBBER

 On Call

*In memory of the loveliest man imaginable
David Delvin (1939–2018)*

First published in Great Britain in 2021

A CIP catalogue record for this book is available from the British Library

Cover design by J D Smith Design

Published by On Call

Printed and bound in Great Britain by Clays Ltd, Elcograf S.p.A.
Typeset by the BORN Group

ISBN 978-0-9954540-8-8

Acknowledgements

This is the fourth novel that I have produced with the same team. They are the talented people at Clays Indie Publishing, Helen Baggott, who is a super-skilled editor and proofreader, the wonderfully creative cover designer, Jane Dixon-Smith, and Daniel Knight, ace typesetter at the BORN Group. I want to thank them all so much because they invariably improve my work more than I can say. We all need experts, and I am lucky to be surrounded by them and am particularly indebted to Coroner Chris Morris, who generously gave me the benefit of his expertise concerning the legal and medical quagmire of people's rights to refuse treatment.

Next, I want to thank Dr Max Pemberton for all that he did for my husband prior to his death, for his support and warm friendship to me over the past twenty years, and also for very generously supplying the cover quote.

And finally, I wish to pay tribute to two of my greatest friends, Gary Avis and Tim Holder, who have been instrumental in helping me settle back in East Anglia. They also invited me to 'bubble' with them – and I greatly value the love, companionship and fun that we share. I also want to thank them for their contribution to *So Many Ways of Loving*. Several years ago, they rescued a miniature schnauzer called Hoagy and gave him the best possible home a pet could have. I've always loved this little dog and he has been the inspiration for one of my major characters, who is also called Hoagy. Luckily for me, the real Hoagy also agreed to pose for my cover! So, a big thank you to him and indeed to all the animals who improve our lives beyond measure.

Chapter One

The Present

'Are we all thinking the same thing?'

Two heads turned to her.

'I'm Jennifer Warboys, by the way,' she went on. 'But everyone calls me Jen.'

'Monica,' announced the woman sitting opposite. 'Monica Charlton.'

'And I'm Lucy.'

Monica reached across the table and picked up one of the A4 cards they had been given, which had the words *Real Hands-On Delivery Person* written on it, in thick felt-tip letters. 'Did you mean what were we thinking about these?' She rolled her eyes.

'Well, actually,' Jen replied, 'I was wondering what you thought about the guy who sent us all in here for some "blue sky thinking".'

'Oh,' sighed Lucy. 'He's a total prat.'

Monica looked relieved. 'That's what I thought too.'

'Exactly! Ridiculously full of himself. And not nearly as bright as he thinks he is.' Jen nodded to emphasise the point. 'So, are we giving up on trying to make sense of this material? It's ludicrous. For God's sake,' she gestured towards another of the cards, 'what does *Ready for the Gridstone* even mean? I haven't a clue what he's going on about, and if that means I'm past it and unemployable, so be it.'

'You're not past it! None of us is past it.' Lucy's tone was vehement as she tossed aside a laminated notice which read *Helicopter NOT Granular Thinking.*

Jen exhaled with such force that her fringe lifted itself off her forehead for a second.

'But what does this say about us? Why did we all answer an advert about working for a new, innovative company. It would suggest we haven't got enough to do, or that we're short of money...'

'Oh,' Monica said, 'it's not the money as far as I'm concerned.'

'Not really for me either,' Lucy agreed. 'I've got an adequate pension. But I suppose I was looking for something different. Something to prove I've still got my uses.'

'That's pretty honest,' Jen murmured.

'Well,' Lucy gazed at her for a moment, then smiled. 'I'm probably never going to meet you again, so I might as well be truthful.'

'This is a bit like *Strangers on a Train* isn't it?' Jen's eyes lit up. 'In a minute, one of you is probably going to ask me to murder your husband!'

Lucy's assemblage of chins quivered, as she threw back her head and laughed.

Monica stared at the other two, blankly. 'This afternoon is going from bad to worse,' she said. 'I couldn't make out what the young man was talking about. And now neither of you are making sense either.'

'Hitchcock movie.' Jen leant across the table and spoke soothingly. 'Two guys who'd never met before were on the same train and got talking and hatched a plan about how they could each murder someone for the other.'

'Oh! Well, I think I've heard of that,' Monica sniffed slightly.

'Good,' Jen responded. 'Look, we're probably all a bit tense after the lecture and realising we're wasting our time. But we don't want to work for this outfit even if they pick us, do we?'

Monica and Lucy exchanged glances, then shook their heads.

'So, how about we all go and get some tea at The Granary?'

'Is that the new arts cinema by the river?' Lucy asked. 'I didn't know there was a café.'

'Well, there is and it's lovely. Great cakes.'

Monica hesitated. 'My husband will be home soon.'

'Look, we were all expecting to be here till five anyway. Still, suit yourself.' Jen stood up.

'I'll come,' said Lucy. 'Presumably, they sell wine all day?'

The three women peeped over their shoulders at the activity in the adjoining glass-walled office, then gathered up their bags and coats and raced to the door.

The Granary was relatively quiet.

'You should have seen it earlier,' said the counter assistant with burgundy hair and a piercing in her left nostril. 'The local WI came in for lunch, without booking. Everyone wanted something different. Then we had a repeat of a Bolshoi ballet production, and three dance schools turned up to see it. Place was packed. Half-term holidays are a total nightmare! Still, all in a day's work. Mind you, I'm leaving today. They keep saying they're getting more staff in. When will that be, I'd like to know? Can't wait any longer. Nice place though. Tea for three was it?'

'No, I'll have a glass of red wine,' Jen decided. 'Will you both join me? My treat!'

'Jolly nice of you,' Lucy smiled broadly. 'And I'll buy us cake.'

'Not for me, thank you,' said Monica.

'D'you mean no wine or no tea, or no cake?' Jen raised an eyebrow.

'Oh, sorry. Maybe a cup of tea. I can pay though.'

'Next time.' Jen dismissed the offer with a wave of her right hand.

3

Monica stepped back and found herself studying her shoes which were new and slightly uncomfortable.

'Cheer up,' Lucy nudged her. 'There's very little that can't be put right with flapjacks and chocolate brownies.' She reached into her capacious satchel-like handbag for her purse. 'One of those and one of those,' she told the young woman. 'Ooh, and a meringue. And three forks if you don't mind.'

Monica decided to engage more with the other two by finding somewhere to sit. But as she headed to an empty table in the corner, she realised that not only had Jen spotted a better one that overlooked the river, but had conveyed to it two glasses of wine, a teapot, milk jug and cup and saucer.

A sigh of defeat escaped from her lips, but she forced herself to walk over and sit on the seat beside the one Jen had taken. Perk up, she urged herself.

Taking a deep breath, she eyed up the teapot in front of her and said, 'I'm ready for this,' and for the first time a glimmer of a smile relaxed her stern features.

Jen tried to think of a question which might establish why this woman with the rather severe hairstyle was so careworn. She was obviously quite well off. The tailored jacket might be Jaeger. The wrap-around jersey dress beneath it was probably Hobbs or Boden. And the winter coat she had discarded on the back of her chair must have cost several hundred pounds. But her demeanour suggested she was someone who was struggling with life.

Lucy and her considerable bulk arrived and collapsed onto the remaining chair, then she put the plate of cakes down noisily on the table before issuing the others and herself with paper napkins and forks.

'Dig in,' she urged, as she shrugged herself out of her green duffle coat.

Monica turned to her. 'My father always used that expression.'

'Mine too, come to think of it,' Lucy replied. 'Probably something they said in the army in the war.' As she divided the cakes into sections and distributed equal shares to the three of them,' she continued, 'I've got no parents now though, have you?'

Jen shook her head.

'My mother's in a nursing home,' Monica explained, 'but she doesn't know me. Might as well be dead, really. My father passed away before I was married. He was too young for the Second World War, but he did do National Service.'

After a pause, Jen said, 'I was thinking of asking both of you why you answered the advertisement that brought us together today. But maybe your reasons are quite personal. I suppose mine are. So, should we just say who we are in a couple of sentences?'

'Is this really necessary?' Monica's tone was defensive.

'No.' Jen put a piece of flapjack into her mouth and sat back in her chair.

'I don't mind,' Lucy responded. 'My surname is Brown. I was a lecturer in English Literature at the university but retired just before Christmas. I haven't quite got my head around that yet. Unlike many of my kind, I never had any ambitions to write myself. And I didn't run any Creative Writing courses either, though the Vice-Chancellor thought that was a money spinner we should get into. What else? I never married. Never had children. But I don't conform to the lonely spinster stereotype – for one thing I hate cats! That's me really. I probably went today because I'm looking for a fresh purpose in life. I've always felt needed; sometimes I've felt so needed, by students and the university, that I was at screaming point! But now that we're well into the spring term, I do feel...' her voice wobbled slightly, 'a tad redundant. And frankly, I don't like it, especially because I feel tired all the time, which I reckon is a reaction to suddenly being jobless.'

The other two made sympathetic noises before all three of them sipped from their drinks.

'I used to be a teacher,' Monica said. 'My experience was mostly in the reception class. I loved it. About thirty-five years ago, I took what I thought would be a short break to have a baby, but

I'd hardly got back into the swing of things when I fell pregnant again. And that second child,' she swallowed, 'sorry, uh, she um, had cystic fibrosis, and looking after her became a full-time job. She was so lovely, and uncomplaining, but she didn't make it, and died eleven years ago. It seemed very unfair. She was on a waiting list for a heart and lung transplant and she was nearly at the top of it. But one day she caught a bug and within hours she was dead.'

'Terrible for you,' Jen murmured.

'Awful,' Lucy added.

'I have another daughter though, who's done very well. She works for the Sydney Opera House. But she's always busy, so we're not in contact much. And the only other thing is that my husband James, who's a solicitor, retires today.'

'So, did you want a job so you could escape him hanging around you all day?' Jen quizzed her. 'Or are you one of the lucky ones with exciting plans like going around the world?'

'Well, we're considering that sort of thing, but I suppose I've been thinking for a while that I'd like a job of some sort... And what about you? Are you married?'

'Uh, I am, yes. And I was, once upon a time, a Fleet Street journalist. But as you know, Fleet Street is no longer the centre of the industry and indeed there's practically no industry. Not in print anyway. And there's less and less money. I was thinking of writing a novel, but it's not very likely I'd get it published even if I finished it. Everyone wants psychological thrillers written by authors in their thirties. I've got no interest in that genre, and at fifty-eight, I'm too old anyway.'

A woman in a smart suit with dark, straight hair, high heels and heavy black-framed spectacles hovered by their table. 'I'm sorry to interrupt you,' she said, 'but I overheard something one of you said, and I was wondering if you were local and might be looking for some voluntary work? We could pay expenses.'

'We are all local,' Lucy replied, 'I think.'

The other two nodded.

'Can I bend your ear for a minute then?' asked the woman and, without waiting for an answer, she drew up a chair and gave them a rather different viewpoint on the staff situation from the one they had heard from the burgundy-haired woman. However, the gist was the same. There were insufficient employees to look after the four screens of the cinema and to serve in the increasingly popular bar and café.

'And so,' she paused, 'we've had a meeting today and I came up with the idea of enlisting local, possibly retired, groups of friends to do shifts together. We can't pay I'm afraid, but the volunteers will get free coffees, teas and cold drinks while they're working, and I'm sure will enjoy the lively atmosphere we have here, plus they'll get a complimentary pass for the cinema every month – including for the opera, ballet and National Theatre relays.'

'We're not actually friends,' Monica pointed out.

'Oh!'

'In fact, we only met today.' Lucy smiled. 'But I think there are possibilities here.'

'Me too,' Jen agreed enthusiastically.

Monica looked uncertain. 'Can we let you know?'

'Of course.' The woman produced three business cards from her pocket, handed one to each of them and disappeared.

'What an odd day this is turning out to be,' Jen said. 'But I like this idea. Particularly being able to see the cinema relays. I'd be booking for those anyway, so to get them for nothing would be quite a big deal.'

'I'm with you,' Lucy agreed.

They turned to Monica. 'Much depends on whether my husband and I are going away.'

'Tell you what,' Jen suggested, 'let's all three of us write our mobile numbers on all of these business cards.'

'Good idea!' Lucy laughed. 'That'll save us the embarrassment of trying to input them into our phones and showing all too clearly that we're of a "certain age"! And the funny thing of course is that we *know* our numbers, which young people never do, do they? Why is that?'

Quickly, they scribbled down their details, and agreed that they would phone or text each other, and then Monica announced that she really must go, and swept up her belongings and left.

Jen sipped slowly from her glass, while Lucy finished her wine and devoured what remained of the cakes before saying that she ought to leave too.

'See you again,' she said to Jen as she reached for her bag, which had spilled some of its contents onto the floor. She bent over and scooped them up. Her breathing, Jen noticed, was quite laboured by the time she had finished and risen to her feet.

'Right. Off I go!'

Jen gave a little wave. 'I'm not in a hurry, so I'll just sit here for a while and finish my Merlot.'

'Enjoy it. Sorry to abandon you. But I think I should go and find where I left my bicycle earlier. I worry I'm getting vague.'

'Don't forget your coat,' Jen reminded her.

Lucy shook her head. 'Oh Lordy! Have I always been like this, or is it getting worse?'

Jen played with a stray strand of hair, which had escaped from her ponytail, then tucked it behind her right ear as she watched the older woman wend her way through the café to the exit. Really, she thought, that's more of a waddle than a walk. She's seriously out of shape. Then she frowned as she inwardly acknowledged that her thoughts were more than a little unkind, as they so often were these days.

His car was in the drive. She had not expected him back so early.

'James, you're home,' Monica called as she opened the front door.

There was a grunt from the sitting room, where she found him, slumped in his favourite leather chair, sipping whisky and looking

8

morose. He did not stand to greet her. Or offer her a drink which, suddenly, she wanted very much indeed.

Why had she not joined the other women in having a glass of wine at The Granary? She wished she had now. But judging from her husband's demeanour, wine might not now be sufficiently powerful for her needs. She wandered back into the hall, dropped her bag and removed her coat, then – suppressing a sigh – rejoined her husband, who did not even glance at her as she made her way to their well-stocked drinks trolley and poured herself a larger than usual measure of Rémy Martin.

What would their life be like now? He had not wanted to retire but the other partners had, as he put it, designs on his income; and he had been urged to go, with promises of consultancy work and a word in the right quarters about non-executive board jobs that would bring respect and kudos if not the large sums of money he was accustomed to.

She hoped something would turn up. The thought of him here, indolent and uncommunicative, all day, every day, filled her with panic. Despite what she had intimated at The Granary, there were no plans for a world trip. He was keen to go to Australia to see Melissa, but the prospect of weeks with her daughter did not enthuse her. Could he go alone? That might be a solution.

He was obviously not going to start a conversation, so it was up to her.

Sitting down on the sofa opposite him, she asked, 'How was your last day?'

He shrugged. 'They threw a lunch for me. In the board room. Various clients turned up. All very laudatory.'

'Well, that was nice,' she said, trying to sound brighter than she felt.

He shrugged again, dismissively.

'And what did *she* have to say? If anything. Your mistress.'

He coughed. Were there tears in his eyes? Surely not?

9

'She ended it,' he snapped. 'Today of all days. After five years. She said it was a natural parting of the ways. I feel absolutely bloody, Mon, honestly. I knew it might not last once I retired. Difficult to arrange. For her, I mean. But I didn't think she would cut me off, just like that.'

'I'm sorry.'

'Thanks.' He drained his drink, put down the crystal tumbler and gazed across at her.

'To be honest, old girl, I could really use a bit of… comfort. What d'you say?'

She stood up. 'Don't even think about it,' she retorted as she strode from the room.

Lucy flicked on the kettle, and then wandered around the ground floor of her house while she waited for it to boil. The old, rambling property was far too tidy. This was a new problem. Until she had left the university there had always been open books dotted around with Post-it notes stuck to various pages, as well as students' essays scattered here and there. She had a study but had tended to expand into the rest of the property. The trouble was that she had cleared away all reference books on the day she had retired – a sort of 'starting-a-new-chapter' exercise, she had thought at the time. And she had given back to her students all that was theirs. So, everything looked different. As yet, she was unsure how she was going to fill her time. She would make some choices soon. She might take a degree in something she knew nothing about. Or pick an area of fiction she had never taught and see if she liked it. But right now, she felt disinclined to do anything. She ought to be seizing the day and making the most of how ever many years were left to her, but somehow, she lacked the motivation. It was odd that just when she had the time to do everything she had never been able to accommodate before, she no longer had the desire. It was like being in a state of suspended animation. She felt tired too, and worried that she was slowing up. Was it just a sort of reaction to being newly retired, as she had said to the other women? Probably, she decided.

Everything would be fine in the end. After all, she had always considered herself to be a resourceful and resilient person. Yet, she was finding it difficult to raise enthusiasm for getting through every day. And this morning, for the first time, it had occurred to her that it was not just today that she had to get through, and not just tomorrow, but every single day for what remained of her life. That seemed a tall order.

Thank heavens she was due a little diversion in half an hour. There were fewer of them now, and she was looking forward to it.

Was she sweaty after her bike ride? She raised each of her arms in turn and sniffed her armpits. Thinking about Napoleon's messaged instruction to his lover when he was returning from battle saying that she was *not* to wash, Lucy stood in the doorway trying to decide whether a pot of tea to revive her was more important than a shower.

'I'm no Josephine,' she declared to the empty room as she made for the stairs. If she abluted quickly, and put on something comfortable, there might yet be time for tea. Anyway, she could have it when he arrived. He was partial to a slice of fruit cake.

Jen put her key into the lock with the same sense of excitement she had had since moving in with Fred thirty-one years ago.

'Darling, I'm home,' she called. 'Shall we have some tea and watch *Pointless*?'

She ran up the stairs.

Pausing in the doorway she found the bedroom as empty as she had known it would be. She felt herself crumple as though she had been punched in the stomach, then she threw herself onto his side of the bed and shed the tears that had trembled behind her eyes all afternoon.

Chapter Two

Six months before the present

'I've never known any woman enjoy sex more than you, Pudding,' he said affectionately, leaning over to pat her Rubenesque bottom. 'How long's it been now?'

'Since when?' Lucy asked.

'Since we first knew each other in the biblical sense!'

'Heaven knows. But hadn't you just graduated that afternoon?'

He picked up his wine glass from the bedside cabinet, sipped, nodded approval, and then gazed into the distance as if he were rewinding the tape of his life to the appropriate day.

'You're right. And that was 1988. God, that makes me feel old.'

Not wanting to think about how much older it made her feel, she came up with a memory of her own.

'You were gorgeous,' she beamed at him. 'Awfully drunk and nervous, but terribly sweet.'

'Well, it wasn't an everyday offer, was it? After all, you were the tutor who'd steered me through the degree and made me work enough to get a 2.1! I was hardly expecting you to school me in the sensual arts too.'

She chuckled. 'You didn't call me "Pudding" till much later,' she remembered.

'I wouldn't have dared.'

She watched him enjoying his glass of Barolo. Guy, or 'Thursday Chap' – as she called him privately – was a nice man and she was fond of him. He was good company, but it was becoming more and more apparent that he was not wearing well. She knew that she was a fine one to talk. Her hair in its untidy bun was always a mess of tangles, and uneven in length because she cut it herself. Her teeth were functional rather than white or even, plus she was several stones too heavy which was probably the reason for an increasing number of aches in her hips, knees and feet. Also, she had much less energy than she used to have.

At no time in her life could she have been called 'a beauty'. But what she had learned early on was that plenty of much lovelier women were not as interested in sex as she was. She adored it, and from the age of thirteen, during a passionate dream, she had learned what a glorious thing it was to feel real ecstasy. Before she had become sexual with other people, she had spent long evenings exploring her own body. And around her nineteenth birthday, she had become so skilled that she could arouse herself by simply squeezing her thighs together and thinking lascivious thoughts. That had cheered up plenty of dull lectures in her youth, she remembered.

Turning her attention back to Guy, she watched as he heaved himself into a seated position. Unfortunately, the movement reminded her of a beached seal, which was a shame because he had been a delectable young man. And it was not just his looks that had aged; once upon a time, after a glass of wine he would have been ready for more dalliance. But now, those days were a mere memory. His appetite was still strong, but his performance greatly diminished. She could also bet on what his next words would be, and felt herself smirk when, within thirty seconds, and as if to please her, he sighed and announced 'I'd better get going. My wife will be wondering where I am.'

'How is she?'

'Well, you know, all right, I think. It works OK. We have a nice lifestyle with good neighbours and plenty of friends. And she usually offers me sex on a Sunday morning. I get the feeling it's on her list of weekend chores, because it's never been very adventurous or joyous. Still, one can't have everything. Thank God for you though, Pudding. You make a man feel appreciated in a unique and highly gratifying way.'

That was her talent, she reflected after his hurried departure as she poured herself another glass of wine. She had not wanted children. Might she have wanted a husband? Maybe a very long time ago, but she had never been sure she was built for fidelity. In truth, she thoroughly enjoyed her single life. She liked not having to do anyone's laundry, or produce dinner every night, and valued the freedom she had to eat baked beans straight from the can if she was hungry but less than keen to interrupt work for a proper meal.

Really, she was lucky, and her wish was to carry on much as she was for as long as possible. It was a pity therefore that there were rumblings about change in her faculty when the autumn term started in a month's time. The new Vice-Chancellor of the university seemed hell-bent on shaking up every department. Everyone felt threatened and the majority of the lecturers were disgruntled and disaffected. But she could not believe that this would lead to the sort of unrest that might dislodge the 'odious one', as she had named him. So, almost certainly, he was here to stay, till something bigger and more prestigious caught his aspirational attention. She shivered suddenly with a sense of foreboding.

Monica turned over in bed and thumped the pillow, then gingerly laid her head in the hollow she had created, in the hope that it would ease the pain.

She longed to sleep. Surely that would help? Anything would, after the events of this afternoon. Soon, it would be time to start dinner. She had planned a sweet potato curry – a recipe she was keen to try from a new cookbook she had bought in Crowbury's independent bookshop. Well, he won't be getting that now, she decided.

It had been bad enough that he had arrived home a few days ago with the news that his firm wanted him to retire in six months when he would be sixty-five. It had come as no surprise to Monica that this might happen. James had been the most senior partner for a decade, and as a leading legal mind on shipping law, his salary was far higher than that of his colleagues. They probably thought the spoils had gone to him for long enough. After all, most of them were still paying mortgages, and putting children through school or university. She imagined those younger lawyers driving past the beautiful detached Georgian house she and James had bought thirty years previously for a fraction of its current worth, muttering that 'good old Charlton' had had the gravy train to himself long enough.

He, on the other hand, had not considered the possibility of retiring and had appeared utterly shell-shocked. His mood had not lightened since. In fact, the terror in his eyes frightened her. Did he really dread, so much, the notion of being at home with her all day? He had taken a week off to think through his future. She had suggested they go to France. He had muttered that it would be an absolute nightmare in August, and that anyway, he was not in the mood and would use the time to sample what retirement at home might feel like.

She had not envisaged that this 'sampling' would involve her in so much lovemaking. Suddenly, he wanted it every night. She had complied, as she always had. That was the deal in most marriages of their type she supposed. The man earned the money and the woman provided food, sex and laundry. She could not imagine her daughter, Melissa, a determinedly feminist woman, settling for that arrangement. And it was depressing that she had.

Still, she and James might have kept the peace and held everything together if today had never happened. But it had. The

15

bitterness and bile that had been exchanged in the past couple of hours had made her feel as if she were performing in a soap opera. Even now, it seemed melodramatic and unreal. Could it have been avoided? Should it have been?

Her migraine had come as a shock. She used to have them frequently around the time of her menopause but, much to her relief, they had died out along with menstruation. Perhaps it was the palpable tension in the house that had triggered it. Or all that unwanted intimacy, which did not fulfil her in any way.

She had felt quite strange early this morning and had been unable to stop yawning. Next, her vision had grown blurry, and she had developed an over-sensitivity to light, and by lunchtime, agonising pain had begun to stab her above the right eyebrow.

She had told James she was going to lie down. He had suggested a back and shoulder massage. It was something he was good at, so when he turned up in their bedroom shortly afterwards, she had been pleased to see him.

He began kneading the top of her shoulders. 'Very tense there, Mon,' he had said. 'Still, I know what'll sort you out.' He had laughed as he flipped her over onto her back and straddled her.

Something deep inside her brain snapped; her mind had filled with a red mist of repugnance and outrage and she had pushed him away from her with as much violent strength as she could muster.

His expression, one of incredulity, made her smile. In turn, his eyes flashed with anger and he lost his balance and slid off the glazed cotton duvet on to the floor. He looked so undignified that she laughed. If only his colleagues could see him now, she thought as, without warning, her mirth was replaced by angry tears.

Somehow then, and for the first time in their married life, they had begun to give voice to all the hidden truths of their relationship. He shouted that her coldness had driven him into the arms of countless other women and that he had been having affairs for decades. And she had screamed at him that his complete lack of interest or concern as she gave up her career to administer chest physiotherapy several hours of every day to their very sick daughter, had killed not only her love for him but her desire.

Spitting words out in her rage she had cried, 'I haven't enjoyed sex with you since we had the girls. I've pretended it was OK just to get you going and get the whole bloody thing over as quickly as possible.'

'D'you think I don't know that? But that's just you. I've never had complaints from anyone else.'

'That's only because women are more polite than men.'

'My God, Monica, you can be so cruel. Sadie says I play her body like a violin.'

'That sounds like something she read in a book! I expect she just says it to make you feel good, where – you see – frankly I don't give a damn. Who the hell is she, anyway?'

'My current lover.'

'Well, she's welcome to you. Why don't you go to her now?'

'If she wasn't married with kids I would!'

At last they had run out of insults and vitriol and had stared at each other, breathing heavily, with hatred in their eyes which was then replaced by horror and disbelief that what had been exposed could never be forgotten or unsaid – and that the companionable and civilised surface that had masked the flaws in their marriage for so long, had splintered into a million pieces.

It was, she reflected, as she lay alone in the bedroom with the heavy curtains pulled shut against the sunshine, the end of everything that she had known. Did she feel relief? Partly. Was she sorry? Not very. What did the future hold? It was unimaginable and terrifying, but maybe in time there would be a fresh beginning that could be different.

'Fred, darling, what *are* you like?'

The noise of the crash in the hall had propelled her out of her study at the back of the house. He stood at the foot of the stairs, his face a picture of embarrassment, as he surveyed the mess of tea splashes on the wall, and the dropped tray, broken cups and teapot that were scattered around him.

'Your Norfolk accent returns when you're rattled, Jen,' he murmured.

'Does it? That's funny.'

'And very, very sweet,' he said quietly.

She watched him trying to process what to do about the chaos he had created. This was something new. A different stage, she supposed. She did not want to consider what it meant and did not want him to start ruminating about it either. He had only just begun to admit to certain weaknesses. He was private and proud and not ready yet to be an invalid.

'It could have happened to anyone,' she said breezily. 'I'm always dropping things – it's just I never tell you. And I hide the damage, so you never know!'

He smiled at her gratefully. 'Sorry, Jen.'

'Listen, don't let it worry you. It's nothing to do with… anything. You're just a bit stressed, aren't you? How many more of those articles have you got to read before you can start judging them?'

'Rather a lot,' he answered, anxiously.

'I've never known there be so many.'

She was lying. Fred had been a judge for this particular journalism award for a decade, and the current schedule was no different from usual. Normally, he loved it. Loved it when he discovered a real talent, but appeared to relish the outcome just as much when he thought the standard was shocking and he could moan to her about how the dumbing down of their industry was producing formulaic robots not writers.

'Perhaps I'm slowing up,' he muttered.

'Not you,' she countered quickly. 'But I think you need a break from it. Let's have tea upstairs. We can put the television on and watch a bit of news and have a rest. I could do with one too; my piece for *The Guardian* isn't going to plan.'

His voice warbled slightly as he said, 'What would I do without you, darling girl? I love you so much.'

'Thank God for that,' she laughed. 'I thought you'd gone off me!'

'What! Because it's been half an hour since I gave you a hug?'

She grinned. 'Just joking. Come on, big man, shall I see you up the stairs?'

Instantly she regretted her words. She did not want him to realise that she knew his walking was becoming unsteady.

He peered at her and she felt in that moment that he fully understood what she feared, and what she was trying to minimise by remaining optimistic and jolly. He had always dubbed her his 'ray of sunshine' and she wanted to live up to his description.

'I'll manage. I'm not in a wheelchair yet,' he said with a chuckle that had little humour in it.

In the kitchen she rummaged under the sink for the dustpan and some spray cleaning fluid which she hoped would deal with the tea-stained wall. Before long, apart from a few wet patches, everything was back to normal and she returned the cleaning materials to their cupboard and switched on the kettle.

They had talked about everything, always. But now they were holding back. She supposed that both of them were trying to avoid facing the truth of a situation that threatened to destroy the life they loved. Did he need to believe that he was just growing clumsy with age, and that it happened to everyone? Did *she* believe it? Standing at the sink, she breathed deeply against the overwhelming distress that threatened. She was not a woman who tended to cry, but when she did, Fred always knew. She sniffed, wiped her nose on a piece of kitchen towel and took a deep breath as she wondered if today was going to be the day when she made a new document on her computer and began listing all his symptoms. Once she did that, she knew it would be a small step to googling them.

Had he looked any of them up? She doubted it, and she would never check on his search history, no matter what happened.

Neither of them ever approached each other's PC unless specifically asked by the other to do so. It was a private workspace. They had never even discussed this habit. It had just evolved.

Back when she had first met him – he the inexhaustible editor of the *Daily Chronicle* and she the keen young recruit from a provincial title beginning her career on a national – he had welcomed her and told her what he valued most in his paper was a journalist's right to confidentiality, and the necessary space and privacy he or she needed to develop ideas or leads.

Within days, someone in the office had told her that the editor's wife had terminal breast cancer, but that he never talked about it and wanted to carry on as normal. Even when she died, Fred had taken hardly any leave and as soon as the funeral was over, had returned to his post and continued to be more energetic and dedicated than any of his staff.

She had admired and respected him, but as a junior features' writer, she had little contact with him, so it was a surprise when he had asked her out for lunch.

They had discussed her career. Did she, he wanted to know, have any hankerings to move into a speciality such as health? Not really, she had said. What about politics? She had pulled a face and he had laughed.

'So, you're happy in features?'

She had nodded and murmured something about how she liked the variety. And he had remarked that she had an eye for the sort of news that could be extended by a timely idea and praised her recent article on parents' anxiety when their children were sitting A levels.

His affirmation had filled her with absurd gladness.

There had been a second lunch. And a third, which took a distinctly personal turn as he discussed his private life and how his marriage had not been happy.

'My wife was a journalist originally, very bright, not bookish like me, but quick-witted and dynamic. However, she wanted to make more money, far more, so she set up her own public relations firm. She was successful. And before long she became a lot more interested in her business than me. Mind you, I was working round the clock and I don't think I was as attentive as I might have been. Anyway, things came to a head within months of Simon, our first son, being born and she asked me to leave. We were apart for over a year, but then she wanted to give it another go, and our second son, Matthew, was the result of that. It was quite turbulent for ages and we split several times, but I kept coming back for the boys. But when she decided to send them both to boarding school – and she could afford it, which I could not have done – that was the end.'

'So, you'd split up before she became ill?'

'Oh, long before. But I went back during her illness and, strangely, we became better friends then, and made our peace with each other before her death. We both felt better for that, and it helped our children. It's been tough for them. Especially Matthew who's only thirteen. They're at the same school though, and very close, which has helped.'

Then, with brutal honesty, he had confessed to a number of relationships in and out of the office which had taken place in the periods he and his wife had been apart.

It was not a total shock. Rumours had been rife that he had had an on-off relationship for years with the Beauty Editor, who had expectations now of becoming the next Mrs Warboys.

There were no more lunches because Jen had gone on holiday to Morocco with a friend, and by the time she returned, Fred was in the south of France with his sons.

Then it had been the political conference season when the editorial staff were based in Brighton or Blackpool or Bournemouth. But one day, shortly after parliament resumed, he had sent her a memo, suggesting dinner the following evening at Joe Allen.

They had talked and laughed, with a new sense of relaxation in each other's company. She had thoroughly enjoyed being with

21

him but had wondered why he sought out her presence, and assumed he was lonely. But on the fourth dinner date, nervously, she had broached the subject of the immaculately turned-out Beauty Editor and asked if it was true that they were to be married.

For the first time, he had taken her hands in his across the table.

'Oh my God, no. Listen, Jen, I've put it about a bit, I'm afraid. And she was probably the most constant companion I had. But I couldn't possibly set up home with her. It would last till about teatime on the first day! She's far too tense. And frankly a bit of a ball-breaker. But since you've asked, and are obviously wondering if my intentions are entirely honourable—'

'That's not it at all,' she had interrupted; not wanting to be the sort of woman who would ask an older man, a boss to boot, whether this was a real date and whether he was hopeful that they might take things further.

'Stop please. And listen… Sorry if that sounds rude.' Then he had confessed that he had loved her for months, and that now that he had got to know her better, he had 'got it very badly indeed.' And that in fact he felt 'sandbagged by love in a way I never have, and never thought I could be.' But then he had, very sweetly, told her that he could not expect someone as young and intelligent as she was to feel the same. And that loads of people would rejoice in telling her that he was unlikely to be faithful. 'But I will be,' he had assured her. 'If only you'll give me a chance.'

She remembered the conversation so well even though it had taken place in 1987. Remembered too the huge feeling of joyous relief that had flooded her mind and body as she realised that she loved him too.

And so, he had taken her home that night and they began the intense and crazily romantic relationship that was, they had kept assuring each other, quite unlike anything either had known before.

Soon afterwards, she became aware that some of the journalists on the paper were placing bets on how long they would be together.

She was mortified and began looking for a new job that day. Much to her astonishment – though Fred's glowing reference might have had something to do with it – she was ensconced before long as Features Editor on a new monthly magazine for 'grown-up women with a brain', which was shorthand for saying that their pages never included items on bridal gowns, childcare, or cookery.

So, the two of them had been free to continue their courtship away from the *Chronicle*, and once his boys became used to the idea, they had married. And we've been so lucky, she thought as the kettle boiled. Lucky and happy in equal measure. It's been a charmed life.

'Jen,' his voice was as strong as ever, 'a man could die of thirst up here! And any chance of a digestive biscuit?'

She grinned. Surely, he couldn't be seriously ill? He sounded fine. She was probably worrying needlessly.

Chapter Three

Three months before the present

'What do you hate most about motor neurone disease?'

Jen and the counsellor had arranged to meet at the café on the ground floor of the hospital. They had had a cup of coffee and a chat about the weather and the parking difficulties, but now they were embarked on their session in a consulting room so tiny that their knees almost touched, and she was not at all sure she was ready to be here.

The older woman seemed to sense her disquiet and continued with a gentle smile.

'I'm sorry. It was quite a brutal question, but it's a brutal disease and most people feel very distressed and angry about it. Also, we're only allocated half an hour in here and I want to move things on, so you get as much benefit as possible.'

Jen nodded. 'I wonder if I could ask you a few things first, like, can I call you Helen rather than Doctor something?'

'I should hope so; it's my name! Anyway, I'm not a doctor, just a therapist.'

'Mmmn. So, where to begin? Hard to know... I suppose I never thought anything would ever happen to Fred. It probably sounds a bit "Princess Diana" to say he's my rock, but he really is. I know he's fifteen years older than me, but he's... he was... so, uh...' she searched for absolutely the right word, 'zestful. We,' her voice cracked, 'we live for each other. He's everything to me. And I suppose what I hate most, to answer your question, is that I might not be a good enough carer for him.'

'I'm sure you will be,' Helen reassured her, 'but while you're caring for him, though you'll probably be able to discuss his death and come to some sort of accommodation in both your minds that he will die,' she paused, 'you might not get round to dealing with your own loss and grief till afterwards. And it may surprise you how bad that feels. I don't want to make things worse by saying that, believe me. However, I am trying to say that you need to think about yourself and your feelings and your own future in this process, as well as about him.'

Jen stared at her shoes, which looked blurry because of the tears she was trying to contain. 'I'm worried about some of the stuff I've read on the net about him getting to the point where he can't breathe or might choke. I feel I'll be useless. In fact, I'm panicking about what he might have to go through.'

There was a short silence. Jen felt herself warm to the other woman and was genuinely grateful that she was really listening, and not jumping in with solutions – because, frankly, those seemed in short supply.

'The illness doesn't take the same path in everyone. And some people go on for ages at a level where they still have good quality of life. Not all, of course.'

'Fred is pretty sure he won't last long.'

'Is he depressed?' Helen asked.

'I don't think so. Obviously, he's reacting to what's happening to him. He's upset about the illness, and about leaving me, and that it's all winding down. But he calls that "appropriate sadness", which I think is rather a good phrase.'

'I agree. He sounds a remarkable man.'

Jen looked straight at Helen for the first time. 'He absolutely is. And his intellect and personality and everything that is the essence of him is still very much intact even though he can't walk up and down stairs now. But when, for example, we watch *University Challenge*, he's still quicker with the answers than most of the students, which cheers us up. So that bit of his brain seems fine. Perhaps that often happens. I suppose you only have to remember the example of Stephen Hawking.'

'True.'

'Can I ask if you have any link to MND yourself?'

There was a long pause.

'Sorry,' Jen said. 'I know some counsellors don't like to give anything of themselves away. It's not allowed, is it? Well not with some schools of therapy anyway.'

'I trained in cognitive behaviour therapy,' Helen told her. 'In that model, it's no crime to disclose details about yourself if it's helpful. And I think it's understandable that you want to know why I'm here and if I have any idea of what impact this has on people. So, yes, I, um, the man I live with has had it for a while. He's a doctor and is very accepting of his own mortality. I doubt if he'll last much longer. Now, my situation may be helpful to you, or it may not. If it's too raw for you that I'm embroiled in the end game as it were, there are other volunteers you could see.'

Jen smiled at her. 'It will help me. Thanks for being so honest. It can't be easy for you. I'm amazed you're here.'

Helen studied her hands for a moment. 'I started by contacting the MND society to find out how to help him. That was a couple of years ago now. But the fact that I had trained as a therapist in the past got me thinking. I suppose I'd begun to feel less useful once we needed a combination of carers and nurses to look after him. Of course, I feed and shave him and try to do personal things, but he's so far gone, the health professionals are pretty much in charge. Doing this – seeing spouses like you – helps me feel of value. The only aspect of the whole business that makes sense.'

*

26

When it happened, Lucy had thought he was playing a trick on her.

It was, she realised, more than a month ago now. They had had a surprisingly energetic encounter. It had been very satisfying for her, but she had kept her eyes averted as he had turned an ugly red colour when he reached his climax. It had taken longer than usual. But all her men valued how she nursed them to ecstasy, and she never let them down. Years ago, they had been quick off the mark. Too quick! Now, it was very different. Well, they were all much older. Sometimes she minded that she would, almost certainly, never again feel the flesh of some rampantly sexual boy in his twenties. Her Monday man, for example, was almost eighty. There must be a time limit on his continuing activity, but he kept himself going with a mixture of Cialis and Viagra. She had worried about him. Worried even that he might drop dead while he was with her. Who would have thought that when someone did, it would be Guy, who was only fifty-four?

It had been a dreadful business. For a start, it had been a huge effort to push him off her. He was a dead weight. Well, he would be, she supposed. She had rung for an ambulance and had been unable to conceal what they had been up to. The paramedics had been kind and efficient, but she had noticed that they had registered the age difference between them, and that their expressions betrayed their bewilderment at the coupling of a man who was quite a handsome, if overweight, specimen and her. And later, when they had left with his corpse and closed the door behind them, she had stared at herself in the bedroom mirror and sighed at the blowsy image she saw staring back.

She had given them his name but had not been able to tell them what his wife was called or where they lived, except that she thought they had a house near the river. She had reached into her mind in an attempt to recall some relevant details of his life, but they would not come to her. So, the paramedics had rifled through his jacket pockets for answers. One of the young men had moved out of earshot when he had called a number in Guy's phone. It had been a shockingly awful day.

She looked at her watch and was surprised at how long it had been since the meeting. Lost in her walking and thinking, some two hours had passed. No wonder she was tired. Sighing, she wandered another fifty yards, to the perimeter of the university grounds where she headed for a bench under an oak tree.

The writing was on the wall now. The Vice-Chancellor had told her that she had to resign, which was, she discovered, the price demanded by Guy's wife.

Lucy had been thunderstruck that the university was prepared to succumb to such blackmail. The deceased was not a student and had nothing whatever to do with the university except for the fact that he had studied there decades previously. But, it seemed, the widow had become obsessed by Lucy. She had engaged a private detective to spy on her and reached the conclusion that Lucy was operating a brothel.

When the Vice-Chancellor had relayed this to her, she was outraged. 'I am not! I would never relinquish my amateur status where sex is concerned.'

The loathsome man sitting opposite her had said that he was appalled by her lack of contrition and called her 'an evil old slag'.

'And what if I don't resign?' She had asked with more bravado than she felt.

'The widow will go to the tabloids and say what a perverse influence you have on this hallowed university and its impressionable students. You'll be hung out to dry and don't think for a moment that the university will support you. Frankly, you're old, and not up to speed with modern teaching. It was only a matter of time before we found another way to edge you out.'

'I could take this to the union.'

'Are you in it?'

'Well, no, actually.'

He had raised a sardonic eyebrow. 'I don't think they'd be any help even if you were. They wouldn't have the power to stop the press. It would be a nightmare for you. Not much better for us.'

'Can I at least see out the academic year?' she pleaded.

'Absolutely not. You must go at Christmas, Miss Brown.'

'*Professor*, if you don't mind.'

'OK, Pro-fess-or! You're...' he glanced at his computer screen. 'You were sixty-five this year. You've had a good innings.'

It felt autumnal now the sun had gone down. A young under-graduate gave her a wary glance as he walked past the seat she was slumped upon. She was nobody now. Nobody at all.

Monica turned over the envelope in her hands, her heart beating loudly. She only heard from Stephen once a year. On her birthday. Every time she had a card from him, she imagined it would be the last. They had not met for almost a decade.

He had been the architect of their extension. Her husband had decided they would add a sunroom to the house. It had been his reaction to the eventual death of their very sick daughter. She imagined he had seen it as a treat for her. It was, in a way. Of course, James was never around to supervise it, so she and Stephen, a quiet, artistic man, had spent many hours together. She had thought that he appeared rather more often to check on the workmen than most architects, but he had assured her that with such an extensive and expensive project, he was keen to keep an eye on the progress.

Morning coffee, or tea and cake had morphed into an early evening drink. She had looked forward to his visits and thought about him so much that she had wondered if her enjoyment of his presence constituted infidelity. But she had been unprepared for his declaration of love.

It had been monumentally sweet and touching. But she had forced herself to ignore it. Her husband depended on her. Anyway, Stephen was newly divorced and probably vulnerable and lonely and not thinking straight.

29

There had been kisses – so passionate and wonderful that they made her tingle all over. He had stroked her breasts once, which had sent a rush of arousal to places that had never felt that way before, but she had reproved him. With just a nod of the head from her, he would have taken things further. And lying hot and wakeful in the nights that followed, she had wished beyond any urge or desire she had ever known, that she might have the courage to consummate their feelings.

She never had.

He had wanted to stay in touch and had attempted to press his personal email address and mobile phone number on her. She had resisted. All she knew was that his company had a branch in Oxford but that he was based in London. It was typical of her husband that he had not believed there could be any good architects in the market town where they lived.

She knew of course that she could have googled Stephen and his firm. Why had she never done so? What kind of a fool was she?

She opened the envelope.

'Sweetest Monica,' the card read. 'You are always in my thoughts. Do you ever think of me? I would still like to light up your life. Fondest love, Stephen.'

Chapter Four

The present

This isn't how I imagined today would go, Monica thought as the ambulance doors closed.

She felt her shoulders relax for the first time since the agitated man in the audience had waved at her across the cinema, pointing at his collapsed companion. Being the only volunteer in Screen Two, she knew it was up to her to do something and had raced to his side while the film, with its excessively loud soundtrack, thundered on.

The woman had been flaccid, unresponsive and glistening with sweat, and suddenly slid from her chair to the narrow floor space between two rows of seats. Monica was not a first aider, but years of dealing with Betsy – her daughter, whose entire life had been punctuated by one medical crisis after another – was training of a sort, she supposed.

She had kept talking to the man's wife to try to prevent her slipping deeper into whatever nightmare was claiming her, determined that Day One at The Granary should not end in tragedy.

An elderly gentleman sitting further forward in the cinema had turned and 'shushed' them. Once he had grasped that there was an emergency, he had gestured an apology, but offered no assistance. However, the disturbance he created had sparked the attention of a young man who turned out to be a nurse. Monica had watched as he strode over, and in that calm, matter-of-fact and confident way health professionals have, had set about coaxing a response from the unconscious woman. Before long, the lady's eyelids had fluttered, and a hint of a smile had stretched the corners of her lips. Embarrassed, she struggled to sit up and began apologising to everyone around her for 'making a scene'.

As the ambulance switched on its siren and drove off, the manager of The Granary – the suited woman with dramatic spectacles they had met on their first visit three weeks previously – put an arm around her shoulders. Initially, Monica's instinct was to shrug it off, but she was shaking, she realised, and found it comforting.

'Bit of a drama for you.'

'You could say that, Mrs Pemberton,' Monica managed a weak smile.

'Oh, call me Liz. Everyone does. Let's get you a cup of tea.'

Since Fred had died, Jen had been busy 'catching up on culture', as she tended to call it whenever her stepsons expressed concern that she always seemed to be out when they phoned. In the seven weeks since she had become a widow – a word she hated and had not used in public as yet – she had been to four plays in London, two concerts in Crowbury, and spent a day in Oxford walking round the colleges before finding herself at a talk on climate change. Keeping active, and being transported and diverted from her aloneness, seemed to be the key to getting through every day. And now, here at The Granary, because of her volunteering role, she was to have free access to a whole range of films as well as theatre, ballet and opera relays.

Today, had consisted of a quick lesson on the workings of the kitchen, being assigned to check tickets in Screen Four, and then sitting at the back of the cinema during its afternoon programme, which was billed as 'a touch of nostalgia'. The film was *Dr Zhivago* and she spent most of it hugging her arms around her body for comfort, but as she was some distance from any of the paying public, she hoped that no one would notice.

In the foyer earlier, she had encountered Helen, the counsellor from the hospital. They had exchanged a 'how are you doing?' and a smile. Bereaved within a fortnight of each other, Jen fancied there was a mirroring of the same expression of shock and sorrow reflected in their eyes. Helen was the only person with whom she had discussed her feelings. It marked her out as special.

She was aware that she ought to tell Monica and Lucy about Fred. They had met just the once since their initial and accidental coming together. She should have done it then but had failed to find the moment. However, she could hardly work with them without explaining that he had died.

Lucy was swallowing the remains of her tea and finishing the custard tart she had bought as a treat for reaching the end of her first day, when she saw Monica, standing with the manager, by the front door.

She had noticed the ambulance before it had driven off, and the sight of it had filled her with horror. Until then, it had not occurred to her that people might fall ill in the cinema. An unwanted vision of the collapsed figure of Thursday Chap dying in her bed, four months ago, came to mind. She had been hope-less in dealing with that trauma. Sometimes, she thought that her inability to deal with any kind of sickness stemmed from the fact that she had never been a mother. Or maybe, to look at it another way, it was *why* she had never become a mother. She had never considered that before.

The manager's arm was round Monica now and they turned in her direction. She waved. They nodded but continued talking.

The trouble was that she had gone through life assuming that her generation, the lucky ones who had been born into a country

33

with an established health service, would all live healthier and longer. However, the evidence around her suggested otherwise. Most people she knew had a litany of complaints. Furthermore, they dwelt upon them, whether it was hypertension, eye problems, or heart disease. As for aches and pains, they could bore for England. Really it was all too tedious.

She suspected she was not very fit herself. But she was coping. She never went to her GP. And she rarely read newspaper articles about health. It had been a miracle that she had had no serious sexual diseases. But perhaps she had picked her partners well.

She looked up as Monica slipped into the seat beside her. Mrs Pemberton hovered.

'I'm going to get Monica some tea. She's had a tough afternoon. Would you like some too?'

Lucy nodded. 'Just common or garden builders, thank you.' She turned to Monica. 'What happened?'

During the explanation, Lucy felt herself growing hot then cold. Should she, she wondered, tell Mrs Pemberton that she was not cut out for dealing with sick individuals and that she should, perhaps, be restricted to the kitchen, or to meeting and greeting in the foyer where there were always plenty of staff milling around.

Trying to focus on Monica she smiled sympathetically and realised that the other woman, though shaken, was not unduly upset, and had regarded what happened as 'all in a day's work.'

Jen appeared, her film having just ended, and Monica began to relay the circumstances of her afternoon all over again. Lucy felt even more anxious as she heard the story a second time. She was, she suddenly realised, drumming her fingers on the table in front of her. It was a habit of hers when she felt rattled but the other two might find it rude, so she clasped her hands together to stop them fidgeting and made herself look around the reception area in search of focal points that might calm or distract her.

Suddenly, she spied an elderly man, in a startlingly patterned Caribbean shirt, which was definitely not a garment suited to the

34

rain, wind and sleety snow outside. He was setting up a music stand in the far corner beside a piano she had not noticed before.

Mrs Pemberton, who had just returned with a large pot of tea and four mugs as well as a plate of cakes, followed her gaze.

'Ah, yes, it's Thursday,' she announced in her very positive voice. 'We're trying out live music, and it's a cello recital tonight. It may be slightly highbrow for some, but it's only for three quarters of an hour, and lots of our patrons are opera buffs and so on. We experimented with a Freddie Mercury tribute band the other night, but it was awfully noisy, and we had more brickbats than bouquets shall we say. Just got to try and get the mix right... Everyone, help yourselves to some tea, can you? And cake.'

'It's so good of you to do this,' Jen said, 'and also very generous to provide live music.'

'Well, it's a bit of a gamble.' Liz Pemberton drew up a chair and sat down. 'You see, the food and drink are excellent ways of making money. You wouldn't believe the markup on a cappuccino for example. So, we need to focus on ways we can encourage our punters to visit the café whenever they come to the venue. We tend to do well at lunchtimes and in the early afternoons, and then get quite busy late evenings with a younger crowd, but the place dies on its feet about now. So, we're trying to provide reasons to keep the afternoon people here for longer, but also encourage those coming through the doors in the evenings to turn up a little earlier to have drinks or supper before the film.'

'Gosh, there's a lot to it,' Monica said.

'You have no idea,' Liz sighed. 'We're lucky we've got some council funding but it's not enough on its own. We've got to make this pay.'

'Yes, you must.' Jen put down her mug to tighten the band that held her customary ponytail in place. 'This town hasn't got anything else remotely as good. It's absolutely fantastic.'

Liz looked delighted. 'I'm glad you appreciate us. Welcome aboard by the way. I think you three are going to make a huge difference.'

35

Lucy, who had not joined in the conversation, was still staring at the couple in the corner. The man's hair was longer than it had been, and he had lost a good stone in weight, but there was no doubt that he was Roy, one of her chaps. Not that he visited her regularly. In fact, now that she came to think about it, it had been weeks since she had last seen him.

He looked surprisingly well, she thought as she continued to observe him. Some months back, he had confided that he had been diagnosed with a neurological condition which would eventually rob him of most movement and which, he had been told, was also likely to change his personality. Apparently, his specialist had run through the possibilities that he might become less risk averse – perhaps more prone to excessive spending or gambling – which might be difficult for those closest to him. As he had relayed this to her over their post-coital wine and fruit cake, he had laughed at the idea of going to the bookies. 'My parents were serious Methodists, and I was brought up to believe that betting was the work of the devil; and though I'm completely irreligious now, that conditioning never leaves you!'

At the time – and it was a while ago, and before Thursday's chap had died on her – she had wondered what would transpire when Roy's ability to recognise what was happening to him, and to discuss it, began to fade, and the new behavioural traits took over.

She had not known that his cello playing was up to performance standard. But maybe he would surprise them all. She hoped it was in a good way.

Lucy's ponderings were disturbed by Jen turning and jumping up to welcome an attractive, older woman who seemed slightly familiar.

'These are my partners in crime,' Jen announced. 'Lucy...' Lucy smiled and gave a little wave. 'And this is Monica, who almost had a death on her hands in the cinema this afternoon. And on our first day too.'

Monica shook her head slightly to indicate that Jen was over-stating the case.

'Too modest, my friend,' Jen laughed. 'I'd be claiming I'd saved the old dear's life and expecting a medal at the very least. Anyway,' she stood back to usher her companion more fully into the group, 'this is Helen. We... we've met once or twice at the hospital.'

'Won't you join us?' Lucy smiled.

'No thank you,' replied Helen. 'I'm waiting for someone off the London train and we're coming to the recital.'

'Another time then.' Monica smiled at the newcomer. 'I feel I know you. Have you always lived in Crowbury?'

'No. We were in Oxford till relatively recently. I've probably just got one of those faces,' Helen grinned.

They all laughed politely as she nodded, then left.

Jen helped herself to a cake and began to regale the others with a story about an excessively large woman in her cinema who had complained that the seats were uncomfortable.

'I had to choke back the words that if she lost several stone, the seats would feel fine. Honestly, some people. They just don't take responsibility for themselves, do they? And then other men and women, who do take notice of all the health messages and exercise and keep themselves in shape just suddenly die. It's not fair is it? I could hit people like her.'

Lucy gave a wry smile. 'I don't think I should comment. I don't do anything right. And there's no excuse really.'

'We all have reasons why we behave as we do,' Monica said, slowly. 'It's probably wrong to judge. No one knows what other people's lives are like behind closed doors.'

There was an uneasy silence.

Jen sighed. 'You're much nicer than me, I think.'

The cellist began to tune up at the far end of the room.

'Are we going to stay and listen?' Jen changed the subject.

'I'm game,' Monica said. 'I haven't got anything to rush home for.'

Jen raised her eyebrows. 'Really?'

'No. My husband decided to go and visit our daughter in Australia, and I had things on. You know how it is.'

Both Lucy and Jen chose to say nothing while, in tandem, they recalled their first tea at The Granary just three weeks earlier, when Monica had implied she had exciting travel plans.

'I've got nothing on either,' Lucy added quickly.

'Nor me,' Jen said. 'Look, he's going to start in a minute, there are some seats in the back row. Shall we grab them?'

'Let's,' Monica agreed.

'By the way,' Jen murmured as they covered the few yards to the other area, 'I've been thinking I ought to tell you that my husband died. I don't, to be honest, want to talk about it. But since we're working together...'

The other two women stopped walking.

'Oh my God,' Lucy exclaimed. 'How awful. I'm so sorry.'

And Monica reached out to try to pat her on the arm but failed to make contact as Jen urged them, briskly, to come and sit down or they would end up disturbing other people.

Almost immediately, there was a stuttering of applause as the accompanist took her seat at the piano, and the soloist walked to his chair and fixed the spike of the cello into the block of wood in front of him, before announcing that he was playing several works by Brahms and expanding on what they were and when they had been written.

Lucy felt relieved as Roy spoke because he sounded just as authoritative as he had over the decades in the lecture theatre. He had always been popular and was one of that rare breed of academics who are highly regarded by their peers but also excellent communicators to those less knowledgeable.

Realising that he had spotted her, she smiled at him, warmly. Was the pianist his wife? She looked lively and attractive and very pleasant, which was not at all how Lucy might have pictured her, given that most of her gentlemen claimed their partners were past lovemaking or had low libidos. This woman wore a proud and slightly proprietorial expression as Roy explained his programme to the audience. More than that, she looked fond and engaged. It was somewhat disturbing.

Since Thursday Chap had keeled over, and it had become apparent that his widow had loved him greatly and was devastated at his loss, Lucy had tried to eliminate a stream of intrusive thoughts that far from providing a public service all these years to sex-starved and misunderstood men whose sanity she had saved, she had simply encouraged husbands, who had perfectly good wives, to be greedy. And if she had, it meant that her ethos for the past thirty years had been based on a lie, which in turn made her question her judgement. She did not want to think that way. It kept her awake at night.

Soon though, she had much more to worry about as she watched Roy begin to sway around dramatically while he played. In her youth, she had been lucky enough to see Jacqueline du Pré in her prime; she had been a most energetic mover while she performed. The difference was that she had drawn from her cello something unquestionably blessed by the gods, which was a far cry from the sound emanating from Roy's instrument.

Monica tried to like the Brahms, but she feared it was too musically clever for her. She could not always understand the melody, and sometimes the cellist seemed to get carried away and she thought he hit the body of the cello with the wooden part of the bow once or twice. Was that an instruction by the composer? She doubted it. Still, what did she know? With her background, there had never been an option to learn an instrument. She was aware that James deplored her cultural ignorance. But then he deplored most things about her.

Her attention wandered to the woman who had collapsed in the cinema. Her husband had been devotedly attentive and concerned and, as she began to recover, had been manifestly relieved that she was looking more like herself. It had been hugely touching. Clearly, his wife was very special to him, and as she recalled the love in his eyes while he gazed at his spouse, Monica had felt bleak and alone in the certain knowledge that James had never regarded her highly. He had been attracted to her in their earlier days, but he had never valued her as a person.

Still, she had probably not valued him either and the truth was that she did not mind that he was away. In fact, she was enjoying the freedom. In October she would be sixty. Till recently, the date had not seemed particularly significant, but now the prospect seemed to be forcing her to focus on whether or not this was as good as her life was likely to get.

She had never thought of herself as someone who would discuss her marriage with friends. It felt too private. Anyway, she had very few. All those years of being at home looking after her daughter had isolated her. Lucy and Jen were possibly going to become closer to her – though that felt a strange concept – but she could not imagine talking to them. Maybe she should see a therapist? A voice in her head immediately responded to that idea by laughing sardonically and muttering, 'Surely not?' But she had to do something.

In between pieces, while the cellist retuned his instrument, Jen glanced at her watch. She was no musical expert, but she was pretty sure this old guy was long past his sell-by date. Of course, they were only using unpaid amateur enthusiasts but even so, she felt he should be much better than this. Thank heavens he was only supposed to go on for another half an hour.

A movement in the doorway disturbed her. Helen was holding out her hands, and as he emerged through the main door, she clasped the arms of a tall, elderly man. He had a very distinguished air to him and was clearly not British. Probably, he hailed from somewhere round the Mediterranean. Shaking his swept-back silver hair free of the snowflakes that had settled there, he smiled broadly at Helen. Jen was about to turn back to the performance when she saw the two of them move into a loving embrace, their lips meeting eagerly and with passion.

Turning away in shock, she told herself it was none of her business. There was no reason why a couple, long past the first flush of youth, should not have a romantic relationship. How censorius she was being. It was just that it felt far too soon. Helen's partner had died a mere two weeks before Fred. She felt sick at the thought that she herself might embrace anyone else with hunger – today, tomorrow, or ever. It would be a complete betrayal. Helen had seemed such a rational and kind figure. Someone to be depended upon. But in that moment, Jen decided that she would never confide in her again.

At last the concert was over. She wanted to leave. Quickly. Since Fred had died, all sorts of happenings unsettled her emotionally just when she was doing quite well. Seeing Helen behaving that way had disturbed her so much that she needed to be alone to walk and think.

'Well,' Lucy sighed. 'So, what did you think?'

'Diabolical!' Jen snapped. 'He was completely past it, if indeed he ever had it. They'll have to do better than that.'

Monica stood up. 'I thought there were some lovely parts actually. Of course, I'm not very musical.'

Roy and his accompanist were surveying the departing audience. No one had stopped to talk to them, and Lucy felt that she must go and say something.

'I thought that went rather well,' Roy announced in her direction as she advanced upon him. He turned to the pianist. 'Barbara, this is Lucy – an old and favourite colleague of mine till she retired. And Lucy, this is my *wife*.' He leant on the word, presumably, thought Lucy, in case she said something out of turn, or had failed to grasp the situation.

'Good to meet you, Barbara.'

'So, how was I?' Roy stood tall and proud. 'All these years I just played in pretty ordinary amateur orchestras, but I realise now I could have done much better. I could have been a professional!'

'But just think what the world of Political History would have missed if you had,' Lucy responded swiftly.

She saw a look of gratitude relax the anxious expression on the wife's face.

'But really, did *you* think I was good?' He was happy. Full of himself and the music.

Lucy turned to Barbara for guidance and saw a tenderness in her that desired to indulge her husband despite any embarrassment she might be feeling. Her pleading eyes peered into Lucy's, while her head nodded encouragement.

What should she do? Really, she should remind her old friend that this is what the specialist had warned him of – risky behaviour, a change in how he thought and acted – and that what he was doing was part of a progressive illness and could never end well. But she could not bring herself to dash his exhilaration, or to leave Barbara to console him if he accepted what she ought to say.

'Roy,' she replied, 'it was lovely to hear you play. You were marvellous.'

Chapter Five

It was her own cry of terror that woke her, that and the pounding in her chest.

She had been dreaming. So, finally, she must have fallen asleep around four, just when she had decided that her wakefulness would persist till morning.

Jen had realised weeks ago that there was no predictability to her night-time hours. And she had adapted to that part of widowhood with surprising ease. Sometimes, she fell asleep early and woke again around two. Usually, when that happened, she switched on the television or radio for company. Sometimes she read. Often, she went downstairs and made a hot drink before returning to bed.

On other nights, she was unable to sleep at all and lay awake for hours, tossing, turning, trying to make herself yawn, subtracting seven from 876,326 and then from 876,319 and so on till she lost the thread and had to begin again.

Often, she directed her memories to specific and particularly happy moments with Fred. She would enjoy them for a while till the reality of his loss clutched at her chest causing such a weight of despair that she could barely breathe. Lack of sleep was just, she decided, one aspect of a life forever changed. And there were so, so many of those.

However, on this occasion, eventually, she must have slept, but now she was alert with memories of a nightmare so hideous that she knew it would lurk in the crevices of her mind all day.

She had been in a department store and suddenly, there was Fred, staggering off the escalator. He was looking for her, she knew that for sure. Yet, he stared straight through her, without a hint of recognition. He was unsteady on his feet and so manifestly lost and anxious that she had longed to run to him, but something was restraining her, and every step she attempted took her away, not towards him. She waved to attract his attention. But it was pointless. Then, it occurred to her that perhaps it was he who was alive, and she who was dead, and that that was why he was failing to see her.

She put her head in her hands hoping to erase the dystopic images. Nightly, she longed to dream of him, but when she did, she was rarely granted scenes from their beautiful life before his illness. Instead, the encounters were disturbing, prompting guilt and mental turmoil.

Defiantly, she shook her head, swung her legs out of bed, then turned and smoothed out the bottom sheet before pulling up the duvet and plumping up her pillows. It was quickly done because Fred's side no longer needed any attention. She thought nostalgically of the mornings when the bedlinen would have been rumpled. Then as she recalled his deterioration, she had a sudden vision of him, towards the end of his life, almost motionless, but somehow summoning up the energy to raise the arm he could still control and waving when she came into the room. She heard herself gasp at its reality and pain.

'The world is such a poor place without you, Fred,' she said aloud. 'Not just for me. But for everyone.'

Could she face porridge? Maybe. Tea certainly. Another day to get through. An endless stream of them stretched before her, for which she had little enthusiasm.

At The Granary later, she forced a smile before pushing open the heavy glass door. A young woman was leaving as she was

44

entering, deaf and blind to the world, as she listened to her iPod while texting on her mobile phone. Jen held the door and waited for her to pass through it. There was no acknowledgement.

'Thank you – very – very – *ve*-ry – much.' Jen's voice was so loud and sarcastic, she sounded like John Cleese in *Fawlty Towers*.

The pretty, unblemished face framed by tumbling blonde curls turned, its expression one of puzzlement.

'What?' she asked as she removed an earbud.

'You should thank people, you little bitch.'

The girl's mouth dropped open in shock.

'Particularly older ones who've got more manners than you'll ever have. We're not invisible you know. And you won't always be the perfect specimen of youth and beauty that you are today. In a few years, no one'll give you a second glance. But meanwhile, trust me, that sense of entitlement you have is most unattractive. Now piss off.'

The young woman gazed around her, eyes wild and wide open, then she shook her head and left, at which point Jen realised that the building she had entered had fallen silent. Some of the gazes trained on her appeared hostile or frightened. Other individuals smiled weakly before turning away. One elderly gentleman shuffled up to her and muttered something to the effect that everyone under forty was 'bloody rude' these days.

Jen surveyed the scene. Her planned coffee and croissant now held little appeal. Her fury was ebbing away leaving shame in its place. Swiftly, she left the building.

The trendy café across the river, where there were so many choices it was exhausting, was busy. She selected Blue Mountain roast for her coffee. Almond milk to go in it. Sourdough for her sandwich. After that she just kept saying 'yes' to all questions, which probably accounted for her beverage being served in a bowl rather than a mug or cup, and a bird's nest of rocket appearing on her plate.

A couple of forty-something women were talking loudly at the next table. She heard all about their recent trip to Tenerife where the blonde one had imbibed so much sangria that, somehow, she had ended up in a young waiter's bed.

'Sooooooo embarrassing,' the woman was saying, though she did not look embarrassed in the slightest, then she recounted how 'Carlos' had needed her to leave promptly the following morning because he had an early shift, but how she was all over the place as she was still drunk and unable to find her shoes.

'You had to laugh,' she screeched.

Both of them then started talking about their spouses and how these men were oblivious to their goings on because they had been on golfing holidays in the Algarve while the women were away.

Even though Jen was aware it was not her business, and that, for all she knew, the loud women might have dreadful husbands, she was so overcome by their contempt for their partners, when at least they were alive, that she glared at them.

Eventually, the pair paused for breath and noticed her.

One of them screwed up her nose, before saying, 'You got a problem?'

Jen said nothing.

'What?' the other woman demanded. 'What's up with you?'

Jen abandoned her half-eaten sandwich and stood up, gathering her bag and coat as she did so.

'You're utterly despicable,' she said, louder than she had meant to.

As in The Granary earlier, the customers of the café stopped talking.

The owner, wiping her hands on a tea towel, stepped out from behind the counter wearing an anxious expression.

It was unfair, she knew, to worry her and damage the convivial atmosphere, and to pick on the stupid out-of-control females who had stood up, spoiling for a fight.

'Sorry,' she muttered. 'Sorry.' She raised her free hand and gestured in an apologetic way. 'I'm going. Sorry.'

Outside, in her haste, as she attempted to put on her coat, she dropped her bag and an assortment of items – make-up, phone, keys and her purse – rolled out of it. A young man stopped to help.

'I'm OK,' she mumbled. 'I don't deserve sympathy or help.'

He stayed with her nonetheless and gathered up her possessions and repacked them in her bag before handing it to her.

'You all right now?' he asked gently.

'Not really,' she murmured. 'I'm making a terrible mess of everything. But my husband died…' And with that, she heard an unearthly wail escape from her throat.

'Must be terrible,' he sympathised.

She nodded. 'Much worse than I ever imagined. You see, when someone's ill, you use all your energy to make their days as pleasant as you can. And you work towards them having a peaceful death, and it doesn't really occur to you then just how empty everything will be afterwards.'

He put his arm round her. 'Can I call a friend for you or something?'

She shook her head.

'No. But… thanks. Very nice of you.'

He backed away, nodding and smiling. 'You take care of yourself, Sad Lady.'

There were pedestrians between them now and she could no longer see him. He had been like an angel of mercy, she thought. And then it occurred to her that Fred had sent him because he could see that she was upset and desolate and needed someone sympathetic in his absence.

'Oh, Fred,' she whispered, 'you always used to say that you would look after me. Are you there?'

The fact that there was no answer did not dent her belief that he had contrived the meeting.

She glanced at her watch. There was still half an hour before she needed to return to The Granary, so she wandered into a recently-opened cosmetics shop.

47

'I'm just looking,' she said as a matronly woman approached her. Then she murmured the same phrase to a middle-aged man who loomed up in front of her. And again, when someone, who looked like his brother, smiled in a syrupy way and enquired if he could be of assistance.

She sighed. Had they no idea that she would most likely make a purchase if only they would leave her in peace to think?

A fourth, eager saleswoman blocked her path.

'Can I show you anything?'

'Are you afraid I'm a shoplifter?'

The assistant glanced behind her at one of the men who had already spoken.

'For God's sake,' Jen muttered. She surveyed the products on the glass shelves around her till her eyes lit on a brand she knew and used. 'I might have some of that serum,' she pointed to a small bottle.

'Ooooh… do you use that then?'

'I have done.'

'Mmmn, I am surprised.'

'Why? Don't you think it's working?' Jen snarled.

'Well, it's really for young skins.'

'Oh, is it? Pardon me for being on the wrong side of twenty-five.'

'Sorry?'

'No, *I'm* sorry. I'm sorry I ever came in here. Still,' she looked the assistant up and down, 'do enjoy your serum. Unfortunately, it won't do anything for your fat ankles, but one can't have everything.'

That was awful, she acknowledged as she headed back across the river. She'll probably get a complex now about her ghastly legs. Ooh, Jen, you are a bitch, she said to herself, then she giggled. However, within a heartbeat, the corners of her mouth headed south and all she wanted to do was weep, or even, she thought – as she stood on the little pedestrian bridge and watched the churning river beneath her – throw herself into the water and abandon herself to it. Her life was pointless now. She was just eking out the time till she too could die. And with that thought she stopped trying to make sense of everything, stopped attempting to look on the bright side and yielded to a visceral emotion that sucked all positivity from her mind and body leaving only a pit of miserable bleakness.

She was cold, she realised. And she could not stand on the bridge forever, so she drew herself up to her full height and walked back briskly to The Granary.

Helen was seated just inside the door. Had she been there earlier? Had she witnessed the incident with the young woman? Had she stationed herself there deliberately, waiting for her return?

'Jen, come and sit down.' Helen's voice was low but firm. 'I've got a quiet table around the corner.'

'Do you mind if I don't? I've got to get going in ten minutes and I need to put on some make-up.'

'I was wondering if perhaps today feels rather too much to cope with and whether you'd prefer to go home?'

'No, I wouldn't. I feel useful here and it's a good feeling. So, if you'll excuse me…'

Helen put out a restraining arm. 'You don't come for counselling to the hospital anymore.'

'You're right,' Jen answered, distancing herself from the touch without looking at her. 'I don't.'

'It's available to people up to a year after their partners have passed away.'

'Someone told me.'

'And yet you don't want to come?' Helen persisted.

'No, thank you.'

'Jen, I know what it is to feel very angry, and so hurt you're like a hedgehog curled into a ball but with his spines on full alert.'

'Spines? Is that what they're called? Aren't they quills?'

49

'Apparently, porcupines have quills. Hedgehogs have spines. They're like hairs filled with keratin.'

'Really? The things you find out.'

'Jen, I know it's very painful.'

'*How* do you know? It's different for everyone, isn't it? It's obviously very different for you.'

Helen looked, Jen noticed, somewhat crestfallen. 'If I'm the problem, you can see one of my colleagues.'

'That won't be necessary. Quite apart from anything else, I don't want to be told that it all gets easier with time. I don't want it to be easier. That would seem like an insult to Fred. And I don't want there to *be* time. Time passing is one of the worst things. Every day that I live on without Fred creates more distance between us. I hate that. We were so rarely apart. So, there's nothing anyone can do. It doesn't help me to talk about it. It helps me to do stuff, so I'm going to go and do my shift. I know… I'm aware that I'm being difficult.' She sniffed, determined not to cry. 'It's probably a stage in the grief process.' Her voice mimicked Helen's immaculate enunciation. She did not want to be cruel to the other woman, or indeed anyone else, but what she did want was to be left alone. Unable to think of words that might bring the conversation to a close in a civilised way, she shrugged and walked away.

As she had foreseen, working had helped. Now she had an evening to fill. She could make a stir-fry, she decided, as she ambled home. Every night, she forced herself to eat properly at the table even though she had little inclination to do so and would really have preferred to overdose on ice cream straight from the freezer.

'We must keep our standards up,' she said out loud to Fred.

It had been one of the phrases which had made them laugh because they were not a couple who cared much for appearances or what other people thought.

As she approached her house, she could see Suzie, her neighbour, walking up the path and ringing the bell.

That was strange. They did not socialise much. Suzie was a somewhat prickly woman who was involved in a number of organisations at the local church and prided herself on being a 'Good Samaritan'. As such, when Fred had fallen ill, she had offered to sit with him. He had agreed only once; he was a private man and did not want to be fussed. Presumably, Suzie had sensed his reluctance as she never suggested visiting again. But after Fred's death, Jen had agreed on a couple of occasions to go next door for a chat and a cup of tea. Mostly however, she avoided contact; the two of them had little in common and Jen was keen to keep her distance from Suzie's rescue dog Mac, who was a most excitable Border collie and rather terrifying.

Suzie spotted her. 'Jen!'

She was holding a lead with a dog at the end of it who was not Mac, but a chocolate Labrador Jen had never seen before.

'Hello! New dog?'

'Thank heavens you're here,' Suzie spoke in a rush. 'Look, can you help me out? This is Archie. He belongs to the vicar. The vicar's wife has had a bad fall. He and his kids are with her at the hospital. I said I'd look after him, but it's Brownie night and I can't get anyone else to step in. And it would be chaos if I left him here with Mac. Could you have him for a while? He's lovely.'

Jen stared at him. She had never owned a pet, nor ever considered herself good with animals. Fred had talked about them having a dog when he retired, but he never fully gave up work, and it was just one of those things – and there were a lot of them, on reflection – that they never fitted in before his days on earth ran out.

She took a deep breath. 'OK. I'll do my best.'

'Great! Thanks.'

'Should I give him something to eat?'

'Labradors never say "no" to food!'

'I've got some steaks in the freezer. Probably past their sell-by date. They've been in there since before Fred got too ill to eat solids.'

'Archie'll think it's Christmas! Look, I'll be back in a couple of hours. Sure you'll be all right?'

Jen nodded vigorously to combat the serious misgivings it would be unhelpful to voice, and Suzie thrust Archie's lead at her and was gone.

'Hello, Archie,' Jen said.

To her amazement, he wagged his tale. It seemed like a triumph; without doubt, the only one of the day. She felt an unaccustomed sense of gladness and found herself smiling at him.

'Come on then,' she said, and transferring his lead into her left hand, she rummaged in her bag with the other one. Eventually, she located her keys and let them into the house. As soon as she had closed the door behind them, she knelt down and released Archie, who gazed at her with his huge brown eyes.

'Let's sort out some supper for you,' she said, then she headed for the kitchen, with the dog padding behind her.

There were indeed rump steaks in the freezer. She pulled out one and put it in the microwave to defrost. Archie, perhaps realising it was for him, wagged his tail again.

It was odd having him here. But odd in a reassuring way.

She cut up the steak and put the dish before him, then laughed as he devoured it in seconds.

He gazed at her, with a look that suggested he could manage more food if it was forthcoming, however as she turned away to make herself a pot of tea, he did not press the point but instead meandered off for a sniff and a look at the vegetable rack while she brewed her tea and sat down at the kitchen table to drink it. Before long, he returned, then lay down at her feet, occasionally glancing up at her.

'Poor Archie,' she said. 'You've no idea who I am, have you? Or what's happened to Suzie or the people who own you? You're so trusting.'

The dog shifted himself into a sitting position and gave her a little nudge with his nose. Then she felt a weight on her thigh and realised that he had put his paw on it. She reached out and shook it as if they had just been introduced, then he replaced it on the floor, his eyes locked onto hers.

Instinctively, she leant over and buried her face in his warm, smooth neck. Minutes passed while a mass of thoughts that had been tumbling around her brain quietened and his body heat soothed her. Archie remained passive throughout, as if a stranger drawing waves of comfort from him was what he was there for.

After a long while, she pulled back and sat up straight calmly trying to fathom how she was feeling. Something strange and different had happened. Something significant. Something healing. Something that had transformed one of her worst days into an evening that promised to be peaceful, wholesome and healthy.

Taking Archie's beautiful head in her two hands, she whispered, 'You're a very lovely boy.' Then, thinking of the other lovely boy she missed so desperately, she added, 'Fred would have said this was a good moment for a digestive biscuit. Shall we have one?'

Chapter Six

The grave beckoned. It was the fourth time this week. Her feet seemed to turn in that direction even when she had not been planning to go there.

'Dearest Fred,' she murmured, as she walked down the grassy slope towards the woodland cemetery he had chosen.

'No hideous gravestones allowed,' he had said to her. 'No plastic ribbons, balloons or other tasteless paraphernalia.'

They had visited it together, not long after his diagnosis. At the time, she had considered the trip to be premature. After all, was she not going to look after him so well that he would live for years yet? That was her plan. But Fred had seemed to think that he would go downhill quickly and was anxious that important decisions might be left till he was too sick to make himself understood. Inwardly, Jen had held to her own beliefs that he would survive for ages, but she had kept them to herself. He was facing his own mortality with curiosity and courage, and if this part of the process helped him to compute what was happening, and how he felt about it, then she must support him.

As it turned out, his estimate of the speed of his deterioration had been depressingly accurate.

'I am cautiously pessimistic,' he told her when they had stopped for coffee in a bakery near the graveyard.

'Darling, don't you mean "cautiously *optimistic*"?'

His eyes had filled with tears as he looked at her and said, 'No, I'm afraid I don't.'

Her own vision was blurry now. Usually at home, when she wanted to cry, she diverted herself by cleaning the windows, or making a cup of tea, or emailing someone. Here, she tended to sob noisily – so long as no one else was about – and her nose began to drip, and she never had more than a scrap of tissue in her pocket, which invariably was not enough.

She could see the grave now, with its newly-engraved natural wood plaque and the remains of the irises she had put there two days previously.

'What am I like, Fred?' she muttered as she brushed the tears from her face with the back of her right hand. She sniffed and then had to resort to wiping her nose on her sleeve.

'Look what I've come to,' she said to him. 'I'm hopeless without you to look after me.'

Then she stopped, because on the mound of earth that lay above him, and right next to her most recent flowers, was a single red rose. A rose that she had not placed there.

It had been windy, so perhaps it had blown over from elsewhere. There was no attached card. Feeling unsettled and surprisingly angry, she lifted it and walked twenty paces, looking at the graves left and right, to see where it might have come from.

It was not obvious to her, but all she knew was that it did not belong on Fred's grave. This was her space. Hers and his. Not wishing to be disrespectful, she laid the flower on a communal expanse of grass before returning to talk with her husband.

Monica jumped as the ring of the phone broke the morning stillness. To her surprise, the call display showed Melissa's phone number.

When James was at home, Melissa often scheduled a Skype session with her father. Monica would always let them speak together for a quarter of an hour or so before joining in for a short time to say 'hello' and dredge up something to say for the last five minutes. She was pretty sure that both her husband and daughter preferred things that way. Melissa had always been a 'daddy's girl'. And in the many arguments that she had had with her daughter over the years, the recurring theme had always been that Betsy was her mother's favourite, that there was never any time for Melissa, that Betsy was not just ill but, despite her sickeningly sweet-natured act, was actually a 'manipulative little bitch'.

Monica knew that she had favoured Betsy, but how could she not? The child had been born ill, and for her entire life had had to battle cystic fibrosis till her exhausted lungs and other organs finally abandoned their fight for survival.

James had resented the fact that most of Monica's waking moments had focused on their sick child. So had Melissa. But had there never been a Betsy, would she and Melissa have been closer? She told herself they would not. But she was aware that that was what she wanted to believe.

Perhaps it was not Melissa at the other end, but James. Could he be calling to see how she was? It seemed unlikely. She could pretend to be asleep, but it was eight o'clock, and all her life she had risen around seven. Eventually, the answerphone whirred into life.

'Mum, I know you're there. Please pick up!'

She reached for the receiver. 'Hello!'

'Hi, Mum. You OK?'

'Mmmn. Fine. Thanks, Melissa. You?'

'Missing Dad?'

Not at all, she thought but she answered, 'Of course. How is he?'

'He's a fucking nightmare.'

Monica instinctively took a step back. This was completely unexpected. 'What on earth's wrong?'

'Look, Mum, I know you and I have had our differences, but I'm not blind. He's never treated you well. I suppose I never wanted to admit that. I was always so cross with you about Betsy. But the thing is, deep down, I know he was critical of you all the time and a terrible snob too. Remember when we were young and you used to say you were cooking our 'tea', and he would snap at you and say that solicitors' wives cooked *dinner* and that tea was something you had with jam and bread earlier in the afternoon. He could be horrible, but I ignored it. I also knew he was unfaithful. I even saw him once with some tart.'

Monica stood, swaying slightly, in the hallway. This was all so odd and so sudden. She felt quite lightheaded. Mind you, she had only had a cup of tea this morning and had eaten little last night after she had come back from The Granary. It was hard to be enthusiastic about cooking for one.

'Are you OK, Mum?'

'Ye-es. Just, it's a lot to take in.'

'Well there's more. Listen, have you had your brekkie yet?'

'No,' Monica admitted.

'Go and get coffee and two rounds of toast.' Her daughter's voice was authoritative but unusually warm. 'You're going to need it. I'll ring off and let you do that. And when I call back, be sitting down. OK?'

'Is Dad with you?'

'Course not. I'm at work. It's five o'clock here. My day's just getting interesting. We've got an opera competition on every night this week. It's madness. Anyway, I don't know where Dad is. But I'm sure he's OK. He always is, isn't he?'

Monica shook her head, feeling utterly baffled. She took the cordless phone with her into the kitchen, poured muesli and milk into a bowl and began to eat it, standing up, while she waited for the kettle to boil. She fancied she might need proper, strong coffee from what Melissa had said. But brewing it would take too long. The instant would have to do.

She had only just sat down, her mouth full of cereal, when the phone rang again. Melissa had given her less than five minutes. She must really want to talk. But why now? After years of them having so little to say to each other.

'Mum, OK this is the thing… I'm a lesbian. Sorry to break it to you like this. Um, I live with someone called Maggs who's lovely and we've been together for two years, and she's a physio, but also very interested in the arts and so on. We're really happy and I should have told you before.'

Monica felt a fluttering in her heart. She had worried about her volatile and somewhat strident daughter and feared that finding the right partner might be difficult for her. But she had never thought to question Melissa's orientation. However, there had been few boyfriends and somehow this conversation made complete sense.

'I'm really happy for you, love,' she said. 'This is wonderful news.'

'Aww, Mum. Thanks. I should have told you before but, you know, I wasn't sure how you'd feel.'

'How has your father taken it? Presumably, as he's staying with you, you had to tell him.'

'He's been quite uber male and sarky about it, which has pissed me off, I can tell you. But now he's totally crossed the line.'

Monica reached for her coffee and took a deep gulp. 'What?' she managed. 'What has he done?'

'Last night I decided it would be nice if I invited Lily, who's Maggs's mother – she's a widow by the way – to meet Dad. I fixed up a fancy restaurant and we had dinner for four. That went quite well. But then I had to go back to work because there was a function at the opera house, and they needed me there. So Maggs came with me, and Dad said he'd get a taxi and take her mother home. I gather, in the taxi he got a bit over familiar and tried to snog Lily and then,' Melissa sighed, 'I can hardly bear to say this… He put his hand up under her skirt. I am so, so mortified. I mean, Mum, what the fuck!'

58

'Oh, no.' Monica sighed. 'Oh, Melissa, I can't believe it. That's so…'

'Gross, I think is the word. Lily told Maggs on the phone this morning and I hauled Dad out of bed, forced him out of the house in his dressing gown and threw his luggage out after him. Unless he fancies a holiday travelling around on his own, my guess is he's going to turn up on your doorstep within hours.'

After the call, Monica made herself the pot of strong Machu Picchu blend coffee she was yearning for and sat down to think. Of course, she was furious with James. But she could not help but be elated by the conversation with Melissa. Could they, after all these years, find some way to become closer? She had always felt that Melissa looked down on her and thought she was not good enough for James. They had been tense and irritable with each other for so long, was there any way back from that? She had always pretended not to mind that they had such a poor relationship. But she had minded. And now James, through his crassness, had for once in his life done her a favour.

But if he was coming home, she needed to act fast. And something she had been putting off, which was to find a therapist to talk to about her future, was now an absolute priority.

Lucy braked so hard she almost fell off her bicycle. She was supposed to be going shopping for vegetables, wine and a couple of items from her butcher. A pork chop perhaps and maybe a couple of chicken breasts. Instead, on auto pilot, she had ridden towards the university and was almost at the entrance to the campus. Several young people swerved to avoid her in the narrow cycle lane. She waved an apology. Shaky suddenly, she dismounted and walked with the bike a few hundred yards to the park adjoining the campus where she knew there was a bench next to a children's playground.

She was still trembling as she sat down. And thirsty, and hot, and anxious.

The trouble was that her mind kept playing tricks. But, she supposed, she was here instead of where she should be, because she wanted her old life back. She wanted to be busy as she always had been, and to moan with the other lecturers about how hard-pressed they were and how long it was till the next vacation.

Life was one long vacation now, which was far too much of a good thing.

She was 'not in a good place' as people said nowadays. Gazing around her, she could see clumps of daffodils blowing in the considerable wind. She ought to feel a sense of gladness. But the trouble was that she was accustomed to her job providing sufficient fulfilment and joy. Now, she often stood in her kitchen, looking around her uneasily, and asking herself out loud, 'Have you done enough with today?'

The answer was invariably negative. Perhaps if she felt livelier, she would be more productive.

There was a café by the playground, and she decided to buy a coffee to steady herself. The place was full of mothers and babies sheltering from the chilly weather, and the entrance was packed with buggies, so she had to pull in her spare tyre and her over-ripe buttocks as she squeezed herself past them all.

I'd probably feel fitter and more energetic, she thought, if I were to lose some weight. Unfortunately, as she reached the counter, she was faced with a pile of tempting, freshly-baked scones dotted with plump sultanas. She ordered her beverage, trying hard not to look at them, but when the young serving girl asked, 'Anything to eat for you today?' she found herself nodding and pointing to the very largest scone in the display, and adding, 'with butter and strawberry jam, please.'

Maybe if she called this 'lunch' she could still cut down on calories later. A wry smile twitched at her lips as she acknowledged that today felt difficult enough without denying herself the reliable comfort of food.

A woman who seemed vaguely familiar was seated at the next table with someone who might be her daughter. There was also a toddler, asleep and sprawled across her pushchair.

'Thank heavens Milly's crashed out,' the younger of the two said. 'Everyone warned me she would become a monster as soon as she turned two, but I had no idea it would be this bad. Anyway, Mum, I'd better go home and try and do some work while she's napping. Keep me in the loop about Dad.' She leant over to hug her parent before reversing herself and her child out of the tiny space and through the scrum of parents, babies, and bags full of the accoutrement they required.

The remaining woman caught Lucy's eye. 'I'm not sure we had "terrible twos" when our children were small, did we?' she asked. 'Of course, they were a nightmare at times, weren't they? Very much so. But I don't think we assumed that our lives were going to be ruined by rudeness and tantrums for a whole twelve months. But now it's very obviously "a thing" as younger people say. You don't remember me, do you?'

Lucy swiftly swallowed the large piece of scone she was enjoying and wiped her lips with the paper napkin. Eventually she was able to answer, 'I do feel I know you. Do you work at the university?'

'No, I'm Barbara, Roy's wife. We met recently when he and I gave a short recital at The Granary.'

Lucy felt hot and wondered if she was blushing.

'Do you mind if I join you?' Barbara asked.

Lucy shook her head before finding her voice. 'Would you like a cup of coffee?'

'No thanks. I've just had one. Some water maybe. They have a cooler in the corner where you can help yourself.'

Lucy followed her gaze and stood up quickly to go and fill glasses for them both.

When she returned, they both drank deeply, not quite looking at each other.

'The recital was good, I thought,' Lucy ventured.

Barbara sat up straighter. 'I think we both know that's not true.'

'Well, you played very well. Impressively, I would say.'

'I've been a piano teacher for decades, so I ought to have a certain facility,' Barbara responded crisply. 'I suppose Roy has told you about his condition.'

'Sort of,' Lucy murmured. 'It was months ago. He mentioned the diagnosis and said that he'd been told by the specialist that he was likely to become more, uh, uninhibited.'

Barbara breathed out sharply. 'That doesn't begin to describe what's happening. Did he tell you while you were in bed together?'

Lucy had just taken a mouthful of coffee; she choked on it and spat out most of the hot liquid, then tried to apologise, before succumbing to a spasm of coughing.

Barbara grimaced and handed her a paper napkin.

Eventually, Lucy gained control of herself. She wiped her face, then dabbed at the coffee stains on the front of her jacket before trying, with the already sodden tissue, to absorb the trail of liquid on the table in front of her. She gave up and apologised again.

'Are you saying sorry for bedding my husband for the past twenty-five years or for spitting at me?'

Lucy swallowed hard. 'Both, I suppose. It was just sex.'

'Well, that's all right then.' Barbara's tone was heavy with irony.

'Genuinely, though. And friendship. It wasn't very personal. I, well, I had a different chap most days of the week. I'm not the settling down sort. As you can see, I'm an ugly old bat, but I love sex. I always have. Men sense it in me and when colleagues have had wives who've tired of them, or who were struggling with bringing up the children, or going through the menopause or whatever, they turned to me. None of it was more than mildly affectionate. And to tell you the truth, till recently, I believed I was providing some sort of service that was keeping them sane.'

'Oh, really? And have you changed your mind about that?'

'Actually,' Lucy stared beyond Barbara, out of the window at a couple of excited infants who were running and jumping around. 'I rather think I have.'

'Why?'

'One of my chaps died earlier in the year, in my bed. He'd always implied that sex was a duty for his wife, so, I suppose I didn't give any thought to her feelings or consider for a moment that she really loved him. But now I've come to believe that she did.' Lucy sighed. 'As a consequence, I've done a lot of thinking and have come to the conclusion that men are just greedy and if they can have sex from another woman as well as their wife – no matter how loving and available she is – many of them will opt for it.'

'Roy and I always had a good marriage. I like sex myself. Possibly not on the scale that he does. But it's been varied and loving. Of course, we've had our ups and downs. I think he felt left out when our daughter was small. Men are such babies themselves. They like to be the centre of attention.'

Lucy smiled warily. 'That's true I think.'

'Do you want to help us now?' Barbara asked. 'It's not going to be pretty. He's deteriorating rapidly. His balance is going and his limbs tremble more and more. Soon, he won't be able to manage anything risky, even if he wants to.'

'Uh, would you mind if I had another glass of water?'

Lucy made for the cooler without waiting for a response. Her mouth was so dry that it hurt, and her heart was drumming its beat in her ears.

'It's awful for Roy,' she murmured as she sat down again.

'Mmmn. And awful for us,' Barbara replied, her voice suddenly quavery. 'He's losing all sorts of abilities and we're losing the relationship we had. I feel a very dilute version of my real self to tell you the truth.'

Lucy nodded. 'I'm sure. What can I do?'

'Well, in the last week he's suddenly wanted to rest more. I need to have some life. I know that sounds selfish.'

'No, it doesn't. You don't know how long this will go on for. Can I contribute financially in some way? Pay for a carer sometimes?'

'I have a carer today and usually on Fridays too. So, I suppose I was thinking that it might be nicer if you came sometimes and sat with him. Read to him perhaps? Literature was your subject wasn't it? You must have favourite books that he'd enjoy.'

'I have a part-time job.'

'I'm sure we could fit something in around that. I'm only talking about a couple of hours twice a week.'

Lucy studied the table. She knew she was no good with sick people. That day when Monica had had to deal with the unconscious woman still haunted her, but she had not found the courage yet to talk about her fears with the manager. Suppose Roy needed the lavatory. Or wanted to be fed? Her insides shrank into a spasm of horror at these prospects.

'To be honest,' Barbara continued coolly, 'I think it's the least you can do. And Roy would like it. He told me.'

Lucy nodded quickly without looking at Barbara.

'Thank you.' Barbara did not sound very grateful as she reached into her bag for a small notebook and pen. Tearing off a page, she scribbled an address and landline number on it. 'Perhaps you'll be good enough to ring me?'

Lucy nodded again.

'It goes without saying,' Barbara's voice was firm and formal, 'that I want no hanky-panky. If he's still well enough for lovemaking, I want it to be with me. So, don't even think about it. If you go near him, he'll tell me – because that's how he is now. No intercourse, no fellatio and not even a hand job under the bedclothes.'

Lucy winced. She suspected that Barbara had rehearsed this section of the conversation over and over in her head, but that the choice of words had been difficult. 'Totally agree,' she whispered.

Barbara stood up. 'I had been meaning to ring you up and talk to you. But seeing you here, on neutral ground, has made it rather easier. I don't understand you at all. But I can see you're an unusual person. And I don't think you're a bad one. I just wonder what made you as you are.'

Chapter Seven

1972

Dalliance in the open air was my idea. Timmy assures me he's enjoyed it, even though – to my astonishment – he's been unable to finish. He seems to be worried someone might see us. I'm surprised he's so strait-laced. But then, I never have been.

'Can we go back to my rooms, Lucy?' he asks. I suspect he's embarrassed.

He's not a bad lover now. Of course, it's several months since we started seeing each other and I've spent the time schooling him in what works for me – and I assume other women. Initially, he was reluctant to do anything except hump away. I had to point out that the clitoris is the equivalent of the penis and that therefore it's pretty crucial it gets some attention. He was quite aghast at some of my suggestions and was very reluctant to try oral sex – well, he liked it when I did it to him, but wasn't keen on returning the favour. Still, we got there in the end. I love that more than anything.

Now, we're back in his rooms overlooking the quad. Enthusiastically, without taking off any of his clothes or mine, he mounts me, negotiates my underwear, and a minute later it's all over and he's making a pot of tea.

Before long, he asks me for help with some work we've been set in the Medieval Literature course we're taking this term. I'm not sure if he just hasn't grasped it very well, or if his brain isn't up to the demands of Middle English. He certainly doesn't have the passion for language that I have. And he admits that his Latin is poor, which certainly is holding him back. I, on the other hand, regard it as my favourite, and strongest, subject. I've always been fascinated by its logic.

I try to explain my understanding of what we've learned so far. Timmy nods a lot. I suggest an angle for his essay.

'Is that something you've pursued in yours?' he asks.

'No,' I reply. 'I did consider it but have gone another way. Still, you don't want to write a carbon copy of mine.'

'I suppose not,' he agrees, without much conviction.

I suspect he's somewhat lazy, and he's definitely not one of Cambridge's brightest, but I don't care because I'm not bedding him for his intellectual prowess.

'You are a wonder, Lucy,' he says.

I feel myself glow with the compliment.

'And your lovemaking is extraordinary. Just so earthy and honest and refreshing.'

I beam at him over my teacup.

'Let's be friends forever.'

I have no idea where this conversation's going. He looks quite serious. Is he going to invite me to our college May Ball? Or could he be about to propose? I've never envisaged being anyone's wife. There's so much I want to do. And I'm aware I was born without that drive to have children which most females have. I rather feel they would get in the way. Still, I don't think many men are natural fathers. They like to be the centre of attention themselves, in my view. Though I know a lot of the posh boys here are keen to make good marriages and produce suitable heirs to manage the family money and estate.

Timmy is quite self-interested. Would he let me be myself if I became Mrs Hinterton-White?

I suddenly realise he's still speaking. 'I don't see any reason why we can't carry on as we are. I mean, we don't need to lose touch, do we?'

I must have missed something. 'Why would we lose touch?'

'Lucy, surely I don't have to spell it out for you. At the May Ball, I'm going to ask Camilla to marry me. You must have realised we've been seeing a lot of each other.'

I know I look bemused. I feel it. 'Camilla who?'

'Oh, Lucy, you are so delightfully vague. Camilla Farringdon-Jones.'

'What a mouthful! Means nothing to me.'

'Her father's something important in the Bank of England.'

'Really? Does that matter?'

'Naturally, it matters. I do like her anyway, but she has wonderful connections. Her grandfather is a viscount. It's OK with you isn't it?'

'Is what OK?'

'That I'm going to propose to her.'

'She might not accept you.'

He laughs. 'Oh, I think she will. You don't mind, do you?'

Surprisingly, I do, so I say nothing.

'After all,' he continues quickly, 'it's not as if I've given you any promises of a future together. Obviously, a chap has to think about what he wants in a wife. Someone to make one comfortable. Someone who'll be an asset to one in business or, you know, if one goes into politics. Someone personable and presentable.'

'Presentable! What the fuck does that mean?'

'You don't have to be so coarse.'

'I thought you liked my fruity language.'

He looks uncomfortable. 'It's one thing in the bedroom.'

I roll my eyes.

'Oh please, don't come over all superior on me, Lucy. OK, you're brilliant in bed, and you have the most remarkable mind

68

and are clearly the cleverest student in our year but there are other things. One of them being that you're so odd looking.'

I'm stung by the remark and my voice warbles slightly as I ask, 'In what way?'

'Well, you're fat for a start. And doesn't it strike you as odd that you often just put your hair in plaits when you're in a hurry? You're not ten years old.'

'It's practical.'

'But not normal though. Nor are your ankle socks. All the other girls wear tights.'

'I've tried that, but they get laddered on the bike.'

'You're wonderfully hopeless.' He smiles at me.

'Well, I'm glad I've provided some amusement.'

'Always, my dear Lucy. Always. So, can I see you next week as usual?'

'What about Camilla?'

'Oh, she's saving herself for marriage!'

'I might be busy. I'll let you know.' Even as I speak, I know that I will continue to meet him.

I really don't understand other people's rules. Or what's important to them. And it doesn't seem as if I'm ever going to be the sort of person with whom someone will want an exclusive relationship. Partly, I'm relieved, because I'm not sure I'm cut out for fidelity. But partly, I feel fearful at having to do things my own way, and alone. Is this how I'm going to live forever? It does seem likely.

Chapter Eight

It had been a long day, they agreed, as they found seats in the café. Monica disappeared for a couple of minutes, then returned carrying two large bowl-like glasses of Rioja.

'I think we need a treat.' She beamed at Lucy as she handed one of them to her.

They had already completed a shift but had volunteered to help with the evening relay of a controversial gender-cross-over production from the Royal Shakespeare Company, which was completely sold out.

'Mmmn! Thanks, Monica.' Lucy smiled back at her friend and wondered whether to mention how much more carefree the other woman had seemed in the past couple of weeks. Instead, she said, 'I'm not usually keen on the Bard being mucked about with, so shall probably hate the bloody thing if I get to see any of it.'

'I doubt if I'll understand it,' Monica said. 'I know I'm not stupid, but I'm from a council house background where there were few books and no outings to the theatre. So, everything I know, I learned at school or college or picked up as an adult. My husband's family were very posh by comparison. He just took it for granted that people grew up learning Shakespeare, did verse-speaking at school, played a musical instrument and had holidays abroad.'

Lucy peered at Monica. 'That can't have been easy. But you're really doing yourself down. You're a bright woman. And this is nice just talking to you. I don't think we've done it before. You seem happier than you were when we first met. Is it this job?'

'Probably. I do enjoy it.'

'Even the day the old lady keeled over?'

Monica grinned. 'Especially that day! I've mentioned before that I had a very sick daughter who died eleven years ago. I not only miss her; I miss having someone to care for.'

'Not sure what that says about your husband.' Lucy leant towards her with a querying expression.

Monica pulled a comically tragic face but made no comment.

'There's that woman again,' Lucy nodded in the direction of someone who had just entered the building. 'She seems so familiar, and it's annoying me that I can't fathom why. We met her with Jen one day if you remember. Talking of which, where is Jen?'

'She didn't want to do another shift. She said she was taking someone's Labrador for a walk. She puts a brave face on everything, but I think she's terribly sad. A couple of times I've caught her looking drained and as if life is all too much. She and her husband were obviously devoted to each other.'

Lucy looked thoughtful before changing the subject. 'Oh, the woman's coming this way. It's so crowded in here I don't think she can find anywhere to sit. Shall I wave her over?'

'Yes, do,' Monica agreed. 'She's very attractive, isn't she? And, like you, I have a sense that I've met her, though a long time ago.'

Helen arrived at their table.

'Do you want to sit with us?' Lucy offered. 'It's mayhem in here this evening. We spoke with you briefly one day when Jen was with us.'

'Yes, I remember. I thought Jen worked with you. Where is she?'

The other two explained how they had been here since mid-morning with Jen but that only they had volunteered to stay on for tonight's big event.

71

'How is she?'

'Not great, I would say,' Lucy replied. 'She keeps things very much to herself. I can't say I blame her. Probably I would too.'

Helen sat down and put her tray on the table before pouring wild berry fruit tea into a patterned cup and saucer from its matching teapot. 'They do things so elegantly at The Granary, don't they?' she said. 'I love it.'

'You seem to be here quite often,' Monica remarked. 'You don't do shifts as well, do you?'

'No, nothing like that. I live nearby. But I'm alone much of the time at the moment and don't feel like eating or drinking by myself every day. So, this has become my "local".'

'You remind me of someone,' Lucy said. 'Or do you remind me of *you*? Perhaps when you were younger?'

'Yes, that's it, when you were younger,' Monica added quickly.

Helen smiled.

'You were on television!' Monica realised. 'At six o'clock on a news magazine programme. In the eighties. Every night. You were a big celebrity.'

Helen shook her head. 'Oh, hardly that.'

'Helen Bartlett,' Monica continued. 'Well, perhaps you're no longer that.'

'I am, actually.'

'Never married?'

'Not quite,' Helen answered quietly.

'I used to love your programme. I spent my days looking after my daughter who had cystic fibrosis. But she was often napping when you were on. So, it was a time I could have to myself before my husband came home demanding dinner.'

'I used to watch you, too,' Lucy said. 'Probably not as much. But you were very famous.'

Helen blushed slightly. 'That was in the days when there were only four channels. But at the end of the eighties, the whole industry changed with Sky starting up. Suddenly there were masses

72

of options. It altered everything. I took a sabbatical, for various reasons, and later decided to train as a therapist.'

'Is that what you do now?' Monica sat forward in her seat.

'Well, in as much as I do anything. I volunteer at the hospital. I see partners and families of people with motor neurone disease. I used to have a small private practice, but Jeremy, the man I lived with, had MND and I stopped seeing clients when he was ill. He's dead now but I haven't gone back to it.'

'I'm sorry for your loss,' Monica said. Then she asked, 'Would you consider seeing someone new now though?'

Helen gazed at her quite penetratingly. 'Perhaps.'

'If someone was at a kind of crossroads,' Monica elaborated, 'and wanted to put things in perspective.'

'That sounds like the sort of thing I might be able to help with.'

'Are you talking about you, Monica?' Lucy asked. 'This sounds pretty private. Should I potter off and leave the two of you alone?'

Monica shook her head. 'No, we're friends now. And I think I've been private for too long. I want to make decisions about my future before I get much older. So, yes, I have been thinking of seeking out a therapist. And, having met you, Helen, I'd like to try it with you.'

'I'm going to keep this entirely to myself,' Lucy announced, her voice gruff with embarrassment. 'Oh, look, Liz Pemberton is beckoning us. Sorry, we better get on.'

Helen reached into her handbag's front pocket for a card, which she gave to Monica. 'Give it some thought,' she advised, 'and if you want to progress the idea, please call me.'

Jen let herself into her house, having walked Archie back to the vicarage. The vicar's wife still had her arm in plaster, and a heavily-bandaged right knee, but she was doing well. It should therefore not have been a shock – though it had been – when she took Archie's lead and said how grateful she had been for all Jen's help, but that she thought she and her family could manage walking him on their own now.

Jen realised she must have appeared stunned or disappointed because the other woman had added swiftly, 'But do come and see him sometimes if you want.'

'I won't be doing that,' Jen said aloud in the empty hallway.

She sounded petulant, she realised. Almost bitter. Then she felt ashamed. Archie was their dog. Naturally, they wanted him to themselves. It was just a pity that she had become so attached to him.

She made her way into Fred's study, and gazed at all the pictures she had put in there of him and the two of them together. The loss of him weighed heavily on her but, as often happened after a moment or two, she began to feel a sense of closeness and comfort. She recalled that when her stepsons had stayed in the house after the funeral, one of them had called the study 'a shrine'. That was too strong a word. It was more a 'Fred Room', packed with the belongings he had liked and used most. She sat down at his desk and switched on his radio. It used to be tuned to Radio Four, but as he became more and more ill, he had said he was unable to work when people were talking at him, and he had changed his allegiance to Classic FM. She had not retuned it since.

The last jacket he had worn before he had abandoned dressing each day, was hanging on the back of the chair. Cold suddenly, she slipped into it. She had bought it as a present the first Christmas they were together. It was a traditional Norfolk design, and though somewhat threadbare around the collar and at the elbows, it was still weighty and warm. Fred had loved it. She told herself it smelled of him though she was not honestly sure that it did. Leaning forward, she stretched out her hand and picked up his pen from the desk and held it. Then she flicked through his last diary, aching anew as she saw again how his writing had seemed normal at the beginning of last year, but smaller and spikier by the summer, then old and trembly by October, and indecipherable by December.

Poor Fred, who had been so keen on keeping an account of everything. She closed her eyes against the pain of accepting that he had no further use for all the items in this room which had once seemed so vital to him.

She swivelled around and gazed at his overloaded shelves and gently swept her fingers over the books she could reach, before selecting the weighty thesaurus that he had continued to prefer despite any number of online versions. A piece of paper, folded over and over again, concertina fashion, fell out of it.

The top of it was dated 1990. 'I love you so much, my darling Jen. You've made me a hugely happy man.'

It was a message from the grave. He had known she was miserable and had directed her to come in here and find what he had written all those years previously. She wrapped her arms around herself, enjoying the slight roughness of the jacket on the palms of her hands. It felt almost as if she were cuddling him. 'How I wish I could,' she whispered to the empty room.

She unfolded the paper and saw that he had added to the initial message every few years.

'1995. And I love you even more...'

'2000. My angel girl, I love you even more...'

'2003. And I love you even more than that!'

Perhaps he had lost the paper for a while because the next writing on it was on his birthday fourteen years later. 'No man ever had a better wife. Thank you. Thank you. Thank you. All my love xxxxxxxxx.'

Then, in the last fold, his script showed the dramatic deterioration in his health. The letters were big but laboriously formed and she could see that he had gone over some of them to make them more legible.

'I will love you forever. Thank you, my dearest, darling, lovely Jen.'

She sat for a while, fighting the urge to wail and sob at the death of the man she had adored. Eventually, she glanced at her watch. It was only seven-fifteen. Not even time for dinner – well not on the timescale they had kept to during their marriage. Who is this woman, she mused, whiling away the hours till she can eat, then searching for something to fill another yawning gap till she can go to bed? This isn't right. I'm nothing. And I'm doing nothing useful. There is no point. No point in anything at all.

Eventually, she spoke her bleakest thought out loud into the gloom. 'It's no good, Fred. I can't do this. I really can't go on without you.'

Chapter Nine

Monica had lived in Crowbury all her life, but she had never seen Helen's house before. It was tucked away down a leafy, unadopted avenue and, she was relieved to see, it was rather grand.

When she had first considered consulting a therapist, she had pictured a tired looking woman, working in a tiny room within a doctor's surgery, or in a small terraced house. And she had been concerned that such a person might not understand her worries about the future. It would be easy for someone less well off than she to dismiss her anxieties as 'shallow'. But the truth was that she dreaded losing the financial stability that her marriage had brought her. She felt ashamed to admit this even to herself. But, having grown up on 'the wrong side' of town, she had a horror of returning to it, and of being cast back to the impoverishment of her childhood.

She was fully aware that, by most people's standards, she was very comfortable. The only question in her mind was how she could ensure that she emerged solvent from any divorce. She was not looking for more than her share, but she had supported James in his career and had been prevented by him from having one of her own.

There had been a party once, at James's firm, when a drunk woman had accosted her and said, 'If you knew what I know about your dear husband, you'd divorce him. You could take him to the cleaners.'

It had been long before the day of her migraine and the confession from James that he had been unfaithful for decades. She had brushed it aside at the time. For a start she had not been ready to acknowledge her long-held suspicions. But now, she was tired of pretence and wanted her freedom. However, she was full of fear that James would become so hostile that he and his legal team would fight to keep her settlement as small as possible.

As she reached the end of the drive, she paused in front of the beautifully proportioned Victorian villa and surveyed the slightly overgrown garden which surrounded it. A sense of peace enveloped her as she took a deep breath and then another. She might have stood there longer but the front door opened, and Helen appeared.

'What a lovely spot this is. Very tranquil.'

'I saw you communing with nature,' Helen chuckled. 'The garden has that effect on me too.'

'You're really tucked away here,' Monica said. She thrust her hands deep into her jacket pockets, which made her shoulder bag slip down her arm and fall to the ground. As she bent to retrieve it, she felt suddenly nauseous and giddy and took her time before straightening up.

Had Helen noticed? What on earth was wrong with her? Should she have come?

'I think it's teatime,' Helen announced in a cheery voice. 'Do come in. Are you happy to have it in the kitchen? I thought it would be more cosy.'

Monica followed the other woman into the house and down the hall into a huge space with a big island of cupboards in the centre, a gleaming green Aga dominating one wall and, at the other end, a refectory table which eight people could have shared comfortably. 'Cosy' was not a word she would have chosen to describe it, but it was pleasingly warm, and light.

'I've had the heating on,' Helen confessed. 'I know we're well into May, but I'm freezing. After that heatwave around Easter, I thought we were set for summer, but I'm back in opaque tights.' She flicked the kettle on and turned to Monica. 'Sorry, I think I'm talking too much. I do that when I'm nervous.'

'You're nervous? What about me!'

Helen grinned. 'Sorry. As you can tell I'm the sort of therapist who tends to share things rather than attempt to be a blank canvas. And also, the truth is that I haven't counselled anyone apart from the MND partners for, oh, maybe three years. And never in this house. When I began in this business, I used to get a stonking headache every time I saw a new client. Honestly, that's not how it's supposed to go! I got over my nerves eventually. But today, I've been quite jumpy.'

'Me too,' Monica admitted.

'Tea – ordinary or Earl Grey – coffee, fruit tea, cold drink. What d'you fancy?'

'Ordinary tea please. Milk no sugar.'

Helen busied herself in the corner beside the Aga, and Monica sat down on one of the seats at the big table, before taking a good look around her. 'This is a lovely kitchen.'

'Thank you. It is. Quite honestly, it's been a sort of sanctuary for me because with Jeremy being so ill by the time we moved here, upstairs began to resemble a nursing home. We had a hospital bed, a commode and a wheelchair, and a Mowbray frame and seat for the loo as well as grab handles everywhere. I've relegated all that stuff to one room, which I never open now as it's too depressing.'

Monica slipped out of her jacket and hung her bag over the back of the chair, before changing her mind and putting it on the floor by her feet.

Helen carried a tray with crockery and a teapot over to the table, before sitting next to Monica. There was a pause till Helen spoke again, 'I was just thinking as we're both a bit on edge about

79

meeting in this way, why don't you tell me your story in here today? We can get into more formal therapy mode next time if we meet again. I won't even take notes. I'll just get an impression of you and your life, and you can see if you like me. I may not be right for you. It's important that you're sure I'm a good fit.'

'That's fine with me. But I must pay.'

Helen did not respond immediately but focused on pouring tea for them both. It was only after replacing the teapot on the tray that she said, 'I was going to talk to you about that. I'm not at all sure I should charge you.'

Monica stared at her own lap. 'It's hard to talk about money, but I won't come if I can't pay. I need it to be a business arrangement so I feel I can see you as often as I want. If you're doing me a favour, it won't work. Can you understand that?'

Helen passed her a delicately-painted teacup and saucer. 'Do you want to add your own milk? We're all fussy about how we take our tea aren't we?'

Monica nodded. When the tea had turned the colour she wanted, she took a sip while she wondered how to find the words to persuade Helen to her point of view. Surely, they were not going to fall at this, the first hurdle?

'I do get it,' Helen murmured after some thought. 'Probably, if I were you, I'd feel the same.'

'Good,' Monica said, still avoiding Helen's gaze. 'Really, it doesn't matter to me if you hand the money to a homeless person on the bridge over the river or donate it to a charity of your choice.'

Helen reached out a hand. 'I understand. It's fine.'

Monica felt her body relax. She looked Helen in the eye. 'That's a relief.'

'So, why are you here?'

'I'm going to be sixty in the autumn.'

'Does that worry you?'

'I didn't think it did, but it is a landmark, isn't it? One feels older.'

'Seems quite young to me! I'm going to be seventy next year. I don't think that's hit me yet.'

Monica smiled for the first time since her arrival. 'You certainly don't look it! But these big birthdays, well, I suppose they remind us that time is marching on... The thing is that my husband fell for how I looked rather than for who I am. I know it's hard to imagine that now, but it's the truth. He's, um, got a very healthy libido, and he was attracted to me in the beginning. I bored him quite quickly though. And, gosh, there's so much to tell you – I had two daughters and, as I mentioned when we met in The Granary, one was extremely ill. Anyway, I can go into all this another time. But the essence of it is that I no longer love him, and now I've admitted that to myself, I want out while I'm still able to build a new life.'

She paused to reflect on the enormity of what she was saying. It sounded so final. Did she really want to be single again after all these years?

'That's a big decision isn't it?' Helen responded.

Grateful for Helen's thoughtful reaction, Monica felt herself exhale fully. 'Yes,' she answered. 'Yes, it is. But I've only arrived at it after a lot of thinking and some very restless nights.'

'I can imagine.'

'Maybe, deep down I'd been considering this for a while but the first time I really let the possibility come into my mind was an awful day, a few months ago now. We had a row and James told me he'd been unfaithful to me for most of our marriage. I think I'd always known, really. And in a way, I didn't mind. In fact, it was almost a relief because, for the first time, I thought it was OK to refuse his demands. And I have ever since.'

'So, you want to divorce?'

'Yes. But I worry about money – though we are by most people's standards quite well off, and I suppose I'll come out of it with enough to live on.' She took a sip of tea. 'There's another thing and I've never told anyone this. Ten years ago, I fell for the architect who did some work for us. He told me he loved me. And he sends me a card every year on my birthday, to let me know he still feels the same. I've never contacted him, though we had been close... we... it's embarrassing... we did kiss and cuddle quite a lot at the time.' Monica's eyes became bright with tears at the memory. 'It was,' she gave a nervous cough, 'very exciting.'

'And now you want to contact him?'

Monica's eyes overflowed and she sat weeping silently for over a minute. Then she reached for a tissue. 'Yes, I think I do.'

'I can understand that so well, Monica,' Helen said gently. 'And as a friend I would urge you to do so. He's waited a long time. And your feelings are unchanged. As a therapist though, I will talk all this through with you quite thoroughly, just to make sure you really know what you want. I mean, quite apart from anything else, I doubt if you've ever spent more than a few hours at a time with him. Never had a meal, possibly. Certainly, never slept with him.'

Monica blushed. 'I wanted to, though.'

'I'm sure,' Helen said, with a faraway look on her face. 'But it does muddy the waters. And if I were a lawyer, I would advise you not to complicate matters by getting in touch with him till you've made your decision about a divorce and you've set it in motion. Sorry, because that may not be what you want to hear. But in terms of a good outcome, I'd certainly say that someone like you, who clearly has a strong moral code, will deal with the unhappiness and guilt that always features at the end of a long-term relationship, if you do things in the right order as it were. You call time on a marriage because it's wrong for you, rather than because there's something that seems so much more promising around the corner. Of course, few of us are that wise. We're all human. We yearn for love. We have needs. And yours have not been met by your husband for a very long time.'

*

Lucy had almost been late. That would have been awful, she knew. But she had kept getting muddled about the time. And she had had to interrupt what she was doing every five minutes or so to have a glass of water, because she was desperately thirsty, and her throat was perpetually dry. She was nervous, she supposed, and she had kept starting tasks at home and then realising she was not in the mood for them. However, just when she should have been preparing to leave, she had become absorbed in downloading more book titles onto her Kindle, and when she next looked at her watch, she had somehow misplaced an hour and had to jump on her bike and pedal furiously to get here in time. Really, she must pull herself together. This was a small thing to do for a man she liked and with whom she had so much history. And a rather more significant act for Barbara, the woman she had wronged over the years.

'Come in, Lucy,' Barbara welcomed her briskly. 'I'm about to go out with a friend. Will you be OK? Have you brought some books?'

'Mmmn, I prefer real books myself, but I thought the Kindle would give us more choices. I've got masses of titles on it, so,' she reached into her capacious bag and produced the device, 'whatever he fancies, hopefully I've got it covered.'

'Good. He's upstairs in bed. I think he's keen to hear some Charles Dickens. He's never read any apart – apparently – from studying *Great Expectations* for O level.'

'Oh, I can certainly help there.' Lucy felt relieved and on slightly firmer ground.

'Help yourself to tea, coffee, or cold drinks. He'll tell you if he wants anything. Don't yield to any request for alcohol. That's strictly rationed. He's quite unpredictable enough as it is.'

'Can he, I mean, is it OK if he needs, the lavatory to, er, let him go on his own? I mean, he's capable of that, is he?'

'It varies.' Barbara gave her a very challenging stare as if she were making the point that there was no way that Lucy could pull out of this arrangement now. 'If he wants to pee,' she said, 'he's quite capable of asking. He's not incontinent. Not yet. He usually says, "I need to take a slash". Awful expression. He never used it till recently,' she sighed, 'but anyway, that's how it is now. There's a bottle by the bed. If I were you, I'd encourage him to use it as he's pretty unsteady if he suddenly gets up and decides to walk to the bathroom.'

Lucy could feel her heart thumping in her chest. She breathed out sharply. This was her worst nightmare. Her hands felt clammy and her throat was parched. But she forced a smile and told Barbara that all would be well and even stood at the front door and waved the other woman goodbye.

What happened next, she never quite knew. But she woke up in an ambulance.

Jen had never been to Florence. Neither had Fred. It was one of the cities they had always meant to visit but ran out of time before they managed it. So, she had decided to go. For both of them. Also, she resolved that if the trip did not lift her mood or help her to feel that her existence had real purpose, she would think about how best to end her life.

It was raining as the plane touched down. She had known it would be, but it was still a disappointment. The May weather they had been having at home was more like April. Very changeable. And she had hoped that Italy would provide some welcome warmth. Sometimes it seemed to her that she had felt cold since Fred's death. Especially in bed. That had never happened when he was alive. Well, apart from her feet of course. What was it about them? They were always colder than the rest of her.

'Put them on me, darling,' Fred would say magnanimously. She had always hesitated, feeling that the last thing anyone would want was someone else's icy toes anywhere near their body. But invariably he had insisted. And before long, she had toasted in his warmth. She missed that. She missed too many things to count.

The taxi ride into the city was crazy. She could imagine Fred nodding towards the ebulliently aggressive female driver, as she wove in and out of traffic hooting her horn loudly at anyone who got in her way, then whispering in her ear, 'Central casting!' She would have laughed and kissed him – full of joy at being away together, happily anticipating good food, wine, wonderful sights and plenty of romance.

The vehicle in front of the taxi stopped for a red light, causing outrage in Jen's driver, who leant on the horn before thumping the steering wheel with her heavily ringed fingers, and screaming, '*Mamma mia!*' So, Italians really use that expression, Jen thought. How Fred would have loved it.

She was first in the breakfast room at seven the following morning, where she ate a pastry and drank some excellent, strong coffee before walking to the Accademia Gallery. It was not yet eight o'clock and they were not due to open till 8.15 but she was far from first in the queue. Still, having read the guidebook's advice about how crowded it would be later, she waited patiently, despite the persistent drizzle. She did not gain admittance with the first tranche of people but before long she was inside.

The Michelangelo *David* was every bit as magical as its reputation. It seemed to pulse with beauty and life. She took pictures from every angle, marvelling at its perfection. The experience was so overwhelming that she decided she had more than had her money's worth and did not venture to other parts of the gallery. Instead, she left, picked one of the nearby cafés, and ordered a cappuccino and drank it while she viewed all the images she had taken. Then she sat doing nothing for a while – not thinking of anything in particular, but aware that her soul had been touched. She was grateful for that. Sometimes it seemed that nothing got past her interior deadness. But *David* had.

'You should have been here, Fred,' she whispered. 'You would have loved this.'

From the Accademia she went to Il Bargello, the National Sculpture Museum, where she saw more work by Michelangelo as well as sculptures by Giambologna and Cellini. There were plenty of others, but not by artists she had heard of. It was a lovely space though and she took her time, enjoying the building as much as the art. Outside, she sought more coffee before walking to the Duomo where she joined a massive queue. After half an hour of little movement, she gave up and wandered off to explore the outside of the vast building as well as Giotto's Campanile. The straggly line of tourists waiting to enter stretched into the distance. She had no appetite to join it. However, suddenly she did have an appetite for lunch, so she turned away from the crowds and walked to a quieter piazza where she found a trattoria with seats and an awning outside it. It was the sort of place Fred would have selected.

The rain had stopped so she risked a seat outside and ordered Insalata Caprese. It came quickly, along with a basket of tempting hot ciabatta and a dish of black olives.

This will be good, she decided. And it was.

While she ate, she scrolled through her Facebook and Twitter accounts and then accessed her emails. All spam. No work. Still, she had not made any contact with editors since Fred had become ill, and if she was going to be commissioned to write anything ever again she was going to have to start networking, and attend some Women in Journalism meetings to show her face and tell people that she was back in business. Would she do it? She should. But something was holding her back. Still, she must do something. She had just about enough money to live on, because she was now receiving half of the amount that Fred used to be paid from his pension. That was going to continue for three years for which she was grateful. After that, probably she would begin to take her own modest independent pension, and in about another seven years, she would get her state pension too. She knew it was more than many people had, but trips like this one would become a real and occasional luxury. Also, wasn't she far too young to be 'retired'? It was a word that Fred had never uttered. He told her once that he didn't really believe in it as a concept. Could she do something entirely different? What though?

The rain started again and within minutes she was shivering, so she stopped her meanderings, exchanged a few rehearsed words of Italian to the jovial young waiter, paid her bill and left. Then she walked to the river to find her bearings and from there, she was able to work her way back to the hotel.

It was a habit. Throughout her years with Fred, by unspoken agreement, they would sightsee themselves to a point of fatigue in the first half of the day, eat a leisurely lunch and then head back to the holiday hotel for a sleep and lovemaking – but not necessarily in that order.

This is what being single is all about, she thought as she suppressed an urge to scream at the emptiness of the afternoon ahead of her. I must be more grateful for everything I've had. And gracious. And less obsessed with my own pain. I honestly want to be. But right now, I just want him back, because somehow, and stupidly, I don't think I'd quite realised that death really is forever.

Monica was at The Granary. She was early, and there was no sign of the other two.

A text message pinged into her phone. She smiled to herself. It was becoming increasingly common to hear from Melissa.

On his return, James had said nothing about his outrageous behaviour in Australia, and she had not told him that she knew about it. They were tiptoeing around each other. Probably, she thought, James is as aware as I am that we need to have a serious conversation, but I doubt if he'll be the one to start it.

After her session with Helen earlier in the week, she had picked a solicitors' practice to consult about her divorce and had made an appointment to see them. She had chosen the rivals to her husband's firm. Even though she was cross with him, it would have been unfair to book one of his partners and lay bare their marriage to a former colleague. In any event, Crowbury was such a small market town, it would become common knowledge soon enough. Did James suspect that she was going to divorce him? She felt he must have some inkling but had so far said nothing. Meanwhile, she continued to do his laundry and always cooked dinner for him if she was in. It was a weird kind of limbo.

'Have you told Dad you're divorcing him yet?' Melissa's text asked.

'No.'

'Get on with it, Mum! It's time you had a life.'

'Are you in touch with Dad?'

'Absolutely not. Maggs says I'll change my mind about him eventually, but I'm still beyond furious. Anyway, have a good day. Mx'

Neither of them yet put 'Love' at the end of a text, but perhaps they would in time. A few weeks ago, she would never have believed that Melissa would become a much bigger part of her life than she had for over a decade. But then, so much in her existence was altering. Two months ago, she would never have believed that she would consult a therapist. At the beginning of the year, she would never have believed she would become a volunteer at The Granary or make two new friends. Where were they, anyway?

She was just finishing her coffee when Liz Pemberton approached her to say that Jen was still on holiday and that Lucy was ill.

'Could you possibly help in the café at lunchtime? And do Screen One afterwards?'

Monica nodded. 'What's wrong with Lucy?'

'Oh, I don't know. Sorry. I was just worrying about how we were going to manage here, rather than about her. That's awful isn't it? I don't like myself sometimes. I had no idea running a place like this could be so anxiety-provoking. Perhaps I should see a stress counsellor or something? You don't know any, do you?'

'Not a stress counsellor as such, but I do know a therapist. You've probably seen her around. Nice looking woman. Bit older than me. Her name's Helen Bartlett.'

'Oh her, yes, I know who you mean. One of the customers was quite excited when he recognised her. He said she used to be a famous TV presenter. I don't remember her myself.'

Monica smiled. 'You're too young. Anyway, to come back to Lucy…'

'Yes, sorry. Well, it was someone at the hospital who rang. Apparently, she had some sort of collapse and they kept her in.'

'No! That's awful. So, she's at the General?'

'Yes. I expect she's fine. But she is terribly overweight, isn't she? And people tend to start getting things wrong with them if they don't look after themselves, don't they? At…' Liz looked embarrassed suddenly.

'…at your age, were you going to say?'

'I'm afraid I was. Sorry. I'm not doing very well today; I keep putting my foot in it.'

Monica grinned. 'Don't worry. You're right. And I'm sure that twenty years ago, I'd have been talking just like you. One doesn't really think about life's stages till you get there. I remember, when I was a young teacher, listening to an older woman in the staff-room going on about her menopause and thinking that I couldn't be less interested. But about five years ago, it almost became my sole topic of conversation. Then, I used to listen to women saying they were dreading their husband's retirements. Again, I thought they were just droning on. Now, I know exactly how they feel. And people do get ill once they get to our age. And sometimes they do, even if they've looked after themselves very well indeed which, I have to admit, I don't think Lucy has. I've grown very fond of her though. I'll pop up there after I finish and see if she needs anything.'

Jen unlocked her front door. It seemed warmer in Crowbury than it had in Florence. Perhaps it was just more familiar.

She sprinted around, looking at the very many photos of Fred she had had framed and placed around the house since his death, and suddenly where there had been numbness, there was joy and even excitement. In their bedroom, she kissed her favourite image of him.

'So glad to see you, darling Fred,' she said aloud. 'Oh my God how I love you.'

She took herself downstairs again and wandered into Fred's study. Nobody messes it up nowadays, she thought. Not that she had ever tidied it during Fred's lifetime. Occasionally, she had suggested hoovering the carpet. Mostly he had not taken her up on her suggestion.

'I like it as it is, Jen.' And she grinned at the memory which, like everything in their history, she treasured in her heart.

'I've been lucky,' she whispered. 'Thank you. Fred, you were so good to me.'

She could almost hear his response. 'It is I who thank you. What a wonderful woman you are. You changed my life. And every day I have with you is special.'

Blinking furiously, she suddenly noticed that there was a light flashing on the answerphone on his desk.

She pressed the Play button.

It was Matthew, her younger stepson. 'Are you OK, Jen? How was Florence? Tough without Dad, I imagine. Hope you're not too miserable. I was wondering if you'd like to come and have a weekend with us in not-very-sunny Norwich? Haven't seen you in ages. I know we haven't spoken for a while, either. My fault. There's been so much happening – and I need to bring you right up to date – but I think about you a lot. The big thing is that Ginny and I have some exciting news. We're having a baby! God, after all these years, who'd have thought it? Load of other changes in the pipeline too. We didn't tell anyone about the pregnancy, because we didn't want to jinx it, but we're around fourteen weeks now and everything's fine. So – you're going to be a granny.'

Chapter Ten

It was a still and sunny day. The rose, a fresh one, was laid in the centre of the grassy mound. Clearly, this was no accident and, much as she might have wanted to, Jen could not persuade herself this time that it had blown onto Fred's grave from elsewhere. It had been placed deliberately. But why? And by whom?

She would stake her life on Fred's fidelity. Since the night she had first slept with him, they had rarely been out of each other's sight. She had never so much as glanced at another man and she was as sure as she could be that Fred had been equally true. Throughout their life together, he had been honest about all the women he had known before his marriage and during all its ups and downs, and had contrasted that with his behaviour in the 'Jen era'.

'I've been lucky to have been given a second chance with the most wonderful woman in the world, so why would I ever stray?' he had said on more occasions than she could count.

So, Fred could not have cheated. Could he?

Against her will, a niggle started in her brain and then an inner voice reminded her that infidelity could be quick; simply an itch to be scratched. She had not been with Fred every single second of every day. Her head spun. She sank to the grass. Who? When? How?

After a moment or two, sanity prevailed. Fred was faithful. Had always been faithful – to her. Shakily she got to her feet and berated herself for allowing such despicable imaginings into her mind. A clear, sharp image of Fred's face flashed before her eyes – his expression one of anguish that she could have, even for one second, questioned his devotion to her.

'Forgive me, Fred,' she murmured. 'That was unworthy. I trust you. I've always trusted you. I know what I meant to you, and you know what you meant to me. Sorry... but why does this keep happening?'

Even as she spoke the words, she knew she was being overly dramatic. A rose had appeared on his grave twice. That was all. Three months apart. Did someone he had consorted with decades ago still love him? If so, who? And surely this person would have come to the funeral? But there had been no strangers there.

'It's a bit of a mystery, Fred,' she said. 'Can you throw any light on it?' She stared at the rose again before moving it to the edge of the plot and placing her bouquet of lilies right beneath the wooden plaque with his name and date carved into it.

Silent as the grave, she thought as she registered the lack of response from her man.

Monica walked up the steps to the hospital recalling the first time she had come here after Liz Pemberton had told her about Lucy.

'I can't remember anything about the collapse,' Lucy had said, looking shocked and confused, as she lay back on the white pillows, her long, grey, wispy hair loose and tangled about her shoulders. 'It came out of the blue. I'm never ill.'

'Well, you are now, I'm afraid,' Monica had responded as she took in her fellow-volunteer's appearance.

Lucy stared into the distance with a puzzled look on her face.

'Did the person who you were visiting when you collapsed bring in toiletries and night wear for you?' Monica had asked.

'Oh no. He's ill himself. You remember the cellist who gave the not very good recital? I was supposed to be spending the afternoon reading to him. But I don't think I'd even started. His wife can't have been pleased. I hardly know her, and my little drama must have ruined her day. I... I rather owed them a favour.'

Monica had asked again about personal effects, but it was clear that Lucy had little interest. Or was she just pretending? Perhaps she had no wish for a comparative stranger to be let loose in her drawers and bathroom cabinet.

In the end, she had gone shopping in Marks and Spencer and bought two pairs of pyjamas, a dressing gown, slippers, skincare, soap and a large bunch of grapes.

Lucy had seemed embarrassed by the purchases and had wanted to pay. Monica had vetoed the suggestion.

'Just let me do this, Lucy,' she had said. 'Quite apart from anything else, I'm very grateful that I know you at the moment because there's a lot going on in my own life and I'd be awfully pleased to discuss it with you, if you wouldn't mind.'

The automatic doors slid open for her and she stood for a moment in the vestibule of the old building, realising that more than a week had elapsed since that conversation, and Lucy was still here.

She had visited most days and had gradually opened up to Lucy, and Lucy had confided in her. Though she had tried not to show it, she had been shocked by her friend's personal life. The idea of Lucy going to bed with so many men was so removed from her own experience it was hard to process. But she came to realise that it was normal for Lucy. Furthermore, to some extent, it explained her new friend's current isolation.

And now, somehow, she had agreed to be named as next of kin, and today they were to meet the consultant to discuss treatment.

'It will be helpful for Miss Brown to have you here,' the Sister on the ward had said.

Presumably then, Lucy had something serious to worry about.

*

The station was crowded. Jen sighed. She had booked herself on a specific train from London to Norwich and had, she thought, allowed plenty of time for the first part of her journey from Crowbury into the capital. But there was a delay, and no one was saying why. She ran through a list of the excuses she had encountered at this station in the past. Too few drivers. A broken rail. A lorry hitting a railway bridge. Trespassers. A person under a train. Leaves on the line. Rails buckling in the heat. Surely, she could rule out the last two as the weather was calm but not hot? Why, in this day and age, with all the technology we have now, can someone not tell us what the hell is happening?

A man standing near her on the platform smiled sympathetically. 'I couldn't agree more,' he said.

She was bewildered. Had she spoken aloud? She had not meant to. How much had she said?

'Sorry?' she smiled at him.

'I agree that it's crazy they don't communicate what's wrong. They must know something.'

'Yes. So annoying.'

'Do you often get this train?' he asked, moving closer.

'No, do you?'

'Well, from time to time. I work, and live, in Crowbury. Like you, I imagine.'

Surely at her age this unknown fellow was not interested in knowing her better. Just in case, she put a stop to it.

'Oh gosh, sorry, I need to... I'm on a bit of a deadline, uh, I better find a quiet corner and make a few phone calls.' She nodded a farewell and walked briskly to the end of the platform and into the coffee shop where she bought a cappuccino before securing a seat in the corner, next to a woman and baby.

'Keep calm, he was just chatting. He's not interested in you, you idiot,' she whispered under her breath, then she gulped at her coffee.

The child was studying her. She grinned at him. Then, from his buggy, he stretched out an arm to try to touch her. His mother was absorbed in texting on her phone. Jen waved at him, but he carried on struggling to reach her. The young mum continued to ignore him. So, Jen leant over and took his little hand and gave it a squeeze, which made him giggle.

He held her gaze for a moment while she smiled down at him, then turned away for a moment to see if his parent was watching. As he did so, it occurred to her that the little curl at the nape of his neck resembled Fred's hair when he allowed it to grow.

Suddenly, it all made sense.

'Fred?' she whispered.

'His name's Dean,' the woman said loudly. 'You must be mistaking him for some other kid.'

Jen felt a pulse beating in her neck. 'Sorry,' she managed. 'You're right. He's like a child who goes to my... my grandson's playgroup. Apologies. He's a lovely little boy, how old is he?'

'Eight months. Yeah, he's all right. When he's not screaming the place down that is.'

Jen nodded and smiled in a knowing kind of a way which she hoped would lend credibility to the idea of her being a grand-mother. Eight months made him too old. Fred had still been alive then. If he had been Fred, reincarnated, trying to establish contact with her, he would have needed to have been born after 4th January.

A man in a railway uniform put his head around the door of the café to announce that the London train would be arriving shortly, but on a different platform.

'System's down,' he explained. 'No public address. No computers. What a day!'

Jen drained her coffee cup quickly, waved goodbye to the toddler, and joined the hustle of disgruntled passengers as they crossed the footbridge and jockeyed for space where they presumed the carriage doors would open.

She was relieved when the train arrived. Relieved to find a seat, and relieved not to be anywhere near the man who had engaged her in conversation, but for all that, she was troubled.

Did she believe in reincarnation? Maybe she wanted to. Why had she lied about having a grandson? Why was she so all over the place? Was she going to implode one day? End up sectioned? Carted away to a grim institution, if such places still existed? Anything seemed possible. Were other widows like her? She wished she knew.

After they had seen the consultant, Monica had volunteered to go and buy cappuccinos from the café on the ground floor. Stunned, by what she had been told, Lucy had agreed. She had little wish for the coffee, but an urgent need for time alone.

It seemed she had out-of-control diabetes. A strict diet was vital. Medication too. Worst of all, she needed surgery to remove a toe from each foot.

She had done her best to answer the battery of questions.

When had she last had a check-up at the doctors? Or a blood test? She had not been sure.

Had she never had an insurance medical?

No.

Had she noticed any difficulty with walking?

Yes, but she had put it down to being overweight and getting old.

Had she thought it strange that she had blisters on her feet and other abrasions that looked painful but that she could not feel?

Not really.

Had she noticed any smell coming from the abrasions?

She thought she had always had slightly smelly feet.

Did she notice she had a raging thirst?

She was, she had reflected, thirstier than most folk, but thought it was healthy to drink lots of water and keep up her fluid intake, so that's what she'd been doing.

How long had she been overweight by four stone?

'Four stone? Really? As much as that?' She had been taken aback. But had conceded that she had probably been this size for a while.

Did she eat a lot of sweets, bread, potatoes and puddings and drink more than two units of alcohol a day?

Yes, to all of those.

She had noticed a slight rolling of the eyes in the consultant, a woman considerably younger than her, but hardly beanpole-thin herself.

'Well,' the doctor had said with a hint of a sigh in her voice, 'we'll leave it there for now, Miss Brown.'

'Professor.'

'Uh yes, sorry. Anyway, there are going to have to be some changes now, aren't there? You're intelligent, quite clearly, though you seem to have no idea how to look after yourself. I hope your friend,' she had indicated Monica, 'can help you. Basically, you have to get your head around the fact that you have a very serious disease which we have not, frankly, caught early enough, and you're going to have to look at ways of opting for a healthier lifestyle if you want to reach many more birthdays. I know that's harsh, but it's how it is.'

But what about my sex life? she wondered, though she decided not to voice the question. As it was, she had seen little action for weeks now. Having been forced to acknowledge that she might have been wrong, all these years, about keeping marriages together, and possibly indeed had damaged these relationships and hurt the partners concerned, she had felt less and less inclined to go to bed with anyone. She had resorted to more solo sex than normal, but even that was not working too well. Perhaps the diabetes was responsible. After all, if her blood supply was inadequate in her feet, was it supplying the clitoris, as it once had? Really this news was too awful to contemplate. She had identified herself for as long as she could remember through her job and her sexual appetite, and now the job had gone, and it looked as though her other great passion might disappear too.

Monica decided to give Lucy time to absorb what she had just learned, so before buying their coffee to take back to the ward, she purchased a cold drink and found a table in the corner over-looking the gardens.

It had been obvious that Lucy was thunderstruck by the diagnosis. Did she realise how ill she was? Monica could remember James's father refusing to take the condition seriously, which was almost certainly the reason why one day he had had a massive stroke and died.

It was distinctly worrying that Lucy, for all her intellectual brilliance, was completely ignorant of all the health messages that filled newspapers, websites, magazines and television news these days. The other worry was how on earth was Lucy going to cope with being on her own. The consultant had said she would be able to leave hospital quite soon after having those two toes amputated, so long as things went well, but that she would have to learn to look after herself, as well as master walking slightly differently – and would need to come back to the hospital regularly to have her dressings changed. People, even those much older than Lucy, usually managed this quite well once they got accustomed to it, they were told. But Lucy, bless her, was so hopelessly impractical, that Monica wondered how she would deal with the situation.

Her life was sex (Monica felt herself redden at the thought) and books. A bit like James really. Perhaps she should introduce them. She giggled out loud at the thought, because Lucy would not be James's type at all.

All of a sudden, an idea so brilliant came to her that it almost knocked her off balance; why not invite Lucy to stay, when she was allowed out of hospital after her surgery? She could then make sure that her friend was cared for, and James would have to be less sulky and sullen around the place if they had a guest. Of course, she would have to tell him about wanting a divorce before Lucy came, but maybe having company would soften the blow. That was assuming he was at all upset. Often, she felt that he had no more wish to be with her than she had with him. She sighed, wondering if she really knew her husband, despite the length of time they had been together. Anyway, she was sure that Lucy and James would be good for each other. And she could cook healthy meals for them both and, hopefully with Lucy there, dinnertime would not be the trial by silence that it had become.

There was always something soothing about being on the train from Liverpool Street Station and gradually being reclaimed by East Anglia. Jen gazed out of the window as it pulled out of Manningtree. The wide expanse of water there, dominated by the endless sky all around, never ceased to touch her heart. It was good that though she was making this journey for the first time since Fred's death, she was pleased to be on her way to Norwich and still felt wrapped in the welcome of her own part of the world and the Norfolk accents of the train crew.

Somehow, feeling more at peace than she had for a while, she found that for the first time in ages, she was able to read. It was only by chance that she had put her Kindle into her overnight bag as the months since Fred had died had been marred by an inability to concentrate on novels. It had worried her. Sometimes, at night, she dipped into a Somerset Maugham short story. Fred had loved them and there were plenty of volumes in the house to choose from. But even those, short and beautifully crafted as they were, usually defeated her. It was a big loss. For as long as she could remember, and way back into the darkest days of her childhood, books had been her friends.

Today, she had skimmed through her Kindle titles – some of which she had started but failed to finish – and had settled eventually on Patrick Gale's latest book, *Take Nothing With You*. She had read everything he had ever written, and before long she was experiencing the same satisfaction and joy that his work always brought her. More than that, she felt like the real her. It was as if she was coming home, which tied in, she mused, rather neatly with her journey to the city of her childhood.

The last hour sped by and soon she was stepping off the train. The configuration of the station never altered, though the retail outlets did. Glancing at the people waiting for friends and family off her train, she fully expected to see someone she knew and was disappointed when she did not.

She had told her stepson that she would take a taxi to their house, but it was such a lovely evening, she elected to walk even though she had a lightweight case on wheels to manoeuvre.

Breathing in the early evening air, she was relieved that Norwich felt to her exactly as it always had. Until his illness, she and Fred had come here regularly. She looked across the road at the old building which had been a wonderful restaurant called Sasses. For years, they had celebrated her birthday here – pleased always to see again the art deco interior and meet with the staff who worked there. But now everything had changed. Sasses no longer existed. Last time she and Fred had been in the city, it had turned into a Prezzo. Now, that too had gone, she noticed as she took in the empty edifice covered with scaffolding.

Determinedly, she shook away the threat of a dark mood as she dodged the queuing taxis on the station forecourt and walked across the river, then onto Prince of Wales Road. Nowadays, it was renowned as a clubbers' paradise though there were still a couple of estate agents, a convenience shop or two as well as a taverna that had been there for decades.

Her mother had worked as a secretary for an estate agent in this street. Suddenly, she saw a man emerge from that very building and realised that it was 'Young Mr Clark', as he had been known when her mother was employed there. He looked to be in his seventies now and seemed rather frail; and his hair, once plentiful and auburn, was thin and white.

She considered speaking to him, but it was probably best not to remind him of those times, so she walked on, trying to ignore how different the street was from the days of her childhood. Life was full of changes. She allowed her heart to ache for Fred for a moment, but then purposefully switched her focus to his son Matthew.

Both Fred's boys had been at boarding school when she had moved into their house, but in the holidays, gradually, she had learned how to be a stepmother and had grown close to them. It had been a particular joy for her that Matthew had secured a place to study Accountancy and Finance at the University of East Anglia. That had given Fred and her a fresh reason for visiting Norwich, which they had enjoyed. Matthew was the steady one. Simon, his older brother, had gone to Oxford for his first degree, and then had crossed the Atlantic to do a Masters at Harvard. Now, he worked in some complicated job to do with policy and politics in Canada that neither she nor Fred had fully understood. But Matthew had progressed from university to a career in Norwich Union, which became Aviva, and married a Norfolk girl called Ginny.

They suited each other. Both good natured and uncomplicated people, they were happy together and with their group of friends from Ginny's childhood and Matthew's time at the UEA.

In their early days, Ginny had worked for her mother in the rather sedate dress shop she owned in Pottergate. But once her parent had retired, Ginny had morphed, remarkably swiftly, into a dynamic retailer, fizzing with innovative ideas. She renamed the business *Indigo* and transformed it into the sort of boutique where women of all ages felt comfortable – and prided herself on never allowing customers to leave her shop clutching an outfit they would regret once they tried it on again at home. Instead, she gave them confidence that she would sell them something flattering and 'just right', even if it had looked nothing special on the hanger.

Fred had loved Ginny and enjoyed her company as much as he did his son's, so they often came to Norwich, though generally they did not crowd the young couple by staying with them, preferring the privacy of a hotel.

They had even at one point, when Fred had been made redundant and decided to go freelance as Jen already was, considered moving here themselves. But they had decided they needed to be nearer London. In any event, for all his fondness for his boys, Fred liked them to have their own lives and their own space, and indeed wanted the same for himself.

She turned up Rampant Horse Street and before long found herself walking past the Theatre Royal.

In her time working at the *Eastern Daily Press*, she had sometimes been allowed to report on the shows that the main critic was not particularly interested in. He had been a gentleman of advanced years who took himself very seriously. This meant that he reserved his attention for plays that were on the Number One Touring circuit, and visits from prestigious companies such as Glyndebourne and Northern Ballet. He always critiqued the big stars too, like Ken Dodd and Danny La Rue. But she had been allowed to cut her teeth on reviewing lesser productions and had felt she had truly 'arrived' in the business when she was invited to Press Night Drinks on Mondays. That thrill of being recognised as someone who wrote words for a living had been so potent, she had never got used to it.

She smiled as she remembered her young self and was still rewinding her life when she reached Chapelfield Gardens where she stopped for a moment beside the bench where she had shared the first kiss with her first boyfriend. They had still been at school. Neither of them knew what they were doing, but it had been a happy introduction to romance. It was just a pity it ended the way it did.

She continued daydreaming and before long, she was in Matthew's street – one of those leading off Unthank Road, in a part of the city now referred to as The Golden Triangle; a term some estate agent must have dreamed up long after she had left.

Matthew and Ginny's place was looking unusually smart. Neither of them had ever been very house-proud and had tended to live more like students than adults approaching mid-life. But now they had painted their door egg-shell blue, and planted geraniums in a hanging basket and cornflowers in a window box. It looked for the first time like a proper 'nest', and soon would not be an empty one.

Her stepson bounded out of the front door and hugged her so hard he lifted her off her feet.

'Jen, so good to see you. Loads to tell you.' He picked up her suitcase and, much to her surprise, put it in the boot of his car which was parked on the road just outside their front gate. 'So much going on. Sorry about the suitcase, but it'll save finding a place for it in the house. We're going to walk up to The George for supper. Ginny's there already, getting us a table. An estate agent's coming round to do two viewings. They say it'll be better if we're out. But when you see inside later, you won't recognise it! We've spent weeks decluttering. It's never been so tidy. I hope we get a sale soon because it'll be a hell of strain keeping it like that! We decided to move because of the baby. We want to talk to you about that... Also, I've gone mad and got a new job.'

He took her arm and marched her through the streets to the nearby hotel, chatting away all the while. She looked up at him, this man with his father's eyes whom she loved.

Matthew pushed open the door that led to the bar and restaurant, and waved excitedly at his wife, before guiding Jen through the bustling Friday night drinkers to their table, where she kissed Ginny on both cheeks before realising that he was still busy talking.

'Ginny can fill you in on everything, but we found out yesterday we're having a boy. I didn't mind what gender it was, but she's thrilled because she says boys are much nicer to their mothers than girls are!'

His wife beamed and nodded.

'So,' he went on, 'we're thinking of calling him Freddie. Just an idea. You wouldn't mind that would you? We felt it would be... well you know, a connection with Dad and a way of linking our son with the lovely man he never got to meet.'

Chapter Eleven

Her mother was sitting in the big armchair in her private room – eyes closed, mouth open. Watching her, Monica reflected that in days gone by, she might have tried to style the old lady's wild hair and perhaps put some lipstick or blusher on her or paint her nails. But fifteen years of dementia to the point where her parent no longer knew her own name let alone anyone else's, had made such gestures so utterly pointless that she, and everyone else, had given up on them.

Not that the nursing home staff were negligent in any way, she acknowledged. But, she thought, they really don't have the heart to do anything except the basics. Who can blame them? Why waste your energy on someone whose life isn't worth living?

'We haven't seen you for a while, Mrs Charlton.' A passing carer put her head around the door.

Monica waved and forced a smile, and the woman disappeared.

Did they, she wondered, think she neglected her mother? She hoped not. But how could she be accused of neglecting someone who was just a shell, who never spoke, and who – on the rare occasions when her eyes were open – showed no flicker of recognition when Monica arrived, greeted her or talked about the past? There was nothing to be done now except keep her parent housed, warm and cared for.

I'm busy anyway, she justified herself. There was a house to run. A part-time job. A friend in hospital she was trying to help. A divorce in the offing. And the tiniest glimmer of hope that she might, after all this time, begin a relationship with someone who genuinely would care for her.

Helen had said more than once that she needed to protect herself from too many rose-tinted dreams about Stephen and had pointed out that the two of them had not spoken for a decade, never spent more than a few hours at a time in each other's company, never been on holiday, never argued about who should take the bins out.

All this was true. No wonder she was scared, even though her heart lifted every time she thought of him.

The next task, which she really must tackle, was to tell James she was divorcing him. It was only fair. And she had decided she could not contact Stephen till she had done so.

'I'm going to ask for a divorce,' she said loudly.

For a moment she imagined that this bombshell might propel the elderly woman back into the real world. But there was no response.

'Did you hear that? I'm going to divorce James.'

Her mother slumbered on.

The two of them had had a complicated relationship which had been made worse by the early death of her father, and her mother's persistence in criticising everything about him till eventually the dementia allowed her to forget that she had been married to 'such a feckless bloke'.

Monica's love for the honest and decent man who had fathered her, was real and fond. He had been part of the National Service generation and – unlike many other temporary servicemen – had loved the army. Having been brought up in London's East End, where opportunities and food had been scarce, he had appreciated the regular meals and the order that the military brought to his life. He had also learned many useful skills and had found a job as a car mechanic when the two years ended. Her mother had looked down on him with his dirty hands and overalls. But Monica thought of him as handsome and clever, and as someone who could whistle a good tune, and fix things with a smile on his face.

His downfall was that he was a heavy smoker, and did not live to see her wedding, or his granddaughters.

It was because of you that I married James, she thought as she stared at her mother.

1982

Mum's painting her nails with scarlet varnish. James is coming over later, so she's probably doing it for him – though to be fair, she has always made the best of herself and James frequently says that he likes how she always makes an effort. Often, he tells me that I get my looks from her and that he hopes I'll wear as well as she has.

It's a mutual admiration society. She thinks he's wonderful, and has said, on more than one occasion, 'I wouldn't kick him out of bed!' which made me feel quite sick. What she really likes though is that he's a solicitor, as his father was, and that he's got his 'head screwed on right' and that all our money worries will be over once I'm his wife.

The trouble is, I'm not at all sure I want this commitment. Is this a good moment to say so?

'You look nice, Mum,' I say.

She looks up and half smiles. Then she says, 'Aren't you going to get out of your work clothes and put on something smarter? James'll be here soon.'

I think I look fine, dressed as I am for comfort in the classroom. I'm doing my final teaching practice at the moment, and when you're in charge of infants you don't want to wear your best clothes. But I'm perfectly presentable in my navy pleated skirt and jumper. Still, I want to please her so I say I will change in a minute.

Then I pluck up courage to deliver my prepared speech. 'Mum, look I know you won't like this, but I'm not sure that I want to marry James.'

There's a sharp intake of breath but I ignore it and plough on.

'At least, not this summer. I'd like to do a year of teaching first and concentrate on that.'

'You should have thought of all that before you let him into your knickers.'

I'm shocked. Shocked that she knows. Shocked that she thinks it changes anything. And shocked that she believes it's shameful in the 1980s.

She notices my discomfort.

'You didn't think I knew, did you? Well James told me. He said he regretted it in a way so he wanted to confess to me that you wouldn't be a virgin on your wedding day. But he said he was careful and won't get you pregnant, and also that you'd wanted to do it so much that he hadn't liked to refuse.'

This version of events is so different from the truth that I am stunned. I've been fighting him off for months, but he kept saying how unfair I was being and that it was only right to test out whether we're good for each other in bed. He kept going on about how the country's morals had changed almost twenty years ago, and that I was well behind the times. And he also said I was cruel and that he was in real pain (in his genitals) and in torment (in his heart) because he wanted me so much.

'I never reckoned you were such a trollop,' my mother snaps. 'You're damaged goods now, girl.'

'Mum, for goodness' sake, the swinging sixties and the flower-power seventies changed all that kind of thinking. It's 1982! Where have you been?'

'Trust me. Keeping your legs closed till marriage is every woman's greatest weapon and you've thrown yours away. Not so bright after all, are you, with all your education? You *will* marry him, Monica. Because you'll never get such a great offer again. And I think you should do it as soon as possible. James and I went and had a look at a venue for the reception earlier, while you were working. He's even said he'll pay for it because he's got so many relatives and friends to invite.'

A carer came in, disturbing Monica's journey back in time. She was carrying a tray with a pot of tea and two cups.

'I thought I heard you talking, Mrs Charlton,' she said. 'So I thought your mother might be awake.'

'She did stir for a moment,' Monica lied. 'But let's just leave her. I expect she'll have a cup of tea later. Thanks for mine though, I'm ready for one.'

After the carer withdrew, she felt slightly mean, and moved over to her parent's recliner, and stroked her hand. 'Tea, Mum?'

Her mother's breathing altered for a few seconds. But then settled again.

I tried, Monica thought as she sat down once more in her own chair.

The relationship had not been awful, she supposed. In the early days, James had been very attentive. But once they had settled into their married life, she had seemed to annoy him. He had resented her taking up her first teaching post, for example, insisting that they had no need of her money as he was making plenty, and completely missing the point that she loved the job and wanted to do something with her days rather than just keep house and arrange flowers and dinner parties.

He had criticised her too. Endlessly. Melissa had been quite right about that. And often he had done so in front of her mother and both of them would laugh. They had been allies throughout.

James had helped her mother buy her council house. He was doing very well by then and his parents had died and left him significant money. Monica had never asked how much.

'I'm a woman of property,' her mother would say, with delight. Then she would add, 'No thanks to my hopeless husband.'

'You were horrid about Dad,' Monica said aloud. 'He was a good man. And he would have made a terrific grandfather if he'd lived. He'd have loved the girls too, in a way you never did.'

The truth was that her mother was squeamish about illness, and cystic fibrosis could be messy.

'You bought Betsy presents sometimes but there were never any hugs for my beautiful girl, were there? Do you think she never noticed? Well, she did. She loved you.'

Her attention moved to her older child. Her mother had been good with Melissa in the early days, but when she became a teenager everything had changed.

'As for Melissa, you stopped bothering with her. You didn't like that she was a tomboy. Or opinionated about politics. And as she grew older, you couldn't see her making a successful marriage, could you? That was all that mattered to you. But she's having a wonderful career now. And she's gay, as it turns out. A lesbian. You wouldn't like that if you still had your marbles, would you?'

Her mother started snoring.

Monica stared at her and felt a deep sadness about her ambivalence towards the poorly old woman.

You're not a bad person, she thought. You wanted the best for me, and you got it, in a way. In *your* way. Still, you can't manipulate me now. I'll be sixty soon. But I'm well and fit, and I think I'm at last coming out of the straitjacket you and James put me in – that Stepford wife, that individual who felt collapsed inside but who was outwardly the upstanding, polite, homemaker, hostess and devoted wife of the town's leading solicitor.

I did all that. I did it as well as I could. But now it's going to stop.

Chapter Twelve

The morning began with the hint of an argument between Matthew and his wife.

'Sweetie, don't fuss,' Ginny snapped.

'But you don't look well, and you obviously don't feel well,' he reasoned.

'Saturdays are always busy. I need to go. I'll feel better later, I'm just tired.'

Jen gazed at the woman who was carrying Fred's grandson. Without thinking about it, she volunteered to accompany her and help in the shop.

'Would you?' Ginny's delight was another of the increasingly touching moments in the visit. 'That would be so marvellous.'

The hours passed quickly. Jen felt useful. It was cheering.

She discussed customers' requirements with them, made suggestions or deferred to Ginny for advice, opened boxes and unpacked new stock, as well as made tea and coffee for the clientele. Then at lunchtime, she found a delicatessen and bought sourdough bread, cheese and Mediterranean vegetables, before making sandwiches in the tiny kitchen at the back of the boutique.

Everything about this trip was surprising. Having worried that she would not be able to sleep in anyone else's house, she had had the most restful night in ages. As for the previous evening, far from feeling surplus to requirements and opting to go to bed early to get out of the way – which was what she had anticipated – she had enjoyed herself as they had reminisced about Fred, and discussed Ginny and Matthew's future plans, including Matthew's new job and the extra travelling it would involve, as well as the houses they had viewed.

Perhaps most amazingly of all, Ginny had given her a copy of Freddie's scan, which had made her eyes prick with happy tears. The truth was that she had not expected to feel such a sense of family. And she was astonished at how excited she was about the baby, though she had kept to herself the hope that he might be a reincarnated Fred.

And now, having spent the day surrounded by clothes, she decided she could boost Ginny's takings by buying a couple of outfits. So here she stood, for the first time in ages, dressed in a summery frock.

'My goodness, that's different,' she commented to her image in the changing room. And to complete the picture, for almost the first time since she had been widowed, she pulled off the band that held her habitual ponytail tightly in place and fluffed up her hair.

'You look lovely, darling,' she heard Fred say in her head. She smiled as she recalled how he had always complimented her on her appearance, and in that moment, she felt real joy at what she had had, rather than the familiar weight of loss.

Next, she tried on blue, glazed cotton cropped trousers and a paler blue and pink cotton top. She looked totally different from normal, but then she had given little care to anything she had worn for months; most of the time settling for a fleece, black top and walking trousers.

As she emerged from the cubicle, Ginny said, 'Wow, Jen, you look years younger and where have you been hiding that perfect figure?'

She remembered her response, a couple of days previously, when someone in Crowbury she had not seen in a while had said, 'You're looking very slim these days. What's your secret?'

She had been brusque in reply. 'My husband died. Turns out that's the best diet imaginable.'

Afterwards, she had regretted her harshness. So, this time, she smiled as she quipped, 'Grief is awfully good for the waistline!' Then she continued, 'Also, I'm on my feet a lot at The Granary and I tend to walk everywhere these days. I probably eat less too, now that there are no lengthy dinners, with me helping myself to second helpings of food while Fred polishes off the wine!'

Ginny moved in for a hug, and though Jen tensed herself momentarily, she did not brush the younger woman aside, but instead allowed the comfort of closeness.

A few days later, back at The Granary, she was wearing one of her new outfits and had been astounded by how many compliments she had received. It just goes to show I've been slopping around looking appalling for months, she thought.

'Gosh, it's crazy again today!' Monica remarked as she appeared with two glasses of wine, flopped into the seat beside Jen and handed her one.

'Mmmn, this rosé is lovely,' Jen thanked her. 'Whoever buys the wine here – and it's probably Liz as she seems to do most things – does a great job.'

Monica nodded her agreement.

'I hope you don't mind my saying this,' Jen ventured. 'But I've been thinking all day how relaxed and different you look now compared with the afternoon we all met and came here for the first time. I don't want to pry or anything, but is life treating you better?'

'I think I've taken control of it,' Monica explained. 'There's a long way to go yet, but maybe we could have lunch tomorrow before we start our late shifts, and I'll fill you in. There's so much going on. I thought mid-life would be all about winding down, but it really isn't like that at all.'

'Tell me about it!'

113

'The crux of it in my case is that I want a divorce, but my husband doesn't know yet.'

'Oh, my goodness! That's quite a shake-up. How do you feel about it?'

Monica looked at her for a moment, then allowed her neck to drop back; she gazed at the ceiling for a second or two before straightening up and replying, 'I do sometimes wonder who's going to massage my back!'

'That,' Jen giggled, 'is the perfect answer!'

Just then, a couple of excited, chattering woman bumped into their table. Monica reached out to steady her glass. The women apologised as they joined the long line of people, snaking round the foyer and into the café area, waiting to show their e-tickets for the six o'clock viewing in Screen One.

'Do you know,' Monica said, 'when I saw that a film called *Rocketman* was scheduled here, I didn't know it was about Elton John. And I certainly didn't realise how popular it would be. It's been on for two weeks, hasn't it? And it's still packed every time. Till I saw it I hadn't realised how many of his songs I knew. I love his stuff.'

'Me too. I actually got to watch it all the way through today. It's brilliant. Fred took me to an Elton John concert once. Probably, from what we know now, he was high as a kite on cocaine, but the whole thing was fantastic. An extravaganza! We had the best night,' her eyes moistened for a moment.

'You must miss him very much,' Monica said, treading carefully. This was the first time Jen had talked of her husband or used his name. Did that mean that at last the pain was slightly less raw? It was probably best not to assume that.

'I do,' Jen said, and she ran a finger around the rim of her wine glass as her expression became more pensive. 'But I'm beginning to feel more gratitude for what we had now, rather than just numbness and as if I'm going through the motions all the time. My stepson Matthew said to me the other day, "You and Dad had a charmed life" and he was so right… As you know, I've just visited him and his wife. They're having a baby, and though of course it won't be a blood relation to me, I do feel quite thrilled.'

'How long have you been Matthew's stepmother?'

'Ages – since he was thirteen. He's forty-four now.'

'Well, that's long enough for him to think of you as a proper granny for his child.'

'I suppose so. Of course, his own mum died when he was only eleven.'

'You must have done a good job with him.'

'I don't know,' Jen's face relaxed and took on a softer expression, 'but I don't think I could love him, or his brother, any more than I do, even if I was a real mother. But then, as I never have been, I've nothing to compare it with.'

'What does the other son do?'

'Simon? He's quite a high-flyer and lives in Canada at the moment, which is funny in a way as my mother's family were from there. She came here to study on some sort of Commonwealth scholarship when she was twenty, and never went back. Simon asked if I'd like him to try to trace my extended family while he was over there – because my mother didn't have any relatives here. But it's the last thing I want!'

'Was your father Canadian too?'

'No idea. I never knew him, or even who he was. And I've certainly never tried to find him. These things are probably best left. What you don't know can't hurt you!'

Monica watched Jen as she listened to her. 'You look lovely today,' she said when Jen paused for another mouthful of wine. 'Really summery.'

'Ginny, Matthew's wife, runs this gorgeous little dress shop right in the centre of Norwich and I went and helped her on Saturday, which was the best fun I'd had in ages. Then, I suddenly realised I'd hardly registered what I've been wearing for months, so I bought a few things.'

115

'It's understandable that clothes didn't matter for a while,' Monica murmured. 'I remember when my daughter died, it was hard to see the point in dressing up.'

'That must have been really awful. I can't imagine what it would be like to lose a child.'

Both women fell silent for a moment till Monica said, 'It was a long time ago. And it's nice when you do recover an interest in your appearance. And you look terrific!'

'Thank you,' Jen responded. 'And Ginny gave me a generous discount, which was very kind.'

'It works both ways, doesn't it? Kindness.'

'I hope so, but I did sort of get the feeling that they both feel a bit responsible for me, which they obviously don't need to be. But knowing Fred, I imagine he said something to Matthew before he died along the lines of "Look after Jen, won't you?".'

Jen's voice wobbled. She swallowed, and then apologised. 'Sorry, I kind of tripped myself up there, just when I was being all bright and breezy.'

Monica reached over and pulled her into a quick hug.

'Thanks, Monica,' she said. 'To be honest, the whole weekend was full of surprises. And the biggest one, a real bolt from the blue, was when they were discussing where they might live and what sort of house they wanted to buy, and then, they actually asked if I'd consider living with them. I think they want to get something a lot larger, and further from the centre, with plenty of outdoor space now they're going to be parents. And Matthew has got a new job with quite a healthy salary, and of course Fred left both boys money, so...'

'People don't ask you to live with them if they don't truly like you! That's far more than Matthew doing his duty by his father. How do you feel about the suggestion?'

'Flattered... Astonished... I don't know though. I do want to help with the baby, but as I've never been a mother, I'll probably be hopeless. Also, I won't be sixty for another fifteen months, and to be honest, I don't think I'm ready to live in a Granny Annexe. But there again, I did enjoy the weekend, much, much more than I'd anticipated. I suppose it confirmed for me that I have a place in Fred's family.'

'Haven't you got anyone else at all?'

'No one. My mum seems to have fallen out with everyone before she left Canada, and there were never any relatives in the UK. She was an only child. I was too, of course. And she died young. I think of myself as being very self-reliant, but I'm not sure now that I am. In fact, I'm not very sure about anything.' She noticed suddenly that Monica had finished her drink and was sitting on the edge of her seat. 'D'you need to go?'

'Well, I'm worried about Lucy. She had her op yesterday.'

'What?'

'Sorry, I can't remember what you know about her.'

'Not much. I'm quite out of the loop, what with going to Florence and then Norfolk. I knew she was ill, but I'd no idea it would require surgery. Is she OK?'

'Hard to say. I'm just going up to the hospital to see her.'

'Would you like me to come?'

'I would! Walk with me and I'll fill you in as we go.'

'How are you now, Miss Brown?'

For once, Lucy did not try and persuade the young nurse to use her title. It was a losing battle. She was retired. She was no longer a professor and might as well accept it. Anyway, she felt so awful, nothing mattered.

'I'm terribly thirsty. Can I have more water?'

The nurse turned to pick up the jug on Lucy's locker, and found it to be empty.

'I only filled this quarter of an hour ago, have you drunk it all?'

'It would seem so,' Lucy replied crossly.

'I'll get you some right away. But I will need to tell Sister that you're drinking so much... Now, have you got pain in your feet?'

117

'No.'

'How are you feeling generally?'

Lucy sighed loudly. 'Not well. But I did have an operation yesterday.'

'Can you be more specific?'

'I just feel awful. Really awful. Is that specific enough? Most of all though, I need a drink. Please, please let me have some water. Now!'

She burst into tears which was as much of a surprise to her as it was to the nurse. Not a teary kind of person, she had probably not wept since she was about fifteen.

'Can I just listen to your chest?'

Lucy nodded through her sobs. Then the room began to spin, and lots of people started rushing about. Everything seemed very weird and almost certainly not going to plan.

Monica and Jen arrived at the door to the ward just as someone was pulling curtains around Lucy's bed. They exchanged glances, but continued to stand, uncomfortable and unsure in the doorway. Then the Sister of the ward, whom Monica had met when the treatment plan for Lucy had been outlined, recognised her.

'I think the two of you better go down to the café for a while. We're going to move Miss Brown to another ward. I'll come and talk to you as soon as I can, Mrs Charlton, as you're next of kin.'

As they retraced their steps to the ground floor, Jen asked, 'How did that happen?'

'What?'

'You being next of kin.'

'Lucy asked me. I know she's got a brother somewhere, but she didn't want to bother him. For all her cleverness, she's completely ignorant about health and doesn't seem to have any concept of what's happening to her, or how serious it is. I mean once they start removing toes, it's pretty dramatic, isn't it? I can't understand how anyone could get that ill without realising it.

She's so… different. Lovely, but she lives in her own world. So, anyway, I agreed. But if things are getting worse, I must try to persuade her to let me contact her family. Ironically, her brother's a doctor. Perhaps that's why she didn't want him involved. She probably thought he would nag or criticise her. He's retired now, she told me. Apparently, he's very religious. So was her dad, who was a vicar, and her mother was active in the church too, I gather, though she was a lecturer, like Lucy. Lucy said she had an idyllic childhood, but I do wonder what they made of her lifestyle?'

Jen looked confused. 'What do you mean?'

'Well, she's had loads of lovers. It's an open secret, it seems. Though perhaps I ought to check with her before I tell you anymore.'

Jen nodded. 'The very idea of Lucy being "louche", is awfully unexpected. I mean, she doesn't look the type.'

'I know.'

They reached the café. 'What will you have?' Jen asked.

'I could do with more alcohol, what about you?'

'I shouldn't think they have any here. Anyway, I've had today's quota.'

Monica looked surprised. 'Do you ration yourself then?'

'Mmmn, I do. I no longer drink at all at home. It would mean doing it alone and that doesn't seem sensible when you're miserable. Not that I'm miserable today. But I generally allow myself up to two glasses if I'm out.'

'That's very restrained of you. I drink far too much. I wish I didn't. I think James has driven me to it! Well maybe a soft drink then.'

'Cranberry juice?'

'That'll do fine. I'll get us a table.'

Jen paid for the drinks and had just sat down beside Monica when a voice boomed from the doorway, 'Mrs Charlton, a word!'

Monica excused herself and went over to meet Sister. The conversation was so brief that she returned before many seconds had passed and sat down heavily, her face pale and anxious.

119

'Lucy's heart stopped, apparently. They got it going again, but she's very poorly and they've taken her to Intensive Care. Sister says we should go home as there's nothing we can do.'

It would be quite crass, Jen thought, to eat dinner when a colleague, or rather a friend, was hovering between life and death. Anyway, she had no appetite and she felt very restless.

In her study, she played around on her PC for a while, checking Twitter and Facebook. She retweeted some messages that were about writers' events or journalists' meetings. Then 'liked' a few posts on Facebook. There were some new Friend Requests. She always ignored those unless she knew the people personally. One was much younger than the rest. Her name was Chloe. Why on earth, thought Jen, would she want to be my friend? Bizarre.

She decided it had been a while since she had cleared out her email inbox, so she went to the oldest messages which were more than a year old and started erasing them.

Then she gasped as she came upon an exchange between her and Fred.

It had taken place on a day when she had been interviewing various teachers about the childhood poverty they were encountering in the classroom. She had sold the feature idea to *The Guardian* and had written the piece already but had felt she needed more quotes from people in the profession. So, she had gone to a school in Birmingham very early that morning, then taken a train across to Norwich, where she had interviewed another teacher, before ending up at a primary school in the Tower Hamlets area of London. She had not returned home till late that night and had worried about Fred being on his own for so many hours. They had not known what was wrong with him at that point, but already he was suffering from the exhaustion that led to his diagnosis.

'Dearest Fred,' one of her emails began, 'what I'm learning today is so awful. Honestly, there are kids who stay at home all the school holidays. Never get out of the house. Never get properly

120

fed. Then they come back to school the following term jumpy and hungry. But at least once they're back at school they get exercise and food. God help us. What is this country coming to? Missing you, darling. See you asap. All love, as ever, J xxx'

He had replied, 'Darling girl. Missing you too. Thanks for keeping me in the loop. You're doing a grand job. The piece will be terrific. You always were a great talent, as I remember from my days as your boss! Counting the hours, sweetheart xxx'

She read on through the other emails they had sent during that long day. They made her cry but at the same time, her heart was gladdened by the palpable affection that flowed between them. 'We were so lucky, Fred,' she whispered at the big photograph of him on her desk. 'So lucky.'

A text pinged into her phone. She looked at it immediately in case it brought news of Lucy, but it was her neighbour telling her she had taken in another rescue dog. Her heart sank.

'What sort is he?'

'A miniature schnauzer. Tiny. Underfed. Nervous. Cute though. Come and see.'

'OK.'

She continued deleting old emails, though not any of Fred's, but before long she gave up and was just about to close down the computer and go to her neighbour's when she noticed that a new email had come in from Matthew asking if she could ring him.

She became aware of her heart beating faster. Surely nothing had gone wrong with the baby.

She reached for her phone.

'Matthew?'

'Jen, hi.'

'Is something wrong with Ginny?'

'Oh… no, not at all.'

'Thank God!'

'It's just there's something I felt you should know – though it all happened a long time before your involvement with Dad. A

121

woman has got in touch, all rather strange, I must say. She says,' he paused for several seconds, 'sorry, it's hard to get my head round this… She says she's Dad's daughter. She's younger than Simon but older than me. She contacted me on Facebook. I don't think she's a nutter or anything. So, I've agreed to have a DNA test, to check. I… um, I'm aware that my mum and dad were apart for a while after Simon was born, so the timing fits. The woman says that she's only just found out, because of an obituary she read about Dad when she was visiting her mother. And then the mum told her she was his daughter. She looked at his Wikipedia entry and of course that lists my name and Simon's. So, she worked out who I was, using social media. Weird, eh? She says she suspects Dad never knew about her. Anyway, it's a bit of a turn up, isn't it? Her name's Chloe.'

Monica rustled up a salade niçoise for their supper – using a tuna steak that was about to go out of date, and adding to it smoked anchovies, hard-boiled eggs, green beans, avocado, lettuce and tomato. She also opened a bottle of New Zealand Sauvignon Blanc.

James enjoyed it. 'I'm not a huge fan of salad as you know,' he had said, 'but this is perfect for a hot July evening.'

Then, she produced a plum and almond crumble – made with fruit from their own garden.

It had been an odd time over the weeks since James had returned from Australia. Her mind had been in a whirl with her plans to divorce him and yet she had carried on doing everything in the house she always had, apart from any carnal activity, which had stopped the day of her migraine, almost a year ago now.

However, Lucy's sudden deterioration tonight had concentrated her mind. And while she played the part of the good wife who could produce a tasty meal at the drop of a hat, she had come to a decision. Life could be so unpredictable. Who knew what lay ahead? Or how long it would go on.

She walked out to the kitchen and took a series of deep breaths. Then, slowly and deliberately she removed her wedding and engagement rings before returning to the dining room table.

'Ice cream, or real cream with your crumble?'

'Ooh, a spot of ice cream, I think,' he answered.

He ate with relish, then poured himself another large glass of wine, and was about to leave her to clear the table while he went to watch television when she reached out her left, ringless hand and stopped him.

'James,' she said. 'I'm sorry. I need to tell you something. I want a divorce.'

Chapter Thirteen

Despite feeling trapped in a dense mental fog, Lucy perceived that she was about to be given a pep talk.

She was unsure what day it was, but she had been moved back to the original ward and now she had been told that the consultant was coming to see her.

The woman appeared almost immediately – exuding an air of determined if exhausted efficiency – and began to run through a list of blood test results, and conclusions.

Listening, listlessly, Lucy took in that her heart was damaged, and that her blood sugar and cholesterol were far too high.

'Do you understand?'

Lucy nodded.

'Are there any questions you'd like to ask about diet or medication, or anything?'

As Lucy shook her head, the doctor launched, briskly, into a speech all about necessary change, beginning with the range of pills that she was prescribing.

Having avoided medicines all her life, it was clear to Lucy that for the remainder of it, she was to rattle like an old-fashioned sweet jar. Next, she was advised that she must find ways to lose weight, and that she would need to take up a 'moderate' exercise plan and also come to the hospital daily, till her feet had healed up, so that the dressings on them could be changed.

'Daily?' Lucy interrupted her.

'I'm afraid so. You do understand don't you, Miss Brown, that you must take this seriously? The cardiac arrest you had earlier in the week is indicative of what the pattern could be now. I'm afraid you're likely to have more such events, or a stroke, if we don't reverse the decline in your health that obviously began a while ago, though you failed to notice it.'

'Until recently, I was busy,' Lucy retorted, and her chin quivered as she recalled the life she had loved before she had been forced out of the university.

'The other thing is that I gather you live alone. Have you given any thought to how you're going to manage? We'll be putting together a care and treatment package and the physio and various other people involved in that will see you later.'

'Not today, I hope,' Lucy protested. 'I don't think I could cope with anything else.'

'No, not today.' The doctor smiled, and Lucy could see that she was quite pretty when her seriousness temporarily rolled away.

Sister hovered as the consultant withdrew.

'Your friends are here,' she said. 'Are you feeling up to seeing them?'

Lucy thought for a moment and then agreed that she was. Perhaps they would help her work out how she might effect all these changes that everyone thought were necessary.

They did not stay long. Lucy tired quickly, having outlined for them what the consultant had told her. She looked ill and helpless, and far from enthusiastic about working towards her recovery. Indeed, Jen was left with the feeling that Lucy believed fate, having blessed her with a happy and fulfilled life till now, had decided it was her turn to be cast into a living hell from which there was no escape.

Outside, the heat of the last few days, which had been almost unbearable, had finally lost its grip and a thunderstorm was raging.

Monica had a tiny, telescopic umbrella buried in her handbag but no raincoat, and Jen was even less prepared in her sandals, long floaty skirt and cotton top.

'I think we ought to stay for a while. Let's go to the café. I don't see how either of us can go out in this,' Monica said.

Jen stared at the monsoon raging beyond the automatic doors and nodded. 'I normally check the Met Office hourly-forecast, but for some reason I didn't today. I'll try and access it on my phone.' She headed towards the café and made for a table by the window.

'Do you want a coffee or something?' Monica called after her.

'I suppose we oughtn't to sit here without buying anything. A mug of tea would be great. Thanks.'

Jen fiddled with her mobile. There was no Wi-Fi for hospital visitors, and the phone signal was poor. But at last the page came up.

'It looks like the heavy rain will pass through in another three quarters of an hour, so shall we stay here till then?' Jen asked as Monica returned with tea for them both.

'I think we'll have to.'

'I'm terribly relieved that Lucy's back on the ordinary ward. I was so frightened we'd seen the last of her, the other night. She's such an interesting person. The world needs to hang on to those.' Jen looked wistful and Monica reached over and patted her arm.

'The thing is,' Jen continued after a pause, 'I'm sensing Lucy is not up for even trying to get better. There just seems to be an air of hopelessness about her.'

Monica appeared to be lost in her own thoughts, but suddenly, in a robust tone, she announced, 'We need a plan. A plan to get her on her feet, literally, and to get her in shape. You know, fitter, slimmer, healthier. I'm sure we could do it. She obviously hasn't a clue how to get started, so we're going to have to help.'

Jen's eyes shone with enthusiasm. 'Yes, we can do that. It would be a tragedy to let her just fade away. She needs motivation and a new direction in life, doesn't she? And I bet as she loses weight, she'll begin to like herself more and, you know, there may be some decent bone structure under that fat face, and we could take her shopping for some trendier clothes. Ooh, and get her hair cut, and we could teach her something about make-up, or maybe even let one of those eager beauty-counter assistants give her a "new look". I think we could achieve a complete transformation!'

Monica laughed.

Jen turned to her, smiling, 'What?'

'I don't know exactly. It was just that you looked as though you were enjoying the idea of a major challenge and couldn't wait to get started!'

Jen laughed too. 'Absolutely! Fred would have said, "Oh God, I feel one of Jen's projects coming on!".'

'Project Lucy?'

'Project Lucy,' Jen nodded before saying, quite seriously, 'Actually, if we get this right, we might genuinely save her life.'

Their enthusiasm was so engaging that the next time either of them looked at their watch forty minutes had passed, and the weather was improving.

'I'm sorry I haven't got around to asking what's happening to you,' Jen said as Monica rose to her feet and announced that she must go. 'Have you told James yet that you want a divorce?'

'I have. I'll fill you in tomorrow. Not that there's much to tell. But I must get going. I'm seeing Helen.'

'Is that helping?'

'I think so. It's certainly useful to run things past her. Anyway, I'm pleased we're both keen to help Lucy. It's probably always easier to change other people than ourselves! It certainly feels more fun.'

They both grinned and, for the first time since they had met in February, they kissed each other on both cheeks before heading off in different directions.

As Jen picked her way carefully among the puddles, she found herself thinking back to Matthew's phone call earlier in the week telling her that he might have a half-sister. Chloe had been on her mind ever since. Was it really possible that Fred had had a daughter? If so, he must have been ignorant of the fact. He would never have abandoned or ignored a child of his had he known about her.

As she thought about him, without warning, she was propelled back in time to a hot morning in a hotel garden in Barbados where the two of them were enjoying the sort of leisurely breakfast that only happens when you're away somewhere warm, with no deadlines. Unlike most of the other male guests around them, Fred was dressed in a crisp, white cotton shirt, tailored shorts and canvas sailing shoes. She and he both agreed that men – with their hairy feet and big toes – should never, ever wear flip-flops unless they were on a beach.

She could picture herself, sitting with Fred; both of them reading a section from a British newspaper which had been printed in the Caribbean overnight. Every now and again one of them spoke to tell the other something interesting they had found on the page. Then they chatted about whether or not to order more coffee, and maybe fetch another plate of the tropical fruits that remained temptingly within reach on the buffet table.

How real it seemed. And how recent. Yet they had had no idea that they were on their last holiday. Would they have acted differently had they known? Probably not, because they could not have been more romantically content, companionable or light-hearted.

She shook her head in disbelief that such happy days would never be repeated and that her attentive and lovely husband now lay in a woodland grave.

Where are *that* Fred and Jen? she pondered. Are they still there? In the Caribbean? In a parallel universe? I really hope so. And where are the even younger couple? The pair of them working together in the newspaper office in a building that had long ago been torn down. The two of them on their wedding day? Are all the Freds and Jens continuing somehow in their own timescale and space, brimming over with their delight in each other?

She had watched a YouTube clip recently in which a bereavement specialist had said that you don't get over the death of the person you love, but that it remains central to your being while you gradually construct a new life around it.

I suppose that's what I'm doing now. Building a different existence around the old one that I wish so very much I hadn't lost.

Lucy would be a good project as part of that new beginning. But then what? Did she want to live in a section of Matthew and Ginny's house? What about the Fred and Jen living in Crowbury? What would happen to them? Could she walk away from their home? She was uncertain that she could, even though often she failed to sense Fred in the tangible and real way she had assumed she would. That was the toughest part of the loss. Somehow, she had thought that she would have such a sense of his constant presence that life in the house they had shared would feel quite normal. She had been unprepared for the vast, endless emptiness, and the fact that she could not always summon him up. It shattered her when she could not feel that he was with her. And when he was not, where in heaven's name was he?

Life in Norwich would help her to tap into a younger Fred and Jen. But what was she to do? Almost certainly she could not spend her days looking after baby Freddie. Wouldn't Ginny want to do that? Anyway, she would be hopeless. Unlike most women of her age, she had never changed a nappy. Never burped a baby. Never known what to say to small children.

She had enjoyed working in the shop, however. Perhaps she could do that regularly, releasing Ginny to be with Freddie more – though a small child could probably come to work with Mum, couldn't he?

If she had a job, then that might be a good enough reason for moving to Norwich, even though up until now, she had never considered earning her living in any way other than writing. The trouble was, having dropped out of that business because of Fred's illness and death at a time when the industry was collapsing anyway, meant that there was less and less work even for people who wanted to write, and the honest truth was that she was unsure that she did. Or perhaps it was that she no longer felt she could.

But was she ready to leave Crowbury? And what about money? The finances were the only aspect of her conversation with Matthew and Ginny that had not been addressed. If she was to have quarters, as it were, in their house, she would want to pay for her part of the property. And that might not be as easy as it sounded. She had written a feature once about home co-ownership and had discovered that if a group of friends wanted jointly to buy somewhere to live, the legal aspects of the purchase were unwieldy and complex.

In any event, unless she could earn a proper wage, she would not be able to fund a new lifestyle, without selling the Crowbury house.

She felt mildly excited at the options available but nervous too. However, as she allowed her mind to wander through all the possibilities, she realised that she was at least beginning to look forward.

'That's probably good isn't it, Fred?' she said aloud. 'So long as it doesn't feel unfair or disloyal to you.'

She was so absorbed in her thoughts that she failed to notice her neighbour until she bumped into her. Suzie had her back turned and was remonstrating with her boisterous Border collie as he jerked and jumped at the end of his lead. Meanwhile, a small white dog, also on a lead, seemed intent on pulling in another direction in his bid to escape the attentions of the bigger animal.

'Oh, thank heavens it's you,' Suzie said. 'Meet Hoagy. He was disappointed when you didn't come over the other evening. I'd told him all about you.'

Jen fought to stop herself rolling her eyes. 'Sorry about that, but one of my friends had been taken very ill that day, and then

I had a long phone conversation with my stepson about something, which was rather unsettling. Sorry. I should have let you know.'

'Oh, well… Can you just hold Hoagy's lead for a minute? He's a very anxious animal, and he's not settled with Mac at all. Mind you, Mac is jealous. He's not used to sharing me.'

Jen took a step back as Mac growled at her now that she was attached to his rival. She had never taken to her neighbour's first rescue dog, but as she looked at little, pale Hoagy, so in need of love and reassurance she felt a wave of protectiveness sweep over her.

In a straggly group, they covered the hundred yards to their adjoining houses. Despite her long experience with dogs, Suzie was having a hard job controlling Mac as he continued to eye up Hoagy in a far from friendly way.

'Border collies are always a handful,' Suzie remarked, at one point, rather breathlessly.

At her front gate, Jen hesitated before handing over the little schnauzer who seemed to be trembling. Then she heard herself say, 'I don't suppose you'd like me to have Hoagy overnight, would you? I'm not quite sure what I'd do with him, but I could probably manage. Is he, I mean, well, is he house-trained?'

'Oh yes. He's no trouble. He'll go out last thing. And he'll let you know if he needs to go out at any other time. He's been fed, but I can bring you round some treats and biscuits. Are you sure you wouldn't mind? I do feel I ought to give Mac some undivided attention. I thought they'd be company for each other, but at the moment it's not working at all. The last two or three days have been a nightmare. Hoagy might have to go back…'

'No!' Jen exclaimed before her mind had caught up with her mouth. 'No, he can't have another failed home. He's so adorable. I'm sure things will calm down.'

Suzie looked at her rather more intently than usual. 'Mmmn, hopefully. Anyway, it would be a solution if you had him tonight. I'll bring his bed over and his blanket and the treats… Sure you're OK with it?'

'I'm sure.'

Inside her house, she gave into her impulse to pick up the little dog and hug him to her. His heart was beating furiously but as she spoke to him calmly, he turned his doleful eyes on her and then, tentatively, licked one of her hands.

She walked through to the kitchen and sat down, still holding him. After a few seconds he wriggled slightly, but she realised that he was simply getting used to the contours of her lap and seeking a more comfortable position. He settled, and she felt him relax as she stroked him, and gradually, his heartbeat began to slow.

'That's better,' she whispered. 'It's all right, Hoagy. You're safe now.'

'Well, it sounds like rather a lot has happened this week,' Helen said after Monica had given her a swift rundown of the events of the previous few days.

Monica nodded.

'Do you want to talk about your friend in hospital first?'

'OK. Jen and I have discussed it thoroughly. Of course, Lucy is very sick, and I get the impression that a stroke or a heart attack could carry her off at any time. It sounds like it's far from certain that all the harm that's been done can be reversed. But Jen and I want to try to help her find the motivation to change things and we're going to give it our best effort. We're calling it Project Lucy!'

Helen smiled. 'I remember when I was training, I was working with a very unfit, overweight woman who had a colossal problem with comfort-eating. I managed to establish with her that there were other ways she could find comfort, rather than through the food which was basically sabotaging her good intentions and leading to various health problems. And we found all sorts of strategies she could deploy to cheer her up, that didn't involve eating. She lost quite a lot of weight and I was feeling really excited on her behalf and saying to my supervisor "and now she might learn a bit more about how to dress well, take up some exercise, maybe meet a lovely man and so on." My supervisor laughed at me, then he said that it was fine for me to enjoy her progress and to be proud of being part of it. However, he added, "Never be more ambitious for your patient than she is for herself." That was such sound thinking. I never forgot it.'

'Are we doing the wrong thing then?'

'No, you're doing the right thing, and it's very kind, but I just warn you that she may not want for herself exactly what you want for her.'

Monica looked thoughtful and slightly deflated. 'I suppose I should tell Jen that, but I'm reluctant to do it because she seems so up for it all and it's nice to see her so enthusiastic.'

'I'm sure,' Helen responded quietly.

'Anyway,' Monica sat up straighter. 'I want to ask you about Stephen, but perhaps I ought to discuss James for a moment.'

'Go on.'

'Right, as I told you, I finally let him know I wanted a divorce on the night of Lucy's big drama. I think something about her life hanging in the balance spurred me on. Even so, I cooked dinner first and we ate it and it was all quite civilised.'

'What did he say to you?'

'Well, after I said that I wanted a divorce, he said nothing for what seemed like ages. And then he said, "I see".'

'That's all?'

'Yes, and he went into his study, where he has his own TV, and watched the cricket.'

'Is he going to agree to make it easy – admit his adultery for example?'

'I don't know. We haven't talked since. I was going to ask you if that's normal. I mean do you think he's planning the next move, or just getting used to the idea, or going to make life difficult for me?'

'What do you think?'

'I suspect this civilised behaviour won't last. But honestly I don't know.'

133

'Mmmn. How do you feel about it all?'

'A bit sad, but mostly relieved. And I've phoned Melissa and told her, and she's over the moon. Funny how she's switched completely from being such a daddy's girl to championing my rights! She says that once her father has got used to the divorce idea, he'll probably get going on internet dating. She says a professional man with a bit of dosh, his own teeth and eyes that look in the same direction will be snapped up in no time. She's a bit of a cynic, my daughter! She also said that's desperately unfair, but it's just how it is. I think she's worried that I'll mind if he gets someone else, but I won't. And of course, she doesn't know about Stephen.'

'OK, so we seem to have arrived at the situation with Stephen. How are you feeling about him?'

'Excited and scared.'

'Have you made any approach to him yet?'

'Not exactly. But the other night when James was busy watching sport, I searched for his company on the internet. It turns out that he no longer has the branch in Oxford, but they do have offices in London... I was worried he might have decided to retire, which would have made finding him more difficult. But I looked at the company website and he's the director, and there was a picture of him.'

'Was he how you'd imagined him?'

'Not exactly, he's got less hair and it's greyer, but he still has that lovely smile.'

'There's a warmth in your voice as you talk about him,' Helen commented.

'There's a warmth in my heart too. I really want to see him. But I've decided that I won't try and email him, though there is an email address on the website, in case his PA or somebody reads it. I did think of phoning, but I feel I'll be so nervous that I might not say the right things. I mean, I hope he still feels the same but, as you say, it's been a long time, and the only indication I've had that he still thinks of me is on my birthday every year.'

'When was your birthday?

'Last October.'

'I doubt if he's changed his mind in the last...' Helen counted on her fingers, 'nine months.'

'But we don't know that.'

Helen smiled at her slightly agitated client. 'We don't, but I think we could make an educated guess!'

Monica nodded then and looked calmer. 'I've decided I'll write to him. Not saying very much except that I have always thought of him and wondered if, after all this time, he'd like to meet. Do you think that's all right?'

'Probably would be best to mark the envelope "strictly private and confidential" but otherwise it sounds fine.'

'I know it's somewhat old-fashioned, but it doesn't put him too much on the spot does it?'

'Will you give him your mobile number or email address?'

'No.'

'So, he'll have to write if he wants to be in touch?'

'Yes, I suppose so. Am I being odd about this?'

'Not at all. It's a big step. You need to do it in your own way. Just one thing. So far as we know, James has never noticed, let alone opened, the card from Stephen that has come every year on your birthday. But it's not your birthday now. And it's just possible that he might be intrigued or suspicious if he notices a handwritten note to you. He may even have wondered, when you asked for a divorce, if you have your eye on someone else. He's a lawyer, after all. You don't want to give him any reason to ramp up hostility, do you?'

Monica looked stricken. 'No, I really don't. Should I use another address then, perhaps?'

'I think it might be wise. Jen's perhaps? Or, if it's any help, you could use mine.'

Chapter Fourteen

Jen had worried that she and Lucy might run out of topics of conversation; it being the first time she had visited the hospital without Monica. But the reverse had been true. Perhaps, simply, they were both in a chatty mood. She had known for months that Lucy was clever, and interesting, but today she was much more animated than she had been for a while and soon they were finishing each other's sentences and talking over each other, eagerly, as they explored a variety of topics. She looked better too. Her hair had been washed and was now caught up in a chignon, and she had lost her deathly pallor.

'You seem much better today,' Jen said when they drew breath.

'Yes, I think I am. Or maybe I'm just getting used to how things are. And you seem more...'

'On top of things?'

'That's a good way of putting it.'

'I am. But as I say that I can't help feel a bit guilty, and almost disloyal to Fred. However, I don't love him any less. That's the crucial fact.'

'I'm sure the two of you had a marvellous relationship.'

'We did. I've been lucky.'

'And he was too, but I imagine he knew that.'

'We both knew it,' Jen responded, and she blinked once or twice before adding, 'that was the good thing.'

'I've never had a great love,' Lucy confessed.

'I'm sorry.'

'Don't be. I've had a lot of great lusts!' And Lucy smiled wickedly before collapsing into peals of laughter.

'Surely you've been in love?'

'No, I don't believe so.'

'Well men must have loved you?' Jen persisted.

'One or two have cried, "I love you, Lucy" in bed at a critical moment, but I think that was about the relief at the excitement and release they were feeling, and a certain gratitude for my expertise!' She laughed again. 'I think I was the only woman most of them knew who loved sex for itself rather than as part of a romantic passion. And I'm pretty sure a lot of them identified with that. I don't mean they didn't love their regular partners. I'm sure they did. But so many males go through life worrying that they're never going to have enough rumpy pumpy and that all other men are having more. One of my chaps used to say that whenever he was about to climax, he started wondering how soon he could have sex again!'

'Did they never say, "Well that was great, but now I can focus on other things for a while", or words to that effect?'

'Never,' she replied.

'Did you?'

'Probably not. Perhaps I'm a man in a woman's body! I expect if I were young now, I'd identify myself as trans. I'm rather glad I was born before all that.'

'Did any of the men buy you presents or take you out for dinner?'

'Good Lord, no.' Lucy looked astonished at the question.

'Why?'

'They were always clandestine arrangements.'

Jen gazed at her sadly. 'Until Fred came into my life, I never believed anyone could love me. I come from an extremely dysfunctional single-parent family and my first boyfriend let me down badly. My intention was to avoid men and focus on my career. Fred saved me from myself, for which I'm hugely grateful. Frankly, Lucy, I think you sold yourself short.'

There was a snorting noise and Jen peered at her friend expecting to see her chuckling, but then noticed that tears were coursing down her cheeks. She was appalled and jumped up to try to hug the other woman but was pushed aside. Eventually when she could speak, Lucy murmured, 'Blasted medication. Seems to be making me tearful. Not like me at all.'

'You've been through a lot,' Jen said gently. 'Don't be so hard on yourself.'

Lucy shrugged her shoulders impatiently. 'Let's talk about you and get off this subject.'

So Jen told her how she was considering a move to Norwich, how she seemed to be suddenly a bit soppy about dogs which she had never been in the past, and how she was going to be a step-grandmother. 'Oh,' she added, 'and I've learned that Fred may have had a daughter before he and I were together. There's some DNA testing going on. Bit of a turn-up!'

Monica felt quite jittery as she knocked on the front door. Helen had rung her earlier to say that a letter had arrived. This meant that Stephen must have replied immediately he had received her note. It was promising, she kept telling herself. And yet she dared not hope.

After the call, she had tried to continue her morning at home as if nothing were different from usual. She had made breakfast for James and asked what he had lined up for the day. She had even dared to query if he planned to see a solicitor soon about the divorce. He had seemed thoughtful for a moment, but then walked away.

And now she was here, her heart beating loudly in her ears.

'O-oh,' she heard herself say as an attractive, tall, elderly, olive-skinned man with silver hair answered the door.

He smiled warmly, revealing perfect, very white teeth. 'You must be Monica, please come in.'

She was surprised. She had thought from his appearance that he would speak with some sort of Middle-Eastern accent, but there was no trace of one. He sounded like any well-off, educated Briton of his generation.

'I'm Sam,' the man continued.

'Ah,' she said, for something to say.

'I've been away rather a lot since we moved here. I had loose ends to tie up in my home country, which is Egypt, as well as in Geneva where I've worked for decades. I've given that up now.'

'Well,' Monica said, trying to remember what she knew about Helen, and feeling surprisingly flustered, 'I hope you enjoy your retirement.'

'Retirement?' he seemed puzzled. 'Yes, I suppose people *will* perceive me as retired.' He looked pensive. 'And I am almost eighty.'

'You certainly don't look it,' she said quickly.

He flashed another smile at her. 'That's kind of you. I sometimes feel it, though. May I offer you a cup of coffee?'

'No thanks. Is Helen here?'

'Sorry, no. She had to go out – something to do with a client whose partner has motor neurone disease. You may know she does some counselling at the hospital.'

'Y-yes, I know that. Did she leave something for me?'

'Oh, yes she did. Sorry.' He turned and flicked through some papers on the elegant hall table. 'Here you are.'

Monica grasped the envelope, thanked him, then turned and tried to open the front door with her fumbling fingers.

He leant over her. 'Sorry, there's a bit of a knack to it. It swells in the rain and we've had rather a lot of that!'

He pulled the door open.

'Yes, we have,' she agreed, and she offered her hand and left.

She almost ran down the drive, then she steadied herself when she reached the leafy avenue at the bottom. 'You made a right 'mess of that,' she told herself aloud. Really this was a most odd morning. Cradling the letter in her hands, she thought of opening it there, but decided she wanted to sit down and take her time, so she dropped it into her handbag and made for The Granary.

Lucy did not react well to Pete, the young Australian physio who was far too informal for her taste. And she had no wish to be here, in this gymnasium, and given metal crutches and told to walk with them. She felt unsteady and unsafe and wanted only to return to bed. The worst part came when Pete placed a small block of steps in front of her.

'No one is gonna let you home till you can climb these beauties,' he told her.

She was exhausted. It would be so good to leave the hospital, but this was literally a step too far.

'I can't,' she protested.

'Come on, Lucy.' His voice was very cajoling. 'Do it for me.'

'You think a lot of yourself, don't you?'

He reeled back as though someone had hit him. Probably all other females fell for the charm that, clearly, he thought he possessed.

'OK, seems you've had enough. But you've got to think about your future. They can't keep you here indefinitely. You're taking up a bed that other people are queuing up for, though I can't say you seem anywhere near being able to manage on your own. You need to get your head round it. Decide to change your attitude, maybe?'

He helped her into the wheelchair and conveyed her, via the lift, back to the ward on the second floor. Neither of them spoke further. And once he had crossed the threshold of her destination, he put the brake on the chair and walked away.

'Oh, back already,' said one of the nurses as she noticed Lucy marooned in the entrance.

Lucy nodded. Last night, apart from that odd weepy episode, she had felt bright and optimistic in Jen's company. Now she felt nothing but despair. And for the first time that she could ever remember, she minded that she was alone.

Jen knew that it was time to leave for The Granary, but she had been keeping an eye out for her neighbour in the hope of finding out how Hoagy was settling.

Unusually, Suzie had not walked her dogs yet and her car was not in the drive. She must have gone out very early.

Since having Hoagy overnight earlier in the week, Jen had thought about him much of the time, but Suzie had not asked her to help out again; worse than that, she seemed to be actively avoiding her. Was that possible? She was such a good person even if she did have occasional and unfathomable moods. It was odd, she remembered, that Suzie had failed to turn up to Fred's funeral, or to the afternoon tea she had arranged at the Station Hotel afterwards. But mostly, though they were not close, the relationship between them was cordial.

She glanced at her watch again. It was ridiculous, she knew, to make herself late unnecessarily. Their shift began at midday, and before that, she and Monica had arranged to meet so they could discuss Lucy.

The trouble was that she had begun to imagine a life that involved Hoagy. It was absurd, she knew; he was not hers to have. And she had never owned a dog. Also, she had been a widow for less than seven months and she had been told it was unwise to make too many alterations to her lifestyle too soon, and preferably none for a year. But the fact was that her existence had undergone a total metamorphosis. Fred had gone and was not coming back. Surely it was only reasonable to make changes in the wake of such a huge event. Changes that might help. Of course, there was the whole issue around Norwich. And if she was going to move to Norwich – *if* she was, which was by no means certain – she would have to talk to Matthew and Ginny if she was considering having a dog. Really it was all too fanciful. Just because she had enjoyed having Hoagy in the house for a few hours and had been unaccountably touched by him sitting outside her bedroom door waiting for her in the morning, and had loved handling and stroking him, it did not mean that she was ready or able to be a dog owner.

She opened her front door one last time to check that Suzie had not returned.

'Come on,' she urged herself. 'You've got commitments. Shape up!'

In The Granary, Monica read and reread Stephen's reply.

'Dearest Monica, I am so happy to hear from you. I want to see you too. Very much. I am going away today on a job in the west country. But I'm free next Wednesday afternoon and could come to Crowbury or, and I suspect you may prefer this, we could meet in London. My office in Wigmore Street is near John Lewis. Not exactly romantic! But I remember it was your favourite store. Could we meet there, at The Place to Eat, on the fifth floor?

Please let me have your mobile number. I would hope to be free by 3pm but am seeing a client in Colchester that morning so I'll give you a call if I'm running late. I enclose a card with all my details.

It looks from your address that you have moved. I'm sure you have lots to tell me.

I have longed for this day. Love, Stephen xxx'

She smiled each time she came to his comment about John Lewis. She remembered she used to say to him that it was the one thing Crowbury lacked. In fact, once he had driven her to the branch in Oxford so that she could choose curtains for the extension he was building. Memorably, on their way back, he had turned the car off the main road and down a country lane, and they had kissed each other feverishly. Like teenagers, she had thought, later.

Jen was going to be here soon, and she would tell her all about it. She could imagine herself saying, 'You know I said that I want to divorce James', and Jen replying with some typically funny comment to the effect that he had sounded absolutely ghastly and the sooner she was out of it the better. And then she would say to Jen that she had not quite told her everything and that there was a man… And Jen would probably thump the table and say 'Great', or 'I knew it'. And then they would laugh, and she would say to Jen 'Am I doing the right thing?' And Jen would reassure her. She was a good friend to have.

A text pinged into her phone. 'Running ten minutes late. So sorry. Jen.'

Ten minutes was nothing, but she was too keyed up now to sit still. So, she wandered over to the café counter and bought one of their postcards with a picture of The Granary on the front.

'Do you have stamps? Oh, and an envelope that I could put it in?'

'No, sorry,' said the assistant. 'But Liz has loads of that stuff in her office.'

Monica looked doubtful. 'Go and ask,' the youngster spoke firmly. 'The management love all you volunteers. You're keeping the place afloat for them. She'll be pleased to do something for you for a change.'

Monica smiled her thanks and then ran over to the stairs and sprinted up them.

Liz chatted for a moment or two about Lucy.

'We – Jen and I – are going to help her,' Monica told her. 'We're meeting in a moment to discuss a plan of action.'

'That's marvellous. It'll be good when all three of you are back working together.'

Monica wondered if she should let Liz know that that particular prospect was a long way off, but decided against it.

Liz searched for an envelope on the stack of filing trays beside her. 'Will this do?'

Monica nodded as Liz rummaged in a drawer for a book of stamps, then peeled one off and put it on the envelope before handing it over.

'What do I owe you?'

'Don't be ridiculous,' Liz laughed. 'It's we who owe *you*!'

Monica thanked her and backed out of the door.

Once in the café again, she scribbled a note to Stephen on the back of the postcard and wondered whether or not to put a kiss at the end of the message. She took a deep breath, and added a little cross, then one more.

'Oh no. Where did I put his card?'

She searched her bag, anxious suddenly that she had lost it, then she looked inside the envelope that had housed his letter, before rummaging through her bag again. She was almost tearful with relief when, eventually, she realised that she had slipped it into her jacket pocket.

'Calm down,' she told herself. 'You're getting hysterical.'

Just in time, as she noticed Jen in the doorway, she realised that she had forgotten to give him her phone number. Hurriedly, she added it, then put the card into the envelope, sealed and addressed it.

'Coffee?' she called across at Jen. 'I've got lots to tell you.'

Jen nodded. She looked quite cast down.

'Are you all right?'

'I am, but Lucy's not. She rang me. I was still in the house because I was already running late. Sorry. She was in terrific form last night. But today she's very gloomy. She had a row with a physio and now wants to discharge herself. I've told her we'll sort something. But what can we do?'

Over coffee they looked at various possibilities.

They could take responsibility for getting Lucy home and arrange private carers to supplement whatever package the people at the hospital might offer her. Lucy probably had reasonable savings as she did not appear to have expensive tastes in anything.

Or perhaps they could persuade her to stay with her brother for a while?

Or could they manage Lucy themselves by taking turns to stay at her house overnight?

Or should they invite Lucy to stay with one of them?

After some discussion, they plumped for the last option. And Monica made it clear that she would like to be the host.

'To be honest, James is so morose now he's retired, and he just hangs around. Maybe if he had someone else to talk to other than me, it would open up his mind a bit. I've actually been thinking about this option for a while.'

'I don't see why it should all fall on you though. My house isn't big. And it's very definitely comfortably chaotic rather than smart. But it might do me good to have the company, and to have someone to care for, rather than just be focused on myself.'

'Jen, you're still grieving.'

'I know. Even so, I could do it.'

'Let's visit Lucy after we finish here at six,' Monica suggested. 'We could discuss this with her and hopefully cheer her up. But what I'm wondering then is whether we should look at both our houses. We can start with yours because it's nearer... Sometimes I wish I still had a car. It's going to be quite a lot of walking.'

'Did you used to drive then?'

'Mmmn, when the children were at home. But when my last car failed its MOT, I more or less gave up. Well, that's to say, I got rid of the car but of course I was always the driver of James's Jaguar if we went out to functions so he could drink as much as he liked. I think he thought that's what wives were for.'

Jen was appalled. James sounded totally unlike Fred, who had had no chauvinistic bone in his body, but she decided not to share that thought. 'I'd offer to drive us, but uh, my old Ford Fiesta is, um actually out of action at the moment.'

'You never mentioned you had a car.'

'Well, I never drive, so I suppose the subject doesn't come up!'

'No problem, I'm used to walking everywhere. But after we've looked at your house then mine, please stay for dinner. I still cook for James, despite our differences.'

'Oh, I don't know. I'm not always good company and your husband doesn't know me.'

'That might be a good experiment then,' Monica responded looking quite serious. 'We could see what he's like with you. Also, now I come to think about it, I'd like you to meet him. You might then be in a better position to advise me about getting him moving on the divorce.'

Jen's expression brightened. 'Well, if I can be of help.'

'Definitely.' Monica patted her arm. 'Would you like to share that platter they do with humous and olives and pitta bread? I fancy eating something before we start.'

'Great idea. But I'll get it, especially now you've invited me for a meal tonight.'

'That's awfully nice of you.'

'It's the least I can do.' Then she added, almost more to herself than to Monica, 'We can sort Lucy, can't we?'

'I hope so.'

'Oh, what was it you wanted to discuss with me?'

Monica thought of the envelope tucked into her handbag. She had planned to tell Jen everything, but now that her friend was to meet James, she decided it would be better to let that happen before she mentioned Stephen.

'Um,' she said, vaguely. 'Oh, you know, only things about Lucy, but you had much more recent news than I had. No need now.'

'Are you sure?'

Monica nodded vigorously. 'Absolutely. Now, while you get the food, I better go and post my letter.'

Chapter Fifteen

They stopped off at Sainsbury's to look for a present for Lucy.

'You're not supposed to take flowers or plants these days, are you?' Jen queried. 'I'm blowed if I understand why, so I suppose it comes down to food of some kind.'

'What are diabetics allowed?' Monica wondered.

'Not sure. Probably not cake or biscuits or chocolates. And I imagine the hospital would frown on alcohol.'

'Probably. Is fruit sugar more healthy than other sorts?'

Jen raised her eyebrows. 'D'you know, we've both been saying how little awareness Lucy has about health messages and how she should have spotted she was doing all the wrong things, but I'm not sure we're as clued up as we should be!'

Monica grinned. 'On the other hand, we are in better shape.'

'True. Well, shall we get a pack of peaches? They're soft enough to eat right away. And maybe some oranges, and blueberries?'

'Why not?'

They had a subdued argument at the checkout about which of them should pay but Jen won the day and they headed for the hospital.

Lucy was toying with the bland white mess on her plate, which she had been told was poached hake. There was also a tiny mound of mashed potato which was equally unappetising. It would all be so much more appealing if the fish was in a rich cheese sauce, and if there were nice, fat chips with it. If it had to be mash though, it needed lots more salt, and a generous helping of butter. She turned her attention to the little strips of carrot and two sprigs of broccoli in a side dish, but they had no flavour either. As for the pudding, it was a fat-free fruit yoghurt which tasted as if much synthetic nastiness was replacing everything that might have made it enjoyable.

A nurse had made her stand on some scales earlier and had told her that she had lost half a stone since she had been in hospital.

'Is that all?' Lucy had responded crossly. She felt she should be a mere skeleton by now.

Her spirits rose as she spotted Monica and Jen coming towards her. They were carrying a Sainsbury's bag. And as they settled beside her, having quickly laid claim to two chairs from nearby, they drew various fruit offerings from it.

'Aww, that's very kind.'

Jen perceived a lack of enthusiasm. 'We didn't really know what to bring you. What you're allowed, you know.'

Lucy shrugged. 'Difficult, isn't it? It's not an exact science, I don't think.' She knew she was lying but hoped the other two women would not. 'The doc said something like, "it shouldn't be torture for you. You can have a little of what you fancy, now and then." And I have been very, very good.' She indicated with a lean of her head, the plate in front of her with its remnants of her healthy meal. 'Could you take this away and put it on the trolley outside? I've managed all I can stomach.'

Jen jumped to her feet, swept up the tray and deposited it in the corridor.

'Would you like something else then?' Monica asked. 'Other than the fruit, I mean?'

'Oh, I don't want you to have to go out again.'

'There's the café downstairs.'

'Well in that case, maybe a little shortbread biscuit and a bar of chocolate?'

'God, I don't want to kill you,' Jen frowned.

'I'll ration myself, don't worry. But I can't tell you how long the nights are in here and how much I long for something sweet, just a tiny morsel, to cheer me up and fill a hole. I feel I'm starving to death.'

Monica and Jen stared at each other – both reluctant to deny their friend, but equally unwilling to damage her.

'I promise I'll just have the smallest nibble now and again.' Lucy leaned forward and eyed them both earnestly.

Monica's face continued to register anxiety, but she nodded slightly at Jen, who stood up again, picked up her bag and strode from the ward.

In her absence, Monica outlined the plans they had discussed.

Lucy remained adamant that she wanted to go home alone and was of the opinion that, because of the lack of beds, they would let her go soon.

'But what about the care package? How soon can they put that in place?'

'Someone came and talked about it earlier. I'll cope. I mean, as soon I get home with my own books, my own television and my own bed, I'm going to feel a hundred times better.'

Monica looked unconvinced. 'Well, let's leave it for now. But Jen and I are both offering to have you to stay. I, in particular, would love you to come to me because you could help cheer up my husband! I know you have a knack with men.'

'What are you suggesting?' Lucy giggled.

'No, sorry, I mean, you'll be there at mealtimes and liven it up no end.'

'I do appreciate it. I do really. I'd still sooner go home though. Let's see what they say tomorrow.'

*

Jen had a sense of viewing her own property through fresh eyes as she showed Monica around. She could see suddenly that everything needed painting and decluttering. It was a home that clearly reflected her lifestyle with Fred, and they had never noticed the shabbiness. It was evident now though. And it felt different too. Having throbbed with the joyful, combined spirit of the two of them, it seemed empty, and devoid of all the positive emotions that had filled it previously.

During Fred's illness, she had rarely thought about 'afterwards', but on the rare occasion that she had, she had assumed that this is where she would feel closest to him. But yet again, she was forced to the realisation that his presence was not as vivid as she had believed it would be, and that their home was a building which had lost its heart.

'Does the atmosphere in here feel soulless to you?' she asked Monica.

'Not at all,' her friend replied swiftly. 'You can tell it's a house that has been enjoyed.'

Jen nodded, though she noted Monica's use of the past tense. They were in Fred's study and a dagger stabbed at her heart as her eyes ran over his computer and printer, wide range of pens, box of headed notepaper and pile of sticky labels. If only he still needed them. Next, though no one else had been in their bedroom since his body had been removed, she took Monica there.

'The walls are a really unusual colour,' Monica remarked, 'but I like it.'

'It's Algerian Red. Sounds like cheap plonk, doesn't it? You're right, most people choose restful colours for a bedroom but around the time that we decided it needed decorating, I was doing a feature with a very well-known interior designer – so well known that I can't remember her name now! Anyway, she went on and on about cool greens, and the palest of blues and so on. As always, I got Fred to read my piece before I emailed it into the magazine and he laughed and said how boring all these ideas were, and how

150

he had never seen our bedroom as being anything other than passionate and vibrant, and the place he most wanted to be. That was so Fred! So, we agreed we wouldn't go "cool" but would opt for a colour that was bold and gorgeous. That's how we picked it. That's how we were.'

'You had a wonderful life together, didn't you?' Monica murmured.

'We really did.'

'Did he die in here?'

'Yes. I felt like I was just sort of helping him over the finishing line. I don't know if people can actually programme their minds to make themselves die. But I honestly believe that once Fred knew he couldn't survive, he wanted to get it over as soon as possible. He often said he wanted to leave me enough time to have a life... I've worried about that since. I wonder if he felt I was fed up with the situation... I was certainly terribly tired sometimes because I continued to sleep in here with him, but he was awfully agitated at night and neither of us got much rest. But did I, in any way, give him the idea that I wasn't coping, or that I was fed up, or wanted rid of him? The thought hammers away at my brain sometimes. But I want to feel and believe that what he got from me was love and strength, and that he felt I was focused on helping him achieve what he wanted – a release from it all. Not that I would ever have agreed to do anything to hasten his death, but I think in a kind of way, *he* hastened it. Every day, he used to say, "I really wouldn't mind if I just popped off now. I feel so awful." And I'm sure he did. But at least he never lived to the stage I was dreading where he couldn't breathe or swallow. I used to have nightmares about that and wonder how I would deal with it. Before he died, he did have some problems in those areas, but they weren't serious. Certainly, his symptoms at that time, didn't seem bad enough to kill him. And our doctor was amazed at how quickly he deteriorated. So, I'm left with questions about why he died so quickly. And I can only think that his mind, which was incredibly strong, willed it.'

Jen stopped, her breathing shallow, looking surprised at all the words that had poured out of her. Monica gathered her into a hug, and the two women stood together, swaying slightly, close and silent.

Eventually, Jen cleared her throat and pulled away. 'I haven't talked about this before,' she said. 'Sorry.'

'Don't be sorry. Do you feel any lighter because you have?'

Jen smiled ruefully, 'Not sure.'

'I'm certain Fred knew that you would have gone on loving and supporting him if he'd taken longer to die.'

'I hope that's true.'

'But he didn't want to go on, did he?'

'He didn't. He used to say that he'd done everything he wanted to do. And that all he minded about was losing me. And I used to say that he would be in my heart forever and that he wasn't losing me but that I would live alongside the spirit of him. But here, in this house, I can't feel it. That's a terrible sadness... It feels empty...' She took an audible breath. 'Right. I must stop this. At this rate dinner at your house will be very late and your husband's going to be starving.'

Monica glanced at her watch. 'OK. Let's go. Your house is lovely though.'

'Do you think Lucy would like it?'

'I'm sure she would.'

'I bet your house is bigger and smarter.'

'I don't know about that, but I was just thinking that your stairs are quite narrow, and she's pretty immobile.'

'Mmmn.' Jen's mind unearthed a memory of the stage when Fred had become more unsteady on his feet and how one day, he had stumbled on the staircase and she had had to summon all her strength to hold him up and prevent him falling to the bottom. 'You may have a point,' she conceded.

As they left the house, Suzie was coming out of her front door. She jumped slightly as though not expecting Jen to be home.

'Hi, Suzie. This is Monica. We volunteer together at The Granary. Monica, this is Suzie my very good neighbour.'

Suzie nodded. 'Sorry must rush. Brownie night.'

'Before you go,' Jen interrupted, 'how are things with the dogs. Is Hoagy settling?'

'I think so,' Suzie said without quite meeting her gaze. 'I've always been so good with dogs I don't understand why these two are playing up. Anyway, I talked it out with the vet and to cut a long story short, I've had them both done today. Cost me an arm and a leg.'

'Done?' Jen looked puzzled.

'Neutered.'

'Oh my God, doesn't that involve chopping their balls off or something?'

'Best not to go into the details.' Suzie's tone made it obvious that she did not want to discuss her decision. 'But they should be a lot more docile now. They're staying at the vet overnight.'

Having submitted to the blood testing and the medication run and a talk with Sister, Lucy lay down, stretched out and tried to think herself into sleeping-mode. She was tired. But it was only eight o'clock. Normally, she would not even have started dinner yet. What a complete change around she had had. This time last year, she had been in Switzerland, enjoying the freedom of a rail pass and relishing the chance to exercise her excellent French, and passable German and Italian.

Before she went, when discussing holidays prior to the end of the summer term, various colleagues had asked if she planned to do some walking in Switzerland. She had nodded so vigorously she had almost deluded herself into believing that she would be trekking up mountains and hiking for miles around picturesque lakes. In practice, she took hotels near railway stations, where she ate large suppers and generous breakfasts before another day of luxury on an amazing Swiss train with its glass, panoramic roof.

Also, wherever she went, there were local shops selling hand-made chocolates, so there had been plenty of opportunities for snacking. Then at lunchtimes, generally she had enjoyed a hearty lunch at an inn, featuring one of those cheese dishes mixed with potatoes that were on offer everywhere, albeit with slight regional variations.

It had been an expensive trip, but at the time she had had every anticipation of another year's salary coming up. Sadly, the death of Guy, her Thursday chap, had put paid to that. Twelve months ago, who would have thought that he would not live to see Christmas?

She remembered too that during the long summer vacation, she had entertained Roy one afternoon. It was just before his neurological condition has been diagnosed, and he had seemed well and spryly active. She wondered how he was now. She had heard nothing since her collapse and had no idea whether or not he and his wife knew, or cared, what had happened to her.

She reached under her pillow and pulled out the little cellophane package containing two fingers of dimpled, buttery Scottish short-bread. Eating it might have consequences, she knew. She had just had her Metformin, but would it be man enough for such a sweet treat? I'll just have one of them, she promised herself, but it was so delicious – without doubt the best taste she had had in her mouth since arriving at the hospital – that she could not resist the second portion.

Feeling more comfortable, she allowed herself to think about her immediate future.

It seemed most unlikely that she was going to satisfy the physio-therapists any time soon. But would they keep her here if she did not, particularly as she had been told that other patients needed her bed? In the days of her youth, there would have been the gentle option of a convalescent home in the country or at the seaside. They had been commonplace at one time. When had that all stopped? Sometime around Mrs Bottomley's reforms, she imagined. She could remember, when she was quite small, her mother going to just such a place in Bexhill, after she had a hysterectomy. Later that week, her father had driven her and her brother to Sussex for a visit, and Mother had been well enough to come out for tea with them at the De La Warr Pavilion.

Her brother, who now lived in Salisbury, would have her to stay, she knew. He was very big on family, and responsibilities, and duty. The trouble was that he had always resented her because she had been brighter than him. He was no slouch though and had had a distinguished career as a rheumatologist.

They had not met for years; not since his boys were still at home. She had enjoyed visiting when they were young, but now the house – which was very similar to the rectories in which she had been brought up during her father's years as a vicar – seemed empty. Also, his wife was dull and so, in many ways, was he. Some time, she supposed, she ought to let him know she was unwell. And if he invited her to stay, she would tell him that she had to be within the catchment area of this hospital.

What she wanted to do, obviously, was to go home where she could have all her things about her, and also eat what she liked.

On the other hand, she did feel quite isolated now that she could no longer move around easily. And Monica and Jen, though they had become good friends, had their own lives and could not be with her all the time. So, it would probably come down to a couple of exhausted carers, popping in morning and evening, heating up some utterly dreadful diabetic meal and giving her 'a little wash'. I don't want to be ungrateful, she thought as she projected an apology to the God of her childhood, but I really think I'd sooner be dead.

If she went to stay with Monica, she would be looked after properly. And maybe the awful husband would have some redeeming features. Supposedly, he was a clever man and well read.

She would need new underwear though, and outfits that she could easily get in and out of. Maybe tracksuits would be the answer. Probably Marks and Spencer sold them. She had never been sporty so was unsure.

Above all, she needed to find a way to stop Monica or Jen when they offered, as they had already, to go to her house and pick up items that she needed. For one thing, she had realised for the first time today that she had left the washing machine going on the afternoon when she had gone to read to Roy. Assuming it had not blown up – she was seriously nervous of most gadgets – there were probably damp, and by now extremely smelly, clothes inside it.

As for the rest of her house, there were bookcases filled with erotic literature. Not that she was ashamed of that exactly, but it was a consideration. Also, her cupboards and wardrobes were in dire need of a clear out. There were lots of rather tired-looking knickers in one drawer and in another there was a tangle of brassieres, again mostly old, and many of them worn more than once since they had been washed and thrown back in to mingle with the freshly-laundered ones.

Perhaps, given what the two other women now knew of her sex life, they would expect to find quantities of exotic corsets, basques, suspenders and such like. But she was not that sort of mistress and had never seen the point of dressing up in scratchy lingerie when the aim of most men was to rip it off her as soon as possible.

So, her friends might be surprised at the state of her undergarments. Indeed, she suspected that Monica, in particular, would be appalled because her own drawers in her lovely house would almost certainly be pristine and smell of delicately scented gardenia or lavender sachets, and her brassieres would be properly arranged in some sort of colour coded system and neatly folded.

Did other people, she wondered, ever consider that at some point they would fall ill and need someone else to view, and help sort, the intimate minutiae of their existence? More than that, were they so aware that such an eventuality might befall them, that their belongings were stored in a way that would not be shameful and embarrassing if someone else had to go to their property?

She had never foreseen such a day. And she had to live with the consequences. It was a worry and she felt very hot, and then, just as suddenly very cold at where her thoughts had led her.

There was online shopping of course.

Perhaps if she rang Barry, the old chap who ran a one-man taxi service whom she had used for years, she could ask him to come here for her keys, and then go to the house and empty out the washing machine and bin its contents. And maybe he could bring in her tablet, which almost certainly was in its usual place on top of a pile of papers on her kitchen table. Her phone screen would be far too small for online shopping. But she could manage with the tablet, and then she could buy such clothes as she needed and have them delivered to Monica's. Might that be a way forward? She could recover there, and before long, be strong enough to go home.

Satisfied that she had mentally assembled some order out of the nightmare her life had become, she fell asleep.

James was shorter than Jen had imagined. And less impressive. Monica had always implied that he had been a real catch and a very distinguished and personable man. Of course, his wife was divorcing him, and he had been more or less forced to retire against his will, so he was hardly going to look his best.

Even so, he was more ordinary than she had imagined. And it was hard to relax in his company as he seemed to be drinking far too much, and also had the very disconcerting habit of addressing her breasts rather than her face.

Eventually, she dipped her head low, so that she was no longer talking to the top of his bald head as he focused on her chest, and they made proper eye contact for the first time.

If he was as intelligent as she had been led to believe, surely he would be ashamed and quick to realise that she had sussed his annoying habit? But after a few seconds, it continued as before. Probably, he had been behaving that way for so long, his mind believed it was normal.

He was, however, quite a good conversationalist. And it turned out he had always bought the *Daily Chronicle* back in the days when Fred had edited it. And he knew Fred's name and reputation and admired him. So, there was an upside.

The dinner was excellent. Delicious chicken casserole with a colourful accompaniment of Mediterranean vegetables as well as tiny and tasty new potatoes. How Monica had pulled this together within half an hour of their arrival at the house, she had no idea.

James's glass kept emptying, she noticed, but he was quick to refill it. Was he getting drunk? She thought so and was even more convinced when his conversation became quite personal once Monica had left them to put the finishing touches to her dessert.

'I suppose,' he said, 'Mon's told you about her UDI?'

At first, Jen thought he meant that Monica had a Urinary Tract Infection, which seemed too intimate a subject for the dinner table. But when she stared at him blankly, he elaborated, 'UDI – Unilateral Declaration of Independence… you're probably too young to remember Southern Rhodesia and Ian Smith. Mid-sixties it all started, as I recall.'

'Ah well, yes, I'd have been about six. Do you mean she wants a divorce?'

'To put it bluntly, yes.'

'She did mention it. I'm sorry.'

He shrugged his shoulders dismissively.

'Still,' she said, and even as she did so, she wondered if it was unwise. 'You won't be on your own for long. You're a guy for a start, and that helps. And you've got assets, a profession, your own teeth, an unbroken nose and a pulse. Trust me, you'll be snapped up in no time.'

There was silence. Perhaps she had offended him, though really – apart from not wanting to upset Monica – she did not care much.

But then he spoke, 'I suppose what I'd really like is to have a lot of sex while I still can.'

Though she was more than a little taken aback, Jen hoped she did not betray it. 'I'm sure you'll be all right there. I mean in these days of the internet, it's easy.'

'And I can always pay for it,' he said.

She almost laughed, thinking he was joking, but then noticed from his expression that he was not.

Fortunately, Monica returned at that point and they were able to change the subject. She must find a way of telling her friend how right she was to be getting away from this man.

The pudding was apple tart with honeycomb ice cream. James attacked it with gusto. He seemed to have cheered up somewhat. Perhaps it was the food. Perhaps it was their conversation. Anyway, he had stopped eyeing up her breasts which was a relief.

He was, though, intent on persuading her to drink more. Twice, she put her hand over her glass. A third time, he batted it away and filled it anyway. He was clearly on the way to imbibing himself into a stupor, which made her very uncomfortable.

As soon as she felt she could, she jumped up saying that she had to ring her stepson that night before bed and she really ought to go and do that.

'Ring him from here.' James's tone was quite dictatorial.

'No, I just need to go.'

'You've only had two drinks,' he pointed out, almost accusingly.

'Don't be a bully, James,' Monica scolded him.

Jen smiled at her friend in gratitude and with a glance that she hoped was reassuring. This was becoming an unpleasant scene and must be embarrassing for Monica.

'Two drinks,' he repeated.

'That's right, James,' Jen agreed, 'two drinks. None when I'm alone, and two drinks if I'm in company. That's my rule.'

'Pretty boring rule.'

'Sorry about that.'

'Why only two drinks?'

'James, I'm not stopping you from having more than two drinks, am I?' Jen heard her voice rising, though she tried to remain calm. 'And I'm not being critical of how much booze you're tipping down your own neck. It's none of your business why I restrict myself. And it's a long story, which I have no wish to explain. Please don't spoil what has been a very nice evening, with Monica's lovely food. I'm going now. Good night.'

Chapter Sixteen

1971

We're queueing for the check-out.

Mum keeps moaning, 'I'm tired, honey, get me out of here.'

She looked quite strange and exhausted when I met her after she finished work. But when she said I'd have to take charge of the shopping I was pleased because I got to choose what we'd buy. I picked sausages, big fat pork ones. They're great. Mum buys little chipolatas but they don't taste nearly so nice. Today, she doesn't seem to mind what we have. She used to make lovely mashed potato, but she hasn't done that for ages. So, I got a packet of Smash. If you put a knob of butter in it, and a tiny drop of milk, it's not bad. I've put butter and milk in the trolley, and Weetabix – because there wasn't any this morning. I've got two tins of processed peas as they're on special offer and six cans of baked beans, we eat a lot of those. And I put in a bunch of bananas because I really, really like them.

I've tried to keep hold of Mum's hand the whole time as she just wants to sit down. Once when she was like this, she lay down on the floor of the supermarket and people had to walk round her. I was frightened that someone we knew would see her. Luckily, that didn't happen.

We're nearly at the head of the queue now. Mum's leaning on the trolley and singing quietly to herself. I hope I'm going to manage to get everything into the two carrier bags. Mum doesn't look as if she's going to be able to carry anything, which is going to be difficult, because I've got a lot of homework and my school rucksack's already heavy.

OK, it's our turn now. The assistant is a nice lady and is helping with the packing. Now Mum has opened her purse and a lot of coins are spilling out.

'It's all right,' I say. 'I can get them. Don't bend down.'

If she does, she'll probably fall over.

Mum hands her purse to the shop lady.

Then the woman leans forward and speaks quietly. 'You haven't got enough money, dear.'

Mum says, 'Jen'll have to put sshome of it back. Sh... sorry.'

The lady looks sympathetic. 'I'll help you,' she whispers to me.

I nod. I can't speak in case I start crying.

She takes away some of the things including the bottle of gin, but Mum begins to make a horrid wailing sound, so the woman looks at me, sighs, and puts it back in the pile we're taking. We end up leaving my sausages and the pint of milk and the butter, and the bananas. I don't argue, even though it means I'll only have beans and Smash for supper.

When I grow up, I'm never going to run out of money. And I'm never going to have children. They cost too much. That's what Mum says all the time.

The way she is, it's going to take ages to walk home. She's sorry, I can see that. But instead of saying it, she says stuff like how difficult life is for her and that that's why she drinks so much.

I hope she might have a sleep for a while when we get in, and then I can write my essay. And if I finish that I can read my book.

162

My best friend, Maria, asked me to help with a wedding in her parents' taverna. They're from Cyprus and they're really nice, and the food they make is fantastic. They always let me choose something to eat from the menu when I help them out, and they also give me five pounds.

We're not officially allowed to work in the restaurant because we're too young, but usually with parties like this one, everything starts very 'proper' and then people have food and drinks and after a while no one is bothered about Maria and me clearing and bringing out coffees. I really enjoy it. And I like being with Maria and her family.

It's our Christmas holidays now and Maria's dad said there are a lot of parties we can help at, so I'm pleased about that because I'll be able to buy myself a new school skirt with the money I earn. And maybe a couple of books.

Today was a big Greek wedding and it's been so happy and lovely. It's interesting to me that no one is drunk and falling around or getting miserable. They seem to drink a lot of water and sip at the wine rather than drink it in one gulp.

The party started about midday and it'll go on for hours yet. I've been dancing as well as helping. The bride's uncle wanted Maria to join in a kind of long line doing their own traditional sort of dance, and she wouldn't do it unless I did it too. I wasn't very good, but no one minded.

It's been a fab day so far but now the son of the man my mum works for at the estate agents – they call him 'Young Mr Clark' – has turned up. He looks worried and cross. I suppose he found out from Mum that I was here; the taverna's only a few doors down Prince of Wales Road from his office.

'Jen, I'm sorry,' he says. 'Your mother's all over the place today. She went out for lunch and took ages, and when she came back, she could hardly walk. You've got to get her to see a doctor or something. She's a nice woman, and when she's sober, she gets a lot of work done. I mean, she's intelligent, and can be very efficient. But Dad's furious. He says we can't have her around when she's like this. You'll have to take her home.'

I feel angry that she's ruining my lovely day, but what can I do?

Maria has heard Mr Clark, and she gives me a big hug. Then her dad comes over and hugs me too and hands me money to take Mum home in a taxi. That will be much easier than trying to get her on a bus. They're so kind. And they're the only friends I've got who are grown up, because Mum hasn't got any.

1978

My boyfriend Keith and I have been in the house together all afternoon. We have been revising for our A level mocks which are happening in four weeks. Keith wants to be a journalist. He says he always has. When he first mentioned it soon after we started going out, I wasn't totally sure what they did.

Now, I know there are reporters who go out and interview people about everything from murders to school concerts. Then there are journalists who have columns, giving advice, or making comment on news and politics, and there are also jobs where you sit in the office and write something called features. Keith's planning to go to university but I think I'll get a job in a shop or something to get some money and then do shorthand and typing at night school. Perhaps if I do OK, I might even become a journalist myself. My English teacher says I 'write very well'.

Keith works hard. He's good to be around because some of my other friends don't take exams seriously. But he does. Maria used to as well. I miss her. Her grandad died and her mum and dad went back to Cyprus. They're looking after Maria's granny now and running the restaurant that Maria's grandad used to have. Of course, they had to take Maria with them. She and I write to each other, but it's not the same as seeing her. Still, I do have Keith.

Mum came home a little while ago and sent me out for cake and a loaf of bread. Keith wanted to come with me, but Mum said he could keep her company.

I've been out a while, because the corner shop didn't have the cake she wanted, so I had to go to the Co-op which is half a mile away.

I'm slightly worried about her because she opened a bottle of wine as I was leaving. She hasn't had a drink for a while and things at home have been much better. Some time ago, the doctor gave her pills that make her really sick if she drinks alcohol, and she has tried to be good and stay off it.

I'm home how and I arrive at the back door and let myself into the kitchen.

I can't believe what I'm seeing. She and Keith are kissing.

She looks shocked when she sees me. I dump the shopping on the kitchen table and try to walk past her.

'Don't be like that, honey, Mummy's sorry.'

'Fuck off,' I shout at her. I've often thought those words, but I've never said them out loud before. It feels good, so I say them again.

'Jen...' Keith walks towards me, tears are rolling down his cheeks. 'I didn't mean. She... she...'

'Yes, I'm sure she started it. And I'm sure it's her fault,' I say in a calm voice that sounds more like a school teacher than me. 'But it does mean we can never see each other again. Ever. You've ruined my entire life.'

The calmness is going now, and I start crying too. Then I race around scooping up his school books and bag and his blazer and I throw it all into his arms. He drops them as he tries to get hold of me, but I gather them up again and run to the front door, open it, and throw everything out onto the street.

'Get out,' I scream. 'And if you ever tell anyone what you did today, or anything about my mum getting drunk, I'll kill you.'

Chapter Seventeen

Monica arrived early at the café on the fifth floor and selected a table near enough to the main cash desk to see the elevators, and the arrival of everyone who came into the seated area.

She had bought a cappuccino, though she was feeling so jumpy caffeine was probably a bad idea.

Three o'clock came and went. She laid her mobile phone on the table, checking first that it was on, and the volume turned up. Then she tried to immerse herself in the *Evening Standard*. When she had read most of the news and features, except for the sport, she turned to the puzzles page and tackled the Sudoku.

It was four o'clock when Jen arrived in the busy restaurant on the second floor of Selfridges. She was pleased she was there first because she was surprisingly anxious. Everything had happened so quickly, and much as she was eager to have this meeting it was unsettling.

Five nights ago, when she had had dinner with Monica and James, she had told them she had to go home because her stepson was expecting her to phone. It had been a ploy to enable her to leave; there had been no such plan. But when she arrived at her house there had been a message from Matthew on the answerphone, so she had rung him after all, and learned that the DNA tests confirmed Chloe was indeed his and Simon's half-sister – and Fred's daughter.

She had headed for bed after they had spoken, but her mind had been whirring with the notion that Fred now lived on in Chloe, as well as in his sons. It was an exhilarating but disturbing realisation. Unable to relax, she had left her bed and gone in search of the details Matthew had given her. It was far too late to ring, so she had emailed Chloe instead.

The next morning, Chloe had replied before Jen was awake, and they spoke on the phone later that day. The younger woman had said she would like to come to Crowbury and meet at Fred's grave. Aghast, Jen had vetoed that idea. She was not ready to share this private space with anyone. It was bad enough that Chloe had visited the cemetery twice and left a red rose on each occasion. Was that an appropriate gesture for a daughter? It had too many romantic connotations for her to feel comfortable about it. If the woman was intent on going again, she could not stop her, she supposed. But certainly, she could refuse to be there at the same time.

Chloe sounded somewhat taken aback at Jen's vehemence, but then suggested a late afternoon meeting in London, where she worked, and they agreed on the following Wednesday.

Jen had told Monica all about Chloe. And Monica asked if they might travel together as she too was going to the capital that day. Then, finally, she had confided her secret about Stephen.

Jen glanced at her watch. It was ten past four. Having been nervous all morning about seeing Chloe, she was now plagued with worry that it might not happen. My nerves won't stand that, she decided. She picked up her phone wondering if she might text Monica to check that all was well with her. Her friend had been stressed during their journey into the capital. Of course, her appointment was rather more crucial. It might change the course of her life. Meeting Fred's daughter, on the other hand, though important was unlikely to impact too greatly on her. So, if she failed to put in an appearance, so be it.

'You must be Jen,' a voice said. 'I'm Chloe.'

Monica had completed the Sudoku, and had also flirted with the Codeword, which seemed beyond her today, though normally she could complete them without difficulty.

She glanced at her watch yet again. 4.15. Had he changed his mind about coming? Surely if he had, he would have phoned her. She remembered very clearly writing her mobile number at the head of her message. Perhaps he had been delayed coming back into London from Colchester, but again, would he not have called? An icy panic stole over her as she wondered if he had had an accident. She tried to dismiss it; she must remain rational.

Her fall-back position was that she had his business card, but she did not want to seem desperate or neurotic, or both, and so far, had resisted extricating it from her bag.

At 4.30, she could bear the tension no longer. She opened her handbag and searched for it. Perhaps she had put it in her purse? No. In the mobile phone pocket? No. Eventually, and feeling stupidly inefficient, she started removing items, one by one, and putting them on the table in front of her. Make-up, telescopic umbrella, hairbrush, a tube of peppermints, antiseptic hand gel, small pack of tissues. Still, nothing. She felt tears threatening but blinked them away as she returned the items to the bag.

Then she remembered that the morning when his letter had come, and she had opened it at The Granary, she had, in her excitement, temporarily lost the card. She had found it, with much relief, in her jacket pocket. Feeling the same relief now, she sensed a smile lightening her tense features. It was short-lived. She put her hands into both pockets, but this time it was not there. It was the wrong jacket. Hot with anger at herself, and the shame of realising that he must have decided against meeting her after all, she swept up her belongings and, with one last hopeless glance towards the row of lifts by the entrance, she walked away.

The big surprise for Jen was how old Chloe was. She was unsure why she felt that way. After all, her stepsons were forty-seven and forty-four and Matthew had told her that Chloe had been born between them. But somehow, when she had tried to picture this new person in their lives, she had imagined her as young, and perhaps struggling to make her way in a career. She had even had some vague idea of offering financial help in Fred's name.

Instead, the woman sitting opposite her was confident verging on bossy, and formally dressed in an expensive but almost matronly way. Perhaps that was what was expected of a medical secretary by her boss – a brain surgeon whom Chloe described in glowing terms as 'renowned and world-famous'– but would her off-duty clothes be much different? It was hard to imagine.

Clearly someone accustomed to organising people, Chloe summoned the waitress, asked Jen if Earl Grey would suit, then ordered it for both of them as well as two portions of carrot cake which, she assured Jen, was not just the best thing they did on the afternoon tea menu but a healthy option too.

The younger woman did most of the talking. She explained how her mother, now living in a nursing home in Devon, had been a foreign correspondent on the paper while Fred was working his way up towards his eventual editorship. He had been the parliamentary lobbyist at the time and Chloe's mother had found him both fearsomely bright, and attractive. She had never, it seemed, wanted a child, in case it impeded her career, until she had woken up one day with a complete change of heart.

'But Fred never knew about you?' Jen checked quickly in one of the few gaps of the monologue.

'No. My mother apparently managed to get him into bed after some late-night drinking and told him she was on the Pill, which she wasn't. Also, unknown to him, she was ovulating. My mother was nothing if not scrupulous in her planning!'

'She certainly sounds very organised,' Jen murmured, as she thought, *and I'm sitting opposite someone just like her.*

The cake arrived, which Chloe tackled with enthusiasm, and in the 'eating gaps' Jen seized the opportunity to ask various questions about the younger woman's life – all the time, watching and searching for similarities between her and the man she loved.

She had, she realised, been full of hope that Chloe would be like a female version of Fred – whimsical, funny, clever, politically aware and charming. And that there would be a shape of a face, a hairline, eyes, ears, or hands that would remind her of her husband. So far, she could find no connection.

'It's complicated,' Chloe said.

'Sorry?'

'You asked about my personal life. I don't have a partner, well, not officially. I'll tell you more when I know you better.'

If you ever know me better, Jen thought, unsure that that would happen.

'Are you like your mother?' she asked.

'God, yes. Spitting image. Probably temperamentally too. Though I've fought against that!'

Jen smiled, feeling for the first time some sense of affinity, though it was more about her ambivalence towards her own mother than anything to do with Fred. But this woman too had grown up without any knowledge of who had fathered her. What must it have been like when the mother, on seeing Fred's obituary, had decided to tell Chloe her secret? Her own parent had never divulged such information. And Jen had drawn the conclusion that she must be the result of a drunken, one-off encounter. How squalid it all was. At least Chloe had a father who was a good man and who had achieved a great deal – even if she had never known him.

'So,' she ventured, 'what can I tell you about your dad?'

'Oh, lots, I hope. But just before I came out my boss said he needed me back in the office as he's... unexpectedly free this

170

evening and, uh, needs me to work. So, I just came to establish we can do this thing.'

'What thing?'

'Well, you know, get on well enough to chat about stuff.'

'Oh,' Jen felt wrong-footed. 'And have you decided?'

'Oh yes, I'm sure it'll be fine. Frankly, I imagined you as somewhat elderly, perhaps a bit slower and less on top of things.'

'Oh, did you?'

'Sorry.'

Jen considered saying that their encounter had been full of surprises for her too, in that Chloe had turned out not just to be older than she had anticipated but totally unlike Fred and awfully ordinary. She decided against it.

'Right,' Chloe jumped up. 'Mustn't keep the great man waiting. I'll pay the waitress on my way out. I'll be in touch.'

Jen had assumed she would pay and be more in control of the meeting, but she said 'fine' and did not argue, particularly as, suddenly, she felt as though she had been run over by a truck. Absent-mindedly, she poured herself another cup of the Earl Grey which she had felt obliged to agree to, even though she would have preferred English Breakfast. Her eyes seemed to be out of focus. She closed them as she tried to assess her emotions. After all the excitement and anticipation of the last few days, she felt nothing but exhaustion.

'Is it all right if I clear the table, Madam?' The question startled her, and she jumped. The waitress was looking at her with some concern. Had she been asleep?

She glanced at her watch. What time had Chloe left? She was unsure. Why was she being so vague?

'Sorry,' she said. 'So sorry. I, uh, it's a bit hot in here. I must go.'

There was a queue of people waiting to be seated in the restaurant. No wonder they wanted her table. She had to push past a couple who were wrapped round each other. Obviously for them,

171

afternoon tea was but a prelude to a whole evening and night of passion. A rush of envy swept over her.

Determinedly, she turned her attention to Monica. If her friend's afternoon was going well, perhaps it would not matter if they returned home separately. Heavy with fatigue, she longed to be out of London, back in her own house, alone, where she could rest and think.

She texted. 'Hope things going brilliantly.'

Monica messaged back immediately. 'What train shall we get? I'm ready.'

That was not the answer Jen had expected, so she rang her.

'What happened?'

Monica sighed at the other end. 'Nothing whatever. He obviously just changed his mind. Perhaps after all these years of thinking he wanted me, he found the reality displeasing or worrying.'

'Wait!' Jen's brain suddenly switched itself back on. 'You mean you've been in John Lewis all this time and he hasn't appeared?'

'Well actually I'm walking down Regent Street, for no reason really except that I couldn't bear to stay there any longer.'

'Monica, listen to me, from everything you've told me about Stephen, I simply don't believe he would let you down like this.'

'Well, he has.'

'Maybe something's happened to him?'

'Oh, don't say that!'

Jen smiled at the anguish in her friend's voice. 'Listen, all sorts of things can delay someone.'

'But he had my mobile phone number.'

'Maybe he's lost his phone, or it's conked out, or been stolen. Where was he coming in from?'

'Colchester,' she said.

'Well maybe the train was delayed. Don't let's give up on this.'

'I don't know what to do.'

'Call his office.'

'I can't. That's the other thing, he'd sent me his business card, but I seem to have lost it.'

'Well you were in a fair old tizz this morning! But you must know the name of his firm.'

'Y-yes.'

'What is it and where is it?'

'S J Falvey and Associates. They're in Wigmore Street.'

'Right, you go back to John Lewis. I'll call his company and find out what's happened.'

'It's a waste of time.'

'No, it's not. Just do it, Monica. You can't give up this easily.'

Eventually, a diffident voice responded. 'All right.'

Jen took herself away from the restaurant area and found a quiet corner. First of all, she brought up the Greater Anglia website on her phone and saw that there had been an 'incident' at Shenfield. Years of using that line meant she knew full well what that meant. If there was a suicide, or a points failure between Chelmsford and Liverpool Street, the whole network of Norwich trains and the commuter routes that fed off it, were thrown into chaos. Next, she googled Stephen's firm. Once she had the phone number, she rang and asked to speak to him.

'And who's calling?'

'He won't know me, but he was supposed to be meeting a friend of mine this afternoon.'

'Was that Monica Charlton?'

'Yes.'

'Oh, thank heavens. He's been frantic about that meeting for some reason. Apparently, he had a note of her mobile number but when he came to call it, there was a digit missing. He was terribly delayed because his train hit a person who'd thrown herself in front of it and they were stationary for ages while the police and ambulance were there. So, it wasn't his fault, but he feels terrible that he was so late. And now the lady has left where he was expecting to find her. He's been back twice. Not sure where he is now.'

173

'Can you get hold of him though?'

'No problem.'

'Well, my name's Jen. Can you let him know that Monica did go for a walk but I've persuaded her to go back to John Lewis.'

'I'll call him right away. He'll be so relieved.'

'I thought you'd had an accident,' they said in unison as they found each other at the entrance to the café.

'Monica, I am so, so sorry.'

'Why didn't you call me?'

'You left out one of the numbers when you wrote down your mobile details. I've actually been trying to guess what it might be and ringing various permutations of it all afternoon. I've spoken to rather a lot of people, not all of whom were polite!'

'Oh, sorry. I'm an idiot.'

'Why didn't you call *me*?' he asked, gently.

'I mislaid your business card somehow, and I felt so foolish that I didn't feel I could ring your office. I mean, it's personal isn't it?'

'Probably not now! I've been on the phone to them constantly. My staff must think I've lost my mind. I even thought of asking if someone could come here and find you, but I was worried you wouldn't like that. I've been here twice. And probably only just missed you. But ten minutes ago, your friend rang the switchboard and told me you were coming back.'

He took a deep breath and so did she, and they smiled, shyly at each other.

'It's been awful,' she said in little more than a whisper. 'I thought you'd changed your mind.'

He took both her hands in his and stared deeply into her eyes. 'How likely is that? I've been waiting ten years for this moment.' And suddenly they were in each other's arms and their lips locked into such a heartfelt embrace that neither of them saw Jen emerge from the lift and stop to watch, with the broadest smile on her face.

174

The junior doctor was one she had not encountered before. He looked about fourteen, she thought, and he was clearly ill at ease as he introduced himself as Ranjit. He was smart though and addressed her as Miss Brown, rather than Lucy, so she warmed to him.

'You've been saying you want to leave the hospital,' he began.

'That's correct.'

'Well, that's good because we need your bed,' he smiled. 'Sorry to be brutally honest.'

'I don't mind,' she returned the smile. 'I like to know where I am.'

'The physio says you're doing better and getting stronger but there's no question of you going home, I'm afraid, unless you have someone else living there with you.'

'Well,' Lucy cast around for some ideas, 'maybe that could be arranged.'

'We feel that you'd be better staying with friends and I gather that your next of kin, Mrs Charlton, is happy to have you.'

'She is, and I've done some online shopping and there are now clothes and other items at her house in readiness.'

'So, are you prepared to go there?'

Lucy shrugged. 'If I have to. What's the alternative?'

'We don't really have a Plan B,' the young man admitted. 'Someone at the meeting this afternoon suggested there might be a bed in a geriatric unit in Oxford.'

'Geriatric!' She spat the word out with such bitter force that she felt her jowls quiver. 'Oh my God, to think it's come to this.'

'Well, maybe Mrs Charlton would be the better option?'

'Undoubtedly. When can I go?'

'Tomorrow.'

She had longed to hear those words but felt suddenly vulnerable and unwanted.

'Lordy! That soon?'

He nodded.

'Fine,' she said, with more bravado than she felt. 'What time would that be?'

'We haven't arranged the transport yet. I'm afraid you may be sitting around in the day room for a while.'

'Can't I be in bed?'

'Not really. Someone else will be in it from mid-morning!'

She pulled a wry face. 'I can get a taxi. The man I've used for years has been here already. I can keep the crutches I've been given, presumably?'

'Of course, and we can get someone to wheel you down to the front door.'

'That seems to be settled then. I'd better ring Monica.'

'Actually, Sister's doing that now.'

What has happened to my control of my life, she pondered as the junior doctor nodded farewell and left her alone to spend her last night in hospital.

They caught the train with less than five minutes to spare. Jen had been at Picturehouse Central in Shaftesbury Avenue, watching *Blinded by the Light*. As Fred had been a Bruce Springsteen fan, it had been a film packed with musical memories.

Stephen and Monica had elected to have dinner at an Italian restaurant in St Christopher's Place, and she had volunteered to ring James before going to the cinema.

He had been remarkably civil while she told him several blatant lies.

'Monica's been so kind,' she had said to him. 'I've got a bit of a family crisis and I'm taking her with me to meet the people concerned. I think she'll bring some sanity to the proceedings. Then I really will owe her dinner! So, we're thinking of getting the ten o'clock train back. You don't mind, do you?'

'I expect I'll manage to open a tin of something,' he had responded, with a hint of petulance, which she had ignored.

'Oh, jolly good. Monica said you'd rise to the occasion.'

'Did she?'

'Oh yes,' Jen lied again.

'Just in case I'm in bed before she gets in, can you tell her that your friend Lucy is coming out of hospital tomorrow. It seems she's staying with us.'

'Oh goodness. Right. Yes. It's very nice of you both.'

He had grunted before adding, 'And since you seem to know everything about our lives you might want to tell Mon that I've set the divorce in motion. Actually, she has you to thank for that. You made me see the other night that there are possibilities.'

'Yes, there are,' she had gushed. 'Loads!'

'Maybe. Anyway, it'll probably go through quite quickly.'

Jen's face had stretched to a wide grin. But she had chosen a diplomatic response. 'Well, of course these things are always sad. But thank you for telling me. She's just in the loo at the moment at the hotel where we're meeting with the family.'

She had felt herself blush at yet another untruth.

'That's OK. On second thoughts, I might go to the pub, so I'll probably see her later and fill her in with all the details.'

'Right. Understood. Thank you, James.'

The train was picking up speed now and Monica was sitting opposite her, beside a large bouquet of yellow roses, eyes shining and looking pinkly pleased with life.

'Thanks for everything.'

Jen smiled. 'Your face tells me it's all been wonderful.'

Monica smiled, dreamily. 'He wanted me to stay the night,' she whispered, with a furtive look at a woman sitting near them. 'I told him I can't till the divorce is under way. He was... fine.'

Jen laughed. 'Fine, but disappointed.'

Monica laughed too.

'How are you going to explain those away?' Jen nodded at the flowers.

'Mmmn, not sure. At least I persuaded him not to buy red ones. They come from John Lewis, not surprisingly. Our favourite shop!' She giggled. 'You can't get much more middle class than that, can you? Conducting your courtship there. What a cliché!'

'Don't knock it,' Jen said. 'Whatever works. And clearly this is going to. You look ravishing.'

Monica raised her eyebrows, before smiling. 'You better let me know what you told James, so I get my story right. Was he OK?'

'He was. I said you were helping me with a family crisis. He said he might go to the pub so would probably still be up when you get back. But he did give me two pieces of news that he said I should tell you.'

'Really?'

'Yes, he said that Lucy's coming out of hospital tomorrow morning and everyone's agreed she's staying with you.'

'Oh, heavens. I hadn't got around to discussing that with him. How was he about it?'

'Seemed OK.'

'That's a relief. Well, we can get on with Project Lucy now.'

Jen nodded. 'The other thing – and I'd get you to sit down if you weren't already – is that James has finally seen the light. He's set the divorce in motion. And it sounds like you could be a free woman by the end of the year!'

Chapter Eighteen

Suzie took ages to open her front door, but as Jen was confident that her neighbour was at home, she continued to wait on the doorstep.

She had no idea why the other woman was distancing herself. The last time it had happened, was after the one visit she had made to see Fred, not long after his diagnosis. Jen had sensed that the meeting had not gone well, but all Fred would say was that it had been a strain because they had so little common ground. Whatever had transpired, Suzie never crossed their threshold again until after Fred's death.

'Oh, it's you,' Suzie said when, finally, she appeared.

'Yes, it's me,' Jen responded brightly. 'Are you OK?'

'Yup.'

'Look, Suzie, I haven't annoyed you or anything, have I?'

Suzie did not meet her gaze as she shook her head.

'I was just wondering how Hoagy is?'

'Both dogs are over their surgery. They're getting on well.'

A sequence of angry-sounding barks from inside the house, which her neighbour studiously ignored, caused Jen to feel uneasy as well as sceptical.

'Could I just come in and see him?'

'Sorry, Jen.' Again there was no eye contact. 'I'm about to rush out. Another time.'

'Of course,' she responded, softly.

As she walked back into her own house, a memory of something that Fred had said, quite out of the blue, came to mind.

'Will you stay in Crowbury afterwards?'

She had been taken aback. He was so ill by then that he spent most of every day asleep. What, she wondered, had prompted him to ask that question? Maybe he had been dreaming about her. Or simply trying to picture in his own mind what her life would be like without him. Perhaps he had realised that she had too few friends here. Maybe, he had thought that Norwich – because of her roots, plus the presence of Matthew and Ginny – would be a better option.

'Are you telling me something, Fred?' she whispered as she put her head around the door into his study.

It takes me ages to get going in the mornings, Lucy reflected as she looked at her watch.

She had always sailed through her ablutions, as she called them. Now, by the time she had raised the energy to remove her pyjamas and negotiate her way to the shower cabinet – where Monica had managed to insinuate a small chair, which allowed her to sit under the water-stream while keeping both feet out of the way so they stayed dry – she was exhausted. Dressing herself, in one of her new brassieres, a T-shirt and tracksuit, was another lengthy business and by the time she was done, she often had to lie down before summoning the strength to tackle the stairs.

Today, when she reached the dining area in the kitchen, it became apparent that Monica had left for The Granary. But James was there, and they had a brief discussion about how difficult it was to summon the motivation to get up once you no longer had a schedule to stick to.

She was surprised by how relaxed she felt in his company. Initially, he had seemed wary of her, but they both liked to talk, and chew over the events in the news, and they discovered they shared a love of Shakespeare, though their tastes in contemporary fiction were different.

He was standing at the range cooker putting the finishing touches to the big fry-up that he indulged himself with two or three times a week, despite Monica's disapproval.

He pointed to some food on the table. 'Mon has left you your healthy option!'

She grimaced.

'Sorry. Not up to much is it? But she has your best interests at heart, you know.'

'I do know,' she replied. 'But it's agony. And I've hardly lost any weight and I'm absolutely bloody starving all the time and it makes me miserable.'

He was silent for a moment, then he looked at her and grinned. 'If we don't tell Monica, would you like one of these eggs and a sausage and some fried bread?'

'Is the Pope a Catholic?'

'Oh God, Lucy, you'll get me in trouble!'

'Can you spare it, though?'

'Of course. Anyway, I'm not totally incapable. I can always make us second helpings!'

'You're talking my language now, you bad boy,' she laughed.

James fetched another plate, slid half of his breakfast onto it and handed it to her.

She sat over it, sniffing happily. 'Scrumptious! Now this makes life worth living.'

He sat down beside her and liberally sprinkled what was left of his own meal with salt and pepper before beginning to eat.

Neither of them spoke for a couple of minutes as they focused on the pleasure before them.

'I say, Lucy,' James turned to her, 'you won't keel over with a heart attack, will you? I've probably just knocked months off your life.'

'I don't care. The important thing for me is that you've lifted my mood considerably. Frankly, I'd sooner have quality of life on my own terms than quantity, if that's dependent on being sensible all the time. Since I got out of the hospital, I've had more salads than I've eaten in my whole life, and loads of lightly-grilled chicken, with no skin on it though that's my favourite part, grilled salmon, poached haddock... Well, you know. I feel bad saying this because both Jen and Monica are doing their very best for me and they're terribly kind, but I feel it's too late and I can't really face what it would take to become even slightly healthier. I'm in a poor state physically, as various nurses and doctors keep telling me, and I don't think they rate my chances. Neither do I. So, I feel I might as well allow myself things that cheer me up. And to that end, I want to go home. That sounds awfully ungrateful. But would you back me up if I suggested it?'

'Probably. I could volunteer to come over and shop for you. After all, I'm manifestly underemployed now.'

'You do see my point of view, don't you?'

'Actually, I do... Tell me, those internet parcels you keep getting from M&S and Boots, they're not all clothes and toiletries, are they? Are you ordering snacks on the quiet?'

'James, you're too perceptive for your own good. I plead the fifth amendment!'

He tried to look stern but burst out laughing.

'You won't tell on me, will you?'

'Don't be ridiculous. Anyway, Monica and I hardly talk now. Frankly, it's made my life easier your being here. It's helped us reach a state of equivalence, I think. Shall I take you to the hospital later?'

'Oh, that's very kind, but I don't have to go today, and tomorrow I've booked my usual taxi driver.'

'Why don't you cancel him? It's silly to pay someone when I'm sitting around. I'll be happy to go with you, and once you don't have to have your dressings changed so often, I'll try and help you move out of here and go home, if that's what you really want.'

How different Monica looked, Jen thought, compared with the woman she had first encountered at the crazy job interview seven months ago. That day, she had assumed Monica was a very buttoned-up sort of a person, formal, set in her ways and no fun at all – which definitely goes to show I'm not a very good judge of character, she reflected.

'You look as if you're sitting in a rosy aura,' Jen grinned. 'Do I take it you've had carnal knowledge of the man?'

Monica blushed and nodded.

Jen felt full of happiness for this woman who had become such a good friend. How marvellous it was that Monica was now having the sort of supportive, companionable, romantic and satisfying relationship she had enjoyed with Fred. She was pleased not to feel envy. And genuinely did not. Of course, there was a pang of regret that she would never again experience this headiness herself, but she felt at peace with the knowledge that she had had it.

'I don't need to ask if it went OK.'

'I surprised myself. I suppose there was a lot of pent up emotion and, to be honest, frustration! Even so, I never knew I could be the sort of woman who, well, could act as I did with him. But I know now, and I can't wait for the next time. Thank heavens we were in his home which is set back from the road and well away from the neighbours!'

'Do you mean you were noisy, Monica?' Jen's eyes sparkled at the thought.

'I *was*. Quite abandoned! Good thing my mother's mind has gone. She wouldn't have coped with this at all! She labelled me a trollop when I'd never really done anything except let James have his way with me before marriage. It seemed to matter to him a lot, but I couldn't understand what all the fuss was about. I know now though. Rather late in the day. But it's fantastic!'

They both began to laugh.

Liz Pemberton, the manager, was at the next table in The Granary café. She looked up and smiled. 'That must be quite a joke, do you want to share it?'

The other two women exchanged glances, and tried to stifle their mirth, but failed. 'You're too young,' Jen gasped eventually, which set them off again.

After their shift, they met again. This time, Helen was sitting nearby but did not approach them. Before long, she was joined by the older, attractive man Monica had been introduced to.

'Your therapist's ignoring you,' Jen nodded in their direction.

'That's OK. Helen explained that once you're in therapy, the counsellor never acknowledges you outside of the consulting room, so as to maintain your confidentiality. As it happens, it wouldn't matter in my case as I've made no secret to you, or Lucy or Liz that I've been seeing her.'

'I saw Helen myself for a while,' Jen told her.

'I wondered if you had.'

'It was a voluntary role for her, seeing partners of patients with motor neurone disease at the hospital. She's probably still doing it, though her husband died, just before Fred.'

'He wasn't her husband.'

'What! How do you know?'

'We were talking one day about me watching her on television in the eighties when my daughter Betsy was alive. And I remembered her name was Helen Bartlett and I said something like "well it was then". And she said it still was, because she'd never married.'

Jen turned briefly to view Helen and the man with her.

'She's very into the new bloke anyway. I find that quite repugnant when you think the other guy, husband or not, died just before Christmas. I mean the very thought of being with someone other than Fred makes me feel sick! Still, we're all different. Maybe she's one of these women who can't be alone. I've never trusted them!'

184

'I met him a few weeks ago. When I used Helen's address to contact Stephen, he answered the door. I... I was quite thrown by it myself, knowing that there had been another partner who'd recently died. But he seemed very much at home. It made me wonder if they went back a long way. I mean look at Stephen and me. We fell for each other ten years ago, but it's only now we're getting together. You don't know what goes on behind closed doors do you? But seeing her reminds me that I must let her know that I no longer need her as a therapist.'

'I shouldn't worry. I doubt if she needs the money,' Jen responded tartly.

'You're probably right. Judging by the house she's got!'

'And I bet the Middle Eastern lover is loaded. He's got that look.'

'You don't care for her much, do you?'

Jen shrugged. 'Not sure. When I first met her, I felt we had a lot in common. But this thing with the new man troubles me, and now I realise we're very different. So, I suppose I don't like her much. Still, I'm sure she won't lose any sleep over that.'

Monica said nothing but stroked Jen's arm.

'Am I being awful?' Jen asked.

'Not at all. I just think you're feeling sad and I'd love it if, in time, you could be happy again.'

'I'm happier than I was, and I'm also beginning to think seriously about what I'm going to do.'

'That's good,' Monica smiled at her, but then her expression changed.

'What is it?'

'Nothing.'

'Yes, there is,' Jen insisted. 'You suddenly looked worried.'

'Nothing much gets past you, does it? I hadn't thought of mentioning this yet but perhaps I should. We've become such good friends and it's only fair I let you in on what Stephen and I've been talking about. He's such a considerate man and doesn't

185

want to hurry me. But at the same time, he feels – we both feel – that we've waited a long time for this and that at our age, it's no point playing games, or hanging around. I mean you can't be sure how long you've got… you know that with Fred, and of course, Lucy.'

Jen nodded, with a faraway look in her eye. 'So, are you going to live together, soon?'

Monica's eyes lit up at the thought as she replied, 'Yes! And the thing is, I've realised that it makes sense for me to move to Oxford. He's used to commuting from there and it's a much easier journey than it would be from here. He's only fifty-seven, he loves his work and wants to carry on as long as possible. And I think he should. And, well, Crowbury isn't exactly full of nice memories, so I think it would be better all round.'

'That's wonderful.'

'It is,' Monica agreed. 'But you and I won't see each other as much. And I'll have to leave The Granary. And there's Lucy to consider too.'

'Oxford's not so far away,' Jen said. 'And heaven knows what's going to happen about Lucy. Anyway, I've begun to think about moving house myself.'

Monica looked shocked. 'I thought when we talked about it a while back you said you weren't ready to go and live in a Granny Annexe.'

'Did I? Mmmn, I probably did. Things change, don't they?'

The women fell silent, each reflecting on how much their lives were altering.

'I suppose,' Jen continued, trying to find the words for the inchoate plans that were buzzing around her brain, 'I've realised that the spirit has gone out of Crowbury for me. It's just not the same without Fred. And my neighbour's being a total pain, and if *you* move…' She sighed. 'Also, I've thought a lot about Matthew and Ginny and I'm kind of getting a sense that Fred would feel I'd be better off with them in Norwich. It makes sense. I mean,

I grew up there, and though that wasn't an entirely happy experience, I love that part of the country, and got into journalism there, and Fred and I have had some amazing times there in the past, and of course I'm soon going to be a granny.'

'When we met,' Monica's voice was low, and slow, 'I'd have sworn that the two of us were so settled here that we'd never leave.'

'I know,' Jen said. 'It just goes to show how uncertain life can become. I'd never have believed it.'

The wounds on each foot, resulting from the amputation of her toes, were not healing up properly. The nurse took swabs from both areas. She looked quite morose, Lucy thought. Had she had a row with her husband before work, or was she disconsolate that this particular patient was not improving as she should? I'm just a nuisance to these people, she decided. A nuisance and a disappointment.

She was asked to return to the waiting room until another nurse became free to take some blood. It was hot and crowded and, annoyingly, she had left her Kindle at Monica's house.

She gazed around the room. It was depressing. Several patients, like her, were hobbling and trying to manage their sticks. Lots of them were as overweight as she was. Some more so.

'God, it's a bloody epidemic,' she said out loud.

'Sorry?' The elderly gentleman sitting next to her was wearing a hearing aid behind each ear.

'Apologies,' she said loudly, and with her lips working overtime so that he could understand what she was saying, she continued, 'I was just talking to myself.'

His eyes twinkled. 'You get a better class of conversation that way.'

She laughed. He looked fitter than most of the patients. 'You don't seem to be as out of shape as the rest of us,' she said. 'Are you diabetic?'

'No, I'm waiting for my wife.'

'I see. How's she doing?'

'Not very well to be honest.'

'Me neither. Bit of a bugger really. Trouble is, I can't summon much enthusiasm to make all the changes they want.'

'Ah,' he nodded sympathetically. 'My wife's determined to see our youngest grandchild married. That's spurring her on.'

'Good for her,' she said warmly, then inwardly she added, *But I have no such motivation. No job. No family to speak of. No partner. No children. I have ploughed my own furrow. I'm an odd-ball really. And I had no concept that one day I would be old and ill and that I wouldn't have a clue how to cope.*

Her ruminations continued until her name was called.

After seeing the nurse, she set off on what she thought of as 'the long and arduous walk to freedom', leaning heavily on her aluminium crutches which, she felt, now defined her.

She should, she knew – if she were a normal person – feel chastened to such an extent by the appointment, that she would garner her resolve to diet properly and embark on all the physio exercises. *I am just not that woman,* she mused, as she struggled along, eyes glued to the ground in front of her, fearful of falling.

James was at the front door. He looked sympathetic, and to her embarrassment, his evident kindness moistened her eyes.

'Coffee, do you think?' he asked gently.

'Not here. Do you mind? Could we go to my place? I'd like to see it. Perhaps we could pick up some milk on the way?'

As soon as they parked outside her house, the weight of her moodiness seemed to lift. And, she noticed, she was speedier on her feet than normal as she progressed up the path and then climbed up the uneven steps to her front door where she managed to balance while she inserted the key in the lock before stepping into her hallway.

James, behind her, carrying a pint of milk, regarded her enthusiasm with a smile. 'Lovely old house,' he said, 'and very pleasant part of town.'

188

She turned to face him. 'I'm glad you approve. I bought it not long after I took up my post at the university. It was cheap – this area wasn't fashionable then. I doubt the present-day lecturers could afford what it might cost today.'

She thought suddenly of Petrina, a very good PhD student of hers who was now teaching in the department. It was strange, because they had had little contact since she had left, but in that moment, she felt a tangible link with the earnest, mixed-race, petite younger woman with the enormous intellect. Life had been tough for her, but she was triumphing over it with energy and spirit.

'Right,' she said to James, 'let's get into the kitchen and have that coffee.'

Everything, including the plate and mug she had used for lunch on the day she had collapsed at Roy's house, was where she had left it. The house smelt somewhat musty and uncared for, but it was home. Thank heavens she had asked her taxi driver to come in and remove the damp washing from her machine. That would have been a serious problem by now.

James insisted she sit down at the kitchen table while he boiled the kettle.

She took out her phone. And texted Petrina.

'Are you still coping? Planning to stay in Crowbury? Where are you living? Still renting? Love, Lucy.'

'Would you like your milk heated?' James asked.

'Thank you,' she smiled, broadly. 'I never do that for myself, but I'd love it. There are some rather lovely biscuits in the tin over there,' she told him. 'You're not going to tell me off for having a little treat, are you?'

'I've decided you're a grown up, Lucy,' he replied with surprising gravity. 'You know what the medics are telling you. You know what you should, by their reckoning, be doing. It seems to me that you've weighed up your chances and your pros and cons and are making your own decisions, as indeed you have all through life. And in a sense, I admire you for it. You're an unusual person and you'll do this period of your life in your own individualistic way, just as you have everything else. Some people might say you're in denial. I don't think you are. I think you've just decided it's not worth your while to adopt all the health messages.'

'Thank you, James,' she responded quietly. 'Frankly, I've thought about this a lot, I don't see the point.'

'Monica thinks you're depressed.'

'Does she? I didn't know that. Do you think I am?'

He shrugged his shoulders. 'I'm no expert on mental health. I think you're a bit low. Is that the same thing? Tell you the truth, I think I'm a bit low too. Probably we both liked our lives as they were before and aren't very keen on the changes.'

'That sums it up, I suppose. But you have options. You have your health. You're a man. You've comfortably off. Monica said you're very keen on sex. Why don't you go out there and get some?'

Without answering, he turned his attention to the saucepan of hot milk and the kettle which had just boiled and spooned generous amounts of instant coffee into two mugs.

'I like sex too,' she said, as he handed one of them to her.

'I rather gathered that from something I overheard Jen say to Monica. Have you ever been married?'

'No, it's all been very clandestine.'

'Have there been a lot of men?'

She nodded, then took a sip of her coffee.

'Any women?'

She looked surprised at the question. 'No!'

'Hmmmn.'

'Why? You haven't had blokes, have you?'

'Good God no. Not my scene.'

'I knew someone… very well… who was into everything. Rumour was that he had even had sex with a German shepherd dog! But I think that story was apocryphal.'

190

She grinned at him.

'To tell you the truth,' James said solemnly, 'I feel slightly lacking in confidence about womanising now. The fact is, and I suspect I shouldn't be proud of this, I've seen quite a bit of action with various partners all through my married life and before it. And I've never before considered that it wouldn't go on like that. But I'm discovering there are different rules now. Making an approach in ways that once seemed normal – though perhaps were quite proprietorial and arrogant, in retrospect – are now not acceptable. Jen more or less said I'd be snapped up by some eager widow or divorcee but, as you know, I can cook a breakfast! And I don't want another long-term relationship, no matter how comfortable it is, unless there's loads of sex. And then I find myself worrying that I may no longer be up to it.'

'But are you still in the mood for it?' Lucy asked.

'I'm not even sure about that.'

'I've got books upstairs that might interest you.'

'Really?'

She noticed that he suddenly looked quite chirpy. 'Come and see.'

'Can you manage the stairs?'

'Well, I need to try, because if I can't, I know I won't be able to persuade you to help me plead my case to come home.'

She was slow, and could feel that her legs were quite trembly, but by pulling hard on the bannister with one hand, and using one of her crutches with the other, she persevered till she got to the top.

'That ghastly male physio might be impressed now,' she gasped.

In her spare bedroom, she sat on the sofa-bed while James perused her erotica collection. Eventually, he pulled out two volumes and showed them to her.

'Good choice, I'd say,' she smiled. 'If they don't get you going, nothing will!'

He looked up and for the first time noticed an oil painting on the other side of the room. It was of a plump, naked woman lying, eyes closed, in relaxed post-coital mode, with a blissful smile on her lips. She was not beautiful by any stretch of the imagination but there was something joyously candid as well as touching about the picture.

'Lucy,' James's voice was almost a whisper. 'Is that you?'

She nodded.

'And isn't it by…'

She interrupted him. 'It is, and you've never seen it!'

'Oh! You're a dark horse. So, you and he…'

She nodded again. 'For decades. But you must never tell.'

'And isn't that painting worth rather a lot of money?'

She smiled. 'I expect it is. Maybe a couple of million.'

'More than that.'

'Do you think so?'

'Definitely. I seem to remember right after he died that one of his works went for ten times that! How did you meet him?'

'At Cambridge. He was very wild even then.'

'I bet it was him who did it with the German shepherd.'

She turned away. 'I'm sure that was just a story,' she said, as she forced herself to her feet and made for the stairs.

Back in the kitchen, she noticed that a text had arrived from Petrina.

'Dear Lucy. Lovely to hear from you. Miss you. Yes, all going well. Keeping out of the way of the hateful Vice-Chancellor. Still can't understand why he got rid of you. Your students were so upset. Come up to the department and have lunch if you could bear to. Or I could meet you in town. Am doing OK. Still renting. I'm that generation! But I love living here. Thanks for everything you taught me. I think about you often. Love, Petrina x'

Lucy looked up from her phone. 'You're a lawyer, James,' she said. 'Could you help me do my will?'

'That's not really my field, but I can recommend someone.'

'No, I want you to do it. Particularly now that you know about the painting.'

*

Jen had walked home from The Granary. It had not been as much fun today because Monica had taken the day off so she could go to Oxford for lunch with Stephen.

And I don't suppose it's just lunch, she thought, and she grinned.

As she turned into her own street, she saw Suzie with the two dogs. She was as sure as she could be that her neighbour had seen her too, but with a sudden spurt, Suzie pulled on both leads, and turned in the direction of her home, twenty yards away. Neither dog seemed enthusiastic about her change of direction. Perhaps they had only just come out. Whatever was going on though, it was clear that Suzie had no intention of sharing it with her.

She sighed loudly. It was uncomfortable living here now. And it did not seem that there would be improvement in the situation any time soon.

Inside her own house, she switched on the kettle and then pottered around the ground floor while it heated up. In Fred's study, the answer machine was flashing.

'Jen, hi. Just Matthew here. First thing is, I've realised that Chloe has gone very silent on us. At the beginning, she was terrifically keen to meet up. Keener than me to be honest. But I've emailed her twice and got no reply. Are you and she in touch? Next thing: we've found a house that seems rather special. Hopefully, you'll like it too. And because of that, and other things, I was wondering if you could possibly come up for a few days soon? I get a bit worried because Ginny's often really tired, and I'm going backwards and forwards to London quite a lot while I get familiar with my new company, so she's on her own much of the time. She says I'm making a fuss and she's fine. But this is such a big moment in our lives, and she is an older first-time mother and there are fewer than two months to go... It would just really be great to have you here, keeping her company and maybe helping with the shop. Would you mind? It would be so nice… I'm missing Dad to be honest and you always bring him closer to me when I see you. Now I'm sounding pathetic. Sorry. No pressure! Lots of love.'

Jen felt a huge sense of belonging in her chest. Fred's boy needed her and wanted her companionship. She was amazed that she mattered to him in this way. Perhaps she always had, but she had never known. There was a real role for her now within the family. It felt good.

Monica had rung ahead and asked Helen if she could pop in and see her.

'Monica, how nice,' Helen said as she opened the front door. 'Come through to the kitchen. Do you actually want a session? Is everything all right? You certainly look well!'

Monica smiled. 'I am! I just didn't want things to go on without me telling you to your face about it. I, uh, everything is brilliant with Stephen. And I, well, I wanted to tell you that I'm very grateful for everything but that I don't actually want to come any more.'

She glanced around her as they entered the kitchen.

'Were you worried that Sam might be here?' Helen asked.

'Not worried, exactly.' Monica sat down at the large table as she had on their first meeting and Helen sat beside her.

'I had rather anticipated this meeting, and indeed what you were going to say, and I was hoping that if you stop coming as a client, you and I might have the odd coffee together? Quite honestly, with everything that's happened, I haven't actually made friends here and sometimes I feel quite isolated.'

'Is your, is… Sam away?' Monica asked.

'Just for the day. A long day though. He's flown to Geneva to sign some papers. He's not as young as he was. He'll be awfully tired later.'

Monica nodded. She did not understand this conversation or Helen's way of life and she found herself wondering what Jen would have said in her place.

'So, Monica, everything is fine with Stephen?'

'More than fine. I just feel so right with him. I've never really believed in the idea of someone being the perfect partner for anyone. But he just seems to be it. And it's all the more lovely in a sense that we have had to wait so long. But it's not awkward at all. It's just relaxing. And then, well, you know, in bed, it's marvellous. You're a therapist. You probably think I'm being too fanciful. But I just feel he is my one true love. Perhaps you don't believe in such things?'

Helen's sudden smile was dazzling, 'Oh, Monica,' she murmured. 'I completely believe in that concept. Far, far more than you could ever imagine.'

Chapter Nineteen

1987

We've just checked-in when Jeremy turns to me and says, 'Helen, I need to sort out details about dinner and so on. Why don't you go on up?'

I look at his eager face and smile. He's excited about this weekend. It's his treat.

'OK, thanks I'll do that.' I squeeze his arm before picking up my hand baggage, taking the lift to the fourth floor and then letting myself into the suite.

Predictably, it's gorgeous. The sitting room windows are open, and the voile curtains that frame them are lifting and billowing in the breeze. The sun, which is surprisingly warm for late March, glints and shimmers on Lake Geneva below. It's truly stunning.

Dropping my bags, I explore the rest of the accommodation. The bathroom also has lakeside views. It's enormous, all gold and silver, and dominated by a huge tub which could easily accommodate two people.

Another reception room, smaller than the other, is cosy, with a lighted wood burner. And the bedroom is, without question, completely 'over-the-top' romantic! I moan aloud as my heart lurches at what might have been, and I struggle to unthink an invasion of thoughts that are not helpful. Jeremy's trying so hard to give me a happy thirty-seventh birthday. I must find delight in it and be grateful.

It's my second birthday without the man I adore. Inevitably, my mind rewinds the tape of my life till it stops at this very day two years ago when we lunched in bed, went to a tea dance in central London, laughed our way through a Tom Stoppard play and then returned to my flat – forgoing dinner – so that we could make love again.

That's how we were.

The loss of Sam punches me in the stomach, tears prick at my eyes and I wrap my arms around my torso imagining the feel of him in his wool and cashmere jacket, hugging me and pulling me close.

As we agreed, we have had no contact since his departure for Egypt eighteen months ago. But I've survived by keeping busy and throwing myself into the construction of a new life around the old one, which promised so much but ended in heartbreak.

Jeremy is Sam's closest friend. He, more than anyone, tried to persuade Sam to ignore the pressure from his homeland, and his mother, and refuse to go back and marry the bride his late father had selected twenty years before.

He was a marvellous support to me too, assuring me frequently that Sam would never leave because we were so obviously meant to be together. But he did leave – because his debt to the past overwhelmed him to the point that he had to walk away from our present and the future we dreamt of.

And on that fateful day, when my boss sent me to interview an ageing pop star at Heathrow – at the very same time, and in the very same terminal, as Sam was due to fly out – we stared at each other across the crowds that separated us, and he mouthed at me that he would love me forever. But then, despite my inner prayers and entreaties, he turned and disappeared through the departure gate and out of my life.

Jeremy, a good, kind man, has done everything he could to console me. Eventually, our relationship took the turn he told me so often that he wanted, and we became intimate.

Had there never been Sam, Jeremy would be perfect, and probably I'd view our liaison as the best of my life. But there has been Sam. And our love was all-consuming, passionate, glorious and not a little insane.

There's no doubt in my mind that he was – and will remain – irreplaceable.

People say how lucky I am to have Jeremy. Some go so far as to say that he's much more 'suitable' than Sam. I nod and agree with them. It's easier. I can't tell anyone that I feel nothing but numbness. Intellectually though, I can see that Jeremy is ideal. A surgeon, like Sam. Interesting. Attractive. Politically aware. Fun to be with. A good father to his two sons. A partner, finally, my parents can approve of. And someone who copes uncomplainingly with my career in television and its demands on us both.

Also, he never appears to resent the fact that he is second best and that, for me, there's always a third person in our bed and in my mind. But he says he loves me. I love him too, just not in the same way that I love Sam. Mind you, I suspect that what he feels for me may be quieter and less thrilling than the emotions he felt for his wife. But she had left him before we met. So, we've been comfort for each other. And of course, Sam's departure is not just a loss for me but for Jeremy too. He misses him badly, I know.

I've always suspected though that the two of them are still in touch. And I'm as sure as I can be that they agreed some sort of arrangement about me. I sometimes think I ought to be insulted about that. But I'm not. Knowing that he couldn't have me himself, I'm aware that Sam wanted me to be with someone decent who would take care of me, and Jeremy was keen to step into that role.

Over the past months, I've often been on the verge of asking Jeremy if he and Sam are in contact, and if so, what Sam feels about me being Jeremy's girlfriend, but I always bite back the words and delay my questions for another day. What good will it do to talk of Sam? To ask what Jeremy knows of his life back in Egypt? It will only aggravate a wound that remains stubbornly open and raw.

Another aspect of my life that's painful is that I long to become a mother before it's too late. Jeremy, well aware of the situation, wanted to help me achieve my aim. But, in a bid to please his wife when their marriage was in difficulty, he'd had a vasectomy. Recently, he paid to have it reversed. Being a doctor, he knew that the success rate was poor. But it was still a blow for us both when he came back from the follow-up appointment.

'No sperm in the ejaculate,' he told me. 'I hoped to be lucky. Sadly, I'm not.'

I hugged him and said it didn't matter, but of course it did.

I'd accidentally become pregnant by Sam a few months before he left, but that led to an ectopic pregnancy and, consequently I lost our child as well as one of my fallopian tubes and an ovary. So, even if Jeremy had started producing swimming sperm again, my chances of conceiving were always going to be slim.

Soon after Jeremy learned that the reversal had failed to work, he arranged this trip.

'Something to look forward to,' he said. 'A birthday in a beautiful place. You deserve it. Let's have a special weekend, away from everything, and then decide if you want to go down the donor route. We still have options. I'll look after you, Helen.'

Is it any wonder that I love this man? I honestly do. Just not enough.

I wander back to the large sitting room and throw myself onto the sofa so that I can look out on the lake. It's mesmeric.

I don't mean to cry. But I do. Then, I hear the click of the door in the hallway. Luckily, in a gold box on the table in front of me, there are tissues. I reach for one and wipe away my tears. I owe Jeremy so very much. The least I can do is to try to be celebratory and enthusiastic.

'My – Lovely – Helen.'

My eyes moisten again. Am I losing my mind? I know I'm imagining Sam's voice. I hear it in my head all the time. But it's not real. And never will be. I must control myself. Not turn around. Not betray my feelings when Jeremy is so kind.

'Darling!'

I must stop conjuring up these words that Sam would have used. Stop tormenting myself.

'Angel, girl…'

I do turn. I see him. I jump up and the room spins.

The next moment, he is steadying me. 'Dearest love, I'm sorry.' He wraps his arms around me so tightly I can scarcely breathe. 'Jeremy thought it would be good to surprise you.'

'Sam?'

'My one and only love,' he whispers.

'Are you real?' My voice cracks.

He nods, his eyes peering into mine. His expression a blend of hope and anxiety.

'I, I've longed for this moment…' I stop, breathless with shock.

His face breaks into the smile I feared I should never see again. 'My precious girl. My dear, dear one.'

Suddenly, we're in each other's arms and I feel his lips searching for mine and he kisses me, tenderly at first and then with increasing passion. I become aware of his tears mingling with mine on our wet faces. We're holding onto each other with a desperation borne of real terror that loosening our grip might somehow end the magic.

At last we pull apart and he takes my face in his hands and gently, with a butterfly touch, kisses the area all around my right eye and then my left. I want it to go on forever.

Eventually, I ask, 'What's happened? How are you here? Why are you here?'

'Before I left you, I had plans for us. Plans I hoped might work out. But I decided not to share them in case it turned out that I would fail. Even now, what I can offer may not be enough. But believe me, Helen, there has not been a moment of any day since we parted when I haven't ached and longed for you and loved you across the miles.'

'But what about Jeremy?'

'We've been in contact throughout, but the latest developments have been sudden. However, he's been as much the architect of our future as I have. He is the ultimate in good friends.'

I nod. Trying to process what's happening and what he's saying.

He gestures to a bottle of wine in a pail on the table in the corner, which I'd failed to notice before.

'Would you like a drink?'

'I would, but maybe later. Could we order coffee? It might be better, while we talk, if I keep a clear head.'

'Have you grown even more wise as well as more beautiful?' He looks boyish and relieved and happy. 'There's a coffee machine in the little sitting room, if it's the same layout as my accommodation next door. Let me make you some. I know I've hurt you, Helen; devastated you, as I have been devastated myself. But now, I want so much to do everything for you.'

I feel my expression relax and a sparkle comes into my eyes that has been missing for a while. 'Well, making a cup of coffee would be an excellent start.'

Chapter Twenty

Jen gazed at the old, stone birdbath in the overgrown garden. The main room, in the part of the property that would be hers if she made the decision to move, overlooked it. Despite a quantity of fallen rose petals littering the bowl, five blue tits were fluttering in and out of it, splashing each other, washing their feathers and pecking at the soggy vegetation which, she assumed, housed a high-protein meal of dead insects.

Ginny was with her. They were both intent on the scene outside and stood, silent and still while they watched. After a couple of minutes, the birds decided that they had cavorted sufficiently, and flew away.

Jen sighed happily. 'Wasn't that fantastic?'

'Magical!'

'Are you OK? Do you need to sit down?'

'No, I'm fine. I think coming here has taken my mind off my tiredness. Being able to have another look around the house, with you, has been great. I'd visit every day if I could but that might seriously piss off the vendors! But your visit to Norwich gave me a good excuse to ask if I could show it to you. Every time I see it, I love it more. It's perfect – especially the fact that it's near the station and yet so rural.'

Jen smiled. 'And the variety of birds is amazing. It does seem ridiculous deciding you must live somewhere because there are so many of them in the garden. But there are worse reasons for choosing a new home.'

'You do like it, then?'

'I do!' Jen laughed.

'Does that mean you'll come and live with us?'

Jen took a very deep breath before replying. 'Actually,' she said, 'I think it does.'

'That's the best news.' Ginny leant over and planted a kiss on Jen's cheek. 'I hope you didn't mind us not going to the shop today, but I'd already booked one of my regular helpers, and I so wanted you to come with me and see this place.'

'I'm really pleased I did. Have you put an offer in?'

Ginny nodded. '*And* it was accepted. Mind you, I keep thinking that someone else is going to come along and gazump us, but the estate agent says the market's very slow and as we've got a buyer for our place, who's desperate to move, we're in a good position especially as the vendors have decided to go into rental accommodation for a while and are happy to leave as soon as we want. Do you honestly think you could be happy here?'

'I do,' Jen replied. 'It feels homely but surprisingly spacious.' She gazed around the room, and then through the window at the expanse of grass and shrubs that stretched away for twenty-five yards or so. 'And the price of the property wouldn't buy a one-bedroom flat in London! Norwich is much more expensive than when I was growing up, but it's still cheap compared with the south of England. So... this would be my main reception room, then I'd have my own kitchen and a small study, and upstairs a bedroom and bathroom. That ought to be enough for one person!'

'Apparently it was built as two properties in the thirties.'

'That explains the layout then, with the two staircases. Honestly, it couldn't be better. Why are the current owners selling?'

'Their youngest child's about to go to university. So, they want to downsize. And they think they'd like to live right in the centre so they can walk to everything, but they're worried it might be noisy. That's why they plan to rent first so they can check it out.'

'Makes sense. Are there two garages? I didn't notice.'

'Yes, so you'll have one of those.'

'That's good. I might need to store loads of stuff in there that I believe I can't do without! Probably in about a year, I'll realise it can all go. Obviously though, I do want to keep lots of Fred's things.'

'Of course you do, and you should.'

Jen smiled gratefully. 'The crucial thing is that you and Matthew love it. But I do too, for all sorts of reasons, like how the garden kind of wraps itself around this part of the house; it makes me want to grow things and make it gorgeous.'

'Are you keen on gardening?'

'I never seemed to have the time before. But I feel I could get into it here. By the way, I know we're British and it's hard, but at some point, we must talk about money.'

'Sure, but let's leave it till Matt's around.'

Jen took a lingering last look at her new accommodation. 'It feels a good place to be,' she said, almost in a whisper. 'I think that Fred would approve.'

Stephen took Monica's hand. 'Thanks,' he said, to the estate agent. 'We'll let you know.'

It was only eleven o'clock, and this was the third house they had seen, or rather not seen – at least not properly. Stephen had raced around each one, shaking his head and muttering, before swiftly negotiating their exit.

Outside, in the front garden, Monica gave him a tentative smile. 'What was that about?'

He looked puzzled. 'I don't know what you mean.'

'You're like a coiled spring today. Obviously, as an architect, you know far more than me about houses, but I thought you'd enjoy this whole buying process. I was quite wrong. You seem out of sorts and jumpy and irritable, and not like you at all.'

He turned to her and holding her face, tenderly, in his hands, he kissed her, lightly, on the lips. 'I want us to have something that's absolutely perfect. And I haven't seen it yet.'

'Maybe I'm not as picky,' she laughed. 'I could live in a shed with you!'

Her attempt at humour did not alter his tense expression. 'Basically, I don't want you to have to put up with a lot of disruption, and frankly none of today's properties are anything like as good as my place.'

'Well, let me move in with you. You've extended and decorated the house beautifully. You've got loads of space, and yet it's easy walking distance to the centre of the city.'

'That wouldn't work. You'd never feel it was yours. We have to start again.'

'But why do we? I like it there. You've got friendly, interesting neighbours too. It's great.'

He shook his head. 'No, sorry.' His phone rang. 'Oh, damn,' he sighed heavily. 'I'll ignore it.'

'I think you should answer it,' she countered, firmly. 'I'm going to wander over to the park we saw on our way here and have a brisk walk. Why not come and pick me up at the gates in half an hour?'

'Monica!' He looked stricken.

'Please answer your phone. We probably both need time and space to ourselves.'

'Your place?' James suggested as Lucy appeared on the hospital steps after her appointment. He tried to take her arm, but she waved him away and managed, albeit unsteadily, to negotiate the descent to level ground on her crutches.

Going to Lucy's home had become a routine which they both enjoyed, and they often lingered there, talking and drinking coffee. But this time, during the car journey, their conversation took a different turn, and she found herself curious as to why, today, suddenly, they were baring their souls.

It started with James telling her that the books he had borrowed from her had 'got his mojo back'. She was never quite sure what that meant, but he looked happier and much more animated as he described feeling a renewed sense of confidence and libido.

He went on to confide about his current fantasy.

'I expect you know you can purchase Viagra over the counter now,' he began. Then he outlined his plan to buy some, take a hotel room in London, and book five sex-workers, spaced throughout the day. His objective was to have some sort of sexual activity with them all, though he also had hopes that a couple of them might perform on each other. As he described how he wanted to experience a variety of shapes and ethnicities, Lucy watched his mouth stretch into a euphoric smile. She was not sure that these days you could legally demand an agency supply a black person, or an Asian, or a white fat one – which were some of the types of females he was considering – but she opted not to interrupt his flow by saying so.

In her turn, though she chose not to reveal her fantasy world, she described one of her most memorable encounters when the famous painter had spent a long afternoon with her and had sent for two of his friends to 'join in the fun'. She chuckled. 'The bed was a mass of bodies, and I just surrendered myself to receiving a seemingly never-ending stream of stimuli and sensations, with every part of me being attended to by a combination of these men. God, it was out of this world,' she exclaimed, with some relish. 'Quite honestly, the most lubricious hours of my entire life.'

Inside her house, they stood in the hall, eyes bright, breathing heavily.

'Oh God, Lucy,' he said, 'are you as turned on as I am?'

She doubted that she was, but she did feel quite cheered by her memories which continued to play on in her mind. 'Do you, uh, need to go and...' she began.

'To be honest, I'd sooner have sex with you.'

'One last hurrah, perhaps,' she murmured.

'Don't, Lucy. You could have years ahead of you.'

Inwardly she dismissed his optimism but kept her thoughts to herself.

'Give me ten minutes to undress. Then, I'll be waiting for you in my bedroom. Could you make us both some coffee, and bring biscuits? I think I'll need all the help I can get!'

Stephen's face was a picture of anguish as his car drew up at the park gates.

As soon as she had taken her place beside him, they looked searchingly at each other. The last half hour had seemed an eternity to Monica and she was sure that her expression reflected her nervousness as well as her relief that he had turned up.

'Was that a row?' he asked eventually.

'I don't think so,' she replied.

'What then?'

She burst into tears and suddenly the distance between them was dissolved and they clung to each other, both apologising and insisting on taking the blame. His lips pressed against hers and they relaxed into the comfort and companionship they had come to depend upon. When, finally, they pulled apart, both of them appeared shaken. He found his voice first, 'We mustn't let this happen again; my heart won't stand it.'

She nodded. 'I agree.'

'What did I do?'

'Maybe it was both of us. We can't quite believe our luck that we've found each other after all this time. I think today, we're both rather on edge, and maybe worried that we don't deserve this happiness, and we're constantly wondering if it might go wrong.'

'That's true,' he admitted, and he studied his own hands before reaching for hers and holding them tightly.

'Perhaps,' she ventured, 'we should accept that we don't need to make it perfect.'

'But I want it to be perfect. Perfection is what you deserve.'

She pulled her hands away from his so that she could smooth away the frown lines on his brow. 'Dearest Stephen,' she said. 'Before I gave up my therapy with Helen, she said something about not making too many perfectionist demands on each other. I brushed it away at the time and said something about how perfect it all was anyway. She gave me a long look as if she wanted to say something but then changed her mind. I think I understand why now. We're lucky, Stephen. Let's enjoy it, but not try to make it more wonderful than it can possibly be. Life's too short.'

He looked out of the windscreen, and she could see his mind considering various responses. 'You're right,' he whispered.

'The properties we've seen, by the way,' she said, 'are not perfect. But whose house *is* before they move in and adjust it to what they want?'

'What it is to be so sensible, Monica,' he teased her.

Relieved that they seemed to be on safer ground, she risked saying what had been in her mind since their earlier conversation. 'Would you reconsider the idea of us living in your house? You've made it so gorgeous that I feel I could quickly feel at home there. And quite apart from anything else, we could be living together, somewhere you're happy with, very soon, rather than have months of anxiety about exchanging contracts and so on. I want us to have a normal life. I want to feel settled.'

He stroked her arm. 'Point taken. OK. It is an idea... shall we go there now?'

'Have you got time? What was your phone call about? Do you need to work?'

'This was supposed to be a day off,' he muttered ruefully. 'But unfortunately, we've got a crisis looming with one of our projects, so I'm afraid I do need to go up to London by late afternoon and sort things. However,' he looked at his watch, 'that gives us a couple of hours.'

'Plenty of time to get naked together then,' she giggled.

He grinned. 'God, you're a brazen woman!'

'I could get used to this.' James was all smiles as he reached for his glass of Barolo. 'Do you always treat your gentlemen this well?'

'Naturally!'

'Your enthusiasm is magnificent,' he said. 'I've been looking for something like this all my life.'

'That sounds a bit dramatic.' Lucy poked him in the ribs.

'Well, in a way it is. John Betjeman's supposed to have said on his deathbed that he wished he'd had more sex. I think that resonates with many men, maybe some women too. I suppose it's about feeling desired and wanted. After all – not that I've done it so far – one can pay for someone to lie down and oblige you. But what I've always wanted is a partner who loved it.'

'Well, that's certainly me!'

'It's not just that though, you have certain... skills.'

She chuckled. 'Like what?'

'Well, just to be serious for a moment, you have wonderful internal muscles. They kind of massage a chap. Very reassuring and arousing.'

'Just as well I'm in good shape somewhere,' Lucy quipped. 'Maybe the next time some health professional is going on at me about how overweight I am and how my blood test results are appalling I can say, "still, my pelvic floor muscles are a thing of beauty".' She laughed so joyously it shook the bed.

Watching, he grinned at her. 'You're a total one-off.'

'I don't know. I mean, leaving Monica out of this as she's my friend, surely you found some prowess or even a real level of keenness in some of the mistresses?'

'Not your particular talent, ever before, actually. Initially, perhaps, a couple of them seemed enthusiastic. And mostly they would say quite kind things – but I suspect it was just to make me feel good rather than genuinely felt. After a while, with all of them, life got in the way. Not unnaturally, some of them wanted me to leave Monica but I was never going to do that. She was, is, a good wife, in many ways. Others didn't really want sex, they wanted romantic evenings, and to be seen out with me. And for someone in my position, being quite high-profile in the town, that was impossible.'

'How pompous you sound, James.'

He grimaced. 'Sorry. I suppose I wanted it all. I realise I haven't always treated women well. Monica included.'

'It's never too late to reform!'

'It is with Monica. She's fed up with me and wants out as soon as possible. I don't blame her. In a way, now it's come to it, I pretty much want that myself.'

'Why not go travelling? I don't mean hitch-hiking with a back-pack. You could do a world cruise or something. I bet you'd get lots of takers along the way.'

He raised his eyebrows slightly, and she could see he was consid-ering the suggestion. But then he said, 'Meanwhile, you and I have each other. Are you up for Round Two?'

Jen opened up the shop and, following Ginny's instructions, quickly punched in the code to de-activate the burglar alarm.

She stood in the centre of the room, eyeing the rails of colourful clothes hugging the perimeter. A sense of excitement, that had been missing from her repertoire of emotions since Fred had become ill, was bubbling inside her.

It was strange that being here alone seemed so thrilling. She remembered suddenly how, when she was at school, she had been allowed on one occasion to accompany her mother to a parents' evening. Normally, pupils were banned, but she had confided in her favourite teacher about her parent's battles with alcohol and had said that the only way she could guarantee her mum would turn up, and not divert herself into the nearest pub, was for her to bring her.

'OK, Jen,' the teacher had agreed. 'We want you to stay on and do A levels and we certainly need your mother to agree to that. So, do come with her, but do me a favour and once you've got her into the building, make yourself scarce. Go to the library or something and I'll come for you when we've finished.'

It had been exhilarating to wander alone through the empty corridors in the half light of evening and then to enter the deserted library with its leathery, welcoming smell. The school was her sanctuary and to be able to enjoy it in isolation gave her an agreeable tingly feeling.

I suppose that maybe, she thought, as she stood in Ginny's shop, I'm a loner. Or a control freak. Perhaps I just like the idea of being in charge and of making decisions and running things.

Writing, after all, she mused, required a lot of unilateral decision-making. What word to put where. How many syllables to use in a sentence in order to make it read easily. How to punctuate and get the rhythm right.

Did she miss it? Sometimes. But that part of her life was so bound up with Fred's career that there was more pain than pleasure in the idea of returning to it. For the first time, she faced the reality of her situation. She had no job, and no real wish to resurrect her previous one, at least not at the moment. It was good to have clarity, but it was terrifying. It was all she knew. And yet, she could see now that she had been working around to this realisation for months. So, might this shop somehow be the catalyst for change in her new, single life?

Her mobile rang.

'Jen, are you OK? Did you get in all right?'

'All fine, Ginny. Just put your feet up and forget all about me and the business till at least lunchtime. I'm going next door to the coffee shop and then I'll come back, sort myself out, and open at ten as you suggested.'

On a whim, she removed a couple of garments from the rails and displayed them more prominently by hanging them on the picture rails that ran around the top of the walls in this quaint old shop. Pleased with the result, she found some silk scarves in a basket and draped them over the arms of the large leather chair that stood in the corner by a heavy, ornate mirror.

'I could get used to this,' she whispered into the empty space.

In the coffee shop, she was surprised to be greeted as an old friend by Maggie, the woman who owned the business.

'It's good you're helping Ginny. Have you got time to sit down and have your coffee here?'

'Definitely. Quite apart from anything else, it will ensure I don't spill it over some expensive outfit!'

'Ginny said you might be moving up here.'

'I might; in fact, I'm pretty sure I will. I grew up here, so it's like coming home.'

'I didn't know that. But it's great. I'm a widow myself. Maybe we could go to the cinema or the theatre together sometime?'

The idea of having friends, new friends, and feeling comfortable enough to accompany them to a film or show was heartening. 'That would be lovely,' she said, her voice breaking slightly.

'Terrific!' Maggie's smile was broad and genuine. 'I just hope that Ginny doesn't sell the boutique. It worries me that I might have real competition next door if she does. Her shop could easily be turned into a café, and most new businesses starting up these days are in the catering field.'

'She's not thinking of selling, is she?' Jen's voice rose in her alarm.

'I dunno. It's just a feeling I've got. Seems to me that her tiredness is more about indecision about the shop than her pregnancy.'

'Really?' Jen encouraged her.

'She said the other day that she had waited so long to be a mother and had never been sure she'd be any good at it, but that now it was finally going to happen all she wants is to be at home with the baby when he arrives. I wonder if cash is another reason.

212

I imagine they're stretching themselves a bit thin with the house in Thorpe St Andrew – even with Matthew's new job. Maybe she could do with getting her hands on whatever the business is worth.'

'We're going to talk about money when my stepson gets back tonight... Look, thanks for telling me. I need to get to the bottom of this. I had begun thinking I might work here and take the pressure off Ginny.'

'That would be great. Better still, perhaps you could be the boss.' Maggie seemed quite thrilled at the idea. 'Or, I mean, could you even buy it if she wants to sell? Sorry. That's a bit bold of me. But it could be a brilliant solution!'

'It wasn't that bad surely?' he asked.

'James, don't be ridiculous. You know very well it was fine. Better than fine. Very enjoyable in fact. And gratifyingly time consuming. We've been in bed for five hours. That hasn't happened to me in a long while! So, this is no reflection on you or your prowess. But now I want to be here on my own.'

'I wouldn't have agreed to bring you today if I'd suspected you were going to do this. Monica's going to go mad. She not only likes having you around, as I do, but she doesn't think you're anywhere near being fit enough to manage on your own.'

'James, please!' Lucy looked over her teacup at him with the sort of stern expression that had silenced a generation of students. 'I'm a pensioner. I'm a professional woman. And I'm poorly. I honestly think I should be allowed to live for however long I've got, in the way I want.'

He looked pensive. 'Will we uh, I mean, did you like this enough to want to do it with me again?'

'I did like it enough for that,' she replied slowly. 'But I don't think it's a good idea. I can't be your long-term fix. You'd tire of me—'

'I wouldn't,' he interrupted her.

'Yes, you would. You're much fitter than me. You need to take your courage in both hands and find yourself a new life and in

213

time, maybe, a new wife. Now could you please go? I need to sleep.'

That was a close thing, Monica thought as she put her mobile back in her bag. James had rung to tell her that Lucy was at her own house and insisting on staying there. He sounded quite panicked.

Then, most unusually, he had asked her how her day was going. Without thinking, she had said she was on the train back from Oxford.

He had sounded surprised, which made her realise that she had probably let him believe she was doing a shift at The Granary. So, she had launched into an elaborate explanation, which she knew was never a good idea with him, all about there having been too many volunteers today, so she had taken herself off shopping in Oxford instead.

She held her breath. James was someone who could be utterly forensic in pinning people down to what they actually meant and what they had done. Fortunately, he sounded too upset about Lucy to query her meanderings. Really, he had become surprisingly fond of her friend.

She would like to tell Jen about this latest development with Lucy, but she was reluctant to inflict this new problem on her while she was with her family in Norfolk. It would be good to discuss it though, and to talk about how she was regularly deceiving James and how badly she felt about it. She justified her lies on the grounds that the divorce was proceeding swiftly and though James had seemed very reasonable of late, she was not sure he would be so affable if he knew she had someone else. But that did not stem her guilt.

She sighed. What on earth could she do about Lucy? She could hardly turn up on her doorstep and kidnap her. Probably after a couple of days the other woman might realise that being alone was too difficult. Let's hope so, she thought as she consciously put aside her worries and chose instead to mentally re-run the earlier part of the day with Stephen.

She breathed deeply, recalling the feel of him. He was obviously thinking about her too because almost immediately, a text from him pinged into her phone.

'I love you and I want more and more and more of you.'

A delightful sense of being special to someone who was so special to her spread through her body as she read and reread it, before sending her own reply.

'It's exactly the same for me. Be safe. Be happy. Soon we'll be together.'

And we will, she thought. In the next moment she found herself thinking about both Lucy and Jen and how they had enlivened her last few months. Helen too, to some extent. Still, Oxford was only an hour away by train. She and Helen could meet regularly. But Jen's plans might well include a move back to her home county. As for Lucy, well she must do something to help her. But what? She considered dropping in on her when she got back to Crowbury, but maybe Lucy would prefer to be alone tonight. Perhaps, indeed that was what was needed in order for her to fully appreciate how difficult it would be to cope alone. She picked up her phone again. In Jen's absence, she would run the situation past Helen.

The house did seem empty now that James had stopped protesting and left. But Lucy had things to do. The big Waitrose by the river stayed open well into the evening. There was no way she could get there herself, and, almost certainly, any online shopping she might do would not be delivered till tomorrow. So, she rang Barry, her old taxi driver friend, and asked him to come and pick up a list and then shop for her. Quickly, she scribbled a note of all the food she longed for: steaks, chicken, a leg of lamb, chocolates, creamy rice pudding, a farmhouse loaf, shortbread biscuits, iced doughnuts, eggs, bacon, mushrooms, black pudding, a case of red

215

wine, a bottle of whisky and a sack of large potatoes. Then, as an afterthought, she added a couple of green vegetables and a bunch of grapes. That would do for now. She had no ready money for a tip, but she would give him her debit card and ask him to pay for her purchases with that, and also draw out £200 in cash which should last for a while.

That done, and while she waited, she reviewed her day. She had had sex. It had been pleasurable and fun but – and she had not confided this to James – the intensity of feeling was missing. Some experts, she knew, would attribute this problem to the fact that she did not find James particularly attractive. But in her colourful past, she had had some of her most thrilling liaisons with men she liked but whose bodies had been far from beautiful. The truth, she was convinced, was that the combination of her perpetual exhaustion, the amount of sugar in her bloodstream, and the unhealthy state of her arteries was having an impact on the parts of her she had always regarded as most reliable.

Not for the first time, she mourned the elements of her life that mattered to her and which had now gone – her job, travelling, her freedom… As for sex, clearly that would soon be a thing of the past too. Her orgasm today – and she had only managed to have one – had been a feeble affair compared with those of days gone by when the whole world had seemed to rock on its axis.

'What is life without the things that made me tick?' she asked out loud.

It was a bleak moment, and in the midst of it, she asked herself if she was ready to meet her maker. A tremor of anxiety indicated that she was not at all sure. But with the next breath she decided that whatever the cost, she had to have more joy, this side of the grave. And almost the only reliable source left to her was eating. So, she was going to indulge herself.

Two days previously, James had taken instructions about what she wanted in her will. Her house was to go to her former student,

216

Petrina, her ISAs to her two nephews and other savings divided between the Salvation Army and Save the Children. As for the painting that James thought would fetch a fortune at auction, they had devised a paragraph saying it was to be left to her old Cambridge college with the recommendation that they used its proceeds to set up a fund supporting state school pupils who studied there.

So, once that's drawn up properly and I've signed it, most things will be in order, she reflected. There was a certain satisfaction in that, along with a sense of relief that she could now do exactly what she wanted. And what she wanted right now, and before Barry got round to doing her shopping, was to order a large, sharing-size, deep pan pizza from her favourite Italian restaurant, and eat the lot.

The evening with James was more pleasant than any Monica could remember. He was complimentary about the meal she had made him, and about her appearance, and had raised a glass to wish her a happy life without him. Then he had explained how, though he was upset about Lucy's decision to be alone, he understood it, and that he was grateful to her for helping him realise that his own life was full of possibilities. He had, it seemed, been to his solicitor after leaving Lucy and was keen to explain that the divorce was progressing well.

'Which is just as well,' he told her, 'as I've gone mad and booked myself on a cruise – a world cruise – and it leaves in five days' time.'

'Gosh, well, good for you. I hope you enjoy it.'

'I hope so too,' he murmured, and she noticed that, briefly, a look of uncertainty expressed itself on his face. But then he seemed to re-gather his confidence and changed the subject by asking if she had thought where she might live after the divorce.

'I've been considering Oxford,' she replied, as casually as she could. Was now the time to tell him about Stephen? There was a pause. The moment came and went.

'Good idea,' he said. 'Make a fresh start. Can I leave you to sell this house? I know it's a bind, but we can really get things moving if we just split everything 50-50. Does that make sense? Even the pensions.'

'That's very generous, James,' she began.

'My solicitor said that,' he laughed. 'But I've begun to view myself in a different way over the past couple of months, and I don't much like what I've discovered. Quite apart from anything else, I did a terrible thing in Australia and I think Melissa will probably never talk to me again. And that is something...' he cleared his throat and tried again but his voice was thick with tears.

She poured him a glass of water and squeezed his arm as she passed it to him. He drank and cleared his throat again. 'Sorry, old girl.'

'James, I know what you did. Melissa told me and she was very angry, but I have to contact her myself. I've got things to tell her, and I'm going to suggest she gets in touch with you. You have, if you don't mind my saying so, become rather nicer than you were.'

'I think I have Lucy to thank for that,' he replied, and he rummaged in his pocket for a handkerchief and blew his nose noisily. 'You too, of course, because you brought her here. She's helped me see things I never wanted to face... I am very afraid that she's not going to make it. I give her six months at most, but I think her legacy will live on in lots of people, including me.'

'I'm not giving up on her, James. I saw my friend Helen, who's a therapist, at The Granary when I popped in there after coming off the train. I've asked her to come round with me to see Lucy.'

She noticed that James shook his head slightly. 'Don't be upset if that doesn't work,' he muttered, gloomily.

Monica jumped up and said briskly, 'Well we all have to make our own decisions, don't we? Where are you going to live by the way?'

He smiled and she suddenly saw in his face the young man she had married.

'I really don't know. I'm going to be away for a good three months and maybe that will give me a fresh perspective and help me decide. If you sell in the meantime, I can arrange to have someone come for all my stuff and store it – though I might not need it if I decide to end up on a beach in Thailand.'

'Is that on the cards?' She grinned at him.

'I've no idea. For the first time ever, I'm just going with the flow.'

Jen was in plenty of time for the train. It had been a momentous and enjoyable few days, but she was ready to be alone and was pleased she had managed to talk Matthew out of driving her to the station.

He insisted, though, on walking with her to the end of his road.

'Go back,' she laughed when they got to a crossroads. 'You two need some time together. Why don't you take Ginny out for some afternoon tea and have a long chat? There's lots going on. She needs you to take care of her.'

'Rubbish! She's so independent, she never needs any support from me, no matter how much I try!'

'Matthew,' she gave him a quick hug, 'trust me, she misses you when you're not here. This is all a huge thing for her. And all this tiredness and everything is, I think you'll find, tied up with the mental challenges of all the changes going on. Maggie, the coffee shop owner next to Ginny's shop, said as much, and I'm sure she's right. Perhaps now that we've discussed finances, and come to some decisions, she'll be easier in her mind. But just cosset her a little. She needs it.'

'No wonder Dad loved you so much,' he murmured, as he hugged her back.

They stood back and smiled at each other.

'We were lucky,' Jen whispered and Matthew nodded before changing the subject. 'By the way, you haven't heard from Chloe at all, have you?'

'No! And I keep meaning to ask you if you have. She was in constant touch till we met up, but that's more than a month ago, and she's gone really quiet since. I've emailed a couple of times. No reply. Weird, don't you think?'

'I do. She seemed so keen to meet us but she's completely off the radar.'

'Perhaps she's more complicated than she seemed. Or maybe she just didn't like me! Anyway, I can't worry about it.'

'No… Sure you'll be OK if I go back to Ginny?'

Jen nodded.

'You're another very independent lady! I'll see if I can get Ginny to come out for a while. If not, we might just lie down on the sofa and watch the Canaries play Arsenal!'

Jen smiled as she walked away. Fred had adored his boys. And she did too. She felt very fortunate that she was so much a part of their lives. It grounded her in a way that she had not expected.

Now that she planned to come back to Norwich regularly, she had left her overnight case with Matthew and Ginny and was able to make speedy progress as she marched along, taking in the familiar landmarks. It seemed odd that this city was going to become her home again after so long. But odd in a reassuring and comfortable kind of way.

'Do you think I'm doing the right thing, Fred?' she whispered. 'I hope I am. It feels right, but it would be good if you could somehow confirm that for me.'

Last night she had felt so sure as she and the younger couple made their plans. Having steered the conversation around to Ginny's boutique, she had learned that the business was indeed a source of worry, so Jen had suggested that she could work in the shop, or even buy it, if that might help.

'Help! Oh my God, that's more than I could possibly have dared to hope for.'

They had talked about the new house too and the couple had insisted that they did not want Jen to contribute to its purchase. They had looked into owning it jointly, they told her, but had uncovered a lot of legal difficulties. Remembering her research when she had written the article on home co-ownership, Jen was not overly surprised.

'Well, maybe that's best,' she had agreed. 'After all, I'd only be leaving my bit of the house to you when I died! Perhaps I could pay your solicitor's fees though, and the survey costs.'

The evening had become more emotional as they looked at all the options ahead of them and progressed from pots of tea to a bottle of wine for Jen and Matthew. There had been tears, but mostly there was laughter and a palpable sense of happy anticipation.

'I'm still pleased about it,' she continued her conversation with Fred. 'I am really. But I do worry that I'll get everything wrong and miss you even more once I've left Crowbury. On the other hand, our house feels so empty without you... Also, there are Lucy and Monica to consider, though there are so many changes going on with both of them, I could well end up alone. And that's what I've felt really. Alone. Especially when I'm at home. I never thought that would be the case. But it is.'

A young man with wild, curly hair, carrying three large boxes side-stepped her as she was about to walk into him.

'Sorry,' he apologised, 'I didn't quite bash into you, I don't think. Hope not. Were you talking to me?'

Jen felt herself redden as she took stock of the fact that she was in Prince of Wales Road and right outside the taverna her friend's family had owned.

'Sorry, no. I'm afraid I was mulling over things aloud. All my fault. Is this your restaurant?'

He nodded.

'I'm so glad it's still going. When I lived here as a child, I knew the people who ran it.'

'That would have been my family,' he told her. And he dropped the boxes he was carrying and opened the front door before picking up his load again and depositing it on the large counter just inside. He gestured to Jen to come in. 'We've rented it out for years, but now we're back. And ready for business!'

'Marvellous! Do you know Maria then?'

He laughed. 'Do you mean my ogre of a mother?'

'What? Maria was the sweetest little girl.'

'Can't be the same person then, my mum's a very tough lady.'

Jen giggled. 'When you're next speaking to her can you say that Jen asked to be remembered to her. I always minded such a lot that we lost touch. I suppose she's still in Paphos.'

'No, she's in Marks and Spencer!'

'She's come back here to live?'

'Yup. Her parents are dead now, and she and my dad have split up. I've been over here for a while, and she suddenly decided to join me. She always loved Norwich and I love it too. So, we're going to manage it together, so long as we don't kill each other in the process!' He guffawed.

'Dimitri, haven't you got those boxes unpacked yet?'

He winked at Jen, then reached out towards the owner of the formidable voice behind them, before pulling her into a cuddle. 'Look who's here, Mum. Your little best friend that you've been going on and on about. How great is that!'

Chapter Twenty-One

Lucy's heart jumped so violently it woke her. Freezing, breathing heavily and groggy with slumber, she attempted to focus on what she could hear. Had there been a noise in the house? In the street outside? Something must have dragged her from the depths of her dreams.

A dream. Yes, that was it. Her father had been shaking his head at her, his whole body signalling disapproval of her behaviour. He had looked like he used to when she was a teenager; in other words, much younger than she was now. She, on the other hand, had been her current age, and ill.

Then, he had spoken, his voice warbling with sadness as well as anger, 'I never approved of your way of life, and what you're doing now is a sin.'

She had tried to engage him in conversation, to put her point of view, but he had buttoned himself into his cassock, pulled his surplice over his head and determinedly turned away from her. He had a congregation waiting. People who deserved him more than she did.

Gradually, her heart quietened. She took a deep breath, then another. She had, she acknowledged, lived her life in an unorthodox way. But she had not committed murder, theft or grievous bodily harm – and she was generous to a whole range of charities.

And did it not count for anything that she had been a good professor, opening up young people's minds, encouraging them in their quest for meaningful literature, providing coffee, tea and hot chocolate in her room at the university for any student who needed a break or a listening ear? Surely, she must have accrued some 'Brownie' points for that?

Was it a sin to wilfully neglect herself? To refuse to go to hospital appointments, and to ignore the phone calls that had come from there as well as those from Monica and Jen?

James had seen her point. But he had gone on his world cruise. She missed him but knew that she had only herself to blame for that, because after their day of dalliance, she had refused all further contact.

Jen was aware of her own happy smile as she put down the phone.

Since she had returned to Crowbury, she had had daily contact with her childhood friend, Maria. They had decades to catch up on, after all. Their conversations energised and amused her – the intervening years dissolving as they spoke. How marvellous it was that they had found each other again and that they could tap into the fondness they had enjoyed as children. Even better, meeting Maria had, she believed, been Fred's confirmation to her that she should return to Norwich.

She reached forward and crossed off today's date on her wall-calendar. This daily routine had begun as soon as she had learned that Freddie had been conceived. It had been a reassuring ritual because – and she knew this was quite illogical – she had often had to battle gloomy fears that something dire would go wrong with the pregnancy. She had asked herself time and again why she was so anxious and had come to the conclusion that Fred's death had stripped away her normal layers of confidence and certainty. Life felt much more tenuous now. She was acutely aware that people who should continue to live, often died. And that individuals who had done nothing wrong might, in an instant, become the victim of a speeding driver, or a violent partner. However, with Ginny's due date in sight, she was more relaxed. Never having been a mother, she was hardly an expert, but surely Freddie was 'cooked' by now and, barring the birth itself going wrong, should survive.

So, now at last, she allowed herself to imagine his arrival and his childhood in the new home. And she gave herself permission to visualise working in the boutique, and to picture herself settling in Norwich, babysitting Freddie, going to the cinema with Maggie and having endless cups of coffee with Maria. Could it be, she wondered, that after all this sadness, and despite her certain knowledge she would always miss Fred, she might be entitled to a happy future?

It was a novel way of thinking. And with it had come a sense of urgency that she must now sell the house, which was why this morning, she was waiting for an estate agent.

She could imagine Fred's laughter at her intense activity over the past few days as she began the process of clearing out their home.

While he had lived, she had never noticed that they had five spatulas, two dozen tumblers, sixteen ill-matched linen napkins and seven teapots. It was not easy to part with any of them, but she had applied various criteria to the sifting and sorting which centred around her own needs in a smaller living space, as well as her attachment to items that her husband had used or bought. Anyway, she reflected, six charity shops have now got far more stock than they had at the beginning of the week.

But it was just a start, and there were larger choices to be made. Their Victorian dresser, for example, was too big for her new home. Perhaps someone buying this house might like to have it – that is unless they were hellbent on transforming her comfy kitchen into a shiny conglomeration of matching cupboards and gleaming chrome equipment.

Then there was their king-sized bed. She had worried it would be too large for her new bedroom but after a panicky phone call to Matthew, he had established that she did have sufficient space. That was a huge relief. 'It would have been like giving away our history, Fred,' she murmured. 'Unthinkable!'

The furniture in the spare room would have to go though. And much though it pained her, she was going to have to choose between her desk and Fred's. Hers had been part of her life since she had bought it from a second-hand shop with her first month's pay in journalism. She could still remember the delivery men huffing and puffing about its size and weight when they were trying to manoeuvre it through the front door of the scruffy flat she was renting. She had had to deal with equally infuriated removal men several times since. It had been central to her life for decades. But, she reasoned, it was just wood and nails and a worn leather top when it came down to it. She had had her money's worth and would survive. Disposing of Fred's desk on the other hand would mean jettisoning yet another part of him, and she had lost so much already.

A text disturbed her meandering thoughts. It was from Lucy asking if she was free to come to see her. Rather than message back she rang her friend's mobile.

'Lucy, I'm sorry. How are you? Monica said you didn't want any visitors. So, I've kept my distance I'm afraid.'

'You were right to do that.'

Jen caught her breath at how weak Lucy's voice sounded compared with her customary robust tone.

'Well, still…'

'I felt I needed to come to terms with things and work out a method of dealing with it all.'

'I understand that,' Jen replied quietly.

'But now I think I need advice. I, uh, I'm not sure but perhaps I'm ready to see things differently.'

'I could come this evening.'

'Might Monica be free this morning?'

'I don't know. She often goes to Oxford now.'

'Do you think I could call her?'

Jen laughed. 'Of course. Why wouldn't you?'

Lucy sounded weakly shamefaced. 'I've avoided her. And I've refused to answer the door when she called.'

'Monica won't hold that against you. She knows, we both know, that people have to,' she sighed, 'you know, deal with this kind of thing in their own way.'

'Thanks, Jen,' Lucy said, and she was gone.

Monica was having coffee at The Granary with Helen, though she planned to go to Oxford later where she would stay the night. With James away, there was no longer a need to rush home, keep up appearances and make him dinner. The day he left, a large For Sale sign had been erected outside their house. And last week, one of James's former colleagues, who clearly had coveted the property for years, had put in an offer, which she had accepted. Later, she would transport more of her clothes to Stephen's house. It was an adventure, and she was enjoying telling Helen all about it.

Their conversation turned to the subject of Lucy. For weeks now, she had tried to make contact but had been thwarted at every turn. She felt, she told Helen, powerless, as well as disappointed that her friendship had not meant more to the other woman. Helen listened in that way she had with her head slightly on one side, alert but not interrupting.

'Monica, I'm sure it's much less a reflection on your friendship than a keen desire by Lucy to deal with this drama how she wants to,' Helen said at last. 'People often look inward as they are dying. It's as if they are no longer fully in this world.'

'Did you find that with, um, your... uh...'

'With Jeremy? Yes, to some extent. Of course, motor neurone disease is very cruel. People with it can have very distressing symptoms.'

227

'Do you mind me asking, and to be truthful, I'm not quite sure how to put this, but was Jeremy actually your partner? I feel a bit confused when you mention him or Sam. Sorry, I'm making a hash of this but I, well, I suppose, I don't want to put my foot in it.'

Helen smiled broadly. 'I think what you're saying is that it's time I discussed my lifestyle with you!'

'Oh heavens. Not at all. I mean, it's your business.'

'True, but I've wanted to explain and just not found the right moment, or the appropriate courage. I'm sure you've seen me with Sam, and I imagine you know and can feel how close we are. So that probably leads you to wonder how that's possible after the recent death of another man I lived with.'

'Yes, I suppose that's it.'

'I get the feeling that Jen's also confused, and – I think – upset. She's avoided me since she first saw Sam and me together.'

Monica picked up a teaspoon from her saucer and stirred her coffee. Without looking at Helen, she replied, 'I believe that's true. But really, I don't want to intrude. Please don't tell me anything you'd prefer to keep private.'

'Our situation is unusual,' Helen began, 'and I know it would be hard for many people to understand it. That's one reason we moved here from Oxford – to be somewhere no one knew us, at a time when Jeremy was becoming desperately ill and Sam was spending more and more time in this country. They'd been close since meeting at medical school and Sam took leave of absence so he could be with Jeremy and help look after him.'

'I see. When I met Sam at your house, he told me he's only just retired. He must be a workaholic!'

Helen grinned. 'You mean because he's almost eighty? Yes, he's very driven. But we've come to the conclusion that we need to spend time doing new things. Seeing Jeremy die reminded us both that no one's here forever. So, Sam has wound down his commitments in both Egypt and Switzerland.'

'And you'll stay in Crowbury?'

'Funny you should ask that. It's something else I've been meaning to tell you. We haven't really settled here, so we're going to move again.'

'Back to Oxford? That would be nice for me – as you know, I'll be there full time once my house sale's gone though.'

'We did consider that, but actually we've decided to live in Geneva to be near our son and his family.'

Monica felt her face betray the shock she felt. 'You and Sam have a grown-up son?'

'We do. And I know I'm biased but he is the most gorgeous thing on two legs. He's a cardiac surgeon, like Sam, and now works for the foundation his dad set up. He married last year, a delightful and clever Swiss woman, and a few weeks ago they had a baby girl, so now we're grandparents.'

Monica beamed at her. 'But that's wonderful news.'

'It is!' Helen's eyes glistened with grateful tears. 'So, let me give you an abbreviated version of our rather strange life. I knew Sam before I met Jeremy. In fact, I met him when I interviewed him on my nightly television programme. We fell massively in love. It was so overwhelming it was almost insane. You asked me, not long ago, if I believed in a one true love. Well, I do, because Sam is mine. But in the autumn of 1985, when we'd only been together about a year, and after a lot of pressure from his mother, he felt compelled to return to Egypt and go through with the arranged marriage his late father had always wanted. He was deeply torn, and it was a horrendous time. Jeremy tried really hard to stop Sam taking what he saw as a ridiculously old-fashioned position. But it made no difference. He went.'

'How awful for you. But presumably you stayed in touch?'

'Not at all. We'd agreed that we'd have absolutely no contact. It was… well, frankly I thought I would die. But naturally I didn't! Eventually, I got closer to Jeremy and we became lovers. He was a very special man. If there'd never been Sam, I'd have counted myself lucky.'

'So how did things change?'

'Well, Sam's marriage was weird by western standards. His wife wanted the status of a home and husband – it was what she had been brought up to expect and do. But she'd been ill and couldn't have children and, rather luckily for me, wanted no intimacy with him. He threw himself into work, launching training projects for surgeons in the Middle East. He achieved a great deal, which I know gave him a sense of purpose. And then someone from the World Health Organization contacted him asking him to speak at a conference in Geneva. While there, he was offered a position that enabled him to replicate in other countries what he'd done in Egypt. He saw it as a solution to all his problems. Obviously, he was keen to have what was a massive career opportunity, but he could also see that if he had a reason to spend several months a year in Switzerland, he could lead a double life. His wife wasn't at all interested in joining him in Geneva but seemed to have no objection to him being there.'

'She sounds odd. Very cold…'

Helen shook her head slightly. 'I'm not sure it would be fair to say that. We're all different, aren't we? Certainly, I never understood her. I'm not sure Sam ever did either. However, culturally, our upbringings were poles apart, so perhaps there's an explanation to be found in our differing traditions.'

'I suppose so.'

'I knew nothing about Sam's changing career initially, but in March 1987, Jeremy took me to Geneva for a birthday treat, and much to my utter surprise…' Helen's eyes flooded with tears and she took a moment to compose herself. 'Sorry, it was just such an overwhelming moment; Sam was there.'

Tears streamed down Helen's cheeks as she continued, occasionally dabbing at them with a tissue. 'The three of us talked and talked and came to a decision about how we could move forward, and from that moment I became exclusively Sam's and Jeremy and I never slept together again.'

'That must have been hard for him.'

'I'm sure it was. But he had always known and believed that Sam and I should be together.'

'He sounds like a very decent man.'

'You don't know the half of it,' Helen replied as she reached into her pocket for another tissue.

'Are you OK?' Monica asked gently.

Helen nodded. 'Shall I go on?'

'Yes, it's an amazing story.'

'Well, the thing was that by the time Sam came back into my life, I'd really had enough of broadcasting. Satellite television started about then, which meant that the whole industry changed, and I found I didn't want to change with it, so I decided to train as a therapist. That gave me a fresh challenge, and also a lot more flexibility, which meant that when Sam was in Geneva, I was able to be there quite often too. Then, when he was in Egypt I worked hard back here and saw family and friends. Jeremy and I remained very close, though he had a succession of women partners and was quite happy, I think. I hope so anyway. I was still based in London, but then Jeremy took a job in Oxford, which was a mix of lecturing at the university and doing clinical work at the Radcliffe hospital. He loved it, and it worked well for him as his two sons from his failed marriage were at boarding school nearby.'

'Oh, so he'd been married?'

'Yes, but he was already divorced when Sam introduced me to him, and that was not long before Sam left for Egypt. Like Sam, Jeremy's work really defined him, but he was a good father and saw a great deal of his boys.'

'And then at some point you had your son.'

Helen's eyes lit up. 'I did. I was so, so lucky. By that time, the three of us were already spending a lot of time together and Jeremy came up with the suggestion that he buy a bigger house in Oxford and that I should live with him so he could help with the baby. We did discuss me moving to Geneva, but in the end, it made more sense for me to remain in England and for Sam to visit when he could, which he did a lot.'

'Did Sam never ask his wife for a divorce?'

'No. Well, actually, that's not quite true. He did, very much later, which was refused by the way. But he would never have broached the subject while his mother was alive. She was a terrifying lady!'

'It sounds like a different world.'

Helen nodded. 'Absolutely. But anyway, we were able to keep all this from Sam's wife in Egypt.'

'Didn't she ever wonder about him having relationships with other women while he was in Switzerland and she was back home?'

'If she did, she never said. I know it's hard to comprehend, but I'm not sure she was interested. She kept their home going, and when he was in Egypt they entertained and so on. Funny what goes on behind closed doors. He felt she was content enough. But it's always seemed to me that though they knew a lot about each other, and shared similar backgrounds, and their families were close, the two of them had little insight into what made each other tick. And that's how things went on for almost thirty years.'

'Surely you minded sharing Sam?'

Helen laid her hand on top of Monica's before speaking. 'After that eighteen months apart, which was absolute torture, I was just grateful that I still had his love and that we had each other and that he was pursuing a career that fulfilled him. Honestly, it worked for us. His wife died a few years ago, which meant that Sam could gradually look for a successor to carry on his work there and then step down. But then Jeremy became seriously ill and we put all our plans on hold.'

'What's your son's name?'

Helen smiled. 'Benedict.'

'And how did he cope with your... arrangements?'

'You could say it was all he knew and therefore quite normal for him. Certainly, he had three adults in his life who totally doted on him. At one point in his teens though he did turn against Sam and didn't speak to him for six months, but I think he just had to work it out in his own way. Thankfully, he adores his dad now. He's very like him too – and will do a great job carrying on his work. He loved Jeremy though. Massively. And he was devastated when he died. But he's close to Jeremy's sons and they all planned the funeral together. We're a weird family! But there's a lot of love. Jeremy's boys are married with children and they always say we're honorary grandparents to their kids. We've been very fortunate.'

As Helen finished her explanation, she fell silent and seemed somewhat smaller in her chair. She appeared, Monica thought, exhausted and – for the first time – she looked her age. Her own eyes pricked with the poignancy of the story she had just heard. How wonderful it was that Helen and Sam had a son – and a grandchild – and that finally the two of them could be together. She felt a warmth in her heart that she and Stephen were a great love too, and that – if the gods were with them – they might have a quarter of a century together or more. She had not had to share her man for thirty years, or anything like it. But she had, and she sometimes wondered why, denied herself all contact with him for a decade. Thank heavens she no longer had to.

The estate agent – a woman called Bryony whom she instinctively disliked – and her photographer had gone. Jen had made them proper coffee, which was the first time she had bothered since Fred's death. She poured out the remains from the tall chrome jug. It was only lukewarm. She gave it thirty seconds in the microwave and then added a heaped spoonful of sugar before sitting down at the kitchen table.

After the first sip, she nodded her enjoyment, and took another, then she said, 'So far so good, Fred. Likes our house, she does. Says it needs a bit of tidying. I laughed. She should have seen it before, shouldn't she? And she was awfully pleased we have a

233

garage. She didn't know that all the houses in the terrace have one in the alley at the back. So, it's all set, and we're going on the market for over double what we paid for it. Still, there's that last part of the mortgage to settle, the solicitor and removal fees, and of course I said I would pay Matthew's stamp duty and their legal expenses and survey. And much of the rest of the money will go to purchase the shop. I need to make that work financially, don't I? I couldn't just sit back and do nothing. For a start it would drive me mad because, you know me, I always want a challenge, but my pension isn't going to be up to much really. I need to work. We thought we were doing so well, didn't we, at one point? But the freelance years after 2008 were pretty diabolical, weren't they? Same for everyone in our business...'

Suddenly, she stopped talking, feeling stupid, almost ashamed, for speaking her thoughts aloud. Most likely, Fred could not hear her, so why was she doing it? As for her future, yes, there was a brand new life opening up before her, the baby, a change of home and a reconnection with her old, best friend, but did any of it really matter?

A wave of emptiness threatened to capsize her. Panicking, she tried to recapture all the good aspects of her existence in an attempt to escape the icy black blanket that might descend at any moment. 'Oh Fred,' she wailed. 'I can't bear it.'

Sniffing back the tears that threatened, she jumped to her feet, washed her mug, and then tried to empty the damp, spent grounds out of the coffee pot into the little composting caddy that the council provided. She made a mess of it. Only a portion of them hit the target and the rest somehow ended up on the outside of the caddy as well as on the kitchen floor.

'Buggeration!' she yelled. 'So much for being the perfect bloody hostess.' And she dropped to her knees, surveying the mess, and wishing for a miracle where Fred had not died at all, and was upstairs resting, and keen for her to pop up with a pot of tea and digestive biscuits.

'What would I give to see you again, Fred?' she whispered, knowing as she said it that she might be tempting fate, and inviting it to solve her problem by giving her some horrible terminal illness. That would serve her right, she acknowledged, and her head spun with longing and sadness and guilt.

The doorbell rang. Perhaps whoever it was would go away, but they rang again, and she forced herself to her feet, rubbed her eyes and, despite knowing that she probably looked a mess, walked to the front door and opened it.

A man carrying a For Sale board and wearing a broad grin nodded a hello. 'OK, for me to put this up, Madam?'

'Mmmn. You haven't wasted any time! Thanks. Do I need to sign anything?'

'No, you're all right.'

'Cup of tea?'

'No, I'll only be a minute. Thanks though.'

She was just about to close the front door when her neighbour emerged.

'So, you're selling?' Suzie said in an accusing tone.

'Seems best,' Jen murmured. Probably she ought to explain her plans, but it felt like too much effort. Instead, she risked asking how Hoagy was.

Suzie bridled. 'Look, I'm the one who knows about dogs. Just lay off. You've never had a pet have you? Just because he stayed over at yours one night, you're suddenly an expert. In fact, you haven't a clue. That's one reason I'm not sorry you're leaving. We're very different people and that's all there is to it.'

Jen felt as though she had been slapped. 'What? But we've always got on OK, haven't we?'

Suzie looked at her with undisguised hostility. 'Not really. You were so wrapped up in that husband of yours and he never had any time for me. He tried to talk to me about the news one day and I wasn't interested. I think he thought I was thick. He never bothered again. Even when he was ill, he couldn't seem to talk about normal stuff, he started off on something about the government. That's why I never came again.'

'Well, news was his life,' Jen explained quietly.

'He was a snob.'

Jen could feel an angry flush spreading up her face. 'He was not. He was the kindest, most decent—'

Suzie interrupted her. 'You won't convince me. And frankly you're no better. I thought you'd change after he died, but you keep yourself to yourself. This street is a nightmare now. Not like it used to be. You knew where you were then. I mean, who'd have thought that we'd get all sorts here, from all over. Used to be the same families that we grew up with. How did all that change?'

Jen took a deep breath. 'I'm sorry you feel this way, Suzie,' she said, trying to stem the outrage she was feeling. 'We shouldn't continue with this. I'm never going to agree with your views on this kind of thing. And you're never going to agree with me.'

'You're right.'

Jen turned, feeling some relief that they had reached an agreement, albeit a fragile one, and was just about to go back into her own house when Suzie's challenging voice announced, 'By the way, I sent Hoagy back to the rescue centre yesterday. He was a total pain.'

Jen stared as Suzie darted into her front door and shut it behind her with a loud bang. There was so much she wanted to ask. When had that happened? Only two days previously she had watched as Suzie had broken up a fight between the two animals. What rescue centre? Where? How would she find out?

Hoagy had been on her mind, she realised, much of every day, and she had meant to try to find a solution to what was going on. But for as long as he was next door, she had allowed the situation to drift; not ready, perhaps, to seriously contemplate dog ownership when she knew so little about animals and was planning to live with other people. She stood, rooted to the spot on her own doorstep, then she found her resolve, marched through the door and straight to her study where she switched on her PC, and waited while it chugged into life.

'This is probably mad, Fred, but I can't give up on that little dog. I've lost you – and God knows I can't bear it – but it would be too much to give up on him too.'

Google revealed just one rescue centre in the area, midway between Crowbury and Oxford. Should she ring or email? How should she approach them? Was Hoagy now forever tarnished with a 'difficult reputation'? And if he was, how could she counter that? She wished she had paid more attention to what had gone wrong with his placement before he came to Suzie. She fancied that it was something to do with bigger dogs. And that was certainly the problem next door. Mac, the Border collie, was entirely to blame. He had been aggressive towards the little newcomer from the beginning, and Suzie had failed to cope with it. I mustn't criticise her though, she decided. Not to the rescue centre. They know her. She took Mac. They probably think she's marvellous.

Suppose they wouldn't rehome Hoagy? Suppose they decided it would be kinder to have him put to sleep. Her pulse quickened with fear at the thought of such a tragedy.

But can I cope with a dog? And will Matthew and Ginny even consider having a rescue animal in the house when they're about to have a baby?

She exhaled audibly and took a deep breath to try to calm herself. There was no time to prevaricate. She would have to ask them.

Monica had been pleased to hear from Lucy, but her pleasure was tempered with anxiety as her friend sounded so breathless and weak.

She and Helen had just embarked on a second cup of coffee – after Helen's account of her history with Sam – when her phone had rung.

As she was soon to start her shift, she told Lucy that she would come round when it had ended.

Helen, who had been listening to Monica's end of the phone conversation volunteered to go with her.

'It sounds like she may be ready to see some sense about her condition,' Monica had said.

Helen had murmured: 'Don't be too upset if it turns out that she's not.'

And now they were with Lucy, who was taking an age to make them a pot of tea but resisting any attempts to help her.

Monica and Helen exchanged glances as they took in Lucy's demeanour and the mess in the kitchen.

There was plenty of food around – in the form of biscuits and cake. And when Lucy opened the fridge to extract a carton of milk, Monica could see that there were joints of meat inside, and several cheeses as well as bottles of white wine.

Always a slightly queasy person when it came to other people's attitudes to hygiene, Monica swallowed hard as she took in the pile of greasy dishes that packed the sink and spilled out onto the worktops around it. She wondered if it would be rude to simply not drink the tea when it finally arrived. To divert her thoughts, she attempted to keep up a bubbly conversation with the older woman.

'You're doing awfully well, Lucy,' she lied. 'How are you getting shopping? Of course, I know you're a dab hand at online purchasing.'

Lucy's hand shook as she poured strong tea into three mugs from a heavy looking teapot. 'I use my taxi driver. Good thing he's an honest old boy because I just give him my debit card and he pays for things, takes money for the taxi and brings me cash from the ATM... I know that's probably a bit unwise, but he's always seemed honest and what's the worst that can happen? He clears out that bank account.' She laughed but it seemed to Monica that there was little merriment in its sound.

Eventually, after Lucy had laboriously lowered herself into the chair at the end of the kitchen table, winced as she stretched out her legs, and propped up her crutches which promptly fell to the floor, she began to talk.

She apologised to Monica for everything – leaving Monica's house, refusing to see James before he left, not answering the door when anyone arrived in the hope of helping her, and generally discarding all good advice.

'I had a dream about my father,' she finished, her voice breaking slightly. 'It made me realise that I am failing to honour the gift of my life. It's set me thinking. I have no religion myself now, but I was brought up by a man who believed in God and the resurrection. For myself though, I just really want it all to stop.' She paused and with a shaking hand, picked up her drink and conveyed it to her mouth. Like a thirsty child, she drained the liquid in a series of noisy gulps before banging the empty mug back onto the kitchen table.

Helen took the opportunity to speak. 'I wonder, Lucy, if you feel you have failed your father and that has left you feeling that you don't deserve comfort or care?'

Lucy stared at her.

Monica watched, holding her breath and fearing an outburst. In the months she had known her, Lucy had always seemed amiable and a woman of reason. But now there was a palpable sense of defiance and danger about her and a feeling that her mood could switch in a milli-second.

Much to her relief, Lucy answered quietly, 'You could be right, but I think I'm a bit long in the tooth for therapy.'

'Fair enough,' Helen responded. 'So, what could we do to help you?'

'I wonder if I should see someone at the hospital. They've probably washed their hands of me, but I can't manage to care for myself properly and two of my toes are now black and, well, they don't smell very good.'

Monica blinked once or twice in a forlorn attempt to rid herself of the unpleasant images that were forcing themselves into her mind.

239

Then she said, 'Well, we know that there's a daily diabetic clinic. I would offer to take you there tomorrow, but I'll be in Oxford.'

'Oh, I wouldn't ask...' Lucy began and then she stopped because she knew she had invited Monica here with the express intention of persuading her to sort things out in this way, and even in her weakened state, she could hear that she did not sound convincing.

'We could go when I'm back towards the end of the week,' Monica added.

Helen shook her head. 'I think we should go before that. I know a lot of people at the hospital because of counselling spouses of patients with MND. Let me sort an appointment for tomorrow and if I promise not to try any therapy on you, perhaps you'd allow me to take you.'

Lucy nodded, mumbling a somewhat indistinct phrase of thanks. Having achieved her objective, she seemed to run out of such energy as she had, so the other two offered to help her upstairs to her bed.

'No.' She managed a firmer tone. 'I'll get myself up there when you've gone.'

'We'll leave now,' Monica said quickly. 'You're obviously really tired. And I must catch my Oxford train. But will you go the hospital with Helen tomorrow?'

Lucy nodded.

'Let's be there when it opens then,' Helen suggested. 'I doubt they'll turn you away and I'll phone a couple of people to say we're coming.'

'Thank you,' Lucy said, then she fell silent.

The other two women stood up awkwardly. Monica wondered whether to try to kiss or hug Lucy but decided against it, so she settled for nodding a farewell and offering gratitude for the tea that she and Helen had not drunk.

Outside, she took a very deep breath. 'Oh dear, I'm normally quite good with illness. But that was so... squalid. And there's a horrible smell in the house.'

Helen gave her a quick squeeze. 'I know. We're witnessing what it is for someone to give up on life. I expect Lucy would just like to go to sleep and never wake up again – and frankly, that might be the kindest thing.'

Chapter Twenty-Two

Just as well my mother is too demented to understand or care what I'm up to, Monica thought as she awoke from her post-coital nap. She'd be appalled if she knew about all the lovemaking we enjoy, especially in the daytime, or early evening *before* dinner!

Still, she smiled dreamily, as she gazed at the fourth finger of her left hand which was now sporting a white gold ring set with two diamonds and a sapphire, although she'd be furious that I've split from James, she would be pleased to know I'm going to marry again – and a professional man at that. What she would never have understood however, is that I'd walk over hot coals for him, and would have 'lived in sin', if that's what he'd wanted, joyously and forever.

She crossed her arms over her chest and hugged herself while she contemplated her new status. How wonderful life was. How amazing it was that she and Stephen had found each other and could be together. She gently patted the left side of her chest where her heart throbbed with happiness.

He had opened the front door to her, a glass of Champagne in his hand which he had transferred to hers as he leant down to kiss her. Then he had led her into his sitting room and produced a little box. She was accustomed now to his generosity, though she felt she would never, and must never, take it for granted. But this gift had been a complete surprise. A marvellous one though; no wonder we ended up in bed, she thought as she looked across at the now empty pillow beside her.

He was downstairs, preparing dinner. 'Lucky, lucky, lucky, Monica,' she whispered.

It had been a strange day. She had been inspired by Helen's story but then very cast down by the visit to Lucy. Now, in complete contrast, she was almost manic with joy. Was it fitting to be so contentedly in love when a friend was nearing the end of life? A chill caught in her throat as it occurred to her that all the pleasure she had with Stephen must in time lead to the ultimate pain for one of them, when they were parted by death. She could not recall having had such thoughts about James. It must be the price one had to pay for genuine and overwhelming love.

'Hello, sleepy head,' Stephen welcomed her as she appeared in the kitchen having had a quick shower and thrown on some casual clothes.

He had made a prawn stir-fry, with broccoli and red peppers and leeks, and flavoured it with his favourite balsamic vinegar. There was only an eight-year age-difference between him and James, but it seemed like a generation. James liked formal food. Always had. Stephen was much more relaxed. Of course, he had lived alone for more than ten years and, Monica imagined, might well have had periods when he ate rather a lot of takeaways or pub meals. He was quite health conscious these days though and she enjoyed the routine they had slipped into which was a mix of his cooking, her cooking and a meal out a couple of times a week. There was a Thai restaurant near his house which had become a favourite haunt. And they also favoured a Sardinian trattoria, which was family-run with home-cooking guaranteed.

She fancied that it was not just because she was in love that she felt fitter and sprightlier. The change of diet with Stephen, plus the fact that she had stopped cooking calorie-rich dinners for James, meant that she had lost weight, and she felt it suited her.

There had been other alterations, not least in her choice of outfits. James had set great store by being the most important solicitor in Crowbury, at least as he saw it, and liked her to look appropriately dignified. He would not have approved of what she was wearing this evening, she reflected, as she glanced down at her blue and pink cotton top, navy Boden trousers and floral Fitflop trainers. She had let her hair grow too. Melissa would be pleased, having more than once referred to her usual hairstyle as a 'helmet head'.

Suddenly, she realised that Stephen was studying her with a gentle smile.

'What are you thinking?' he asked.

'I'm thinking I'm a changed woman – and I like it!'

His dancing eyes were full of fun as they met hers. They held each other's gaze for a moment. Then, he said, 'I was wondering whether before we give up for the night, we could tell a few people about our engagement?'

'Yes,' she grinned. 'Why not? Mind you, I was never going to let you out of my sight anyway, so you didn't actually have to place a ring on my finger!'

'I never wanted to do anything more. I love you and, well, this is rather old-fashioned, but I want you to take my surname and be mine.'

'Delighted, kind sir,' she responded in a mock west-country accent. Then she stood up so she could curtsey.

'You're mad,' he giggled.

'Who will you phone?' she asked, slipping back into her chair.

He named his two adult children – neither of whom she had met. 'And what about you?'

She looked at her watch. 'It's late. I don't think I'd better call Jen. But I'll text and suggest we meet at the end of the week when I'm back in Crowbury, then I can tell her face to face. I'll call Melissa though... actually, could you take a picture of us together and I'll WhatsApp it to her? When I told her about you, she asked me to send her one, but as I never have, she's no idea what you look like. Also, she doesn't know how I've changed. She'll be pleased about the engagement, but what she's really going to be thrilled about is my hair!'

The phone was ringing as Jen let herself into the house. She heard the answerphone click into action, followed by the sound of Matthew's voice. Interrupting him mid-sentence, she picked up the handset.

'Hello, lovely boy.'

'Jen! Sorry not to call back till now but I've been in London all day. Only just home.'

'No problem. I've been doing my volunteering and I was on the late shift which I don't often do.'

'So, what did you want to ask? Your voicemail sounded very mysterious!'

'Sorry! Yes, look, you may hate this idea, so I need you to be totally honest with me if that's the case.'

'I'm fascinated now. Dad always said you had to have a project on the go. Is it something you think we won't approve of?'

Jen giggled nervously. 'Well, I don't want to run a brothel in your house if that's what you're worried about!'

She had to move the receiver further from her ear as Matthew's loud and genuine laugh rang out.

'I don't know whether to be relieved or disappointed!'

She took a deep breath. 'Actually, I was wondering what you'd say to the idea of us having a dog.'

There was a long pause. She winced as she realised that not only had she put him in a difficult position, but that he hated the notion.

'I can't believe you've just said that,' he responded, eventually.

'Sorry. Just forget it. It's mad. Sorry.'

'No, no, Jen... stop! It's the best possible suggestion. What I was going to say was that only last night, Ginny and I were talking about the future and about the fact that, probably, Freddie is going to be our only child. He's a total surprise as it is. You don't know this, but for years we kept trying for a baby and it never happened. We never told you as, to be honest, we decided not to go down the treatment route because we thought we might not get enough help on the NHS – and we didn't want to put you and Dad in the position of feeling you must subsidise us if we had to go private.'

'But we'd have been happy to help.'

'I'm sure. But it could have been thousands of pounds. Anyway, gradually, we just kind of gave up. So, the pregnancy was a shock, but a great one. But what Ginny was saying was that she'd been an only child, as you know, and she thought she'd turned out much less selfish than she might otherwise have been because they always had a dog in the house. And she told me she'd been wondering how you'd feel if we got one.'

'Really? How synchronistic is that?' Jen laughed. 'Right, if you're sitting down, I'll tell you the story of Hoagy, the sweetest white miniature schnauzer you ever did see!'

Lucy had struggled to be ready in time for Helen. It would have been so easy not to go and instead crawl back to bed and ignore the front doorbell when it rang. However, it had been her decision to call her friends for help and, she reasoned, it would be ungrateful and irrational now to discard their advice. What a hideous effort it was though. And what a waste of time.

Glancing at herself in the hall mirror as she edged past it on her way to the front door, she saw an image of a very sick, elderly person whose spirit had left her. And that's me, she thought as she registered the concerned look in Helen's eyes before the other woman assembled her professional, caring face and somehow manoeuvred them both down the steps and into the car.

She felt too tired to talk on the journey and was grateful that Helen did not attempt to cajole her into believing that the situation might not be as bad as it seemed. It was that bad. She knew it, and it was clear that Helen knew it too.

The nurse was not one she had encountered before, but she could see in the younger woman's expression, an amalgam of compassion and unease bordering on disgust, as she re-dressed Lucy's toes for the first time in over three weeks. Neither of them mentioned the smell. But they both wrinkled their noses against it.

'Are you still taking the ciprofloxacin?' the nurse asked.

'Of course,' Lucy replied, hoping she sounded convincing. There had been so many drugs prescribed for her that she was unsure how often to take them all, and indeed what many of them were for.

'You ought to be admitted, really,' the nurse murmured as she finished.

Lucy forced a smile. 'I doubt if there's any capacity. And anyway, I've had my chance. I feel any more days as an in-patient would simply be taking a bed from someone who might actually benefit. I know the score.'

The nurse turned away as she said, 'Will you at least come in and get these dressings done more regularly? It doesn't have to get as bad as this. With some care—'

Lucy quickly interrupted. 'Yes, OK.'

Helen was waiting outside the consulting room with the wheel-chair she had commandeered on their arrival. Not so long ago, Lucy remembered, she had managed to walk the long corridor to the exit knowing that James would be outside waiting. That would be impossible now.

'How was it?' Helen asked gently.

'You know,' Lucy replied gruffly.

And Helen nodded as though she did.

For the second night running, Jen had stayed late at The Granary. But this time, it was so that she could view the 'touch of nostalgia' offering, *Some Like It Hot*.

247

It had been Fred's favourite film, so she had sat right at the back with a free seat on her right-hand side and pretended that he was sitting in it. Every now and again she had leant over and laid a hand on the seat and imagined that Fred was holding it. I could never tell anyone about this, she thought; they would think I'd totally lost the plot. However, it was comforting, and she continued to do it till the end credits rolled.

It was gone eleven by the time she opened her front door and switched on the hall light. 'I'm such a dirty old stop-out, aren't I, Fred?' she called out into the emptiness.

Shrugging off her coat, she put a mug of milk in the microwave to warm up and pottered through to Fred's study. The answerphone was flashing. She knew it would be Matthew.

'Hi, Jen. I'm leaving this message at nine. Don't call me back because Ginny's really tired and we're off to bed. But lots to tell you. Oh, just while I think of it, I've had another go at contacting Chloe, but her mobile doesn't seem to be working and there's an out of office reply when you send an email. So odd… Anyway, next thing: suddenly, there's progress with the house. Both our buyer and seller have agreed they can exchange and complete on the same day, and they've asked for next Monday. Of course, we're pleased but we weren't expecting it to be that soon. I just hope Freddie won't come early now! Also, I've been in touch with a woman at that rescue centre. They do have Hoagy. They seemed worried about rehoming him. But when I said I live in Norwich, they got more interested – something to do with Crowbury having not suited him twice over – and also they like the idea that Ginny's so experienced with dogs. I had to say how I knew about him, and I told them you lived near his last placement. I kept it simple. I didn't say you were a neighbour or anything. They seemed OK with it. So, as long as our references tick the right boxes, we can have him. Now, I'm going to have to go to London next Wednesday, which is not ideal so soon after the move and I hate having to leave Ginny to cope. But, since I have to be there, maybe we can get Hoagy that day. What do you say? I can't take the car because parking where our offices are is impossible, so I thought I'd travel down by train and then in the afternoon after my meeting, I'll take another train out to Oxford. Could you meet me there in your car, and we could go to the rescue centre, which is in the middle of nowhere, and then we could go on to Norwich? I hope you won't mind doing all that driving. And then could you stay for a few days? To help us settle in, and also get Hoagy used to being with us? I hope you're pleased. Everything seems to be happening at once. It's bloody mad! Lots of love. Good night.'

Trying to ignore the tentacles of panic that were squeezing the breath out of her chest, Jen wandered back to the kitchen and retrieved the hot milk from the microwave, before sitting down at the table.

She felt lightheaded. Of course she was thrilled about Hoagy, but until now she had not really thought about where they would live if they were allowed to have him. Naturally, it made sense for it to be Norwich. Her neighbour Suzie would hate it if he were here. But she was not able to move yet; no one had even viewed the house so it might take months. Still, she supposed she could get a man and a van to move some furniture to Matt and Ginny's so she would have a desk and a bed. And the idea of being in the new place with Fred's son and his wife, plus the little dog she loved so much, was very appealing. And it would be exciting to help unpack boxes and get the place straight. But there was so much to arrange... If only she could avoid the driving. It wasn't Matthew's fault. He had no idea why that would cause her anxiety. She sighed and sipped at her milk. I should have sorted this out ages ago. What was I going to do? Move to Norfolk and leave our car here in the garage? Of course not.

'You're a bloody idiot, Jen,' she cried angrily. Then despite the million and one thoughts that were racing around her brain, and the almost certain knowledge that she would never sleep, she switched out the kitchen light and headed for bed.

*

Lucy sat in front of her enormous fried breakfast. Cooking it had worn her out, and though she kept telling herself it was 'splendid', for the first time ever she was having difficulty in finishing it.

It was not yet light, so an endless day yawned open in front of her because, apart from eating, reading and sleeping, she had nothing to do.

Helen had turned up at her front door the previous day, or was it the day before that, trying to persuade her to go to the clinic again.

'I don't need new dressings that often. I can't take up all their time,' she had protested.

Helen had hovered on the front path, but in the end had not challenged her. However, she had gone on to say, 'Lucy, I've been thinking that if you've got as little time as you seem to think you have, perhaps you might want to see some of your family. Monica said you had a brother.'

Lucy had nodded but said nothing more and Helen had turned and walked away.

She had been thinking about her family most of the night, which was undoubtedly why she was awake so early.

'Damn it,' she said aloud as she swallowed the last mouthful of fried bread.

For weeks, she had pushed all thoughts of her brother out of her mind. In fact, the last time she had focused on him had been when James asked her about bequests while drafting her will. That reminded her, she must ring his firm today. It worried her that she had heard nothing from them since James's departure. She must check that he had made a note about her ISAs going to her nephews. Also, had she signed it? Probably, but those details seemed vague. And was there a copy where people would find it easily? Maybe she should write a big note and paste it on her filing cabinets in her study saying who the solicitor was. The other anxiety was that she had not as yet received a bill. Did that mean the will was not complete or legal, or that James had done the work as a favour? She hoped he had not – because that would make her feel even more guilty about refusing to see him to say goodbye before his departure.

As for Thomas, her brother who had never answered to the name of Tom, there seemed little point in contacting him now. Long ago, she had decided that her chaps, plus other friends, were all the 'family' she needed.

'Damn it,' she said again. She should do the decent thing and phone Thomas, but what was she to say? Could she write a note instead? That might be easier.

With some sort of decision made she decided she would have a milky coffee and a piece of shortbread, just to keep her strength up. For one thing, she was trying to read Ian McEwan's *Machines Like Me*. It was very interesting, but hard to follow. She wanted to believe that the way her mind seemed to hurt when she attempted to assimilate the plot was due to the author's lack of clarity. But suppose it was she who was unclear? If her brain really was deteriorating, after her relishing – and relying upon – her intellect for as long as she could remember, then there would be nothing left to live for. Not even food could compensate.

Restless now, she decided to abandon the novel for a while and ring the solicitor.

'Yes, Miss Brown,' said the young woman. 'What can I do for you?'

'Your former senior partner wrote a will for me. He was very kind to do it, but we are friends. I just need to know if it is complete and legal and...'

She heard a sigh and felt herself bridle. Young people were so rude these days, she thought. 'How dare you sound so bored with me,' she snapped. 'I've a good mind to take my custom elsewhere.'

251

'Miss Brown, Miss Brown... sorry, are you still there?'

'Of course I am. What's the matter with you?'

'Miss Brown. Sorry. It's just, well, do you remember we had this conversation a few days ago?'

'No! What conversation?'

'About your will. It's all legal. We've got a hard copy in our files and it's also in our system. As for the bill, two weeks ago, you asked us to send it to you, though Mr Charlton had said it was not necessary. You received it, and wrote a cheque and then your taxi driver friend brought it in. I rang when it had cleared and thanked you. Do you remember that?'

Lucy's heartbeat seemed to be tap-dancing in her ears. She pressed the red icon on the phone to terminate the call and threw the handset onto the kitchen table. The world was going mad. Were people deliberately lying to her? And if so, why?

She grabbed at her metal crutches and slowly edged her way through to the hall and round to her study. A tall grey filing cabinet faced her. She propped herself up on one crutch so she could open the top drawer.

Inside was a large piece of white card. In big black felt-tip writing that did not look like hers, it read: WILL AT SOLICITOR and below the text, someone had stapled an old business card of James's to it, with the address and phone number of the solicitor's.

Her head felt as if it were full of mist as she collapsed into a nearby chair and tried to fathom her next move.

Monica hugged Jen on her doorstep then pulled back and nodded at the For Sale board.

'It's funny to think that till recently, neither of us had a clue we'd ever leave Crowbury.'

'I know. So many changes. Who knew that that would happen in mid-life?'

'Not me, but there are some amazingly good changes in mine. Including...' Monica held out her left hand.

252

'Oh, my goodness! Well, to be honest, hardly a surprise the way you two are, but very, very good news.' Jen hugged her friend to her, then shivered. 'What on earth are we doing out here on the doorstep? It's quite autumnal, isn't it? Come and have coffee. Unless you'd like to celebrate with something stronger?'

The two women wandered through to the kitchen chatting as they went.

Jen poured hot water onto the ground coffee in the cafetière and then left it to stand while they discussed the engagement and who knew about it so far.

'I've got to meet Stephen's daughter next week. I'm dreading it. Suppose she doesn't like me?'

Jen laughed. 'Don't be ridiculous! She'll love you. I bet she's been worried about her dad being on his own for so long.'

Monica sat down at the table. 'I hope you're right. Stephen rang her and said she was delighted. He might have over-exaggerated though. On the other hand, he didn't pull his punches about his son.'

Jen turned, with a querying look on her face. 'The son? Sorry, I'd forgotten he had one.'

'Yes, he's something in the City and he lives in Richmond or somewhere posh like that. He and Stephen aren't close. Apparently, he adores his mother and thinks she did the right thing when she walked out on his dad. The man she left for is very wealthy and it seems the son likes that.'

'Why should he care one way or the other about you then? After all, Stephen's wife was clearly the guilty party.'

'No idea.'

Jen brought two full mugs to the table and sat down with her friend.

'Does Stephen mind that he and his son don't really get on?'

'He says he doesn't but I'm sure he does... what were your stepsons like when you met Fred?'

'Well, their mother had died, and of course they were much younger, and away at school. I'm sure I was hopeless with them

253

initially. But I kept out of their way quite a lot so they could do masses of stuff in the holidays with their dad. And then I suppose I gradually got to know them and their friends. It took a while, but it wasn't awful. It might not have been so easy if they'd been around more. But of course, Fred was editor of the paper at the time, and often worked well into the night. He couldn't have managed if they'd been at day schools, but they'd been boarding for two years before his wife died... Sorry about Stephen's son though.'

Monica shrugged her shoulders but still wore a worried expression. 'Enough of him. I rang my daughter and told her. She's really pleased. I think she'd assumed I'd be alone forever, which, come to think of it, isn't very flattering! She wanted lots of details and said she'd like to come over for the wedding. Also, she and her dad are in contact again. Apparently, he's in Honolulu, and will be in Australia in a few weeks and she's agreed to meet him, so that's good.'

They carried on talking till they had exhausted the pot of coffee.

'Are you sure you won't have a proper drink?' Jen asked.

'Stephen and I've been doing rather too much celebrating! I'm going to give my liver a rest for a day or two.'

Jen giggled. 'So, you're obviously going to spend more time in Oxford now?'

'I am. In fact, I've contacted The Granary and told them I can't do any more shifts unless they're desperate.'

Jen nodded solemnly as she registered how this really was the end of a significant chapter in their lives. She too needed to speak to Liz Pemberton about future plans. Perhaps she should do it today.

'Are you OK?' Monica asked, softly.

'Sorry, yes. Just thinking. What brings you back to Crowbury today, then? How's your house sale going?'

'It'll be all right in the end, but you know how you have to answer all these questionnaires nowadays, I'm afraid I don't know a lot of the answers about boundaries and so on. It sounds hopelessly "old-school female" to say that I left all that to my husband. But he was a lawyer for God's sake, so I did.'

'Understandable.'

'Mmmn. The other thing is I need to check with Helen what the state of play is with Lucy. They went together to the hospital earlier in the week, but I don't think they've been again. By the way, you know how you turned against Helen because of her new man?'

Jen exhaled loudly. 'I know that I got into a ridiculous tizz about it. Now, I'm not sure why.'

'Well, you were hurting a lot. Still are, I'm sure. But the other day, she told me the whole story, and it's not what we thought at all.'

'Sounds intriguing! Shall I make more coffee and you can tell me everything?'

Monica nodded and began the saga. When she had finished, some fifteen minutes later, Jen's face was wet with tears. She reached for a piece of kitchen towel and wiped her face. 'I think that's extraordinarily romantic. How marvellous. No wonder they're so wrapped up in each other.'

'I know. Her one true love.'

Jen nodded as more tears flooded her eyes. 'I owe her an apology. I must see her. Also, to be honest, I'd like to talk to her about something that's kept me awake most of the night – though I don't see any reason why she should help me given how awful I've been.'

Barry, her taxi man, was standing over her. Lucy had no idea why she was lying on the carpet but probably she would remember in a moment.

'Did you fall?' He bent down and helped her to sit up, and then supported her while gradually, and very unsteadily, she got to her feet.

She found she was trembling. Why was she in her study? Hadn't she just decided she needed coffee and a couple of biscuits? Maybe medication would help.

'I don't quite know what happened. I expect I will in a moment,' she said slowly.

He helped her back into the kitchen and she opened the drawer where all her pills in their respective boxes were kept. She took one of everything, and then – just in case – took an extra one of the diabetic medicine. And maybe, she thought, if she'd fallen asleep without meaning to, or had blacked out, it would be sensible to take another pill for hypertension, so she did that too.

Barry made her a cup of coffee with hot milk and sugar.

'Just as well I have a key,' he remarked at one point.

She nodded. 'Have you been to the supermarket yet?'

'No, you asked me to come here for a list.'

'Yes, of course. But I'm not sure I've written it yet.'

He walked over to the noticeboard at the end of the kitchen and unpinned a scrap of paper.

'Is this it?'

She felt more than slightly cross. Did he think she was senile? Still, she had no wish to fall out with him, so she said nothing at first, then muttered, 'I think it's an old one actually, but it will do.'

'Could I have your debit card?'

'Ah! Don't you have it?'

'No, you took it back last time.'

'Do I owe you money?'

'No. I told you I took my fare and the shopping amount the other day. Shall I do the same today?'

'Good idea. Not sure quite where I put the card.'

'You put it at the back of your wallet. You said it would be safe there. Shall I look?'

'Can you?'

He left, eventually. Everything seemed to be taking so long. Also, she was hungry now. Well, she would be. It was two o'clock. Where had the morning gone?

*

256

Jen walked into The Granary, almost hidden behind a floral arrangement of autumn flowers. She noticed that Helen was watching out for her and jumped up in readiness to greet her.

That is a very decent woman, she thought as she walked towards her. Thrusting the peace offering at Helen, she said, 'This is enormously kind of you. I can only apologise. I've been so, so dreadful. I've been blushing all my way here as I've gone over it in my mind. Is my face still red?'

The older woman took the bouquet and leant over to kiss Jen's cheek before answering, 'Not at all. In fact, despite a slightly worried expression you look a lot more peaceful and recovered than that day all those months ago when we discussed whether hedgehogs had spines or quills!'

Jen felt herself blush again. 'Oh, dear God. I was behaving very, very badly that day. I had rows wherever I went.'

Helen sat down again and gestured to the chair beside her which Jen took.

'You were awfully distressed, and hurt and sad,' Helen responded quietly. 'And it didn't help that I had been, hopefully, of some use to you in the beginning, but that you then came to feel that my relationship with Jeremy could not have been as powerful as yours with Fred if I was ready for a new relationship so soon after his death. It was unsettling for you.'

Jen stared at the floor. 'Well, I know now that your situation's completely different from the one I'd imagined.'

'No one could blame you for not guessing! Our romantic history is slightly bizarre.'

Jen peered at her for a moment. 'Well, yes, it is. But it's also marvellous. I keep crying about it because it's such a triumph of true love.'

Helen passed her a tissue before saying, quietly, 'Thank you, for understanding the magnitude of it. I hope that doesn't sound overly dramatic or exaggerated.'

Jen shook her head, and then blew her nose. 'No, it really

doesn't. It's wonderful.' She reached in her own bag for another tissue and mopped her eyes. 'What a state I'm in,' she muttered.

Helen reached over and patted her hand. 'Would you like a glass of wine? I think you could do with it, and we can go and talk upstairs. I cleared it with Liz. The admin staff have all left by this time of day.'

In the tiny office, where their knees almost touched, reminding Jen of their first counselling session, Helen prompted her by saying, 'Monica said you'd got something on your mind. And that you couldn't sleep. Do you want to tell me? You can get as emotional as you like up here!'

Jen sipped from her glass. 'I do feel emotional about it because it involves Fred and me... I've tried so hard not to think about it since he died, but now something's happened that has forced the issue.' She cleared her throat and then began to tell Helen about Matthew's phone message and about how he and his wife were being so kind and were even going to offer a home to Hoagy as well as to her.

'It's clear that they really love you and want you to be happy with them,' Helen said.

'I know. I'm so fortunate. And all I'm required to do, next week, is to drive to Oxford to meet Matthew and then drive to the rescue centre, then on to Norwich. But that's actually,' she sighed heavily, 'a very big ask.'

'So, is it the driving that's the problem, and has it brought back a bad memory?'

Jen nodded, then sniffed as tears began rolling down both cheeks. 'I haven't driven since Fred died, well, actually since a few weeks before that. I was never a great driver and mostly he drove, but of course, he'd had to give up because he'd lost all his coordination. But sometimes during the illness, he'd get quite vehement about something he could no longer do. It was frustrating for him, I'm sure. Anyway, we were in a supermarket underground car park, prior to shopping, and I was looking for a space and he pointed to a tiny one between two pillars. But it was an area designed for a motor bike or scooter and wasn't wide enough. I tried to drive on, but he got cross, which was totally unlike him. Then he insisted I reverse into it. I was panicking, but he was determined I should do it because it was near the lift and he wouldn't have to walk far. So, I tried, but I scraped the side of the car. It didn't really matter, and it didn't damage the pillar, so I didn't have to go and confess to an attendant or anything, but I was ridiculously upset. And then he became tearful because he realised, I suppose, that his spatial awareness was all over the place. I should have just kept quiet and driven him home and discussed it quietly over a cup of tea, but I shouted at him that he was never to make me do anything I didn't want to again, and that I had to make the decisions now, and it was hard enough without him interfering.'

Jen leaned right back in her chair and began to sob noisily. Giving up all attempts to staunch her tears, she cried and cried.

Eventually, she stopped and tried to speak, but the stream of words that she uttered made little sense.

Helen interrupted her, 'And was that the only time you ever lost control with Fred in all the months of his illness, when you were doing more and more and more for him?'

'Yes,' she whispered.

'Do you think he blamed you?'

Jen took a very deep breath and raised her shoulders to her ears and then let them drop. 'I really hope not,' she croaked.

'After that, did he carry on telling you how grateful he was to you?'

She nodded.

'Did he tell his carers and the nurses who came in that you were a nightmare? Or did he constantly say what a marvel you were?'

'He never said I was a nightmare.'

'And did he praise you to your face and to other people?'

'All the time.'

259

'Would he want you to carry that horrible car park incident in your mind for the rest of your life and allow it to weigh you down?'

Fresh tears sprang into Jen's eyes as she shook her head slowly.

'I think we need some tea,' Helen suggested.

Jen peered at her mistily. 'Thank you,' she replied, and then she closed her scalding eyes on her painful memories.

Ten minutes later, Helen gently shook her awake and handed her a mug. 'This is so tough for you. No wonder you haven't wanted to drive. But I think you'll be able to tackle that now. And I hope that you can also come to see that what happened that day was not typical in any sense of how you behaved normally in your love and care for Fred. It just got too much. We all have a breaking point. But you're a brave person.'

'I don't feel brave,' Jen admitted.

'I know, but you are. And I suggest that when you get home, you go to your garage, and see if the car will start. If it will, just go for a five-minute drive, and then take it back.'

'And that's exactly what I did,' Jen told Monica on the phone later as she recounted everything that had happened with Helen. 'The scrape down the side doesn't look as bad as I remember, and, well, the car's ten years old, so I don't think it's worth worrying about. Miraculously, it even started first time and I took it to Sainsbury's and parked it, and then I drove home.'

'Well done. And did you enjoy that?'

A phrase came into her mind that Fred had tended to use when he was less than keen on something. It had always made her giggle. 'Modified rapture, I think,' she replied, and she grinned as she heard Monica's laughter.

Chapter Twenty-Three

'You're going to be fine,' Stephen whispered in Monica's ear as they walked towards the table in John Lewis where his daughter was waiting.

Emily turned towards them, then threw herself into her father's enveloping hug. Suddenly, Monica found herself looking into the younger woman's smiling face. She seemed familiar. Those blue – almost violet – eyes, that prettily tumbling, black, shoulder-length hair, that porcelain skin.

'Well, this is wonderful,' Stephen said, 'to get the two of you together.'

Monica held out her hand shyly, but Emily leaned over and kissed her warmly on both cheeks.

'So lovely to meet you, Emily,' Monica said. 'And I almost feel I know you, because, in a strange way, you remind me so much of someone.'

'Ooh,' Emily looked intrigued. 'Well, I hope it's a nice memory.'

'What are we having, girls?' Stephen's face settled into a fond smile as he looked from one of them to the other.

Monica suggested tea and Emily nodded before taking her seat again. She sat beside the younger woman. 'I've been quite nervous about this meeting,' she admitted.

'Me too,' Emily agreed. 'I was so worried you might not be right for my dad. But you very obviously are. He's been so happy since you got together. Well, I already knew that of course. But having just seen how he looks at you, well, that's magic!'

Monica swallowed the lump that had risen in her throat. 'So nice of you,' she murmured.

'Honestly, Monica... can I call you that?'

'I hope you will!'

'Good. Well, naturally, I love my mother, but she isn't the easiest person, and my parents really weren't right for each other. They have different values quite apart from anything else. Dad seems so upbeat now. I feel as if he's become an even lovelier version of the father I've always had. He's more fun. Best of all, he's got something else to talk about now instead of wall to wall architecture!'

They both laughed. In the pause that followed, Monica wondered what to say. Knowing that Emily was an English teacher at a high school in Oxford, she decided to ask about that.

'Oh, the teaching's fine,' Emily told her. 'It's just all the admin and policy documents and spreadsheets and data dashboards and what have you.'

'Sounds grim.'

'Well, let's just say, it's not where my natural talents lie. Still, I'm enjoying producing the school play. Perhaps you and Dad could come? It starts on Wednesday.'

'I'd love that.' Monica's eyes shone with happiness. She felt she was drawing energy and youth from this lively woman. She had often wondered what Betsy might have looked like as an adult, had she recovered. And Emily who, she knew, had been born in the same year, was providing a realistic impression of how her lovely girl might have turned out. 'I hope this won't upset you,' she went on, glancing across the room at where Stephen was to check she had time to confide in Emily before he returned, 'but the person you remind me of is my daughter Betsy. She was born in 1985 too, but unfortunately she died eleven years ago.'

'I'm very sorry. I remember now that Dad told me about her. It's hard to imagine how awful losing a child must be.'

Monica nodded. 'But meeting up with you, well, I suppose it offers me a vision of what she might have been, which is surprisingly comforting.'

'That's a lovely thing to say,' Emily responded.

'Here we are, tea all round.' Stephen returned with a laden tray. 'I bought these,' he laughed as he put a plate of scones on the table. 'Can't have my two favourite people fading away. Monica was a teacher, Em, did she tell you?'

'Only primary children though so probably not as challenging. And there was much less bureaucracy in my day,' Monica said. 'I'm not sure I'd have coped in this era at all!'

'That seems to be that, then,' the young man said as he and his brother returned from packing their vehicle to check with Jen that they had left nothing behind. Then he added, 'I suppose there's no chance of you booking us to do the big move when you sell the house?'

She raised her eyebrows as she considered the idea. These two energetically bouncy lads, who hardly looked old enough to shave, were impressive. They were quick and efficient and had accommodated far more in their Luton van than she had imagined possible. Having begun with the essentials – her dismantled king-sized bed, two Victorian bedroom chairs, plus her dressing table – there was space to spare, and they had urged her to use it. So, she had packed a couple of sets of bed linen and a duvet and some pillows, and then asked the brothers to put in Fred's desk, chair, computer and printer. Finally, having seen a clothes rail at the back of the van, she had hung up her best winter coat, several dresses and her collection of black trousers, smiling as she remembered telling Fred over and over again that she would probably die before she ever found the perfect pair.

'I hope not,' he would say in response. And they would laugh.

'So, we'll get off then,' the older lad said.

'Sorry, I was miles away,' she replied. 'But I was just thinking that because I'm going to have to seriously downsize, I'll probably get rid of the other desk and the twin beds, as they're not going to fit into the new house. And I won't need both sofas. So, I suspect when I do the main move, your van would be big enough. I'm hardly going to need a pantechnicon.'

'Brill!' The two youngsters rubbed their hands together in unison. 'Make a change for us – most of our jobs are around Crowbury. We're gonna go out on the town tonight in Norwich. Never been there!'

She grinned. 'It's a fine city, as they say on all the signs as you approach it. Have a good time. Don't get lost on the way!'

'No worries, we've got satnav.'

Jen nodded, though in her head she could hear Fred saying that he hoped they had a decent map as well, because gadgets were not infallible.

'Safe travel,' she called as they sprinted away, eager, she supposed, to embark on their adventure. She watched them go, closed the front door and ran up the stairs to her almost empty bedroom. 'This all looks very strange,' she whispered, as she scooped up her favourite photo of Fred and took it into the spare room where she would sleep before driving to Norwich tomorrow.

Suddenly weary, she sank on to one of the twin beds and stared deep into the photograph at Fred's smiling eyes. As she peered at him, she had a weird perception that his expression changed in response, as if he was actually looking at her. She blinked and retrained her eyes on his, which again seemed to respond warmly as he appeared to gaze at her. She found herself smiling broadly, reassured at their closeness and connection.

Gently, she placed his photo on the bedside table, then lay back on the bed, and began to think of all the significant changes she was negotiating, including the reality of the almost ready-to-be-born baby who was her husband's grandson. And from tomorrow, there would be Hoagy too, she thought, and the challenge of settling him, as well as getting used to living in the same property as Matthew and Ginny and turning her rooms there into a new home.

She was so fortunate to have all these exciting prospects. But even as she framed those thoughts, her pleasure was brutally and abruptly swept away and replaced with sorrowful emptiness and the darkest of thoughts.

I must press on, she protested, trying to stem the negativity that was taking hold. But why? Why must I press on? What's the point?

She had proved that she could survive the biggest loss of her life. But just because she could, did she want to? Might it not be better for everyone if she gave up now? Stopped fighting to get through every day. Stopped having to make her own entertainment. Stopped having to deal with the crushing loneliness that was her constant companion. Stopped having to force herself to get up and go to The Granary and do a shift. Stopped, when alone at home, struggling to fill those in-between hours between four and seven till she could decently have dinner and watch TV before giving up on another Fredless day.

Once I get to Norwich, she reasoned, I can't kill myself. It would be awful for Ginny and Matthew. They'd think it was their fault and blame themselves and decide they hadn't been welcoming enough. So, if I'm going to do it, I have to do it here.

Why was she thinking this way?

Because... because... because my recovery is a fragile thing and I'm hanging on by a thread that is finer than gossamer, and I don't think I even want to.

She curled into a foetal position and surrendered to the bleakness of it all.

The phone was ringing. She wondered why it was not being picked up by the answerphone. On and on it went. Then she remembered that she had had to dismantle the machine, because the cables had been wrapped around the legs of Fred's desk, which was now on its way to Norwich. She should have reconnected it. Eventually, there was silence, but then her mobile rang. With a heavy sigh, she reached into her pocket and answered it.

'Jen, it's Helen. How have you been since our conversation the other day?'

'I, uh… yeah, been fine.'

'How are you, really?' Helen's voice was low and concerned.

'Not sure.'

'Are you working today at The Granary?'

Yes, she was supposed to be. She glanced at her watch. What was she doing lying here? She needed to get going. 'I… yes. Sorry, to be honest, I've just been having a monumental wobble.' She exhaled loudly. 'Sorry.'

'Jen, you're dealing with a hell of a lot. You don't have to apologise. Shall I pop into The Granary late afternoon? We could have a cup of tea.'

There was a pause during which Jen found herself thinking of Fred and how he always looked after her, and she imagined him sitting beside her and hugging her to him.

'I'd really like that,' she replied.

The phone woke her.

Lucy considered making the effort to leave the sofa and answer it but remained lying where she was. She was hot, she noticed, which was quite unusual. And she could detect a smell of cooking, or was it burning?

She groaned with the exertion required to reach for her crutches and heave herself to a standing position. The answer machine clicked into action.

In the kitchen, she turned off the oven and opened its door, balancing awkwardly as she attempted to fan away the smoky fumes. The chicken was quite charred looking. Pity. She had been looking forward to that. Propping herself up, she managed to pull out the roasting tin and put it on top of the stove. Sighing, she surveyed the dried-up bird. Some of it might be edible when it cooled down.

What day was it? Her iPad, lying on a nearby work surface, could tell her but, like her mobile phone, it had stopped working because its battery was flat. Where had she put the charging bits and pieces? She engineered herself into a more stable standing position and managed to navigate herself back into the hall and then into her office where she switched on her PC, before pressing play on her answerphone. There were four messages. Yet another from her GP's surgery who kept asking her to call them. One from Helen, and the other two from Monica and Jen. She was fortunate to have such good friends. They called regularly. She had spoken to one of them... hard to remember who now... yesterday, or was it the day before? And she had told whoever it was, that she was fine for shopping and was coping, and that Barry brought her provisions every day.

Where was he though? And when had he last come?

As she sank into the chair in front of her computer she saw, rather than felt, her right foot hit the desk leg. There was a crack. It was not a good sound. Had she hurt herself? They had warned her at the hospital that it would be easy to break a bone. Pressing on the desk in front of her, she levered herself upright. Glancing down at her feet, wrapped in their grimy dressings and fluffy slippers, she could not see, or feel, anything untoward. But suddenly, she was staring at a growing puddle on the floor beneath her and she registered that, without any warning whatsoever, her bladder had given way. This was a fresh horror, and an indignity too far. Could she, she wondered, broach the subject with Barry and ask him to buy incontinence pads? And even if she did, would she be able to manage to put them on by herself? The room blurred around her as tears filled her eyes. How quickly one can go from being a respected professor to this. Surprisingly, the tears stopped almost as soon as they had started and were replaced by a ghostly sense of calm and curiosity.

She rotated on her crutches and slowly padded back into the kitchen where she transferred the roasting tin to the kitchen table. Then, attempting to ignore the cold dampness between her legs, she eased herself into a chair and began pulling the chicken apart with her fingers and nibbling around the burnt bits.

A phone call the previous day from her solicitor had brought Monica back to Crowbury where she had slept for what, she decided, might well be the last time. The truth was that having found love and companionship with Stephen, she really missed him when they were apart. Each day was filled with pleasure at his company; she felt indeed that their spirits were melding and that every hour brought them closer together. Her heart beat a little faster as she enjoyed the heady sensation of belonging to someone so remarkable and special. I would never have guessed this could happen to me, she thought for the hundredth time.

Still, there were legalities to be sorted and she had to empty the marital home – and the solicitor had suggested she should make that her priority as it seemed the exchange of contracts was imminent.

So, she had risen early and, breakfast quickly over, was trying to decide where to begin with her packing. Of course, most of her clothes and other personal items were already at Stephen's, but the accumulation of kitchen equipment, crockery, cushions, book-cases and other furniture was going to take some shifting.

Stephen had urged her to bring whatever she wanted, but as she surveyed the shelves and cupboards in her kitchen, she felt no sense of connection or nostalgia. Everything belonged to the other Monica. The formal Monica who was good at dinner parties. In any event, Stephen's house was perfectly well-equipped.

Shrugging her shoulders, she told herself to get on with it. So, though her heart was not in it, she began dividing up everything in a way that she thought was fair to James. But every twenty minutes or so, she paused and sighed at the scene before her. It was not as if her husband had expressed any interest in keeping any of these items. Perhaps he had no more desire than she to be reminded of their marriage.

Nonetheless she soldiered on and packed up the Waterford crystal for herself and boxed the Edinburgh crystal for him. There were two dinner services, so she elected to keep the Wedgewood and allocated him the Myott.

She had been labouring at this unwanted task now for over two hours and it looked, and felt, as though she had barely scratched the surface. She sighed loudly. What if she simply gave the rest of it away. She had a feeling that charities like the Salvation Army would come and clear houses. That would make much more sense. Would she regret it? After a couple of minutes thought, she concluded that she would not.

Jen wedged her two holdalls full of clothes into the boot. Then she covered the whole of the back seat with a travelling rug, before laying out her purchases from the internet – a pack of doggy treats, a couple of chew toys, a squashy bed, and a clown made of brightly knitted cloth. Lastly, she fetched the dog carrier with its sheepskin interior she had bought and wedged it tight against the back of the driver's seat so that it wouldn't move around. That looks so comfortable I wouldn't mind travelling to Norwich in it myself, she thought. Mind you, Hoagy might prefer to be held by Matthew, but at least she had covered all the options.

She felt a rush of happiness; not only would she soon see the little schnauzer for the first time in ages, but she was going to keep him. He had touched her heart in a way that nothing and nobody else had since Fred had gone – apart maybe, from the vicar's dog Archie. She had a role now; she was going to give this little animal the best possible life.

But there were hours to go before she needed to leave, and time seemed to be moving excessively slowly. She would have more coffee, and perhaps a brunch of scrambled eggs on toast.

As she prepared them, her thoughts, as they so often did, turned to Lucy. She had left a message every day and only once had it been returned. It was a worry, but both Helen and Monica had said that Lucy was determined to do things her own way and that they had decided to respect that.

Resolutely, she pushed her anxieties to the back of her mind and went in search of her Kindle. She was reading *Agent Running in the Field* by John le Carré and would enjoy another chapter while she ate.

Half an hour later, her mobile rang; she glanced at the display before answering. It was Bryony from the estate agents.

'Good news, Mrs Warboys. I've lined up two viewings on Friday.'

'Oh, great, thanks – but I won't be here.'

'Not a problem. Quite the reverse, in fact. It's probably going to be much easier to sell the house if you're not around.'

That was rather blunt, Jen thought. Perhaps it was not a personal comment, but it certainly felt like it. What was wrong with her? Or did estate agents generally dislike home-owners to be around?

'Why would that be, exactly?' she asked, trying to keep her voice friendly.

'Oh, you know, just one of those things. Anyway, I've got a key, so all good. Can you take your old car out of the garage by any chance?'

'I just have – I'll be leaving in it shortly.'

'That's certainly going to help.'

'Hmmn, the other thing is that I've sent some of my furniture off to Norwich already, which means that my husband's study and our bedroom are more or less empty.'

'Brill! The less clutter the better.'

Jen breathed in sharply. Their marital bed and Fred's desk were not, in any way, clutter. She was about to make that point when the young woman breezily wished her a good day and rang off.

She took a deep breath. It would be madness to fall out with the estate agents. After all, the sooner she found a buyer, the better. Now that she was going to have Hoagy, it would be increasingly difficult to divide her time between Norwich and here – especially once the baby was born. And anyway, now that she was set on returning to her home city, she was becoming more impatient about being settled there.

A thought that had been hovering just below the surface of her 'must do' list suddenly bubbled into her mind. What about The Granary? She had put off deciding what to tell Liz Pemberton. She had thought about it the previous day during her shift, but the manager had not been in the building. Now, she was embarking on a whole week off, but she was scheduled to be back at work in eight days' time and, she realised, she had no appetite for it. Probably, it was because Monica had already left, and Lucy would never be going back either.

'You've got to let them know,' she said aloud.

As it turned out, Liz Pemberton was not remotely surprised by what she had to say.

'The three of you were marvellously helpful in keeping the place going at the beginning of the year,' she said. 'But we're doing well now and have plenty of volunteers. You need to focus on your future and your new life. Just like Monica is.'

There was a silence and she could tell that Liz was thinking of Lucy, as she herself was, and how there were no words to sum up her loss to both The Granary and life itself.

'I'm very grateful to you, Liz,' she murmured after a pause.

'Not half as grateful as we are to you,' replied the other woman, 'stay in touch.'

Jen agreed and rang off. 'So, that's another thing done, Fred,' she announced.

In that moment, she had a sudden image of Bryony the estate agent poking her nose into various cupboards and units before the potential buyers turned up. She felt a sense of outrage that the young woman might come across Fred's Norfolk jacket which was hanging in her wardrobe. The idea that anyone other than her would touch it made her feel quite sick. She shook her head. That simply could not happen, so she ran up to the bedroom and collected it, then ran back downstairs and out to the car where she laid it on top of her holdalls in the boot.

It was still too early to leave; perhaps she should try phoning Lucy again.

The answer machine responded, so she left yet another message, 'Lucy, I'm sorry to have missed you again. Maybe you are at the hospital? I'm off to Norwich as I think I've already mentioned. I won't be back for a week. Please call me sometime or text me. I can always get help to you even if I'm not around, though I know you don't want any. Sorry. Hope you're OK.'

Next, she texted Helen.

'So grateful to you for yesterday. I feel much better. Thank you. Not quite sure what you said that made the difference, but it really worked. I suppose there will still be ups and downs but I'm quite excited about getting my dog and then going to Norwich. Hope to see you soon. Btw, when was the last time you had any real contact with Lucy? Have you actually spoken to her, or seen her, since you took her to the hospital? That seems ages ago. I suppose her driver is still going in every day. It's just worrying that she never, ever answers the phone.'

Perhaps she could talk to Monica? But she was so rarely in Crowbury these days and was probably with Stephen. She settled for a text.

'How are things? Are you still in your rosy glow? How did meeting the daughter go? I don't suppose you've seen Lucy? I haven't, but I keep ringing her. She never answers. I suppose we'd hear if things had taken a turn for the worse as that driver goes in every day, doesn't he? I hope he does.'

Her mobile rang soon afterwards.

'I thought you'd be on your way to the rescue centre by now.'

'Oh, Monica. Good. Thanks for calling. Where are you?'

'In Crowbury. I'm making a half-hearted attempt to pack up my goods and chattels. Tonight, Stephen and I are going to a play in Oxford. But I'll be here for a while yet. When are you off?'

'Not for an hour and a half. I want to go now really but would end up driving around somewhere for the sake of it. It's silly, I know, but I'm quite unsettled. I can't seem to focus on anything.'

'Are you OK?'

'I'm fine. But, embarrassingly, I had a kind of meltdown yesterday. The removal lads had just packed up a load of my furniture and left for Norwich, and I suddenly felt completely bereft. Luckily, Helen phoned as it was happening, and she was really helpful. And then we met later, after I had done my shift at The Granary. Honestly, she's a marvel. So, everything's good. I just want to get going.'

'Have a wonderful time. Hopefully, you'll feel really happy as you start settling yourself into the new house. And I know you're going to be thrilled with your dog. Don't worry about Lucy. Just go and forget everything for a week.'

'Are you sure?'

'Yup absolutely. I did manage to talk to her a couple of days ago. She sounded pretty tired, but she said she was OK, and absolutely and definitely did not want visitors at the moment. Though she did say that her taxi man Barry comes in with shopping all the time. So, what can we do? We don't have a key. We can't insist she has us round.'

'Suppose she just drops dead?'

She heard Monica's sharp intake of breath at the other end. 'Well, that's what she wants, I think. Her life is over as she sees it. Before us, I don't think she ever had any female friends who weren't academics. And I get the impression that the only people who ever visited her house were her gentlemen callers. She doesn't even know her neighbours. She's just unusual, isn't she? I really, really like her, but she's very determined, and I doubt anyone can alter the course of what's likely to happen. It's obvious she doesn't want to die in hospital with tubes in her arm and what have you. She just wants to slip away.'

'But should she be allowed to do that?'

'That's a very big question,' Monica's voice was grave. 'I keep feeling we should do something or tell someone. But who? And, I mean, don't we all want to do things our own way?'

Thinking of how quickly Fred had died, and his determination not to have a slow, lingering death, she replied, 'I suppose we do.'

'How was Helen, by the way?' Monica asked. 'She told me they've got a lot of interest in their house and are going off to see some property in Geneva that her son has found. I'll miss her when she moves.'

'Well, we're all leaving Crowbury, aren't we?'

'True, but I'd assumed that you and I would stay in touch. I'd like to visit Norwich. Stephen says it's lovely.'

'That would be terrific,' Jen responded warmly.

'And I know you're going to be busy in Norwich with the shop and the dog and the baby,' Monica went on, 'but Oxford isn't so far away.'

'No, I'd love to visit you. And I'll come back to Crowbury regularly, because of Fred's grave.'

'Of course you will.'

'You know,' Jen said, thinking aloud, 'Geneva's only a two-hour flight. We could invite ourselves to Helen's for a weekend!'

'Now that *is* an idea. Do you think we could?'

'She's said several times she'd like us all to keep in contact, so maybe... I think I'm just getting my head around the fact that I really won't ever again have to rush home to check on Fred. I think something in me, perhaps for self-preservation, kind of thought of his death as being temporary. It's... it's hard to believe it's not. But at the same time, I'm beginning to see that I have different options now that might be interesting and enjoyable.'

'That's an improvement, isn't it?' Monica asked gently.

'Definitely. Oh, what happened with Stephen's daughter?'

'It was fine. I needn't have got myself in such a panic at all! In fact, we'll see her again later. She's a teacher and she's produced the school play, and we're going to it tonight. The strange thing is that she's the same age that Betsy would have been and is quite physically like her. And I feel very comforted and almost thrilled that I know her. Do you think that's strange?'

As Jen recalled some of her own bizarre thoughts about Fred over the past months, she answered, 'No, not at all.'

Talking to Jen had been a welcome respite, thought Monica. She ought to continue with the packing, but she decided she could probably allow herself a cup of coffee first.

While she prepared it, her thoughts returned to Lucy. She was aware that, like Jen, she felt a constant undercurrent of anxiety as well as unreality, that their friend – an educated, financially solvent, interesting person who lived so close – was choosing to refuse treatment and live in increasing squalor till she died.

She took a sip of her beverage and found herself worrying that perhaps she was committing some sort of crime by not insisting that Lucy had treatment. But how could you insist? Her thoughts were interrupted by the phone.

The solicitor told her that the exchange of contracts on the house was happening the following day. Then he transferred the call on to the divorce lawyer, who explained that her decree nisi was through, and that the divorce would become final in just over six weeks.

She was about to ring Stephen to tell him when Melissa called, full of the joyful news that she and Maggs had decided to become parents. They had picked their sperm donor and had elected that Melissa would be the birth mother this time around, as she was older, and then Maggs would become pregnant, they hoped, by the same man in a couple of years. Melissa had always been quite indifferent to children. Come to that, she had never even played

275

with dolls, but now she sounded blissful and soft and hugely lovable, and a world apart from the young woman who had quarrelled with her frequently and ferociously from the age of ten. Monica shivered as some of the harshest words of their encounters troubled her brain. But that was the past. She would never forgive herself that she had handled their relationship so ineptly, nor for the fact that Melissa had been quite right in her assumption that she had favoured Betsy. Sometimes, she felt their new fondness was more than she deserved.

'And Dad is coming in a fortnight,' Melissa was saying. 'So, hopefully he'll behave himself this time. But he sounds different on the phone. Apparently, he's got a girlfriend and it sounds quite serious... So, to come back to me, I thought I'd come over and spend Christmas with you and meet your feller if that's OK, and if you're getting married soon, maybe I could stay for that, so long as I'm not away from here longer than a month... Maggs wouldn't be able to get the time off and I'm going to miss her like hell. Also, we want to try and get pregnant as soon as possible!'

After the call, Monica realised that her coffee had gone cold, so she made another. For a moment, she was tempted to have a brandy with it as she felt lightheaded after all the happenings of the morning.

Till now, she had resisted communicating with James but perhaps it was time to tell him that the sale was almost through, and to check if he had changed his mind about what he wanted from the house.

He responded swiftly to her email which led to a whole series of them – all surprisingly affable. Indeed, he was gracious in a completely untypical way about all the clearing and packing she was doing, and promised to sort out storage for his items. Then, though she had vowed to keep her love for Stephen a secret till after the decree absolute, she found herself telling her almost-ex-husband all about him, though she left out the information that he had been the architect of their extension.

Her opening up about romance prompted him to reveal his own liaison. Her name, it seemed, was Sapphire. She was a singer on the cruise and he really liked her. Loved her, maybe. She came from Bolton, he wrote, and had a broad Lancashire accent.

Monica smiled as she read the details. James would once have mocked the voice of his new beloved. He had hated the vogue for regional accents among television announcers and had written furious letters to both the BBC and Channel Four about them. How he had changed.

With the next email, he attached Sapphire's picture. This was another surprise. The lady was definitely what James might once have described as 'brassy' with her false eyelashes and impossibly long – probably fake – nails. It was obviously a promotional photograph, so the chances were that she looked somewhat different when she wasn't performing, but the fact that he was falling for her was still a shock.

Her next message put him in the picture about Lucy.

His reply showed how fond he was of her friend, and also how he was completely accepting of what she was doing to herself. The email ended, 'She has a right to live and die as she wishes.'

Having eaten two bowlfuls of muesli with double cream poured over them in lieu of milk which seemed to have run out, Lucy eyed the quiche which, she had decided, might have to do for lunch later. For some reason, it wasn't in the fridge. It had dark patches on it. Blue cheese probably. Or could it be mould? She had never been rigid about sell-by dates at the best of times but now she was unsure how long she had had it. Still, Barry came in every day, didn't he? She ought really to look for the box that the flan had come in. She swung around on one crutch, ignoring the pile of dishes in and around the sink, which she must tackle at some point. There were boxes and carrier bags lying around the bin, which was full. But she was far too tired to rummage through them to find the right one. It would be OK. Anyway, her supplies were somewhat depleted, which was annoying. She would have a think about it over a cup of tea and some shortbread.

If I go now, Jen thought, I'll have to hang around there, and Oxford is always hectic, and it will be impossible to park or wait.

She decided to put on some make-up. But even after applying two coats of mascara, some blusher and lipstick, she had only used up five minutes.

The doorbell, for once, was a welcome distraction.

'Chloe!'

Fred's daughter stood in front of her, pale, make-up free, dressed in a T-shirt, jeans and puffer jacket and carrying a large handbag. She looked wan, but somehow younger than the matronly figure Jen had encountered back in the summer.

'Gosh, this is... extraordinary,' Jen said. 'Matthew and I've kept saying we've heard nothing from you. We were bewildered, to be honest. I mean, it's months since you and I met.'

'I know. Sorry... Can I stay here?'

'Stay here?'

Chloe nodded.

'Look, come in. Tell me what this is all about.'

'Have you got time? You're not off anywhere are you? Is that your car, packed full of stuff?'

'Yes, it is. I'm going to Norwich, via Oxford, but I don't need to go quite yet. Come through. You look like you could do with a strong cup of tea.'

In the kitchen, Chloe slipped out of her jacket before sitting at the table.

'My goodness, you've lost a lot of weight.'

Chloe nodded. 'I've been on the heartbreak diet.'

'Oh God, what's happened?'

'In a nutshell, I'd been having an affair with my boss, you know – the brain man – for seventeen years. He's finally left his wife, but not for me.'

278

Jen sat down beside Chloe. The younger woman stared straight ahead, her face a study of utter devastation.

'I came to Crowbury,' she said, 'to see if I would feel better for seeing my father's grave. I think I do. Then I decided to drive past this house, so I could see where the two of you had lived. And then I saw the For Sale sign…'

'Mmmn. Things have changed since we met; I'm planning now to move to Norwich and live with Matthew and Ginny. Sorry… seeing the sign was probably a shock for you.'

'I guess, but it got me thinking. I hope you don't mind that I knocked on your door, but I suddenly wanted to talk to you, and also find out if you have a buyer?'

'Not yet. But how did you know where I live?'

'I asked Matthew for your address, after you and I had met in Selfridges. He and I were emailing a lot at that time and I told him I wanted to send you a card. He was a bit reluctant to be honest, so don't be cross with him. I can be very persuasive just not, obviously, when it really matters.' Chloe's eyes pooled with tears and she reached into her pocket for a tissue to wipe them away.

'I'm sorry you're in such pain.'

'It's just so, so awful.'

'I'm sure it is. Let me get you that tea.' Jen switched on the kettle before opening the fridge and extricating some cheese to make a sandwich.

'D'you remember when we met you asked me something about men?'

'Did I? That sounds somewhat presumptuous.'

'It wasn't at all. But I gave you a vague answer. I had a feeling even then that I was losing him, and I was panicking. So, when that day he had asked me to work late, which was his usual code for saying we could have time together at my flat, I jumped at it. I'm embarrassed now. You probably thought I was rude to cut our meeting so short. And, as it happens, he did just actually mean "work late" and about ten days later, he ended the relationship.'

'That sounds brutal.'

'Yes, it was. He wasn't remotely interested in how I was going to cope or get over the split. I went mad. He left me screaming and shouting. I think his last words to me were "For God's sake, get a grip".'

Jen sighed. 'Nice man,' she said, sardonically.

'After that, I can't really remember what happened for around a week. I know I gave in my notice. And that I was planning to go to Devon to stay with my mother but then, sod's law, she had a stroke. She can't talk now though I think she understands most things.'

Jen put a mug of tea in front of Chloe and a sandwich. 'What a lot has happened, and so quickly. I'm sorry... Eat that,' she said. 'Your dad had a theory that there was nothing bad in life that couldn't be improved by a cheese sandwich.'

For the first time, a glimmer of a smile warmed the younger woman's expression.

'I wish I'd known him.'

'I wish that too,' Jen said, automatically and then she realised that she meant it.

'I can see now that I've been a complete mug. You have no idea how many birthdays and Christmases and other holidays I've spent alone just in case he could get away. I've pissed all my friends off big time because I've cancelled on them far too often over the years, and now basically no one wants to know. It's a mess.'

Jen leant over and gave her a hug. Somehow now that Chloe was thinner, sadder and quieter, she looked more like Fred, which was disconcerting and comforting at the same time.

'I've taken a temporary job as a medical secretary at the hospital here,' Chloe murmured.

'What?' Jen released her and stood up straight. 'Really? My goodness, this is all moving so fast, but surely that'll be awfully low key compared to what you're used to?'

'That's the plan. I need to do something normal. Stop being on a treadmill of high-powered work and high-powered sex and all the drama of being either in seventh heaven or lonely as hell. Thing is too, I had a lovely flat in London, in Maida Vale, which my mum helped me buy twenty years ago when I moved there. I put it on the market, and it sold in a day. A Russian guy wanted it, complete with all the existing furniture and white goods – and he paid cash. It was unbelievably quick. So, I'd already thought of renting down here till I found somewhere to buy, but if you're going, I could buy this house. Then I'll get more of a sense of my father, and of course you could stay here when you visit friends or go to his grave.' She rooted around in her handbag for her phone and quickly brought up the details of her bank account.

'Look!'

The balance was over £800,000.

'Oh my God, Chloe, this is all so sudden. Do you always make such snap decisions?'

'I haven't before. But my life has turned upside down. Well, to be more precise, my life as I knew it has ended. So, I kind of figured I might as well go with my instincts.'

Jen's heart went out to Fred's daughter as, for the first time, she felt a real connection to her. Her own life as she knew it, had ended too. And she was fully aware of how difficult it was to build a new one when you had no wish to.

'You may have a point,' she replied, quietly.

'I expect you're keen to get on with your move to Norwich.'

Jen flopped into the seat beside Chloe. 'Yes. Quite apart from anything else, you probably don't know that Matthew and his wife are about to have a baby.'

'What are you asking for this place?'

'Uh, five hundred grand, but I feel I should let you have it for less.'

'No, you shouldn't. I can afford it. That's a fair price.'

'Chloe, we don't have to decide this now. You've obviously been through a great deal and maybe you're not thinking straight. I mean you don't know anyone here. What will you do? And are you sure you want to live in a house owned by the dead father you never met? It's all a bit odd isn't it, almost macabre?'

'I don't care. I want to live differently for a while, and this would suit me. It probably won't be my forever-home. But I'm thinking I might do a language course at the university and join a gym and maybe a book group. You have no idea what all these years have been like – loads of exotic travel, long hours, expensive presents. But I think that all I really wanted was love. And I've never had it. Not really. I'm sure now *he* never loved me, though he did love my blinkered devotion and that I was available all the time, more fool me. I'm not even sure that my mother loved me. I can't ask her now because she can't talk. But she's been such a career person that I had a whole series of childminders. There was a lovely nanny once, but Mum fell out with her. Seriously impressive woman, but hopeless parenting material. I like to think your husband would have been a dad to me. And that's why I want to be here.'

'Well look, for what it's worth, I want you to be part of our family and I think Matthew and Ginny will too. Certainly, you can stay here, but don't decide yet about buying it. It's a mess at the moment. Some of my stuff has already gone. And more will be going though not everything. It's nothing like you're used to. I think you should reserve the right to change your mind.'

'Well, are you leaving the cooker, and has it still got a bed?'

'Yes, to the cooker. And there are twin beds, which I can't take. Plus, as you can see, I do have a rather lovely Welsh dresser that I was going to have to get rid of. And there's a desk and sofa.'

'More and more perfect. Please let me stay here. And please let me buy it. Can I tell the estate agent that you're withdrawing from the sale? I don't see any reason why you should pay them commission, do you?'

Thinking back to Bryony's brusque attitude and rudeness about clutter, Jen's eyes sparkled with fun. 'No, I don't. But they won't take that instruction from you, so I'll do it – and to say it will be a pleasure is an understatement. Now, please eat your sandwich.'

Chapter Twenty-Four

The quiche will have to do, Lucy decided as she put it into the oven. Sighing with the overwhelming effort of living, she decided to ring Barry. It was a bore that she had to use the landline, her mobile still lying dead to the world on a crowded kitchen worktop. She had to look up the number too, which took a while.

'I thought,' he remarked, once she finally got through, 'that you never, ever wanted to see me again.'

'What are you talking about?'

'You told me not to come. You said, "How dare you speak to me like that" when all I did was ask if any of your friends were coming to see you. And then you shouted at me, "Never contact me again".'

'Is that Barry?' she asked.

'Of course it's Barry.'

'You must be confusing me with someone else. Can you bring food? Usual things...'

There was silence at the other end of the phone.

'What?' she demanded.

'This can't go on,' he said at last. 'You falling out with me, and not remembering.'

'How dare you,' she retorted.

'There you go again. You aren't fit to be on your own. You should be in hospital.'

She swallowed the angry response that was forming on her tongue. 'Barry, please, please, don't... I am sorry. Sometimes I feel slightly out of it. If you won't come today, please come tomorrow. I'll pay extra.'

'All right,' he said.

'God, this is more than flesh and blood can stand,' she muttered. 'And is it still Wednesday?'

Jen looked at her watch again. Matthew had been gone twenty minutes. It seemed longer. Surely, there was no problem? Her pulse quickened at the thought that his references might not be acceptable, or that her neighbour could somehow have heard she was going to adopt Hoagy and persuaded the rescue centre not to go ahead. She switched on the radio, sampled various programmes, but failed to find anything to hold her attention.

After leaving Chloe and trying to come to terms with the younger woman's appearance and change of circumstances, she had driven, very carefully, to Oxford. As she had feared, there had been dense traffic in the area around the station, but Matthew had already arrived and positioned himself in a spot where it was simple for her to pick him up. Like Fred, he always made life easier for her.

They had talked briefly about Ginny, and then Jen had launched into an account of the sudden reappearance of Chloe.

'Well, in a way,' Matthew had said, 'it's a relief to know what's been going on. She was so up for meeting in August but then disappeared without a trace. I'm sorry she's in such a state though.'

'Well, she'll either miraculously get herself together, or it'll be a disaster, but I guess buying the house will be as good an investment as any and, you never know, a bit of somewhat dull, market-town life might be just the ticket. Also, assuming she doesn't change her mind, I'll be free to move properly now, instead of dividing my time between you and Crowbury. Funnily enough, this morning, I gave in my notice at The Granary, and that's before I knew about Chloe. Perhaps I'm psychic!'

They had left the subject then and moved on to Hoagy. Quickly, they had reached the conclusion that Matthew should handle the formalities at the rescue centre and that she should stay in the car. So, she had. But now she was impatient.

'Bloody hell,' she cried in frustration. 'How can it be taking this long?'

She reached for her phone and checked her texts and calls. There was no urgent communication from Chloe, which was good, but there was nothing from Lucy either. Even after her conversation with Monica earlier, she was finding it difficult to shake off her anxiety and guilt about being away when her friend was so ill.

She decided to contact Monica again. Quite apart from anything else she wanted to tell her about Fred's daughter. Her friend's mobile went straight to voice mail, so she left a message.

'Hi, it's Jen. Hope all well. There's been a bizarre development. After we spoke, Chloe turned up at the house. Will tell all later but basically she wants to buy it! You couldn't make it up, could you? Still, if she goes ahead, it will make life a lot easier. Just collecting Hoagy now. Enjoy the play. Speak later.'

As she re-pocketed her phone, finally the tall figure of Matthew came into view. He looked like a giant beside the little dog. Hoagy was clearly timid, so much so that her stepson was having to stop every few yards, then pull the lead gently to encourage the animal forward a few more steps. Presumably, this place had been a sanctuary of sorts, and had felt safer to the schnauzer than his previous billet with the boisterous Border collie.

She saw Matthew crouch down and tickle Hoagy behind the ears. Her heart warmed as she watched him display his characteristic kindness and patience with their new pet. Feeling a wave of love for her stepson as well as for the dog, she jumped out of the car and sprinted towards them.

'Hoagy!' she called.

His head lifted. Suddenly his tiny tail began to wag, and he started to pull Matthew towards the car rather than away from it. Then, as Jen reached him, and squatted down beside him, he leapt onto her lap and licked her face enthusiastically.

'Gosh, someone's pleased,' Matthew laughed. 'He knows you! Hopefully he'll get used to me in time, but there's no doubt his mood's completely changed now.'

Jen looked up at her stepson, her eyes shining with happiness. 'Isn't he gorgeous? You do like him, don't you? God knows how we're going to manage with us all getting used to a new house and you and Ginny having a baby but—'

'It's going to be fine,' Matthew interrupted in a confident voice that was so like his father's. 'Let's help you up. Here, you take the lead. Do you want to walk him around for ten minutes? I want to phone Ginny before we set off. Also, I was wondering if you'd be insulted if I suggested that I drive?'

Jen grinned. 'Did I make you nervous then, after I picked you up from Oxford?'

'Not at all. But Norwich is a fair way – getting on for two hundred miles, I think. And what's just occurred to me is that Hoagy's going to be much more content if you sit with him for the journey rather than me.'

She transferred the lead into her other hand so she could use her nearer arm to pull Matthew into a hug. 'I'd be thrilled if you'd drive,' she admitted. 'You have no idea! But what about insurance?'

'Are you still with the same company?'

'Dear boy, I'm an *old* person! We don't change providers of anything unless we have to. Anyway, I think your dad always used Aviva out of loyalty to you. I know that you've left them now, but I'll probably stay with them forever.'

He chuckled. 'I'll make a quick phone call and sort it.'

'That would be so good. What do you say, Hoagy?'

In response, the miniature schnauzer bounced around excitedly, like Tigger. Giggling, she tried to encourage him to walk with her, but her laughter seemed to excite him more and he began to jump up and down, with all four of his feet leaving the ground, as if he were on a trampoline.

'What fun you are, little dog! Come on, let's have a quick run around. We're going to be in the car for quite a while.'

The play was called The Pauper Princess and was based on Mark Twain's The Prince and the *Pauper*. It had a suitably large cast and was lively and engaging, though it took Monica a while to absorb herself in it after the events of the day.

The combination of phone calls, emails and serious packing had preoccupied her so completely that she had almost missed her train from Crowbury, which then had travelled exceedingly slowly, because of a points failure in the area. Luckily, thanks to Stephen's knowledge of the back streets of Oxford, they had made the school hall just in time for 'curtain-up'.

And now it was nearly over. In the half-light she noticed that he could feel her gaze on him and, in response, he turned to her and stroked her arm. How marvellous it was to be with someone who always seemed to be in a good mood.

The curtain fell to the accompaniment of boisterous cheers and whistles from the audience.

'I thought that was excellent,' Stephen said as the lights came up. 'Let's go and congratulate Emily.'

Lucy had finished the quiche, even though it had, she thought, tasted slightly strange. Still, it had filled a hole and was probably fine.

She had been asleep. It was dark now. Where had the day gone? Was it too early to go to bed? She longed to lie down, but the stairs were becoming too much of a challenge. She was pretty sure that her foot had swelled up since she had knocked it. Was that today? Or yesterday? Had she slept on the sofa last night? She rather thought she had. Perhaps she would do the same tonight. Really, she needed a wash, but had no energy to do it.

Uncertain, and hazy, she made her way slowly out to the hall with the vague intention of using her downstairs lavatory but then she noticed some post on the mat inside the front door. There was rather a lot of it. Perhaps she had forgotten to check for it yesterday.

Wobbling precariously, she laid one crutch against the wall and leant on the other while she picked up the envelopes. With some difficulty, she negotiated the few yards back into her sitting room where she edged herself into an armchair.

There was an appointment card from the hospital saying she needed her eyes checked. Well, there was no way that was going to happen. Now she came to think of it, one of her eyes was feeling painful. It had seemed blurry today as well, but maybe that had been when she had shed a tear about something that no longer seemed important.

There were two bills, a bank statement, and a leaflet from a new Mexican takeaway. Their food might make a nice change. The last envelope yielded no clue as to its contents from the outside, but when she ripped it open, she saw that it had come from Dignitas. A while back, probably weeks ago, she had written to them and become a member so that, if she chose, she could journey to them in order to die.

It had seemed a good idea at the time. It still did, if only she could magic herself to Switzerland. But the travel was way beyond her now. She should have sorted it earlier. A tranquil, civilised death would have been infinitely preferable to her present undignified situation.

For the first time since she and Matthew had arrived, Jen was alone. Except that she was not, because Hoagy was with her. And that had changed everything. She looked across her kitchen to his bed where he lay.

'So cute,' she murmured.

289

There was a burst of laughter from the other end of the house which caused her to smile. It seemed she had found her ideal location, though it had taken her a while to be sure about it. She still had enough space of her own but was a mere ten seconds away from the company and comfort of Fred's family. It felt right.

'You're pleased about this, dearest Fred, aren't you?' she asked into the stillness, knowing with peaceful certainty that he was.

And she knew too that Ginny and Matthew were happy about the arrangement, which was so touching it made her want to cry. Over supper, she had put Ginny in the picture about Chloe and told her that she could now start work in the shop immediately and embark on the process of buying it. With considerable difficulty, but palpable enthusiasm, the younger woman burdened by her enormous baby bump, had pushed herself out of her chair and come over to offer a big hug.

'Wonderful news. I'll be able to focus totally on Freddie now,' she had said, with a blissful smile that spread over her entire face.

Jen smiled at the memory, as her eyes returned to Hoagy. What a day he had had. No wonder he looked worn out. He seemed to be snoozing, but every now and again, he would jerk his head upwards and his eyes would open in an anxious expression till he registered that she was really there.

It had been astonishing to her that he had remembered her, and a real thrill that he had been so pleased. She had anticipated that he would be nervous and unsure who she was, so his rapture had been a welcome surprise.

Ginny had been wonderful with him – producing a couple of new toys and various treats.

'I won't be going on like this,' she had explained to Jen, her eyes dancing with humour. 'But he needs to associate this new place as being comfortable and safe.'

He certainly seemed settled, and had lain, contentedly, under the table in Ginny and Matthew's kitchen, while the three of them ate their Indian takeaway.

There was no oven in their kitchen, and the new one was not due to be delivered for a week. 'Best excuse ever for not having to cook!' Ginny had giggled, looking as relaxed and happy as Jen had ever seen her – despite the house being stuffed with packing cases and there being no curtains at the windows.

'It's all going to be great,' she had continued. 'There's plenty of hot water. There's a warm airing cupboard. Working central heating. Plenty of people would think we're already living in the lap of luxury! And I don't believe I'll ever get used to how big the house is. It's fab!'

So, here we are, Jen thought. In Norwich.

The estate agent's details had described this room as 'in urgent need of modernisation', but now that she was here, she realised that it would take little effort to make it perfectly suitable for her needs. There were some cupboards on the walls that would be fine with a coat of paint. She had no great urge for matching shiny units with everything hidden behind them. What she did want was to have a table, where she could eat, and sit and read. There was insufficient space for a big one like Matthew and Ginny had in their kitchen, but maybe she could buy a gate-legged type which would open up to seat four people. That would do. And she knew where she would find it.

In her youth, there had been a china shop in Norwich that she used to walk past, longing for a time when she might be able to buy cups and saucers and dinner plates that all matched. Funny what seems important, she thought. But with her disordered upbringing her older self could see why, as a child, she had had a desire for beautiful things. Unfortunately, the shop had not survived, but in its place was an extensive second-hand store called Loose's Emporium. She would go there, and almost certainly find any furniture she needed.

'Fred and I weren't really into sprauncy kitchens,' she said in Hoagy's direction. 'I'll just make it comfortable.'

So as not to disturb him, she tiptoed away. When she and

Matthew had arrived, having stopped to pick up the takeaway on the nearby ring road, Ginny had been so keen to sit them down and distribute the food, that it was only now it occurred to her to explore upstairs and venture into her bedroom.

The removal boys had promised they would reassemble her bed, which they had, but what she had not anticipated was that Matthew and Ginny would have found time to unpack her bedding and put the sheets and duvet and pillows on the bed, making it look just like it used to in her old home. She gazed at it longingly. Her dressing table was in an ideal place too, and in front of it, stood one of her Victorian chairs.

She had temporarily forgotten that there was a wall of built-in wardrobes in the bedroom, and she opened them up eagerly, pleased with how much storage space there was. And then she found that in one of them, the younger couple had hung up all the clothes that had been on the rail in the removal van. Fred's Norfolk jacket was there too. Matthew must have brought it up when she had been occupied washing up after their meal. She grasped the two arms of the garment and brought them to her face so she could inhale the scent of the fabric.

Just then, Hoagy walked into the room.

'Oh no,' she said firmly. 'Your bed's in the kitchen.'

He gazed at her, all eyes in a tiny face, then retraced his steps but only as far as the threshold, where he slumped down and curled up.

'Come on, Hoagy,' she urged him. 'The kitchen's warm. You'll be comfortable there. I'll see you in the morning.'

He followed her downstairs and returned to his bed. She played with him for a moment or two, squeaking one of the toys, and then tucking the knitted clown close to his chest.

Back upstairs, she saw that Matthew had also brought up her holdalls from the car boot. She unzipped one of them in search of her toiletries, but a movement in the doorway distracted her; Hoagy was back. This time though, it looked as though he

292

understood he must respect her space, and he contented himself with curling up on the landing carpet just outside her open door.

'Oh Hoagy,' she groaned. 'I don't want to battle with you.'

His head angled to the left, and his eyes bore into her.

'Come on, it's bedtime, let's go,' she said briskly, before running quickly down the stairs. He followed, rather more slowly.

'Bed, Hoagy!' Then she giggled because she realised she sounded like Barbara Woodhouse.

He jumped in but remained standing, staring back at her.

'Yes, good boy. Good dog. Bedtime, Hoagy.'

Upstairs, she continued rummaging through her bags, but before long, Hoagy reappeared and hovered in the doorway. He made a little whiny sound, then yawned and settled himself again on the landing carpet.

'Awww, I love you, Hoagy,' she said. Then she added, 'I know it's hard. This is very new for us both... Look, if I bring up the bed, and put it here just outside my door, will you promise me that you'll stay in it?'

She glanced behind her, feeling embarrassed. 'Oh my God,' she murmured, 'I'm talking to a dog. Asking him questions. Negotiating with him. I've completely lost the plot. He can't possibly comprehend what I'm saying. This is ridiculous.'

But then it seemed to her that, just possibly, he had understood. He yawned again. He must be exhausted.

'OK, stay,' she said. And he did, while she ran down to the kitchen, scooped up all his belongings, carried them upstairs and put them down beside him. He jumped up, then he gave a little yelp and stepped into his bed. Within seconds, he had settled himself and closed his eyes.

'Promise me you'll stay there,' she whispered. 'No coming into my room.' He looked up at her out of one barely opened eyelid. She bent down to tickle his tummy and he licked her hand.

Picking up her washbag, she wandered through to the bathroom where she cleaned her teeth but neglected to floss. Then she

293

cleansed her face but did not bother with the facial exercises she had learned when she had interviewed the author of a book on the method.

'Standards are slipping, Fred,' she murmured as she padded back to her bedroom.

Hoagy did not move. Finally, fatigue had overcome him. And she was tired too, she realised, and all she wanted was to slip into her own bed in her new room and give up.

'Awwwww, so lovely,' she murmured as she stretched out under her duvet. 'They've given me a hot water bottle. How kind is that?'

'I really wanted to make love to you tonight,' Stephen whispered as he curled round Monica and nuzzled her ear.

'Well, be my guest,' she replied softly.

'I'm too tired, I'm afraid. I don't feel I can raise a canter. What it is to be old and exhausted when you're in bed with the loveliest woman in the universe.'

She chuckled and pushed her bottom back against him.

'We had a great evening, didn't we?'

'We did,' he agreed. 'It's wonderful that you and Emily get on so well.'

'She's a delight. I like to think that Betsy would have turned out like her if she'd lived.'

Stephen tightened his arms around her. 'Sorry.'

'Don't be. By the way, were you listening when she said that her school is desperate for teaching assistants? I was thinking that I could do that. I mean, you're still working full time and there are only so many carrot cakes I can make! I know you don't see me as a Stepford wife, thank goodness.'

'I certainly don't! And that sounds like a terrific idea.'

'I'm glad you feel that way. I'll have to see what the procedure is, after all it's decades since I was in a classroom.'

'I shouldn't think there'll be too many obstacles. They'll be crawling over themselves to have you!'

'Not everyone has your rose-tinted spectacles! Oh, and another thing I've been meaning to tell you all evening – and there's been a lot, hasn't there? – is that Melissa wants to come for Christmas and she's talking about staying for the wedding. Though she more or less implied that if we didn't get on with it, she'd have to go home. I think you're going to find her rather more – what shall we say – brutal, than Emily!' Monica giggled. 'Still, in recent months she does seem to have softened a great deal. The other thing is she wants to make us grandparents!'

'Really! How will that work exactly?'

'God knows. I think they've found a donor, but I didn't like to ask whether he's going to do the deed the good old-fashioned way. Knowing my daughter and her pronounced preference for women I doubt that very much. I expect a clinic will handle it.'

'Makes sense.'

She reached for his right hand, which was wound round her waist, then she raised it to her lips and kissed it. 'Thanks for everything.'

'No, thank you,' he replied. 'I don't think I'll ever get used to it. By the way, it's your birthday in two weeks and for the first time in ten years I won't have to send a forlorn card reminding you that I'm still alive and lusting after you.'

'No, I suppose you won't.'

'What would you like to do? We could go to Paris.'

Monica recollected that the last time she had been there with James, he had been moody throughout. It was not a pleasant memory.

'We could, but we were talking about driving through France for our honeymoon.'

'True. In fact, now that you're going to be a free woman in six weeks why don't we get the date sorted for the wedding and maybe book a hotel just the other side of the Channel for the first couple of nights before we go off-piste, as it were.'

'That would be fantastic,' she responded. 'In which case, could we do something nearer home for my birthday? Perhaps we could go to Norwich for a couple of days? We could meet Jen and her family, and see her shop, and do the cathedral, as well as have time for us, and… you know…'

'I like the sound of the "you know" best of all.'

'Naughty boy!'

He kissed the back of her neck. 'It's hard to think of anything else when you're around. Which is why I'm disappointed about tonight. But there's always the morning.' Reaching behind him, he switched off his bedside lamp. Then in the darkness he murmured, 'Good night, wonder woman.'

She snuggled back to get as much contact with his warm body as possible and promptly fell asleep.

Lucy woke. Everything hurt. She was shivering, but then as a wave of nausea swept over her, she felt hot and clammy.

Some weird sense of appropriateness about where she should be sick forced her to her feet, and she reached for her crutches before hauling herself up the stairs so she could use her bathroom rather than vomit in the downstairs cloakroom. But on the last step, a devastating pain in her chest felled her, and she screamed as one crutch and then the other fell away from her, and she collapsed in a heap, breathless and in agony.

The door to her spare room was open and the light from the landing spilled onto her portrait. Despite the pain, she smiled to herself, remembering the wild boy who had painted it, and the celebrated artist he became. He had told her once that her talent in bed would never be surpassed. That's something, she thought.

She heard herself whimper. Her head was swimming. This was the moment she had wondered about. Would she, she had pondered, when the crisis came, find herself panicking and doing all she could to ring 999? Her breath was coming in angry, rasping wheezes. So that's what people mean by a death rattle… Curious. Well, she had no decision to make now. She was beyond summoning any intervention.

Fragments of conversations from years ago drifted in and out of her head. Some she could identify.

'You're brilliant in bed, and you have the most remarkable mind and are clearly the cleverest student in our year.'

What had his name been? Timmy something. She had enjoyed her brain and how clever she had been.

Then Guy, her Thursday chap who had died in her bed came to mind. He had always been fulsome in his appreciation. 'You make a man feel appreciated in a unique and highly gratifying way.'

A more critical voice replaced him. 'You always did do things your own way.'

That was her father. He was so loud, it sounded as if he was next to her. In this house. How could that be?

Struggling to remain conscious she searched in her memory for his last words to her. 'I'm ready to go,' he had said, in a whisper. And with that recollection, the noise of her breathing quietened. This was it, then. The moment. And with that recognition, she realised that, just like her father had, she was aware she had reached the end.

'*I'm* ready to go,' she murmured. And the world stopped.

Chapter Twenty-Five

Monica stifled a sigh and shifted in her seat; the eulogy seemed endless. Obviously, Lucy's brother loved the sound of his own voice. Worse than that, whoever it was he was talking about was not the Lucy she and Jen had known. For one thing, he kept calling her Lucinda Mary which sounded like something out of an old, but not very good, novel.

She allowed her eyes to roam around the church; a location that had figured significantly in her childhood. Her mother had believed it was important to come to St Mark's, though she was hardly a spiritual person, or even a kind or Christian one. For a while Monica had attended a Methodist Sunday School because one of her friends did. She had enjoyed that. But Mum had frowned on it and insisted that it would benefit her much more to mix with people who went to the 'C of E'.

There had been school carol services here too. And then, she had been a Girl Guide for a while, in the hall next door, and had marched, crocodile fashion, in and out of the building for church parades. She had never felt she quite fitted in – probably because the other girls had been more middle class. And when she had outgrown her uniform, and her mother had made noises about how expensive it would be to replace, she had told her to save the money because she would prefer to leave. It was a relief. They were due to go camping a fortnight later, and not only had she little desire to light a fire out of doors, but the thought of being incarcerated in a tent with girls who had matching underwear and pretty hair brushes had induced panic in her young mind.

As an adult, she had never been a regular churchgoer. She thought she probably did believe in God but was not at all sure that if he existed, he was Church of England. The next time she would set foot in here, she imagined, would be after her mother died.

James had talked about flying back for the funeral from Australia where he was mending his relationship with Melissa, but she had told him that Lucy would not have expected it. He was the executor of the will and had taken his responsibilities seriously. It was strange how close he and Lucy had become.

The brother was droning on now about how his sister was a free spirit and not easy to understand. She glanced at Jen, who was staring into the distance, lost in her own thoughts. As she watched, Monica saw one solitary tear trace its way down her friend's cheek. It was not a year yet since her husband had died. Grief took much longer to be contained. She knew that. Her dead child would live on in her heart forever and there would always be a sadness attached to the unfairness of her brief life. But it was a real bonus now to be in contact with Stephen's daughter, who so often reminded her of Betsy. They had become close, and Emily was helping to heal the gaping hole that her beloved girl had left.

The other death she would never cease to grieve for was that of her father. He had been the best of parents. Much to her mother's annoyance, he had stipulated that he did not want a funeral at St Mark's. Her mother had borne a grudge about that, as indeed she had about so much else, until her mind deteriorated to the point that she no longer remembered it.

'The crem will be good enough for me,' he had said. Monica hated that place forever after her father's coffin disappeared behind a curtain. Every time she had thought about it, for at least a year, she had cried. It had seemed so stark and final. Today, they were supposed to be going there after the church service because Lucy's body was due to be cremated later. She had gained the impression that neither Jen, nor Helen and Sam who were sitting behind them, had much enthusiasm for attending. In any event, maybe the family would prefer that last rite to be personal to them. Dare she hope that was the case?

A light touch on her right hand caused her to turn towards Stephen. He gave her a gentle smile. Her heart gladdened. With him, she had grown into the Monica she had always wanted to be.

Fred would have hated this, Jen decided. He had no religious beliefs and his funeral had been conducted by a Humanist he had found on a website when he was putting his affairs in order. She had written the eulogy, re-drafting it time and again till she was happy that it captured the spirit of her wonderful man. She had delivered it herself too. Matthew and Simon had queried whether that was asking too much of her, but she had been adamant that it was her job. Her voice had croaked and wobbled once or twice but she had managed it. And then Simon had recited a Shakespeare sonnet that his father loved, and Matt had read a funny article that Fred had penned decades previously about bringing up teenage boys alone.

The day had been packed with love, tears and laughter and had been a world away from these awkward proceedings.

She had not been inside St Mark's before. And probably, she would never set foot in it again. Since returning to Norwich, she had ventured into the Catholic cathedral a few times and lit a candle for Fred. Her mother, completely lapsed throughout Jen's childhood, had regained her faith in her last years. Jen had found it comforting to go to Mass occasionally after that. And now she felt it held some new attraction for her, though how that would develop she had no idea.

The brother had stopped damning Lucy with faint praise and had embarked, for some peculiar reason, on lauding his father. You'd have thought the late rector had been Archbishop of Canterbury at least for all the approbation being heaped upon him. Jen caught Monica's eye and pulled a face.

This funeral had been hijacked utterly by the relatives whom Lucy had chosen not to contact during her illness – and it had become a seriously formal business, with a hearse and two huge gas-guzzling limousines.

Monica had told her that James had given in about the funeral arrangements. He had said it was a battle worth losing if it stopped the family challenging the will and Lucy's wish for her house to go to her former student Petrina. Apparently, James had rung the brother and persuaded him that Lucy had known her own mind, had believed her own family to be more than comfortably off, and wanted to give stability and security to a young woman whose spirit she admired, and had enjoyed nurturing.

It would not, Jen reflected, have looked good if the prosperous brother – tall, thin, dour and the complete opposite of Lucy in every respect – had fought to deprive the young woman of her bequest. Maybe James had pointed that out. She had not liked Monica's husband on their brief acquaintance, but what she had learned of his diligence in helping Lucy, had changed her view of him.

Apparently, Lucy had also owned a very expensive painting. She and Monica had never seen or known about it, but James had had it removed from the house swiftly before the family descended, like vultures, to paw over Lucy's belongings. How unseemly it all was. And how different from Fred's death. Different too from how her own would be; living as she did now with Matthew, Ginny and little Freddie, her affairs would be very straightforward.

Lucy's had been complicated because she had not seen her GP in the weeks leading up to her death. This had meant that the police and the coroner had had to be involved. It had been quite a drama, and she and Monica had worried that someone might try to claim they had been complicit in Lucy taking her own life, or negligent in not trying to force their friend to accept more medical intervention. But in the end, there had been no inquest. James had offered his opinion by Zoom to the effect that Lucy had been positive she did not want to receive more health care. And eventually, it was concluded that she had died of complications from diabetes and that 'if a competent adult chooses not to avail themselves of recommended treatment, they have an inviolable right to do that, irrespective of how unwise others might think this is'.

So dear, spirited, idiosyncratic Lucy had given up and was… somewhere.

She hoped there was a somewhere because that meant Fred was somewhere too.

They were onto communal prayers now. She and Monica were silent as the congregation joined in. Sam, behind them, must have been brought up as an Anglican, she realised, because she could hear that he knew all the words. She fancied Helen had told her he had gone to Marlborough or Harrow or somewhere equally elite. Probably there had been a lot of churchgoing when he was a boy.

At last, it was over.

The heavy wood coffin – preceded by the head undertaker – processed down the aisle and out of the front door. Following it were the black clad figures of Lucy's brother, his wife and their two sons and partners. Their eyes stared straight ahead, making no attempt to engage with anyone in the congregation. They had come to be seen to do their duty. Nothing more.

Monica spoke first as the family passed their pew. 'This is absolutely not what Lucy would have wanted.'

Jen, hearing the tremor in her friend's voice, realised that Monica, normally so reasonable and mild-mannered, was furious.

She reached for Monica's hand and held it briefly. 'I'm not going to the crematorium,' she whispered. 'I hate that place. I was so grateful that Fred decided to be buried in the woodland cemetery. I thought Lucy would go for something like that.'

'Unfortunately,' Monica replied, 'I don't think she recorded precisely what she wanted though there was a mention of a willow coffin and she had said to James that she didn't want ridiculous funereal cars or a church service. That family are total bastards!'

Jen had never heard Monica sound so critical of anyone. She put her arm around her friend and said, 'I doubt if she'd have liked being referred to as Lucinda Mary either!'

Monica shook her head as another of the undertaking staff began to shepherd the mourners out of the church. Along with Stephen, they filed into the aisle when it was their turn, with Helen and Sam following close behind them.

'Fine display of passive anger there,' Helen muttered, as they reached the church door and stood watching Lucy's relatives, who were grouped together, not shaking hands with anyone, and not even speaking to each other.

'You're off duty,' Jen told her. 'Perhaps therapists never are though!' She caught Sam's twinkling eyes and he smiled broadly at her remark, before putting his arm around Helen.

'So, what did you think of all of that?' Jen went on as they moved out of earshot of the glum brother and his group.

'Awful,' Stephen said. 'Obviously, I didn't know Lucy, but from what I know about her, I can only hope she's looking down and saying to herself, "How right I was to avoid my brother for most of my life".'

Everyone laughed, their mirth breaking the tension of the previous hour.

'To be honest,' Sam said, 'I rather enjoyed the readings and responses as I had no idea I'd still have a memory of all of that. It's sixty-two years since I was in an Anglican church. If only one had that much recall of more recent events!'

'Were you a choir boy?'

'I was. And a server. The whole works. And the thing is, even now, the language is comforting to me, despite the fact that I'm not a believer.'

'I bet you were cute,' Jen grinned.

'There's a picture,' Helen responded. 'And he was.'

'So, the two of you aren't getting married here?'

'No way,' Helen answered. 'We're doing it in Geneva. In February. We hope you'll all come.'

'Oh! That'll be really lovely,' Monica looked much more cheerful at the prospect.

'Absolutely,' Jen added.

'And you can stay with us. There's plenty of room. Sam and I've decided we're too old to go off on a formal honeymoon!'

'Never too old for that!' Stephen chuckled.

Sam laughed. 'You could say every day for us is a honeymoon since we've waited so long. And we love our new house so much, I think once we shut the front door after we've moved in next Friday, we might never leave it again!'

Monica nudged Jen as she realised that Lucy's coffin was being loaded into the hearse. 'What do we do now?'

'Well, my proposition is that we should all have a drink, as far away from these hideous people as possible,' Sam replied.

'Good man,' Stephen agreed.

'How about we all go to The Granary?' Jen suggested. 'We could have a glass of wine and some cake – cakes that Lucy might have picked.'

'Better and better,' Stephen replied. 'Why don't Sam and I go on ahead and get a table, and you can take your time and talk to anyone else you know once the family have gone? Invite others to join us, maybe.'

'That would be helpful,' Monica said. 'I feel I want to wait and see Lucy's coffin as it leaves here.'

'I do too,' Jen agreed.

304

'I'll stay as well,' Helen said.

'Look,' Jen gestured, 'the monstrous brother and co are getting into those cars and not saying goodbye to anyone. How rude is that?'

'Very,' Monica nodded. 'It's obvious they don't want anyone else to come to the crematorium. Isn't that Petrina, the young lecturer Lucy's left the house to, standing near them?'

'It is, and they've totally ignored her. Just frozen her out.'

'I'm actually not surprised at that,' Helen told them. 'Sam heard the brother refer to her as "that bloody chit of a girl".'

As the hearse pulled away slowly with the limousines following, the three women stood, watching. And as the coffin passed them, Helen put a protective arm around the other two and they bowed in unison.

'Goodbye, lovely Lucy,' Jen whispered, and then there was silence until the funeral party disappeared from view.

Monica wiped her face with an already damp tissue. 'It feels so, so sad. But the only thing you can say is that once Lucy was aware of just how ill she was, she really had no wish to go on, and particularly if it meant giving up everything that for her made life worth living.'

Jen, struggling with her own emotions, studied the ground. 'I know. She was such a lover of life with huge appetites in so many directions. But once that changed for her, compromise wasn't in her nature, was it? Anyway, I think she was in such a poor state, she might not have extended her life for long even if she'd followed the health advice to the letter.'

Monica dabbed at her face again. 'Right, shall we... Oh, where's Helen?'

They looked across the church car park to where their friend was talking to Petrina.

'Oh good,' Jen said. 'I was wondering if we should invite her to join us. Looks like Helen thought of it first... I don't remember Lucy ever mentioning Petrina to me, but she must have been close to her. Perhaps she thought of her like a daughter.'

'Will she come though, do you think?' Monica queried. 'It can't be easy for her, not knowing anyone.'

Petrina exchanged a few more words with Helen, but then shook the older woman's hand and turned away.

'Sorry,' Helen apologised as she rejoined them. 'I thought one of us should talk to Lucy's protégée, especially as I'm pretty sure she heard how rude the brother was about her.'

'Did you ask her to come to The Granary?'

'Yes, I hope that was OK. But she says she'd prefer to go off and have a bit of a weep on her own and then she's going to be busy with tutorials later. She's overwhelmed by Lucy bequeathing the house to her, and said she didn't think she deserved it, but I told her that, knowing Lucy as we all did, she would have thought all this out very carefully. I'm sure Lucy really loved her. And I suggested to her that she should enjoy this generosity and that one day, she might have the opportunity herself to do something equally beneficial for a younger colleague.'

'You're very good at saying absolutely the right thing,' Monica said, 'as I know from experience.'

Jen nodded. 'Yes, me too.'

Looking pleased but mildly embarrassed, Helen changed the subject. 'Right, come on, let's go and see what the men have sorted.'

'Might you take up therapy again once you're settled in Geneva?' Jen asked her.

'Definitely not. Sam and I are going to learn how to be retired people and enjoy our son and his family. None of us know what's round the corner and we need to make the best use of the rest of our lives together.'

Monica smiled. 'I know just what you mean.'

'And of course, you are going to be newly-weds with all that that entails!' Jen giggled.

Helen blushed. 'Enough! Which way shall we go?'

'Actually, I need to go via my house – well, soon to be Chloe's now. Ginny and Freddie and I spent last night with her and I'd love them to come to The Granary so you can meet them. Chloe's working unfortunately, but you will get the chance to see my pride and joy.'

Helen looked bewildered, then laughed as she realised what Jen meant. 'Ah, your dog!'

'Your house isn't far off the direct route,' Monica pointed out. 'Let's all walk that way.'

Fifteen minutes later, Monica held open the door to The Granary while Ginny wheeled in Freddie's buggy. Helen followed with Jen, who was holding Hoagy.

'I rang Liz Pemberton earlier saying we might end up here,' Jen told her. 'She was fine with me bringing the dog so long as he's quiet and we're discreet! So,' she whispered in the miniature schnauzer's ear, 'don't let me down, little boy!'

Stephen and Sam waved from the other side of the room where they had put two tables together overlooking the river.

'That's exactly where we sat with Lucy on that very first day,' Monica commented softly as they walked over to the men.

Sam pulled a chair out from the table and seated Jen, then Helen, while Stephen helped Ginny to settle in the corner before turning to Monica.

'Are you OK, dearest?' he asked her quietly.

'Yes, thank you. I'm fine,' Monica whispered, then she reached up and pulled his head towards her and kissed his forehead.

'Right, I'm in the chair,' Sam announced. 'What's everyone having?'

'I could murder a glass of Rioja,' Helen replied.

'Sounds good to me. Is that fine for everyone?' Stephen asked. Everyone nodded except Ginny and Jen.

'Could we have tea?' Jen asked. 'Ginny's breastfeeding obviously and I need to drive us back to Norwich later.'

'Fair enough. And did someone mention cake?' Sam asked.

'Definitely!' Monica and Jen answered as one.

'You ex-volunteers better pick then,' Stephen suggested. 'You've probably sampled quite a selection over the months.'

307

Monica punched Stephen on the arm. 'Rather too true, I'm afraid. Perhaps we should have what Lucy bought for us that first day, which was meringue, chocolate brownies and... some sort of muffin?'

'Wasn't it a flapjack?' Jen contradicted her.

'Yes, you're right! So, something like that?'

'Consider it done,' Stephen said, as he and Sam made for the counter.

Ginny plucked Freddie from his pram, chatting softly to him about how gorgeous he was and how good, and how he was her very best boy.

'He's such a beautiful baby,' Helen murmured.

'Have a little cuddle if you like,' Ginny offered.

'Could I?'

'Oh yes, he loves people cooing all over him. Especially women!' She passed him over.

'He's adorable. Can I have a little hold afterwards?' Monica asked. 'It's been far too long since I had a baby in my arms.'

Jen looked on with a huge smile on her face. 'I don't think I'd ever held one before Freddie. But even I seem to be tolerated by him. He's so great.'

'It must feel tough that Fred never saw him,' Monica said gently.

Jen's eyes misted. 'It is, but I hope he's looking down and seeing for himself what a terrific grandson he has.'

Helen passed Freddie onto Monica, then turned towards Jen. 'You'll be the best granny.'

'I doubt it. I'm not even a blood relation.'

'That doesn't matter,' Helen insisted. 'You'll be an integral part of his upbringing and he'll love and depend on you, and you'll see Fred in him.'

Jen swallowed. 'I do already. It's quite overwhelming. In a very good way.'

'And you have your little dog.'

Jen gazed down at the miniature schnauzer lying by her feet.

'Is that going well?' Helen continued.

'It is. He's not perfect. I think he may always have problems with other dogs. He certainly barks noisily at them. And we've had our battles about me being in charge, and he hates being left alone – but as I live with the family now, I don't think that's going to be an issue. The fact is that he's mine, and another heartbeat in my part of the house, and I'm special to him, as he is to me.'

Jen stopped talking and watched as Helen and Monica's men, each bearing a tray loaded with drinks and cake, returned to the table.

Helen nodded. 'Being special to another being is like food and drink to us,' she murmured as Sam leant over and passed her a glass of wine, his eyes settling on hers, which gleamed in response.

Monica stood up and passed Freddie back to his mother, then she and Stephen sat down in adjoining seats.

Spent suddenly, no one spoke for a moment or two. Then, while the wine drinkers took their first grateful sips of the emotional afternoon, Jen poured tea and passed a cup to Ginny, whose face lit up at the prospect. The two of them beamed fondly at each other over baby Freddie's head.

Monica raised her glass. 'Shall we drink to our friend, Lucy?'

'A friend we were very lucky to know,' Jen added.

The others raised their glasses, 'To Lucy', and then all of them spontaneously applauded before sinking back in their seats to think their own thoughts.

The silence was broken suddenly by Hoagy waking, yawning loudly, then giving a little bark and bouncing up and down till Jen reached for him and settled his body on her lap.

She stroked his head as she surveyed the two happy couples on the other side of the table, as well as her daughter-in-law and grandson. 'So much has happened since Monica and I sat here with Lucy ten months ago.'

Monica nodded. 'I certainly never anticipated then that I'd be embarked now on this whole new adventure.' Her eyes met Stephen's before she smiled at the others.

Jen lifted Hoagy so that he was nestling into her chin. 'I could never have imagined everything that would happen to me either. I've learned a lot this year, not least that it's impossible to avoid pain and loss as you grow older. It's part of the deal of living. But something else I know now, that I certainly didn't back in February, is that there are so many ways of loving... and that's a truly marvellous thing.'

'It is,' Helen smiled at her. 'We've all had our challenges, haven't we? To be honest, I wouldn't mind if we could have a period of calm now. Perhaps 2020 will bring fewer surprises.'

The End

About Christine Webber

Christine Webber tried various careers in her younger days – she was a classical singer, a Principal Boy in pantomimes, an undistinguished actress as well as a piano and singing teacher. Fortunately, for her, when she was thirty, she managed to get a job in television as a continuity announcer, and shortly thereafter she became a news presenter at Anglia TV. Finally, she had found an occupation she liked that other people thought she was good at. This was a massive relief.

In her early forties, she married the love of her life, David Delvin. Soon afterwards, she decided it was time to leave news presenting to train as a psychotherapist and she also became a problem page columnist for various publications including *TV Times*, *Best*, *BBC Parenting*, *The Scotsman* and *Woman*. In addition, she regularly broadcast relationship advice on *Trisha*, *The Good Sex Guide …Late* and from the BBC's Breakfast sofa.

In her fifties, she and her husband set up a practice in Harley Street, and they worked together there and collaborated on several books. They also wrote the sex/relationships content on www.netdoctor.co.uk and penned a joint column for the health section of *The Spectator*.

Over the decades, Christine was commissioned to write ten self-help books including *Get the Happiness Habit*, *How to Mend a Broken Heart* and *Too Young to Get Old*.

Now, in her seventies, her focus is on the issues of mid and later life. She makes video podcasts on positive ageing and writes a column for various regional papers on that theme. She is also a life coach specialising in health and ageing. But she has no plans for any more non-fiction books. Instead, for the past five years she has concentrated on writing novels for and about older people. Previous titles in this genre have been *Who'd Have Thought It?* and *It's Who We Are.*

So Many Ways of Loving is about the major life changes we have to expect as we age, but it also highlights the possibilities of numerous new beginnings as well as our crucial need for strong bonds with friends and families – and pets.